I0533666

THE DRAGON HUNTER

Book Two of The Dragon Stalker Bloodlines Saga

D.K. DRAKE

Dream Doers Publishing LLC
North Carolina

Cover designed by Karri Klawiter
Visit her website at www.ArtByKarri.com

This book is a work of fiction. Names, characters, places, and incidents either are products of the author's imagination or are used fictitiously. Any resemblance to actual persons, living or dead, events, or locales is entirely coincidental.

Author D.K. Drake
Visit my website at www.AuthorDKDrake.com

Published in the United States of America by Dream Doers Publishing, LLC

Print ISBN: 978-09907463-3-1
EBook ISBN: 978-0-9907463-2-4

FOR MY SISTERS, LAURIE AND JULIE

*Your support gave me the freedom to follow
my dreams and helped make this book possible.*

NOVELS BY D.K. DRAKE

The Dragon Stalker Bloodlines Saga

BOOK 1: **The Dragon Collector**
BOOK 2: **The Dragon Hunter**
BOOK 3: **The Dragon Protector**
BOOK 4: **The Dragon Destroyer** *(coming soon)*

Get Exclusive Access to More {FREE} Stories Today!

When you become one of my email buddies, you get FREE access to the D.K. Drake starter library that includes the short story "Cops, Robbers...and Dragons?" (This is the story that sparked the idea for the entire Saga!)

You'll also get notified about new books and deals, have a chance to join the Advanced Reader Team, and keep up with my real-life adventures as an author, a runner, and a foster parent.

All you have to do is visit **www.AuthorDKDrake.com** and sign up to the Insiders mailing list for FREE today.

What are Dragon Stalkers?

Dragon Stalkers live in the Land of Zandador, a place where both dragons and men can live anywhere from 700-1000 years. Four types of dragons roam the Land of Zandador: Midnight Stalkers, Dawn Stalkers, Noon Stalkers, and Dusk Stalkers. They eat once a day and are named for the time of day they prefer to eat.

About three hours before their peak feeding time, their scales change from grey or white to their designated colors. If they are not fed before all their scales turn colors, their appetites become insatiable. They will go on a hunting rampage and enjoy feeding on as many humans as they can find.

The Midnight Stalker's scales change from grey to black as midnight approaches. The largest of all the Stalkers, the Midnight stalker grows up to twenty feet, breathes electric bolts, and lives in mountainous territory. This type of stalker is characterized by pointy wings, impressive strength, and high intelligence. Its weakness is loud noise.

The Noon Stalker's scales change from grey to gold as noon approaches. It can grow up to fourteen feet tall, breathes fire, and lives in the jungle. This type of stalker is characterized by round wings, invisibility, and a light-hearted, humorous nature. It's terrified by ants and ladybugs.

The Dawn Stalkers' scales change from white to rainbow colors of red, orange, pink, and purple as dawn approaches. It grows no taller than ten feet, breathes acid, and lives where waterfalls abound. It has no wings and is characterized by its vanity and ability to teleport. It is terrified of winged insects.

The Dusk Stalker's scales change from white to rainbow colors of pink, purple, blue, and green. It grows no taller than ten feet, breathes poison, and lives in the Forest of Crooked Trees. It also has no wings and is characterized by its sensitivity and speed. It is scared of water.

When man couldn't agree how to coexist with the dragons, four factions developed:

- The Collectors believed man should work with dragons and that dragons thrive when given a purpose: to serve and protect man.
- The Hunters believed dragons should be enslaved and used as tools to gain power over their fellow man.
- The Protectors believed dragons should be free and have no one to look after except themselves, so man should protect the dragons from harm.
- The Destroyers believed dragons were dangerous creatures and should be eliminated.

Since these four factions, or Bloodlines, couldn't agree how to govern, they chose to fight it out.

Whoever collected, hunted, protected, or destroyed each of the four dragons first would assume the throne for 100 years. Then, in the last year of the king's reign, another Battle for the Throne would ensue to determine who would rule for the next 100 years.

If no one won the Battle, the current ruler would keep the throne for another century. And if dragons were to become extinct while a ruler was on the throne, he would become the King of Zandador for the rest of his life, and his descendants would rule after him.

A Hunter is now on the throne. King Omri has ruled for nearly 500 years and uses his dragons to control every aspect of the people's lives. With dragons on the verge of extinction, he is set to rule for the next 500 years.

But he lives in constant fear of the Prophecy:

The war between the Bloodlines will divide the nation and cause the people to scatter. Many kings will rise to power, but one who masters the dragons and their scales will remain on the throne for centuries. He will rule with a cruel hand, suppress the will of the people, and seek to annihilate all dragons but his own. If his power remains unchecked, he will expand his rule to the world beyond the portal. Gaining control of that world and its resources will allow him to reign for a thousand more years, bringing death and destruction to those who dare defy him.

All hope is not lost. A young Collector whose eyes shine like emeralds and whose ears can hear the thoughts of any dragon will enter the competition in the final months of a Battle for the Throne year. He will be the only one capable of dethroning the king and must collect all four Stalkers by sunset on the final day of the battle year. If he succeeds, however, collecting the four Stalkers will not be enough to defeat the king.

The dethroned king will use his dragons and loyal subjects to wage a war unlike any Zandador has ever seen. The Collector must therefore unite the four opposing Bloodlines for only the united front of the four Bloodlines led by the young Collector will be strong enough to win a war against this most powerful of men.

If such a war is fought, the outcome thereof will determine the fate of the dragons once and for all.

YOU ARE NOW ENTERING THE LAND OF ZANDADOR...

PROLOGUE

At age thirteen, Micah hated his life.

Ever since he got his father's approval and moved into the castle three years ago, all he did was train, eat, and sleep. He never got to see his mother, his father, his half-siblings, or any other kids his age. His life consisted only of sword training, exercising, and reading about sword training, Dragon Hunting, or the laws of Zandador.

He wanted more adventure. More excitement. And more attention from his father. But Omri was an elusive, powerful man. Micah was only able to catch glimpses of him now and then. When he did see him, Micah noted how he walked, how he talked, and how the people around him catered to his every demand. Someday he was going to be just like his Dad.

Today, though, he wanted to escape the confines of the castle. He was supposed to return to the training room after dinner. Instead, he walked right past the room, down the stairs, and snuck out one of the back doors of the castle.

He breathed in the evening air, took a stroll through the woods, climbed a few trees, and tossed some rocks into the lake. He really should come outside more often. This was much more fun than spending his life in that damp, dark, windowless training room.

The sound of a twig snapping behind him caused him to turn around. A dragon stood ten feet away, and his colorful scales indicated he was a hungry Dusk Stalker in search of food.

Micah gulped. This was why he wasn't supposed to exit the castle through the back. He had walked right into the feeding grounds of his father's four dragons.

"You must be Eli," Micah said, trying to sound calm and confident. He found himself fascinated by the ten-foot high, wingless, beautiful creature. The dragon stood his ground while Micah took a step closer. "My father is your master, so you aren't allowed to eat me."

The dragon nodded as though he understood, and Micah walked even closer. He was only an arms-length away now and noticed the dragon had a collar with spikes protruding into his scales wrapped around the base of his neck.

1

"Why do you have this on? That must make eating painful. Bend down, and I'll take it off for you."

Eli complied with Micah's instructions. Micah unlatched the heavy collar and freed it from the dragon's neck. As soon as he took it off, Eli nudged Micah's shoulder as if to say thanks and sprinted away.

"What do you think you are doing?" Omri's booming voice startled Micah, and he dropped the collar, cutting his leg with one of the spikes in the process.

"I was helping the dragon. He looked sad and hurt."

"You are never to help the dragons, especially that one. They deserve no mercy and are to be treated like the slaves they are. If you cannot understand that, you will never be a Dragon Hunter."

"No mercy. I understand now, sir."

"I don't think you do, but you will."

Omri was right. After spending the next six months in the dungeon wearing a collar like the one he took off of Eli, Micah understood the meaning of no mercy. And he vowed to never again treat any dragon as anything other than a mindless slave.

CHAPTER 1
UNEXPECTED REACTIONS

"You...you can't go in there." A shaky, scrawny soldier holding a spear stepped in front of the double wooden doors. Like that was going to stop Micah from entering the throne room.

"Of course I can, you twit." Micah purposefully let his black dreadlocks fall in the man's pale face as his 6'3" muscular frame towered above the runt. How did this guy earn guard duty for the King?

"I am King Omri's son," Micah said. "His favorite son. The son who just won him another dragon. I go where I please, when I please. Now move." Micah shoved the wimp out of the way and burst through the doors.

A handful of the king's advisors huddled in the corner chatting amongst themselves. King Omri paced alone on the stage in front of his throne at the far end of the room.

Moonlight shone through the wall of windows behind him, casting long shadows on the red carpet from his tall height and wide shoulders. His white shirt popped against his black skin, and his short, tight braids looked more regal than Micah's long dreadlocks. Maybe Micah would change his hairstyle once he became King.

"Father!" The word bounced off the marble floors and stone walls of the spacious room. "You can congratulate me. Your newest dragon and I have destroyed the rebel city of Gri."

"Congratulate you?" Omri stopped pacing and began walking towards Micah.

Micah smiled and waited for his father to approach. Omri had to be pleased with him. So pleased he was bound to lavish him with gifts.

It would probably start with a feast. Perhaps followed by awarding him a wing of the castle. Along with a wife.

Sure, he was still underage, but he had earned that kind of privilege. The laws of marriage everyone else had to abide by didn't really apply to him. After all, he was Micah, the thirteenth son of the King. A fierce captain in the elite Justice Unit of the army. And now Dragon Hunter.

But as Omri reached Micah, Micah's smile vanished. Instead of pride, he recognized rage in his father's harsh brown eyes. He had seen that rage before and braced himself for the beating he knew was coming.

"After the way you humiliated me," Omri said, punching Micah in the gut, "I ought to kill you."

◊　◊　◊

Javan let himself drift off to sleep on the back of Varjiek as darkness settled in. He trusted his dragon to carry him back to the capital city to face Micah and didn't need to be awake to navigate the flight.

Only he didn't feel rested at all when they landed a short time later. "Why are we stopping?" Javan asked.

I thought landing was a better option than crashing. Listening to you snore makes me want to sleep.

Javan cringed. He should have known better than to ask Varjiek to keep flying after already making one intense cross-country flight that day. After covering thousands of miles, the dragon had to be beyond exhausted. "Sorry, buddy. I forgot you're not a robot."

What's a robot?

"And I forgot you're not from earth." Javan sighed. How to explain this? "A robot is a like a person, but it's mechanical. You tell it what to do and it does it. It never gets tired or hungry or talks back."

No, I am not a robot. Varjiek yawned. *Get some sleep, young Collector. We will fly again in the morning.*

Javan slid off Varjiek's back and stretched his sore, stiff body. Carefully. He wanted to reach his arms to the sky and clasp his hands behind his back and pull, but either exaggerated stretch would bust the sealing mud and cause his chest wound to split open. Right now, sealing mud was working like stitches to keep the sword cut that spanned from his belly button to his clavicle together.

At least he had gained some muscles beneath his tan skin during his month or so here in Zandador. Otherwise that cut would have sliced right down to his ribs. Nevertheless, he had lost a great deal of blood thanks to that cut inflicted by Micah and was feeling the fatiguing effects. Getting a solid night of sleep on the ground was probably a better idea than dozing fitfully on the dragon's back.

Javan did like the looks of his room for the night. The dragon had found a nice little grassy spot by the river where the moonlight danced off the water.

The water.

They shouldn't be near the water at all. And they certainly shouldn't be on the south side of the river. What was this dragon doing?

"Varjiek," Javan said between gritted teeth as he walked around to face the dragon. His grey scales made the dragon easy to see in the dark. His massive size helped. The dragon stood twelve feet tall from his legs to his back, and his long neck added another six feet to the distance from the ground to his head. At only five foot nine inches tall, Javan felt like a dwarf next to the dragon. That didn't mean he couldn't still be mad at the creature whose thoughts he could read.

"Why are we on the southern shore of the river? We're supposed to be heading east, toward Japheth."

Ah. I was wondering how long it would take you to notice we weren't going in the direction you wanted.

"That doesn't answer my question."

We're heading south because you need to collect a Dawn Stalker. We won't find any Dawn Stalkers in Japheth.

"I don't want a Dawn Stalker right now. I want Micah."

You need to collect dragons, not humans. Collecting a Dragon Hunter is not going to help you win the throne.

Javan rolled his eyes. "I know that. But I can't focus on dragon collecting until I make Micah pay for what he has done."

I agreed to let you ride me because you promised me Skylark. The sooner I help you collect your other three dragons, the sooner I get to see Skylark. So we're going after a dragon, not a Dragon Hunter.

"Hold up there, buddy! I may only be fifteen in earth years, but I look like I'm 150 here in Zandador."

I have seen many humans in my time, and you don't look a day over a hundred.

"Not according to my mother, thank you very much. She told me I looked older than her, and she's 147."

You don't. She was just trying to instill confidence in your young soul.

Javan had grown accustomed to the idea that he looked like he was a good 150 years old. It did help his confidence and made him feel like he was old enough to be a king.

If this dragon was right, and he only looked like he was a hundred, would the people still be willing to follow him if he were to collect all four Dragon Stalkers and win the Battle for the Throne?

Then again, in a world where people lived to be 700-1000 years old, did fifty years really make that big of a difference?

"No matter how old I look, I still look like an adult who can make his own decisions. Besides, you let me ride you. I am your leader now. You are part of my dragon collection. You have to obey me. Your job is to do what I tell you to do."

Is that so? Varjiek stood and towered over Javan. *I don't just look like I'm 623 here in Zandador; I have actually been alive for 623 years. That makes me much older and wiser. You gained my lifelong loyalty the moment you first rode me, but I remain able think for myself and make decisions that are best for both of us.*

He bent his head so his large black eyes were even with Javan's bright green ones. *If you wanted a robot, you should have become a Hunter and cut off my tail.*

The dragon covered Javan with a puff of smoke and walked away.

CHAPTER 2
DRAGON ROUND-UP

"I don't understand. How did I humiliate you?" Micah lifted himself up on his hands and knees while swallowing a mouthful of blood. His father would kick him again if he dared get a drop of blood on the floor. "I sliced that Collector's chest open and left him for dead the night I won Mertzer."

"You should have made sure he was dead." Omri stomped on Micah's back, sending him crumpling to the floor. "Not only did that Collector survive, but he collected a Noon Stalker. He forced me to release the prisoners and made me look like a fool in front of my people. Now Javan has a flying dragon with the power of invisibility. All you have is a wingless dragon who can't even teleport."

Micah eased himself into a sitting position and looked up at Omri. "Mertzer is the last of the Dusk Stalkers. Javan has no hope of winning the competition since I already claimed that dragon."

"Now you are the fool!" Omri pulled Micah to his feet by his hair. "All the Collector has to do is kill you, and the dragon becomes his. I'm tempted to go ahead and kill you myself just to prevent that from happening."

"Father, please." Micah had to find a way to keep himself alive; he knew his father didn't issue idle threats. "Keep me alive, and I'll hunt you more dragons. Imagine how powerful you'll be with eight dragons under your control."

Omri released Micah's hair. "I'm only letting you live, because I want more dragons. Clean yourself up. Gather soldiers. Go to midnight territory. I want a Midnight Stalker next."

Micah's blood-soaked mouth went dry. "A Midnight Stalker? Shouldn't I get a little more practice hunting the other dragons first?"

"Those are my orders. It's the only way to show the people that I am more powerful than that Collector." Omri glared into Micah's eyes. "If you return here without a Midnight Stalker, I'll feed you to my dragons. I've seen the way you treat them. They'll be happy to tear you limb from limb. Now go."

"Yes, sir." Micah nodded and left the room.

As he made his way down the long spiral staircase to the Dragon Quarters, rage and confusion masked the pain of the beating he had just endured. How could his father hurt him after Micah brought home a dragon for him? That was a feat no one else had ever done or even thought of doing. So why did his father hurt him? He had done nothing wrong.

That's what the boy Micah whipped a little over a week ago told him. Micah had whipped him anyway. Had he been wrong to punish that boy?

No. The boy had violated curfew. He should have returned from hunting before dark. So what if his family was hungry and wanted the food? He broke the law by ignoring the curfew. It was Micah's job to make sure people respected the King and the King's laws.

Maybe that's why Omri had beaten Micah. To instill respect.

He would let his bruised ribs serve as a reminder to be more respectful. He hoped he had a chance to demonstrate his increased respect for his father. This trip to hunt a Midnight Stalker could easily turn into a suicide mission. Did his father expect him to succeed in capturing a Midnight Stalker or die in the process?

After being humiliated by the Collector, Micah didn't think Omri cared one way or the other about Micah's life.

"So I'll make him care," he muttered to himself. He would hunt a Midnight Stalker. Then a Noon Stalker. Then a Dawn Stalker.

Once he had all four dragons and was able to keep his father in power, Omri would have to care. Then Micah would finally know what it felt like to be loved by his father.

His entire life had been dedicated to pleasing his father, making him the favored successor. The fact that he grew taller and stronger faster than others his age didn't hurt. Most weren't strong enough to join the army until they reached 100; he became a soldier at age fifty. Now at seventy-seven, he had already accomplished more than most men twice his age.

He knew he would have to wait several hundred more years, but he was still young. By the time his father retired in another two or three hundred years, Micah would be plenty young enough to rule for a good seven hundred or so years.

At least that was the plan until Javan came along. That Collector had to pay for the damage he was causing. He needed to die. And he would. After Micah captured himself a Midnight Stalker.

◊　◊　◊

Micah stormed his way through the double doors at the bottom of the stairs. He hated coming to the Dragon Quarters. The packed dirt floor made everything about this wing of the castle feel dirty. The wide hallway and thirty-foot high ceiling made it spacious enough to house the dragons, but no windows and poor lighting created a depressing atmosphere. The stone walls and ceiling left a constant chill in the air.

It didn't help that Omri wouldn't allow the dragon keepers to clean the stalls more than once a month. Micah understood the need to not pamper the dragons, but he wondered if the dragons would be less temperamental and easier to control if they didn't have to live in their own excrement.

The filthy stalls made the stench unbearable for any humans that entered the area; it had to have been worse for the dragons with their heightened sense of smell. How the dragons lived with the smell or how the dragon keepers stayed down here for eight hours at a time without puking their guts out baffled Micah.

The current keepers on duty were closing the massive stone door at the end of the hall. It was too big and heavy for one man to close alone. The two of them thus had to work together to pull the door closed using a thick, rough rope connected to a pulley on the ceiling. The system had been devised centuries ago to open and close the door for the dragons when they needed to leave the castle to hunt.

The dragons didn't have to go far to hunt. A wooded area behind the castle was constantly stocked with animals and vegetation the dragons enjoyed eating. Years ago, the keepers brought the dragons their food. The dragons didn't appreciate being caged up at all times and being given their food without having to work for it.

They took to feasting on the keepers just for sport. Omri tired of having to replace his help every other day and re-established the dragon hunting grounds.

Now Micah had added one more dragon to the mix. Once he finished his job and captured three more, they were going to have to increase the size of the grounds and the food supply. Otherwise the dragons would start fighting each other, and that would defeat the purpose of Micah working to hunt more dragons.

He would let Omri deal with the feeding problem. Right now, he had to do whatever was necessary to acquire a Midnight Stalker.

"Harness the dragons," Micah said. The keeper looked familiar, but he had never cared enough about the help to bother learning names. "I need them ready to ride in ten minutes. Don't bother with Eli, though. I've got Mertzer." Besides, Eli was unpredictable and never cooperative.

"Sir, that's impossible. I just sent Serenity out to feed. She won't be back for at least an hour."

"Fine. Get her ready when she returns, but get the other three ready now. While you're at it, gather the captains of the Justice Units. I need all of them and their units prepared to leave with me."

"It's getting late, sir. They're all settling into their quarters. There's no way they'll be ready to leave--"

"I don't care what time it is," Micah said, interrupting the man. "Just do as you're told. I am on a mission for the king. It is your job to assist me, and it is their job to follow orders. Got it?"

"Got it."

"I'll be back in an hour. I expect to see all of the dragons and Justice Units prepared to leave."

Micah turned and left. Next stop: the kitchen. He needed food now and for the journey. He just might have to hurt someone if any of the cooks tried to talk back to him.

He kind of hoped one of them would. He was itching to fight. Beating someone to a bloody pulp would improve his darkening mood.

CHAPTER 3
THE DRAGON'S SECRET

Nestled on the soft grass fifteen feet from the shore of the river, sleep easily overtook Javan. He kept his stalker swords within reach just in case he had to fend off wild animals or enemy soldiers who were sure to be tracking him. First, however, the offending party would have to get past Varjiek. Knowing he had a dragon to protect him allowed him to sleep without worry.

He didn't think about waking up until he felt something sharp poking his back. Figuring it was just a rock he rolled onto, he adjusted his position.

A few minutes later, a warm breeze shot over his face. Annoying. He hadn't slept long enough. He covered his face with his left arm and kept sleeping.

Until the shaking ground startled him enough to open his eyes. It reminded him of the tree tremors he experienced in Dusk Stalker territory. But that shouldn't be happening here. Not by the river.

Earthquake. It had to be an earthquake.

Javan sat up only to discover Varjiek running toward the river, causing the earthquake.

The dragon ran forward, sailed through the air, ducked his head, and curled his wings and legs into his body. When he was about to the middle of the wide river, his balled-up body splashed into the water. It was the coolest cannonball Javan had ever seen, but he was so entranced by the sight that he didn't bother getting out of the way of the resulting wave.

The water splashed up and over Javan, drenching him from head to toe. The entire shore was soaked as well.

Varjiek popped his head up from near the middle of the river. *Ha! I finally got you to wake up.* Some of the scales on his neck were gold, indicating that noon was less than three hours away.

Javan stood and pushed his wet black hair out of his eyes. "You couldn't have tried a gentle nudge on the shoulder?"

I tried all sorts of things. I yelled at you, but you apparently can't hear my screaming thoughts when you are asleep. So I poked you with my tail. I snorted smoke over your face. I almost blew a stream of fire over your head but was afraid the fire might get too close and burn you. Then I came up with the jumping in the water idea. Glad I did. That was fun.

"Are you always this perky in the morning?"

This is the time of day I feel most alive. I'm just starting to get hungry, and hunting for food is the most excitement I have all day. He dove into the water and came up chomping on a fish. *Tasty!*

Javan's stomach started to rumble, but he didn't want a fish for breakfast. He'd make a meal out of some of the food his mother had packed for him. That food would only last a few days. Soon he'd have to hunt right alongside Varjiek. "Hurry up and find you enough food. We need to get going."

We do have a long trip ahead of us. I'll probably have to hunt several more times before we get there.

"What are you talking about? Dawn territory is just to the south of us. I was able to get there in several hours riding an okty not too long ago."

Javan had thought himself to have achieved the epitome of coolness the day he first rode that overgrown dragonfly with its fuzzy body, six legs and pink wings—all eight of them, four on each side with one shorter pair stacked atop a longer, thicker pair. Now he rode a dragon. Definitely cooler.

We're not going to Dawn territory.

"Where else am I going to track down a Dawn Stalker?"

In Keckrick.

"Keckrick? You want to leave Zandador?"

Indeed. All of the Stalker territories are going to be patrolled by soldiers. They are unsafe for us. So we're going to Keckrick.

"But I need to collect another dragon."

You will. In Keckrick.

"You're not making any sense. Dragons live in Zandador, not Keckrick."

Correction. Most dragons live in Zandador. I have heard rumors of a Dawn Stalker born not too long ago who is hiding out in Keckrick.

"That can't be true. Dragon eggs can't hatch in this dimension. They can only hatch on earth. The Dark King hasn't allowed anyone through that portal with a dragon egg or a dragon in centuries."

These rumors began about fifteen years ago, right around the same time there were rumors that a baby had been smuggled to earth. How old did you say you were, boy born in Zandador but raised on earth?

"Fifteen." The possibility that a dragon as old as him weakened Javan's knees. He plopped to the muddy ground. "How can you be sure the rumors are true?"

I can't. Not until we get to Keckrick.

CHAPTER 4
DISSENT

Micah hated having to move at the speed of Dahlia the Dawn Stalker. He didn't expect her to be any help in the fight to capture a Midnight Stalker and thought about leaving her behind. But he needed her for her teleportation power.

Once the mission was complete, he would have Dahlia teleport them back to the castle. He would have had her teleport them here, but she could only pop in and out of places she had been before. It was an annoying limitation to her skill, but it did mean they only had to make a one-way trip to Midnight Territory.

They only had about 500 miles to travel from Japheth to Midnight Territory and could have been there by now had she not been slowing them down. The winged dragons could fly that distance in less than two hours, and with Mertzer's Dusk Stalker speed, he could run it in less than three. Even the slowest of okties that the soldiers rode could fly three times the speed that Dahlia could run. With Dahlia, however, their trip had turned into an all-day adventure.

The four captains of the Justice Units each rode a dragon and utilized bridles and reigns to direct the beasts. Mertzer hadn't yet been fit for a saddle, so unlike the other captains, Micah was forced to ride bareback.

Micah led the way on Mertzer. The twenty-four soldiers in his unit flew behind him on okties, six men wide and four men deep.

He made the other three dragons walk behind him and his unit; just because the Noon and Midnight Stalkers could fly didn't mean they had to. His dragon couldn't fly, so no dragons should be allowed to fly when traveling with him.

He had to allow the soldiers with them to fly on okties since no other animal ran fast enough to keep up with the slowest dragon, but they couldn't fly ahead. They had to remain in formation behind the dragons.

The one hundred men had traveled through the night over the hilly, rocky terrain, pausing only for Dahlia and the Noon Stalker Vasilis to feed along the way. Now Mertzer's white scales were beginning to change to blue, indicating that his feeding time was approaching.

At least they had reached some promising hunting grounds. The base of the mountain range that led into Midnight Territory was just ahead. The trees and lush vegetation that grew on the mountainside along an abundance of streams were sure to house ample food for Mertzer to find.

He didn't want Mertzer to have to work hard to find food and water. The dragon had covered over two thousand miles running at top speed to Gri and back over the past few days. Micah knew his dragon was exhausted, so he reasoned that walking at Dahlia's speed was a good thing for Mertzer's sake.

Micah was a bit exhausted himself and wanted to hide under some shade for a bit. He had been riding in the blazing sun on the back of a dragon all day, and his black skin was starting to feel like it was on fire. He also wouldn't mind catching a quick nap. This was day three without any sleep, and he was starting to feel cranky.

As they reached the tree line, Micah held his hand up in a fist so everyone could see him. "We'll stop here. It's time for Mertzer to feed."

While men and women on okties landed all around him, he slid off Mertzer, pulled the saddlebags of food with him, took off his bridle, and gave the dragon his orders. "Eat and return when you're full." When he saw Mertzer eying the feast of okties surrounding them, he slapped the dragon's leg with the flat-edge of his backsword. "No okties. Go hunt your dinner."

Mertzer didn't obey. Instead, he scanned the colorful sea of the eight-winged creatures. The fuzzy bodies of the okties were all black, their big, round eyes were all brown, and their tiny noses were all white, but no okty had the same color of wings. Every color on the rainbow seemed to be represented, and that apparently looked appetizing to the dragon whose scales were changing to pink, purple, blue, and green.

Micah was about to slap the dragon again when Mertzer finally huffed his displeasure and walked into the woods. "That's what I thought," Micah said and re-sheathed his sword. The dragon better do what he was told. Micah had earned the right to control him the second he cut off that dragon's tail days ago.

The other dragons had to obey him because their master Omri ordered them to. Micah preferred having direct control, even if Mertzer technically belonged to Omri. He could say he ceded the dragon to his father, but he knew he was the one who had actually cut off Mertzer's tail, not Omri.

He washed his face off in a nearby stream, inhaled a sandwich prepared by the kitchen staff, and found a place to rest under a huge oak tree. Just as he leaned against the thick trunk of the tree, covered his face with his wide-brimmed hat, and closed his eyes, he heard footsteps.

"This is a good spot." Micah recognized Galiron's deep voice. He had been the captain of the Midnight Justice Unit since the beginning of Omri's reign and was one of Micah's many trainers. He was the reason Micah was so good with a sword. "Should we set up camp here?"

"Set up camp?" Micah slowly opened his eyes and glared at Galiron. The tall, red-bearded man stood with his arms crossed over his wide chest. He looked like he thought he was the one leading this mission. Micah needed to correct the man, so he stood and matched Galiron's height. "We're not camping. We're headed north. Into the mountains. To catch a Midnight Stalker."

"To carry on without a good night's rest would be foolish. We've been traveling all night. Some of these men have been traveling for days without any rest."

"They are my men. They don't need rest."

"We all need rest. Especially in this situation. No human has been in these mountains for centuries. Any dragon we face is not going to like having company. We'll be in his territory during his feeding time. It's dark and cold. He's smart and strong. We need time to scout the territory in the daylight when he's sleeping and not hungry."

"We have four dragons with us, one of whom came from this territory. We'll let them do the fighting while I cut off the dragon's tail. We don't need to be rested for that."

"At least let us skirt west and go through the Rocky Way."

"And lose several days traveling there? No." Micah had to stick to his decision. He was the leader now, not the student. Galiron needed to understand he could not dictate travel plans to Micah the way he did in training sessions. "The most direct route is due north through Fury's Pass."

"The most dangerous route is due north through Fury's Pass."

"Afraid of a little danger?"

"I'm not afraid. I'm wise. That's something that comes from centuries of experience. Which you don't have."

"Now you're going to bash my age? I may be young, but I've already conquered a dragon. How many have you hunted in your long lifetime?"

"You know I'm not from the Hunter Bloodline."

"That's right. You can't hunt dragons. You have to assist those of us who can."

"I have devoted my life to assisting your father and you. Part of my duty includes keeping you out of death traps like Fury's Pass."

"One person dying while attempting to travel through the pass does not make it a death trap. We'll be fine." Micah had to show no fear, no weakness. He couldn't back down from this course of action, even if walking through Fury's Pass did make him a little nervous. "Now tell your men to eat and be prepared to move out as soon as Mertzer returns from feeding."

Galiron stepped so close to Micah that the hairs from his beard tickled Micah's cheeks. "This is a mistake, Micah."

Micah pushed him away. "I don't make mistakes, Galiron."

Galiron shook his head and began walking away. He only made it a few steps before turning back and saying, "That kind of attitude is going to get us all killed."

"Nonsense. Now gather your men. They've had enough time to eat and rest. Head north to Fury's Pass. My unit and I will meet you there."

Galiron tensed and looked like he wanted to argue. But rather than say anything, he simply nodded and left.

Micah had never doubted his decisions before, but now Galiron had him wondering if he was right to continue on this course.

Of course Micah was right. He was always right. Right?

◊   ◊   ◊

A blur. That's the only word Javan could use to describe how his afternoon had passed riding on the back of Varjiek as they raced south toward Keckrick. He had spent hour after hour straddled at the base of the dragon's neck clinging tightly to his triangular grey scales.

The land below him remained a steady streak of green all day. He had to close his eyes after a while to keep from getting airsick. Even with his eyes closed, he didn't dare relax. Varjiek was flying too fast, and Javan didn't want to risk falling off.

He wished he had a speedometer so he could clock the dragon's speed. Javan recalled from his training time with Astor that Noon Stalkers could fly as fast as 350 miles per hour. That sounded like a ridiculous figure when Javan first heard it, but now that he was actually flying on a speeding dragon, he wondered if that figure underestimated Varjiek's top speed.

One thing he learned that Astor hadn't taught him was that dragons don't like to chit chat when they are focused on flying fast. Varjiek's thoughts had been mind-numbingly boring to listen to. The only three thoughts Javan could hear were, "Wing speed. Stay cloaked. Reach the desert."

Then again, Javan was glad that the dragon talked to himself and didn't want to carry on a conversation. Javan could hear Varjiek's thoughts, but Varjiek couldn't hear his. That meant Javan had to actually speak to communicate with the dragon. Talking was difficult with his face pressed against the dragon's neck while traveling in the equivalent of an open cockpit at hundreds of miles an hour.

With the sun beginning to set in the east, Javan noticed a sudden drop in their cruising speed. *Feel that?*

"You slowing down? Yeah."

No. The air. It's changing. Warmer. Thicker. We've almost reached the desert.

"Great! I would like to make a pit stop before we go much further, though."

A pit stop? I do not understand.

"I'm hungry. I want to eat." He also needed to find a bathroom, but the dragon didn't need to know all the aspects included in a pit stop. "Then we can fly over the desert at night when it is cool."

I think we will need to rest a few days before carrying on.

"A few days? You're the one who wouldn't let me go after Micah and wanted to rush to Keckrick to collect a Dawn Stalker. Why take time to rest now? We should just keep going."

I have never traveled across the desert before. By day or night, it is a dangerous place.

"I've got my stalker swords and stun balls, and you're a dragon. Nothing is gonna mess with you."

With all the flying I have done with you over the past few days, I am wearied. You are still injured. We both need rest. If we are not at full strength before carrying on, we may not survive the journey. Plus this is a good place to hide. I wanted to reach this point before stopping because there are not many humans around to run into.

Javan didn't want to stop and rest. He wanted to be tough. To keep going. To show no sign of weakness. That's what a leader did, right? It was his job to make and stick to his decisions, even if those he led disagreed.

Or should he listen to Varjiek? The dragon did make some good points. Javan could benefit from a little downtime. If he had to use his swords to fight whatever awaited them in the desert, he didn't want to have to worry about his chest wound splitting open. It needed to heal, and that was going to take time.

"All right," Javan said. "Let's find a place to hide out for a few days."

CHAPTER 5
FURY'S PASS

The sliver of light from the moon on the cloudy, starless night didn't offer much assistance as the dragons marched their way up the steep mountainside. Micah felt Mertzer fumble his way over the rocks and boulders in the dark and let the dragon set his own pace. They were traveling slower than Micah preferred, but if Mertzer hurt himself by going too fast, they wouldn't be going anywhere. Micah didn't want that.

Besides, the slow pace helped them all adjust to the altitude without getting too sick. Micah had felt lightheaded since they passed the tree line hours ago, but he wasn't sure if that was from the altitude or from fatigue.

He was glad he had sent the flying dragons on ahead. As long as they didn't have a problem with altitude sickness, they would be a bit more rested and prepared to lead the way through Fury's Pass.

More importantly, it gave Serenity a chance to eat without holding everyone else up. Judging by the position of the moon, midnight had already come and gone by the time Micah and the two units with him reached the pass.

He had never been here before and did his best to assess the terrain in the dark. The ground leveled out, but the path ahead was blocked by a rock wall that stretched so high and wide that he couldn't see the top or the end on either side. Trying to climb or fly over the wall was impossible. The air grew too thin towards the top; neither man nor animal could breathe at that altitude.

Many had tried. None had succeeded.

A few had survived the journey through Fury's Pass, however. It was the fastest, most direct route into Midnight Territory, so that's the route Micah was going to take, even if the howling winds and burning rocks made the trek a touch dangerous.

Spotting the entrance to the pass was easy. The dozens of soldiers and okties milling about carefully avoided an opening in the rock wall just wide enough for a dragon to walk through. The noise of the wind whipping through the gap in the wall also drew Micah's attention to it. No wonder they called it Fury's Pass. The wind sounded furious.

"It's not too late." Galiron approached Micah before Micah even dismounted Mertzer. "We can still turn around and enter through Rocky Way."

Micah shook his head. He wanted to retreat, but he wasn't about to give Galiron the satisfaction of being right. "Not a chance. We're here, and the wind is blowing. As long as the wind is blowing, we don't have to worry about the rocks heating up and burning us."

"Micah, my men are tired, and half of them are sick. Let us rest until daylight."

"And have to wait for Dahlia to feed at dawn? The only food she'll have to eat around here are okties. Or us. So no rest. We go. Now." Micah urged Mertzer forward until he was positioned in the clearing the soldiers had created. He whistled, directing all eyes to him. Once he had everyone's attention, he stood on Mertzer's back and shouted his orders. "Mount up. Serenity is the biggest dragon, so she'll go first to help block the wind for the rest of us. Then Vasilis, Dahlia, and Mertzer. The rest of you will fly low and follow us. Let's move!"

Mumblings and grumblings accompanied the scrambling of the soldiers. He didn't know what they were complaining about. This wasn't a boring training exercise. They weren't having to deal with people or punish lawbreakers.

They were on a dragon-hunting expedition. They finally had a chance to do something that mattered. The adventure of helping him catch a Midnight Stalker should trump any feelings of sickness or fatigue they might be experiencing. Maybe they would learn to appreciate the experience once they reached midnight territory.

Galiron glared at Micah as he marched by him on the back of Serenity. At twice the size of Mertzer, she was an imposing dragon with mean black eyes and generally nasty attitude. She was not going to be happy about taking the brunt of the wind through Fury's Pass.

Having her angry would help in the hunt for another Midnight Stalker, though. She would relish the opportunity to fight a dragon her own size. It would be much easier to cut the tail of a dragon who had expended all his energy fighting one of his own kind as opposed to attempting the same feat on a fresh dragon.

Phalloz, the wiry captain riding Vasilis, stared straight ahead as he walked by on his Noon Stalker Vasilis. Typical. Phalloz hadn't talked to Micah since Micah had beaten him in a boxing match a decade ago. That man sure could hold a grudge.

Vasilis, a good five feet taller and wider than Mertzer, seemed disinterested in the entire affair. He followed Serenity with a nonchalant air about him.

Dahlia, however, had her nose stuck up as high as it would go. With her white scales and wingless body, she was similar in size and appearance to Mertzer. But she was a prissy dragon who never liked to get her scales dirty. Shara, her captain, constantly had to take her to the lake for bath and reflection time. That dragon seemed happiest when she could gaze at herself in the water.

She didn't have any water around right now, but Micah wasn't all that concerned with nurturing the dragon's vanity at the moment. All he wanted to do was get through Fury's Pass.

Accomplishing that simple goal soon turned into a more difficult task than Micah ever anticipated.

◊　◊　◊

Micah leaned against the frozen scales on Mertzer's neck and listened to the only thing he could hear: the wind. It blew above and around him. Relentless. Cold. Loud.

The okties had refused to fly into it. Fighting their fear wasn't worth it, so Micah decided to leave half a dozen men to care for the okties and ordered the remaining soldiers to follow behind the dragons on foot.

He knew they were behind him, but he couldn't hear their footsteps. He couldn't see them, either. He couldn't see anything. The darkness was too thick. It took away his ability to see as well as his sense of time. He had no idea how long they had been in this narrow pass.

He wanted out of this place. With no end in sight and the walls close enough for him to touch on either side, he felt trapped. "Move faster!" He belted out the command, but the wind blew it away before it reached the ears of the caravan in front of him.

At least he had three dragons ahead of him. The wind would be ten times worse at the front of the pack.

"Deep breaths, Micah," he told himself. "Deep breaths. You'll be out of here soon enough."

After what seemed like hours, he finally noticed a break in the darkness ahead. "Ha! We're almost through," he said, keeping his eyes on the dot of grey at the end of the stone tunnel. "And Galiron thought this was a bad idea. I'll be able to capture a Midnight Stalker and be back at the castle before we would have even made it to Midnight territory following his route."

An aggressive gust of wind swooshed past Micah, nearly knocking him off of Mertzer. "Whoa!" Micah clutched the reigns and pulled himself back into an upright sitting position. The wind picked up speed, howling and swirling along the rocks.

Then silence. No wind. No nothing.

Until the rock walls started glowing, wiping out the darkness. Heat replaced the cold in an instant. If they didn't get out of here in the next few minutes, they were going to be caught in the impending firestorm. "Run! Fast! Get out of here!"

Serenity and Vasilis zipped ahead and disappeared. He assumed they made it through the exit. Which meant he wasn't far from freedom.

Only Dahlia couldn't run as fast as the bigger dragons and blocked Micah's progress. "Make her move, Mertzer!"

Mertzer snorted, put his head down, and rammed Dahlia from behind. As he pushed her along, tiny sparks began shooting off the walls. Screams from the soldiers singed by the sparks pierced Micah's ears.

That's when Micah remembered the soldiers weren't on okties. They were on foot. There was no way all ninety of them would escape before the pass burst into flames.

Should he leave them and escape, or pause to save as many as he could?

His training told him to protect himself.

An unfamiliar internal voice told him to stop and help those behind him.

Not sure why he was listening to the unfamiliar voice, he trusted his instincts, pulled on Mertzer's reigns, and yelled at Shara. "Shara! Stop!"

Shara stopped Dahlia and looked behind her. "Stopping is going to get me killed!"

More sparks began shooting off the walls.

One slapped Micah's face. Another burned his leg.

"Just for a minute. We have to save as many soldiers as we can!" Micah turned and yelled at the men and women running toward him. "Hurry! Climb on Mertzer and Dahlia!"

A swarm of people rushed onto the dragons, clawing their way up the scaly bodies. When no more could fit, he nodded at Shara. "Go!" As he urged Mertzer forward, he tried not to think of the fear he saw on the faces of those who couldn't reach him or listen to the sound of their screams.

Maybe he could still save them. Mertzer was the fastest dragon. Micah would get everyone on him and Dahlia out, then send Mertzer back in to rescue as many men as possible.

The exit was fifty feet away.

The heat intensified, making him feel like he was in a furnace.

Exploding rocks drowned out the screams of the people behind him. "Faster, Mertzer!"

Twenty feet to freedom. Ten. Five. Free!

Micah breathed in the cool night air and turned Mertzer around. No one left on foot had made it out yet.

"Everyone off!" Micah pushed the soldiers off the dragon and dismounted. "Mertzer, you've got to go back in there. Save who you can."

But he was too late.

Micah watched in horror as the pass burst into flames, incinerating everyone still stuck between the stone walls.

CHAPTER 6
RED CLAWS

The heat from the fire warmed Javan's skin and helped dry his drenched black hair as he fried one of the three fish he caught earlier that day. The post-fishing swim in the lake not too far from his wooded campsite left him feeling cool, relaxed and clean.

After swimming, he had covered his eyes with the color contacts he retrieved from his room in Gri. He didn't want to draw any unnecessary attention to himself in case he came across any people, and making his eyes brown rather than their natural glowing emerald green color would make him appear to be just another normal human being. Having someone identify him as the potential answer to the prophecy might jeopardize his dragon-collecting mission.

He still didn't want to believe the prophecy referred to him, but the similarities were too uncanny too ignore. Ever since reading it for himself, those words had been burned into his memory:

A young Collector whose eyes shine like emeralds and whose ears can hear the thoughts of any dragon will enter the competition in the final months of a Battle for the Throne year. He will be the only one capable of dethroning the king and must collect all four Stalkers by sunset on the final day of the battle year. If he succeeds, however, collecting the four Stalkers will not be enough to defeat the king.

The dethroned king will use his dragons and loyal subjects to wage a war unlike any Zandador has ever seen. The Collector must therefore unite the four opposing Bloodlines for only the united front of the four Bloodlines led by the young Collector will be strong enough to win a war against this most powerful of men.

If such a war is fought, the outcome thereof will determine the fate of the dragons once and for all.

He shook his head to relieve the pressure of those haunting words and focused his attention on his present situation.

Fortunately his chest wound was healing nicely. Two full days of laying around doing next to nothing had helped. So did the ointment Varjiek had somehow acquired. The dragon had told him not to ask questions.

Javan didn't need to. He had noticed several of Varjiek's scales were missing on his back left leg. Varjiek must have snagged the ointment from a nearby town and left some of his scales in its place as payment.

The logistics of the swap baffled Javan. Varjiek's ability to become invisible could easily allow him to fly around town undetected. That part made sense. But how did that big dragon get a hold of a small bottle the size of a soda can? Did he tear the roof off of a house to get to it? Or did it just happen to be in the open, allowing Varjiek to swoop in and make the trade without having to hurt anyone or destroy any property?

Javan was grateful the dragon had gone to the trouble to secure the ointment and had more important things to think about than how he came to possess it. Like where were his grandmother and the other missing townspeople of Gri? Had Ravier and his mother found them yet?

How was his mother? Everything had happened so fast after he rescued her from the Dark King. They never had a chance to talk before he took off on this mission with Varjiek, and he didn't like what he saw. She looked gaunt and lifeless after being paraded around Zandador like a criminal for the better part of a month, then stuck in the dungeon to rot.

He was less concerned about his grandfather Ravier. The man was a seasoned soldier, and the week he had spent in the dungeon didn't seem to weaken him. If anything, that had only sharpened his resolve to battle the king. What had seemed to suck the life out of him was the moment he had realized his wife Hannah was missing.

The gruff man who had trained Javan had been reduced to a puddle of mush in that moment. Javan was happy to learn that his grandfather had a heart capable of feeling, but he didn't like witnessing Ravier's anguish. Hopefully he had pulled himself together and now led the hunt to find Hannah.

Surely Astor and Hamilton were helping with the search.

He wished they were helping him. He missed the boxing lessons with the big, burly Hamilton and the Zandadorian survival lessons with the old, knowledgeable Astor. He even missed the dreadful but challenging sword fighting lessons with Ravier.

What if he hadn't learned enough to be able to make it on his own? He did fail miserably in his attempt to collect Mertzer and would have a scar to show for it for the rest of his life. Although he had managed to collect Varjiek on his own, that was only because the dragon had gotten himself caught in a time trap. It was either allow Javan to ride him or remain frozen in time for however long it took for the time trap to run its course.

What if the next dragon Javan met decided Javan made a better meal than Collector? Then Micah would win the throne on behalf of Omri, and the Dark King would remain in power. The people of Zandador would continue to suffer for centuries, and the remaining dragons in the land would not survive Omri's reign.

Javan pulled the fish away from the fire. It was cooked to perfection and ready to eat, but his appetite had vanished.

If he was back home in Montana, his biggest worry right now would be lack of playing time on the junior varsity football team. That seemed so insignificant now.

A soft breeze rustled the fire and tickled Javan's cheeks.

Varjiek. The dragon could make himself invisible, but the wind from his wings gave him away every time.

"I know you're here, Varjiek," Javan said. "You might as well let me see you."

A puff of smoke floated toward Javan from across the fire. Then the dragon's grey-scaled body appeared. *How do you do that? How do you know every time I'm near? It's annoying.*

"It's my job to know." Javan cocked his head and smiled. He might have failed with Mertzer, but he had won Varjiek. He could win again with another dragon, especially now that Varjiek was on his side. "You're my dragon."

His stomach growled. Good thing he had a fish ready to eat.

◊　◊　◊

"Next!" Micah could barely feel his frozen hands as they clutched the handle of his sword. As cold as it was in the valley they had traveled to over the past two days, he should be wearing gloves. But he didn't like anything covering his hands when he fought.

After watching thirty-seven soldiers burn in Fury's Pass, he preferred to be cold anyway. Trying to warm himself by the campfire only brought back images of those flames surging through the mountain walls and the sounds of the men and women burning to death.

Why did losing the soldiers bother him? It wouldn't have bothered his father.

Ryiah, a dark-skinned soldier about the same height and build as Micah, stepped into the circle Micah had carved into the snow. Micah vaguely recognized him as one of the men in his unit, but he didn't recall ever hearing the man speak. That's what Micah had liked about him: all brawn, no fuss.

Without a word, Ryiah tossed his coat aside and threw the hat that was covering his shaved head on top of the coat. Drawing his backsword, he nodded at Micah.

The bonfire to the right of them provided enough light for them to be able to see each other in the late-night darkness, prime hunting time for

Midnight Stalkers. They had yet to come across any, but this was not the time of day Micah wanted to find one.

Since Midnight Stalkers hated loud noises, Micah knew none would approach their camp if they maintained the steady sound of clashing swords. Still, Micah had each of the dragons with him positioned around the camp, and soldiers were stationed between the dragons to create a full perimeter.

He had allowed Serenity to leave her position to hunt for her own midnight meal. Now he was facing the soldiers one by one in the sword-fighting ring he created. None of them stood any chance of beating him, but it was good exercise.

Ryiah thrust his sword toward Micah. Micah smiled and blocked it with his own sword. The fight was on.

The sound of steel smashing steel echoed off the mountains around them. Round and round the circle they went, trading blows. Ryiah wasn't backing down. Or getting tired. Actually, he seemed to be getting stronger.

Who was this guy? Why hadn't Micah ever trained with him before? He was proving to be a challenge, something Micah wasn't used to encountering.

Micah had to concentrate to stay in control of the fight. Considering he hadn't slept or eaten much since this journey began, concentration was difficult. Good thing he was so well-trained that he could almost fight with his eyes closed.

Ryiah was also well-trained. But by whom? Micah needed to know. While blocking blows to his head, waist, and chest, he managed to spit out, "Who trained you?"

Ryiah paused with his sword in mid-air. Sweat dripped down his face. Fear flashed in his eyes. He looked like he didn't want to tell who his mentor had been.

Micah moved the tip of his sword to just under Ryiah's chin. "I asked you a question, soldier."

"You're not going to like the answer."

"Tell me anyway."

Ryiah lifted his head and lowered his sword. "Ravier."

"Ravier? The traitor?"

"Told you that you wouldn't like the answer."

Before Micah could respond, a streak of lightning flashed through the sky. A tree just beyond the range of the camp's perimeter crashed to the ground. More lightning streaks. More crashing branches and trees. The growls and grumblings of dragons added to the nightly noise.

"Excellent! Serenity has found us a Midnight Stalker!" Micah shouted. "Captains, mount your dragons and prepare to fight. All else, grab your weapons. Soldiers with bows, shoot the stalker's wings to keep it from flying. Those of you with swords, stab at its legs to keep in from running. Now charge!"

The men and women scrambled to retrieve their weapons and began a stampede toward the lightning show. Micah sheathed his sword, flung it over his back and ran the opposite direction to retrieve Mertzer.

He found the dragon curled into a ball. Snoring. The dragon looked uncomfortable with the bridle still on his long snout, but Micah hadn't taken it off in case he needed the dragon in an emergency situation. Like this.

He'd reprimand Mertzer later for falling asleep when he was supposed to be keeping watch. At the moment, he needed Mertzer awake and running at top speed toward the fighting dragons.

Micah grabbed the reigns as he jumped on Mertzer's back. The jerk of the reigns woke the dragon. "Get me to the Midnight Stalkers." Mertzer shook himself awake from his head down to his tail, stretched out each leg, and took off toward the fighting dragons.

Past the soldiers. Through the snow. Over rocks. Around trees. Until they reached a clearing. The Midnight Stalkers whose scales were slowly turning from grey to black circled each other. Every time one attempted an approach at the prize in the middle—a dead bison—the other would breathe a bolt of electricity to keep the offender away.

Serenity did not appear to be winning. She had a stripe of missing scales along her right side and was favoring her front left leg. The other dragon bore no battle scars and appeared to be in perfect condition. Its red claws matched its red eyes. Considering its size, Micah was surprised Serenity was still alive.

The dragon was a good ten feet taller than Serenity and made Micah feel like a midget sitting on top of Mertzer. Midnight Stalkers weren't supposed to be as big as this one was. And they certainly weren't supposed to have red eyes. If Micah could capture this unusual and frightening dragon, his father wouldn't just forgive Micah; he would be bound to surrender the throne to him.

Micah's breath hung in the air as he watched the dragons battle over their dinner. He could hear the stampede of approaching soldiers behind him and was aware of Vasilis's presence above them. Neither Midnight Stalker seemed to notice the commotion. They were too focused on dinner. As much as they hated noise, that focus wouldn't last much longer. Micah needed to take advantage of this opportunity while he could.

He maneuvered Mertzer so that he was standing sideways to the Midnight Stalkers rather than facing them. Micah drew his sword, stood on Mertzer's back, and waited.

Red Claws was approaching from Micah's left with his long tail dragging along the ground behind him. All Micah had to do was jump on the dragon's tail and slice through it. Then the dragon would be his.

"Come on, come on, come on," Micah muttered. He had practiced this tail-jumping move thousands of times. Even so, Micah felt his heartbeat kick up a couple of notches. The real deal was always more exciting than training.

The black tail inched closer. "Almost..." Micah made himself wait another second, then jumped.

His feet landed exactly where he wanted them, right in the middle of the tail.

The dragon's scales were slicker than he expected. He slid a few feet but managed to stay on, drop down, and wrap his legs around the thick tail.

"You're mine!" With both hands on his sword handle, Micah reached up. Just as he was about to slash the sword through the dragon's tail, a bolt of lightning hit the sword, shooting it out of his hands. "What the...?"

Micah couldn't finish his sentence. Not when he was staring right into the flaming red eyes of a hungry dragon.

CHAPTER 7
DEFEAT

"Mertzer! Vasilis! Attack!" Micah shouted the command as he dove off the tail, barely dodging another lightning strike from Red Claws.

Vasilis breathed fire down from above. It took the dragon's attention away from Micah but seemed to make Red Claws mad. The dragon spread his wings and shot straight up into the sky, ramming Vasilis in mid-air.

The collision took Vasilis by surprise and sent him spiraling out of control into the darkness. Red Claws remained unfazed. He kept his composure and swooped straight back down to Serenity. He kicked her head several times with his front feet. She didn't put up any kind of a fight. All she did was yelp and crumple to the ground.

Mertzer looked ready to fight the super-sized dragon, though. As Serenity lay on the ground whimpering and covering her head with her wings, Mertzer charged forward. Except he was no match for Red Claws. One swipe of the giant dragon's tail flung Mertzer into a nearby tree. Mertzer grunted as his head hit the tree trunk, knocking him out.

That's when the first of the soldiers started to arrive. One managed to launch an arrow that zoomed past the ear of Red Claws. That was all the firepower anyone could muster before Red Claws turned around and, hovering in the air, fired back with a steady streak of lightning streaming from his mouth.

One by one, the soldiers in the first wave fell. No second wave approached. The men and women who witnessed the destruction of their comrades chose to turn and run away rather than face the same fate. Including Dahlia, the only uninjured dragon left on Micah's side.

Cowards. All of them. Cowards.

Micah, however, wasn't about to retreat, not while the tip of the dragon's tail was brushing the ground. All he had to do was get to it and cut it off before the dragon tired of attacking the soldiers and flew away.

He picked up his sword and charged toward Red Claws from behind. Even though the soldiers were withdrawing, the dragon continued his assault. The noise of the screaming, running soldiers had the dragon half-terrified and half-crazed. Which was good for Micah. It gave him a chance to approach without being noticed.

As he ran, he kept his eyes on the tail. Ten steps. Five. Three. Close enough. He swung his sword at the tail. He missed. By a hair. Because just as Micah swiped at the tail, the dragon banked to the right, snatched the bison that started the battle, and disappeared into the night sky.

◊   ◊   ◊

He…lost. He lost the dragon. And nineteen more soldiers. Thirteen men and six women according to Shara's count. He had put her in charge of burying the dead. She hadn't been thrilled with the assignment.

He wasn't about to handle such a task. He needed to focus on more important things. Like analyzing what had just happened. How could he have lost the battle with that dragon? He was Micah, son of King Omri. He was a victor. Trained to win. Always.

What had gone wrong?

Micah considered the answer to his question as he paced in front of Serenity. She was slowly eating the deer and antelope he and Galiron had brought her while the remaining thirty-four soldiers and two captains buried the dead by moonlight in a mass grave dug by Vasilis and Mertzer.

His father's dragons were the problem. They were too soft. They could easily destroy defenseless people in defenseless towns, but they were no match for dragons who were used to surviving in the wild on their own.

Now he had to bring Serenity food because she was too beat up to hunt for herself, patch up Vasilis after his collision with Red Claws, and calm Dahlia down because she was spooked from the sight of the attacking Midnight Stalker. Five hundred years of being taken care of by humans had weakened the dragons.

Mertzer was a different story. He had awoken from being knocked out angry and ready to fight. Which meant Mertzer was his best chance at helping him hunt another dragon.

"It's done," Shara said. She approached with Phalloz and Galiron trailing behind her. Both men were taller than her, and her long brown hair blew in the cold wind. Without her bow on her back, she seemed as dainty as Dahlia. Micah wasn't sure if the strained look on her ashen face was because she was tense or tired. "The other captains and I have been talking."

That was definitely tension in her voice. Somehow the men had selected her to be their spokesperson. "You have, huh?" Micah said. "About what?"

"It's time to return home. One more encounter with that monster we just faced will be the death of us all."

Micah crossed his arms and studied the trio of captains. They stocd shivering in the darkness. Looking weak. Defeated. These people were no longer of any use to him. Just like his father's dragons.

"Have Dahlia teleport everyone back to the castle. Then send her back for me and Mertzer. I have somewhere else for us to go."

One thing was certain. He couldn't return to the castle. Not without another dragon. One with wings. One that currently belonged to Javar..

CHAPTER 8
NEW TERRITORY

Micah found himself in a strange predicament. No one knew where he was. No one knew where he was going. No one knew what he had planned. And he had no one to turn to for help. No friends. No mentors. No one.

He had been surrounded by people his whole life. Strategically placed people. People he wasn't allowed to get attached to. Mentors never trained him for more than a month at a time. They only discussed skills, technique, logic, rules, facts. Never emotions or feelings or anything personal.

The same held true for those he trained with. Because his heritage made him better than the people around him, Omri would not permit Micah to become buddies with his colleagues. Micah was more important than the people he worked with and had to behave accordingly. He couldn't be an effective leader if people he served with saw him as their equal and their friend.

Micah understood his role. He liked being independent and having the ability to suppress his emotions. That made him powerful. Just like his father. He thus willingly complied with all of his father's instructions and learned how to cope with not confiding in anyone about anything.

What he didn't understand was why Omri kept him away from his brothers and sisters. They might not all share the same mother, but they all shared the same father and thus the same bloodline. That made them equals, right?

Then again, it also made them rivals. Only the strongest among them would be able to win the throne. It would be easier to fight his own siblings if he didn't know anything about them.

He knew something about one of them, though. That's why he had Dahlia transport him and Mertzer here to the middle of Zandador, right outside the fishing city of Madai.

Perhaps he shouldn't have sent everyone else back to the castle. Had he kept some members of his unit with him, he would be able to order them to set up shelter, hunt for food, and do whatever else needed to be done. Now he had to take care of those pesky survival details on his own.

He knew how. Years and years of tough training made sure of that. He just didn't like it. He preferred having people around him to do his bidding so he could focus on more important things. Like how to hunt dragons.

Lack of sleep had to be the problem. He didn't make mistakes like Fury's Pass, losing fights with dragons, and cutting himself off from his team when he had adequate rest. He blamed Omri.

His father should have let him hunt a Dawn Stalker first. At the very least, he should have let him sleep before heading to midnight territory. Then he would have been able to return triumphantly to the castle with a new dragon, not find himself hiding in the woods fighting sleep early in the morning. All by himself.

He didn't want to be by himself. He wanted to be walking amongst the millions of other people inside the city.

He had the travel papers he needed to enter the gated city; his pass got him into any city any time. Usually his face was enough to get him in, anyway. He couldn't remember the last time a gatekeeper had asked to see his travel papers.

Too bad he couldn't use either asset. Everyone thought he was still in midnight territory hunting a Midnight Stalker. Dahlia knew the truth since she transported them here, but she was a dragon and couldn't talk. He was certain his secret remained safe with her.

Now his face was a hindrance. If someone spotted his very recognizable face or his very recognizable dragon and word got back to Omri, Micah was as good as dead. His father didn't mind deceiving others, but he didn't tolerate being deceived.

The lie wouldn't matter if he returned home with a dragon. But how was he supposed to get the information he needed if he couldn't barge into the city with a bunch of soldiers by his side to scare people into submission?

He had to find a way. His brother lived inside the city. They hadn't seen each other in decades, but Karl was the only person Micah could talk to who might know where Javan had gone to collect his next dragon.

"Think, Micah. Think." He rubbed his eyes and shook his head to wake himself up. "What's your next move?"

Micah had plenty of connections throughout Zandador, but they were all tied to Omri. They all followed the law of the land and played by the rules. Like Micah, they punished people who played outside of the rules. Now he was about to become one of those people. If he wanted to survive, he had to operate outside of the system.

What if the people he had punished—such as the boy who was hunting after curfew—operated outside the system so they could survive?

What if the system didn't work for them the way it wasn't working for Micah at this moment?

"Nonsense." Micah sat a little straighter and shook his head. "Everyone I punished deserved it. They were being rebellious. My motives are pure. I'm trying to win a dragon for the King."

How he went about achieving that goal didn't matter as long as he met his objective and pleased his father. If that meant breaking a few of the king's own rules along the way, so be it.

"One thing is for sure, Mertzer," Micah said. "I have got to get some sleep if I want to start thinking clearly again. We'll find a way into the city after dark. You keep watch while I sleep. When you get hungry, hunt your dinner, then come right back here. Don't bother waking me up."

Micah grabbed his gear and dismounted Mertzer. This wasn't an ideal camping spot, but he was far enough away from the city and the road to not be spotted by any people passing by or soldiers patrolling the area.

He didn't much care if anyone did find him. Mertzer wouldn't let them live to tell about it. All he cared about was closing his eyes and finally getting the sleep he needed.

◊ ◊ ◊

This is it, Varjiek said. He landed in the lush green grass of a meadow just south of where they had been camping for the past three days. The grass faded in front of them and gave way to wimpy patches of grass and scraggly scrubs that dotted the auburn-tinged sand. *We're standing at the edge of the desert.*

With the sun setting to his left, Javan adjusted his position on Varjiek's back and stared at the flat landscape that stretched out before him. It looked different than what he expected. He expected to see only sand, not any kind of plant life. Besides the grass and shrubs, he spotted a few towering trees in the distance. "It looks a bit bleak, not dangerous."

Just because we can't see the dangers doesn't mean they don't exist, Varjiek said. *The weather is the biggest problem. Storms strike without warning, and the heat makes it too difficult to travel by day. We'll have to keep moving at night to avoid freezing, but that's when the animals of the desert also like to lurk about.*

"Then it's a good thing we can just fly right over them. If I remember my geography correctly, the desert spans about 350 miles from north to south. As fast as you fly, we should be across long before the sun even rises."

The air here is thick. It slows my speed. We'll probably be able to move faster if I walk.

"Walk? Why would you want to walk when you can fly?"

Varjiek hummed to block Javan from reading his thoughts. His right ear began twitching. The tip of his tail tapped nervously on the ground. He shifted his weight back and forth. The dragon was hiding something.

"What are you not telling me?"

Varjiek took a deep breath and lowered his head as he exhaled. *According to Zandador legend, the wings of those who attempt to fly across the desert become crippled, and they are never able to fly again.*

"A legend? Is that why you had me pack three days' worth of supplies on your back? Because you planned to walk this whole time?"

Perhaps.

Javan wanted to scream. He had spent the entire day climbing uxe trees and cutting down leaves for them to eat on their trek through the desert. Each leaf looked like a dog's paw and was the size of a placemat. The top was smooth, and the underside had ripples like potato chips. Each ripple contained a streak of water, so they doubled as a water source.

Piles of them were tied to Varjiek's back with vines. They tasted like broccoli but were as filling as steak. Varjiek loved them. Javan didn't but was willing to endure them until they found something tastier to eat once they reached Keckrick.

Javan didn't think he would actually be stuck eating them for three days and only packed as much as he did as a precaution. If they ran into trouble, he wanted to make sure they had food to eat and water to drink.

"Any reason you why you didn't want to share this plan with me until now?"

You didn't need to know until now.

"Listen, buddy," Javan said, "we're a team. We need to be on the same page."

I do not understand. What is a page? Why would we need to be on the same one in order to cross the desert?

Javan rolled his eyes. He missed being around humans who knew how to interpret common sayings. "I mean we need to work on our communication skills. You've got to tell me what you're thinking. It's not like I can read your mind."

Umm…you can read my mind. That is how we are communicating right now.

"Oh. Right." Javan crossed his arms. "Then why didn't I know about your plan?"

Maybe I only let you hear the thoughts I want you to hear.

"You can block thoughts from me?"

Apparently.

"Okay. Fine. I guess I wouldn't like it if someone could read my every thought either. But you have to share your important thoughts, like the ones that involve where we are going and how we plan to get there."

You are right. I will work on my 'communication skills.'

"Good. Now forget this walking nonsense. Wings up. Let's fly."

But the legend!

"How reliable is this legend? Have you ever met any dragon or okty who tried to fly across the desert but ended up crippled?"

No. I have not.

"It's probably just some story a parent made up to keep their kid from hopping on an okty and running away from home across the desert."

What if it is true?

"What if it's not?"

It is a great risk.

"Face your fears, Varjiek. I trusted you once when you had me jump from a tree in hopes of landing on an invisible dragon that I couldn't see. It's your turn to trust me. Let's fly."

The dragon nodded. *As you wish, young Collector.* Varjiek spread his wings and lifted them into the air.

CHAPTER 9
GROUNDED

A cool breeze floated into Micah's tent, tickled his hair, and rattled the cloth walls. The second time he felt it waft across him, he opened his eyes to see the last rays of the setting sun bouncing around the inside of his makeshift room.

The breeze bothered him yet again. This time he sat up. And saw nothing but Mertzer's giant nostrils pointed directly into the open doors of his tent.

The dragon was sleeping on his back and breathing right into Micah's face from his upside-down nose. "Ugh. Mertzer, move." Micah freed his feet from his blanket and kicked the top of the dragon's nose with both his feet.

Before Micah could blink, Mertzer was on his feet and glaring into Micah's eyes.
"Whoa. How did you move that fast?"

The dragon snorted and narrowed his black eyes, eyes that seemed to be filled with hatred. Hatred toward Micah. Did this dragon have...feelings?

"You won't hurt me." Micah's voice cracked as he spoke. He cleared his throat before speaking again to try to sound tougher. "You can't. I'm your master. Now back off."

Mertzer held his ground. Micah held his breath. All the dragon had to do was spit one little drop of poison on him, and Micah would be dead. Perhaps it wouldn't hurt to treat the dragon with a little more respect. "Sorry I kicked you. I won't do it again."

That seemed to appease Mertzer. He bowed his head as if to say he accepted the apology and backed away.

"Did I just apologize to a dragon?" Micah plopped back down and covered his face with his arms. He clearly needed more sleep if he was allowing a dragon to dictate his manners. Micah wasn't the apologizing type.

Oddly enough, though, Micah found himself admiring Mertzer. He kind of liked that the dragon had a mind of his own and demanded respect. Which was unlike his father's dragons who took his abuse without question.

Demeaning the dragons the way his father did made Micah feel powerful. He knew, however, that it was a false sense of power. Had Omri not cut off their tails, they wouldn't hesitate to turn Micah into a meal. They were mean and cruel and had no regard for Micah.

Now he wondered how mean and cruel they really were. Had they always been that way? Or had centuries of being enslaved by Omri made them reflect the nature of their master?

Since Micah strived to be like Omri, would Mertzer end up reflecting his ruthless nature? Is that what he wanted for the dragon?

Is that what he wanted for himself?

Yes. Of course. He wanted to be ruthless. He wanted Mertzer to be ruthless. He wanted both dragons and people to fear them. That was true power. His father taught him that.

But if he was feared, would he be respected?

Which was more satisfying: to rule mindless cowards or to lead intelligent, confident beings who shared a mutual respect for one another?

Micah shook his head and sat up again. "Stop thinking. You know who you are. You know how to control dragons and people. Respect isn't important. Fear is power. Be ruthless. Make people fear you."

Micah looked to his right and saw Mertzer's silhouette through the thin cloth of the tent. The dragon was bound to obey him, but his spirit had yet to be broken. Micah needed to fix that. "Make Mertzer fear you."

He picked up his sword and whip and crawled out of the tent.

◊　◊　◊

A dim slither of the moon barely lit the cloudy night sky as Javan and Varjiek flew south. Slowly. So slowly Javan's black hair didn't rustle from a breeze. "Any chance you can pick up the pace and fly a little faster?"

I would if I could, Varjiek said, *but I feel like I'm flying through mud.*

"Can you run faster than this?"

I can walk faster than this.

"I guess flying wasn't such a good idea. Go ahead and land. Looks like we'll be crossing the desert on foot."

Thank you. Varjiek pointed his nose down, then promptly leveled out again. *Wait. What is that?*

Up ahead, Javan saw tiny specks of light sparkling against the dark night sky. "Think we should fly through it?"

Maybe they are stars. I've always wanted to fly through stars.

Javan felt Varjiek's muscles churn as the dragon worked to churn through the thick air to reach the low-hanging stars. The closer they inched toward the dazzling white lights, the more entranced both became. Nothing mattered except getting to the light.

After what seemed like an hour of struggle, they finally reached their destination. Varjiek eased his way into the midst of the lights that turned out to be thousands of round fuzzy dots the size of marbles floating all around them.

The dots moved to accommodate the large dragon and his rider. "Stunning," Javan said. "What do you think they are?"

Who cares? They are beautiful. We should take some with us. It will be easier to travel by night if we have them to light the way.

"Good idea." Javan tried to catch one, but it scurried just beyond his reach. He tried another. And another. All darted away. "They're scared of me."

Try talking to them. Varjiek swayed back and forth, his wings moving just enough to keep them airborne. *Tell them it's okay to land on my wings.*

Javan adjusted his seat at the base of Varjiek's neck and looked up to address his audience. "So…ummm…light thingies in the sky? We'd like you to come with us and be our light in the night. You can travel on Varjiek's wings. We promise not to hurt you."

None of the dots responded.

That wasn't very convincing. You need to work on your powers of persuasion.

"I convinced you to let me ride you."

That's because you promised me Skylark. The only thing you promised these lights is not to hurt them.

"They're dots of light. I don't know what they want; they aren't sharing their thoughts with me like you are. What else could I promise them?"

Better think of something because I'm not going anywhere without these things

Javan sighed and ran his fingers through his hair. "Maybe they like to fly on their own and will follow us. Try landing and see what happens."

Varjiek looked down but didn't move. *I can't. The lights below me are too pretty to fly into.*

Javan leaned to his left and looked down. The dots had formed a solid floor of light a few feet beneath Varjiek's claws. "Then fly forward."

And scare the lights in front of me? I think I'll stay where I am. Varjiek's words started to sound sing-songy, as though he were in a trance. *I like looking at the lights.*

"The lights are pretty." Javan knew he should be concerned, but he too was entranced by the lights and the smooth swaying motion of the dragon to let the alarm bells ringing in the back of his mind worry him. "Come, lights. Come land on the dragon."

One by one, the lights began to listen to Javan's beckoning call. Within minutes, they covered both of Varjiek's wings on the top and bottom.

This tickles, Varjiek chuckled, *but I like it.*

"Me, too," Javan said. "Your wings are so bright! And check it out. The lights are starting to blink."

Varjiek craned his head to admire the blinking lights on his wings. *Impressive!*

"I bet it will look even cooler when you flap your wings. Let's fly!"

I…I can't.

"What do you mean?"

I mean I can't move my wings. I can't feel my wings. Get the lights off me!

The blinking accelerated as Javan crawled over to the left wing and began swiping the lights away with both of his arms. But no matter how many he shoved off, more landed in their place. "It's not working!"

I can't keep us in the air. Hold on, young Collector. We're going down.

Javan had just enough time to latch onto the edge of Varjiek's wing before they plummeted to the ground.

CHAPTER 10
MICAH SEEKS HELP

Micah packed away the last of his gear into his dragon bag, threw it over Mertzer's back and mounted the dragon. The strip that held the two weighted bags together sat flat on the dragon's back. He found the hole in the middle of the strap and latched it to the tip of a scale before settling in at the base of Mertzer's neck.

The sun had yet to rise, but Micah wanted to make his way into the city before first light. "All right, Mertzer. I need to enter the city on the east side. As soon as I jump the fence, you return to this spot. Remain here until I return for you. That should be tonight, but it all depends on how fast I find Karl and how much he knows."

Micah tapped his whip against the dragon's tender scales to remind him about the beating he endured last night. "Understand your orders?"

Mertzer flinched and nodded.

"Good. As long as you continue to obey me, I won't have to use the whip again. You lost the right to do what you wanted when you lost your tail." Micah grabbed the reigns and leaned against Mertzer's neck. "Let me feel your speed. Get me to the eastern fence!"

Mertzer snorted, lowered his head, stomped the ground, and dashed toward the city.

The dragon seemed to sail over the land. Micah didn't even feel the bumps of the trip even though he knew several hills over several miles separated them from the fence.

Before Micah realized they had gone anywhere, the fence that seemed so far away now towered above Micah's head. "Whoa!" No dragon he had ever ridden had been able to go from zero to super speed that fast. His dragon could fly. He simply used his feet rather than wings.

"Impressive, Mertzer," Micah whispered. "Now hold still. I'm going to use you as a ladder to get over the fence. The instant I jump, run back to the woods."

Mertzer took a deep breath and made himself rigid. Micah smiled. He loved having a creature like this under his control.

Micah could easily reach the top of the fifteen foot fence from his stance atop the back of ten foot tall dragon, but he would still have to work hard to pull his own tall frame up and over the sharp wooden pickets. Mertzer's neck gained him an additional five feet, making his neck even with the top of the fence. The top of the dragon's head would provide a nice platform and minimize the work Micah would need to do to get over the fence.

He left his supplies with Mertzer, secured his sword to his back and his whip to his waist, then made his way up Mertzer's neck. He peered over the fence. Even though the darkness prevented him from seeing the ground, he knew it was a long way down. A wave of queasiness rolled through him at the thought of plummeting into the darkness below.

He could make out the top of a building about five feet away from the fence, though. He would just need to jump out rather than down. That thought settled his stomach and kept him from wanting to throw up.

"Here goes." Micah stepped from Mertzer's head to the top of the fence and pushed himself forward. He landed on his feet on the flat tin roof, took a few running steps, and dropped to his stomach once he finally gained control of his momentum.

He waited for the residents of the building to investigate the crashing sound they were sure to have heard. When no one came, he breathed a sigh of relief.

He had made it into the city. Undetected.

If he wanted to stay that way, he needed to steal some clothes. He shuddered at the thought of having to wear the ugly brown garments of the commoners, but he wouldn't be able to walk through the city without being noticed if he kept his uniform on.

Just one more reason to hunt Javan and make quick work of killing him. The sooner he got rid of Javan and captured his Noon Stalker, the sooner he could return to the castle and make his father happy again.

◊   ◊   ◊

Every time Javan closed his eyes, he relived the crash landing from the night before.

Wobbling from side to side at an angle perpendicular to the ground. Watching the ground get closer and closer as the dots on Varjiek's wings glowed brighter and brighter. Falling faster and faster. Yelling at Varjiek to slow down. Varjiek yelling that he had no control.

Clinging to Varjiek's neck. Praying the dragon would land on his feet and not his head. Flying off Varjiek's back when the dragon's front legs collided with the sandy ground. Rolling in the dirt. Seeing Varjiek's wings spread over the dirt while his body remained motionless.

Running to Varjiek. Thanking God when the dragon looked up at him and said he survived. Listening to Varjiek moan while he brushed off the light dots and gently folded the round wings into Varjiek's body.

Javan opened his eyes and wiped a layer of sweat off his forehead. Even under the makeshift blanket he had made after the crash last night by tying uxe leaves together, the heat from the desert sun made life miserable.

He had tossed the uxe blanket over him and Varjiek just as the sun began to rise, curled up in the crook of Varjiek's back left leg, and attempted to sleep. Sleep had eluded Javan but visited Varjiek. The dragon continued to snore, even though his scales were beginning to change from grey to gold.

"Better feed him," Javan said. He unrolled his long sleeves to protect his arms from the sun, tied a spare shirt around his head to help prevent sweat from dripping into his eyes, and plopped his wide-brimmed, floppy hat on over the shirt. After donning his shades, he crawled out from beneath his shelter.

Sand, sand, and more sand covered the flat land behind them and to their left. Way out in the distance, the flat land turned into rolling hills of dunes. Ten feet to their right, the land disappeared.

Javan jumped over Varjiek's tail and walked over to investigate. The land hadn't disappeared; it dropped off and formed a deep canyon several miles wide and as long as Javan could see. Ragged red rocks formed the walls and floor of the canyon, rocks that surely would have killed them had they landed on those sharp edges rather than the soft sand of the desert floor.

"Wow. That sure was close."

Javan? Javan, where are you?

Javan turned around to see Varjiek stirring under the uxe leaves. "Coming."

I still can't feel my wings. He stood and shook the blanket off of him. *You should go on without me. I am a useless dragon who will never be able to fly again!*

"Calm down." Who knew dragons could be such drama kings? "I'm not going anywhere without you, and it may just take a little while to get the use of your wings back. Even if you don't, you are still quite useful."

You want me even if I can't fly?

"Of course." Javan stroked Varjiek's snout from his eyes to his nose. "We're in this journey together."

Thank you, young collector. Varjiek stretched each of his legs. *At least my legs have suffered no injuries. But they are still sore from the rough landing. Will you feed me so I don't have to walk anywhere to find food?*

"Sure." Javan tore several leaves off the edge of the uxe blanket. His dragon knew how to milk an injury. "You get to fill up on uxe leaves today."

◊   ◊   ◊

Micah didn't know how much more of this sitting and waiting and watching and observing he could handle. He had no problem being patient while hunting prey in the woods, but trying to blend into the background around people proved challenging. He usually demanded the center of attention and preferred being the one giving orders.

Instead, he had spent all morning dressed in uncomfortable clothes hiding in the shadows of a fish shop located in the middle of the Madai harbor hoping to spot a brother he hadn't seen in over fifty years.

A wooden boardwalk connected one end of the city to the other along the bank of the River that Runs Through Zandador. The bank curved inland, creating a huge U in the middle part of the boardwalk. Dozens of piers branched off the boardwalk and stretched into the water. Fishing boats of varying sizes docked sporadically at the piers.

Young boys and girls serving their required tenure learning the fishing trade unloaded cargo and cleaned the ships under the supervision of the older career fishermen. Soldiers patrolled the boardwalks and piers ensuring no one left or arrived without proper documentation.

Micah had missed out on all of this. He had spent his childhood learning how to fight and hunt dragons, not learning how to fish or farm or learn any trade. He wasn't even technically old enough to be in the army yet. At his age, he should be serving a decade-long stint learning a trade. He looked older than he was, though, and passed himself off as 177 rather than his actual age of 77.

Only a few people knew his true age. His brother Karl was one of those people. He was Omri's fifth son and Micah's only other sibling from the same mother. Because of that bond, Karl had taken Micah on his first official hunting trip.

That trip had not ended well for Karl and was the reason Omri had kicked Karl out of Japheth and sentenced him to a lifetime of fishing here in Madai. It was also the reason Karl would be easy to pick out of a crowd. Not many people walked around with a piece of wood for a left leg.

"What are you doing here?" The man who whispered the words in Micah's ear also gripped his shoulder and shoved the tip of a knife into Micah's back.

Micah forced himself to remain relaxed and casually kept his eyes on the water. "Looking for you."

"Why? Shouldn't you be out hunting dragons instead of your outcast brother?"

"I am hunting dragons, but I've run into a little trouble. That's why I'm here. I need your help."

"The last time I helped you, I lost a leg, my position in the army, and my father. I ought to repay the favor by cutting one of your limbs off and sending you back to the castle. I doubt you'll still be the king's favorite son when he sees you're no longer perfect."

"That's an option." Micah resisted the urge to disarm Karl and decided to let his brother continue to feel like he controlled the situation. "Or you can help me and get yourself back in our father's good graces. I may not be able to do anything about your leg, but I can restore your place in the castle."

"Impossible. You know Omri never reverses any punishment."

"He will if I ask. As you said, I am his favorite son. Besides, if you help me accomplish what he wants more than anything—which is to stay in power—he'll be happy to welcome you back home."

Micah felt the breath of his brother on his neck as the man considered his words. Finally, the iron grip on his shoulder loosened, and the sharp point of the knife went away. "He'll never welcome me back home, but I do want something he may be willing to grant me if you ask on my behalf. What do you need?"

"What do you want?"

"Answer my question first."

"Information." Micah turned around and looked into a pair of eyes that matched his own. "I need to know where to find Javan and his dragon."

CHAPTER 11
ON THE HUNT

It took Micah all afternoon to walk from the harbor to Karl's house at the other end of the large city. He could have taken one of the horse-drawn carriages that shuttled people from the docks to their homes, but he wanted the exercise. He needed it to keep his edge and maintain his physical superiority over Javan. Unfortunately, this past week had left him with not enough sleep and no chance to run. The loss of sleep and lack of exercise left him feeling cranky and weak.

The walk through the city revived him. He kept to the western path under the trees that separated the homes from the community buildings in the middle of the city. Unlike the eastern side of the city dominated by rows of barracks for the interns and soldiers stationed in Madai, rows of houses dominated the western side. Families lived in the three bedroom houses in the southern end while all the single residents, such as Karl, lived in the one bedroom houses in the northern end.

Despite his trek in the shade, Micah smelled like fish, sweat, and dirt by the time he walked into Karl's small home on a dirt street cluttered with similar small homes. As the door creaked closed behind him, Micah took in his surroundings.

A few cabinets, a sink, a woodstove, and a cooler comprised the kitchen on his right while a single rocking chair in front of a fireplace completed the living space on his left. Nothing hung on the shabby wooden walls. What a bleak and boring place to live.

It did at least have power. He noticed a string of scales lined the top of the walls along the ceiling all around the house. What he didn't see was the activation scale he needed to turn the lights on.

"Maybe it's in the bedroom, which I sure hope is cozier than this." Micah crossed the room in five steps and opened the door to the room behind the kitchen. "Nope. Just as blah."

A cot topped with a green blanket and white pillow filled the middle of the room. The only other furniture was a short brown dresser with two drawers in the far corner beside the bathroom door. After checking out the bathroom that was barely big enough to turn around in, Micah returned to the bedroom, sat on the cot, and stared at the blank walls.

This is how his brother lived?

While Micah lived in the castle with a bed as big as this room and a room twice as large as this house, Karl lived…here. Micah felt a twinge of guilt sear through his conscience, but he shook it off. "It's not your fault, Micah. Karl chose to fight that bear."

To convince him of his innocence, Micah's memory took him back to that night. He was just a kid in his twenties, and Karl was escorting him on his first official training mission. All was going well. Until night fell. And the bear appeared at the water's edge not far from their campsite.

Micah wanted to kill it. The meat would last for weeks, and the black fur would look great as a rug on his floor. Plus his father would be so proud.

Karl warned him to leave it alone. He said Micah wasn't old enough, experienced enough, and strong enough to defeat the six-legged beast yet.

Micah disagreed. He grabbed his sword and slithered toward the bear in the tall grass. When he was inches away from stabbing the bear in the back, it roared, turned, and swiped Micah to the ground with one of his claws.

The blow left Micah bloody, shaken, and swordless. Before he could get up or recover his sword, the bear attacked. Micah saw the bear's teeth and smelled his rancid breath as his gigantic mouth closed in on Micah's head.

Then it screeched. Roared. Left to chase Karl.

Karl wasn't fast enough. It caught him.

They fought.

The bear took Karl's leg, but Karl took the bear's life. Micah stood by and watched it all happen, too paralyzed by fear to help his brother.

That's not the story Karl had told their father, though. He later told Omri Micah had saved him from the clutches of the bear, fought valiantly, and killed the beast all on his own.

Micah didn't correct the lie and had been Omri's favorite ever since. Karl had ended up here.

"Not my fault." Micah stood and shook his head. "He didn't have to save me or lie for me." He hadn't backed down from a fight since, but he knew his reputation as a warrior had been built on that lie.

Micah staggered into the bathroom. He needed a shower to wash away the memory.

◊   ◊   ◊

Once the sun set, Javan had put on every last stitch of clothing he had with him. That consisted of brown pants, a t-shirt, a long-sleeved brown shirt, and the blue jacket he brought with him from Montana. None of it seemed to help. He felt like he needed about forty more layers to insulate him against Varjiek's ice-cold scales and the frigid night air of the desert.

The good thing about the cold was that it motivated Varjiek to get up and move. The dragon had been strangely quiet and still all day, but as soon as the first chill washed over him, he stood and said he was ready to walk.

His pace had been slow at first but had picked up significantly once he got used to walking with his lifeless wings. They had been walking for hours and were finally approaching the sand dunes Javan had spotted earlier that day. Judging by the light from the moon and stars, mini mountains of sand now blocked their path.

Varjiek paused in front of the changing landscape and sighed.

"What's the problem?" Javan asked.

The problem is that my wings still don't work, and I have to walk over all these hills. How do dragons with no wings handle all this walking? It's exhausting!

Javan chuckled. "Experiencing the walking woes of us wingless creatures is good for you. It builds character and gets you in better shape."

I don't want to be in better shape. I want to fly.

"Do you need to stop and rest for a bit before continuing?"

No. It's too cold. Besides, we have company. It will be easier for them to attack if we stay put.

"Company?" Javan looked around but didn't see anything. "What company?"

A pack of wolves has been trailing us for a while. I think they are waiting to pounce after we get over the first hill so they can jump on me from above.

"Say what? A pack of wolves is hunting us?" Javan drew his swords and restlessly scanned the area around them again. He still didn't see or hear anything. "How many? Where are they? What should we do? And how can you be so calm about this?"

I am often hunted and know how to win these battles. Varjiek started up the hill. *I can usually fly away to escape my predators, but tonight I shall have to rely on my defense mechanisms. It will be a fun test of my skills.*

"Being hunted by wolves is not my idea of fun, but okay." Javan gripped his swords tighter as they climbed. "Why don't you make yourself invisible?"

I am. The wolves are tracking my scent.

"Oh."

They can also hear you talk and are getting closer.

"Oh. Shutting up now."

Javan stretched his cold, tight muscles and watched his clouds of breath fade into the darkness as they trudged upward. Looking down, he could see a semi-circle of four legged beasts at least nine wide climbing the hill behind them. How were they going to defeat an entire pack of wolves?

Varjiek walked slower and slower the closer they got to the top of the hill. The wolves, however, picked up their pace. Javan could hear the growls and snarls of the pack as they closed in.

"Why are you slowing down?" Javan whispered. "These guys are about to attack."

I know, Varjiek said, sounding giddy. The threat of a wolf attack seemed to be the cure for the dragon's depression. *That's why we're going to attack first. Keep your swords ready but hold on.*

Javan barely had time to hug Varjiek's neck before the dragon spun around and lit up the night with a stream of fire. Several wolves caught fire, shrieked, and ran away. Others howled and charged forward.

Varjiek fended them off with his fire breathing. All but one. Javan tracked it as it ran to the top of the hill and leaped on Varjiek from behind.

Javan stood on Varjiek's back and faced the animal. "Got a problem here, Varjiek."

Got lots of problems out here, Javan. Just be loud and look intimidating.

The huge white wolf that stood waist-high to Javan crouched and inched toward him, growling and showing his razor sharp teeth.

"You may have sharp teeth, buddy, but I have sharp swords. Bring it on."

Javan hoped the wolf wouldn't accept his challenge. He wasn't all that confident in his ability to best a strong, mean, hungry wolf. What he really wanted to do was jump and run. But he'd lose a foot race in a heartbeat. He'd be better off dropping his swords and curling into a little ball to protect his face and neck if the wolf attacked.

Hoping to prevent an attack and scare the wolf away, he heeded Varjiek's advice by standing his ground, swishing his swords through the air, and yelling as loud as he could. He tried not to let the bursts of light from the fire and loud screeches from the other wolves distract him from acting like a mad man. One wayward glance and he could end up as this wolf's next meal.

The wolf bared his teeth, inched closer, and lowered his front paws. The pack of supplies strapped to Varjiek's back was the only thing separating Javan from danger.

"He's about to pounce, and I don't know how to stop him!"

I do, but you need to duck.

Javan dropped to his stomach as the wolf leapt over the supplies. At the same time, Varjiek's tail whipped through the air and collided with the wolf's body, sending him sailing into the sand. Varjiek followed the beating up with a stream of fire that singed the wolf's fur. It whimpered and disappeared into the darkness along with the rest of the retreating pack.

And that is why you don't cut off a dragon's tail, Varjiek said. He sounded jubilant. Victorious. Happy. *Otherwise we can't use it as a weapon to keep you humans safe.*

"I am glad I'm a Collector and not a Hunter." Javan laughed, re-sheathed his swords, and reclaimed his seat at the base of Varjiek's neck. Now he, too, felt giddy. The dragon's attitude was contagious. "Let's keep going. Maybe more animals will attack us as the journey continues."

I like the way you think, young Collector. Varjiek stuck his head in the air and pranced the rest of the way up the hill. *I like the way you think.*

◊　◊　◊

The creaking sound of a door opening woke Micah from a deep sleep on Karl's deceptively comfortable cot. The noise seemed to have come from inside the dark, windowless room, but the door leading to the living space remained closed. A piece of the floor along the wall beside the dresser, however, was now raised up.

Micah slowly reached under the pillow and latched on to the dagger he hid there before falling asleep. If anyone other than Karl came through the floor, he'd be ready to fight.

"You can put the knife away, Micah." Karl lifted himself through the floor. The lantern he pulled up with him lit the dark room. "It's just me."

Micah left the dagger where it was and sat up. "How did you know I had a knife?"

"If you didn't, I'd be ashamed to admit I once trained you."

"You're lucky I didn't take your head off. What are you doing under your house in the middle of the night? The curfew law dictates you shouldn't be out doing anything after dark."

"Are you going to turn me in?"

"I should."

"Enforcing laws that keep people small and restricted isn't as noble as our dear father would have you believe."

Micah wasn't entirely sure what his brother meant by that, so he changed the subject. "Did you find Javan?"

"I reached out to everyone in my network and didn't come up with anything until a few hours ago. One of my guys brought me this."

Karl limped over to Micah and tossed a golden sliver on his lap. "An active noon stalker scale? This is incredibly valuable and could power the castle for centuries. Where did your guy find this?"

"It showed up in Posa--"

"Posa? What is he doing in Posa? That's directly south of here and nowhere near any stalker territory."

"A bottle of healing ointment disappeared in the same spot two fully active noon stalker scales appeared."

"Javan would have needed ointment. I cut his chest open when we fought over Mertzer. But how did he get two scales off his dragon during its feeding time?"

"Anyone that can manage that is a serious threat to the throne. You might be better off hunting dragons rather than this Collector."

"Nonsense." Micah stood and shook off Karl's warning. "He's ruining my life. I have to take him out and make his dragon mine."

"Then you should head south. If we leave now, I can get you out of the city while we still have the cover of darkness to protect us."

"You can get me out of the city? How?"

"Underground tunnel." Karl smiled and shrugged. "Don't tell Dad."

CHAPTER 12
EXCHANGE OF FAVORS

Micah listened to the rhythm of Karl's wooden leg echoing against the brick walls as they walked along the stone floor of the tunnel. Its rounded ceiling left plenty of room for them to walk through without crouching, and its width gave them enough room to walk side by side. Karl made Micah walk behind him anyway in some sort of power play.

Micah didn't like following. It made him feel weak. He wanted to lead, to be in charge. He also wanted to carry the lone light in the dark space, but Karl refused to give up the lantern. If Micah didn't need Karl's help, he would have snatched the lantern from him at the start. He hated playing nice.

Omri wouldn't play nice if he knew this tunnel existed. He would send his dragons and level the entire city. Maybe that's what Micah should do once he became king. That would get the attention of the people. They would wonder how he knew their secrets and fear him more than they feared Omri.

What if every city had tunnels like this, though? He couldn't wipeout everyone and everything or he would have no one left to rule.

Why did the people feel the need to build the tunnels in the first place? Was it because Omri's laws were too oppressive? If the people were allowed to travel when they needed to go somewhere—regardless of the time of day—they wouldn't need a secret tunnel system.

Such thoughts made Micah's head hurt. Everything used to be black and white. The law clearly dictated the difference between right and wrong. Obey the law or suffer the consequences.

But Micah wasn't obeying the law at this very moment. According to the law, he should be tucked away in his home sound asleep. Not breaking curfew by being out after dark. And certainly not walking in an illegal tunnel to travel outside of the city without travel papers approved by the local travel administrator.

He also wouldn't be seeking help from a fisherman whom Omri had banned from the capital city. He had been banned because of Micah. So why was Karl helping him now? Why had Karl helped him all those years ago? Perhaps now was his chance to find out.

Micah halted and crossed his arms. "Karl, stop."

Karl ignored the order and kept walking. "We don't have time to stop."

"I need to know why you saved me from that bear, then told our father I killed it."

Karl paused and turned. The lantern light now lit up both their faces. "You were in trouble. I was the only one around to save you, so I did."

"But we were trained to protect ourselves, not each other. Plus you made me out to be the hero. Why?"

"If Omri knew how scared and shaken you were, he wouldn't have hesitated to disown us both. Losing my leg sealed my fate; Omri would never keep a disfigured son in his presence.

"But you? You were young and strong and smart. Killing a six-legged bear at an age when most kids couldn't hold a sword would set you up for life. And it did. You're becoming a legend. If people knew your true age, they would be even more amazed at your accomplishments."

"I still don't understand." Micah stepped closer to Karl, closing the gap between them. "You had nothing to gain by protecting me and enhancing my reputation."

"I'm your brother, Micah. Family looks out for each other, even if one has to make sacrifices to raise the other one up. Our mother taught me that."

"Our mother?" Micah had been too obsessed with training and working to please his father to spend much time around his mother. "She didn't have a chance to teach me much of anything. I only see her once every few years."

"When you get home," Karl said, his eyes tearing up, "you find her, hug her, and tell her I love her."

"I will." Micah found it odd that Karl missed their mother more than their father. She was nice, but his father was the one with all the power. Shouldn't Omri be the one Karl missed?

"Let's carry on." Karl cleared his throat and dried his eyes. "We've wasted too much time already."

They walked the rest of the way in silence, which didn't help Micah's headache. The silence forced him to think, and thinking made him question his relationship with his parents, the laws of the kingdom, and the validity of his quest to hunt dragons in order to keep his father in power.

Just when he thought his head was going to explode from too much thinking, they reached the end of the tunnel.

"We're here," Karl said, pushing open a stone door. The smell of water whooshed through the opening. "Watch your step. The ledge is only a few feet wide, and one little misstep will have you swimming in the river below us."

Karl crept out, followed by Micah. Sunrise was still hours away, so the lantern remained the sole source of light as they inched along the narrow path that led up the rocky cliff. Once they reached the top, Micah could make out the silhouette of Madai about a mile away.

"All right, brother. We're out of the city. Go find the Collector and his dragon. When you are successful, I expect you to return for me." Karl looked around, waving the lantern. "Where are you hiding your dragon?"

"Just north of here." Micah glanced at the river behind him. Mertzer was terrified of water, and Micah would never be able to get the dragon to swim across. "I'm going to need one more favor before we part ways."

"You want my boat, don't you?"

Micah smiled. "You read my mind."

"I figured you would need a way across the river. Some of my men are set to meet us at Schrader's Pier about three miles south of here. But there's only one way I'm going to let that dragon on my boat."

"What's that?"

"Just get your dragon to the meeting spot. I'll tell you there." Karl winked and began a lopsided jog south along the bank of the river.

Guided by the light of the moon and stars, Micah sprinted through open meadows, patches of woods, and farmland to reach Mertzer's hiding spot.

The run revived him. Being woken in the middle of the night and spending hours winding through a confined space had his nerves on edge. But the open air and intense exercise cleared his mind and made him forget about his lost sleep.

The sight of Mertzer curled into a ball and sleeping underneath two giant oak trees also relaxed him. Fortunately the dragon was right where Micah ordered him to stay. The sun would be up soon, and he didn't have time to hunt Mertzer down or beat him for not complying with his orders.

Mertzer opened his eyes as Micah approached him.

"Good," Micah said, "you're awake. Time to get up and travel south." He loaded his gear on the groggy dragon, hopped on, and led Mertzer back over the path he had just taken.

Mertzer covered the miles in the blink of an eye, but Micah pulled him to a stop just before they reached the water's edge. If the dragon caught a glimpse of the water, he would freeze the way he did when Javan tried to collect him.

That ridiculous fear of water had given Micah the window of opportunity he needed to steal Mertzer from Javan, but that fear could work against him now. So he needed a way to work around it.

"All right, Mertzer. You're not going to like this, but tough. Do what I say anyway." Micah took a blanket out of his bag, dismounted, and walked around to face the dragon. "Lower your head, close your eyes, and remain still."

Mertzer cocked his head and squinted before finally complying. When he dropped his head low enough, Micah wrapped the blanket around his eyes and tied it behind his ears. Mertzer flinched and snorted but didn't attempt to remove the blindfold.

"Good boy." Micah stroked the dragon's snout to keep him calm. "I'm going to hold your reigns and walk in front of you. All you have to do is listen to me and follow my lead. I'll take the blindfold off soon enough."

Mertzer huffed and shook his head, loosening the blanket.

"Whoa!" Micah yanked on the reigns. "Stop that. Try it again, and I'll have to get my whip out." Mertzer settled down, and Micah retightened the blindfold. "Let's go."

They walked steadily along the river until they reached the pier. Karl stood on the sandy shore in front of the pier, and his boat floated in the water at the end of the pier.

"Glad you made it," Karl said. "We weren't going to be able to wait much longer."

"Let's just load up and get across this river as fast as possible." Micah started leading Mertzer toward the pier, but Karl stopped him.

"Wait. Remember that favor I mentioned?"

"Yeah. What is it?"

"I want to ride your dragon onto the boat."

Micah hesitated. "I don't think that's a good idea. He's unsure of his footing with that blindfold on, and he's never had anyone but me ride him."

"Take the blindfold off."

"I can't. If he sees the water, we won't be able to get him to walk anywhere."

Karl crossed his arms and shrugged his shoulders. "If I can't ride your dragon, you can't ride on my boat."

"Fine." Micah sighed. He wanted to tell Karl no, take over control of the boat, and be on his way. He also didn't want to share his dragon, but the man was missing a leg because of him. The least he could do was let him ride Mertzer for two seconds. "Mertzer, bend down, and let my brother ride you."

Micah tugged on the reigns to convince Mertzer to crouch low enough for Karl to climb on. Karl approached from the left side, grabbed on to Mertzer's neck, and pulled himself up onto the dragon. Once he got situated, he motioned for the reigns. "Hand me the reigns. I'm ready to ride."

"No. I'll lead him from down here."

"Nonsense. I'm not a child. Hand me the reigns."

Karl put his hands out and stared at Micah. Not wanting to waste any more time, Micah grit his teeth and complied.

"Thank you. You go ahead and get on the boat. We'll be right behind you."

Micah grumbled the whole way down the pier and walked up the plank that led to the deck of the boat that was going to be just big enough to hold Mertzer. Three gruff, bearded men standing beside the cabin at the bow of the boat didn't even notice when he walked aboard. They were too focused on the dragon headed towards them.

Mertzer did make an impressive sight. His white scales practically glowed in the dark, and the thunderous sound of him trampling along the wooden boards shook the boat.

Micah smiled at the wide grin on Karl's face as the pair approached the plank and decided letting him have this moment of glory wasn't such a bad idea after all.

As they began walking up the wobbly plank, though, Mertzer's legs began to shake, his tail began to twitch, and his body began to tremble. "Hurry and get him on board," Micah said. "I think he knows he's near water."

"Up we go, boy," Karl said. He urged the skittish Mertzer forward, but as soon as he stepped on the deck of the boat, the boat swayed back and forth. The swaying seemed to upset the dragon. He spun around, balked his head, and started spewing poison in every direction.

The crew ran to the front of the boat, Karl yelled at Mertzer to calm down, and Micah grabbed a jolt blaster hanging on the side of the cabin. He shot Mertzer in the side, sending bolts of electricity through the dragon's body.

"Quick," Micah screamed at the retreating crew, "get us out of here and to the other side before he recovers from the shock!"

CHAPTER 13
SOUTHWARD BOUND

Javan didn't want to move. After traveling all night in the cold going up and down one sandy hill after the other, then spending the first few hours of the morning in the blazing sun with nothing but a hat to protect him from the heat as they walked across a barren, cracked earth, he liked the cool tree Varjiek had found to camp under at the edge of a dry riverbed.

The trunk of the tree was hollowed out in the shape of a teepee and had an opening just large enough for Javan to crawl inside. The long, thick branches were covered with leaves and thus provided Varjiek with the shade he needed to escape the heat of the sun.

They had been quietly resting for hours when Javan heard terror in Varjiek's words. *Javan! I'm being attacked! Help!*

Javan grabbed his swords and scrambled out of the tree. "What is it? What's wrong?" He looked around to see if the wolves had found them again but saw nothing.

It's this bug. Right here. On my dinner. Kill it!

A spattering of Varjiek's scales had turned to their typical golden color, and he had the half-eaten blanket of uxe leaves spread out before him. Javan had to strain to see the tiny ladybug crawling around on one of the leaves. "Really, Varjiek? You can fight wolves without a second thought, but you're scared of a cute little ladybug?"

These things are lethal!

"Lethal? That bug is lethal?"

I ate one once and almost died. My throat swelled up and I couldn't breathe.

"Oh. You must be allergic to them. For a second there I thought my dragon was a big baby." Javan walked over and flicked it off the leaf. "There. I saved your life. Now we're even. You can finish your meal, and I can finish my nap."

Javan made it halfway through the door when Varjiek called for him again. *Javan, there's another one.*

Without a word, Javan walked over and flicked it away. But three more appeared in its place. He swatted them off the leaf only to find five more show up. "Where are they coming from?" All he had to do was look up to answer his own question. "Uh oh."

Thousands of the red-bodied, black-spotted insects swarmed in the branches above them. "We should probably get out of here, Varjiek."

What? Why? The dragon's eyes followed Javan's. As if on cue, the bugs dropped all at once, covering Varjiek, Javan, and their precious food source. *Leave the leaves! Save yourself!*

With that, Varjiek sprinted away.

"Wait for me!" Javan swiped as many of the bugs off as he could, snatched his hat, backpack, and sword belt, and ran into the hot desert sun after his petrified dragon.

◊   ◊   ◊

Shooting Mertzer with the jolt blaster got Micah's trip south off to a bad start. Although it calmed Mertzer and kept him from destroying the boat or inadvertently jumping overboard in his traumatized state, the short trip across the river didn't give the dragon enough time to recover from the shock. As Micah, Karl, and the crew of three discovered, dragging a dazed dragon off a boat was not an easy task.

It took them until sun up to get Mertzer off the boat and onto the swampy south shore. The only way they had been able to do that was by wrapping Mertzer in fishing nets and pulling the dragon inch by inch down the plank.

Micah wasn't sure what story Karl was going to tell the authorities to explain his missing boat at the dawn check in. It better have been a good one, or Karl faced a lashing at best and imprisonment at worst.

Soon his brother wouldn't have to worry about following the law; he would be able to enforce it again once Micah completed his dragon-hunting mission, returned triumphantly to the castle, and convinced Omri to reinstate Karl's place as a soldier. At least he thought that's what Karl would ask for when Micah returned for him. He never did say exactly what he wanted in return for his help.

Half the morning had gone by before Mertzer had been alert enough to walk, but Micah couldn't travel on a walking dragon through south Zandador once they got to the edge of the marshland.

The lack of wooded areas in this part of the country would make Mertzer easy to spot even if they avoided the roads that connected the assortment of villages, cities, and towns throughout the open land. Since Mertzer couldn't become invisible, Micah needed to wait until he could run too fast to be seen.

By noon, Mertzer had regained his strength, so Micah pushed him hard in a zigzag pattern through meadows and farms as they headed south toward Posa.

He still didn't know why Javan had come to Posa for healing ointment. It was the southernmost city of Zandador and more than 1500 miles east of Dawn Stalker territory. Plenty of other towns closer to stalker territories could provide healing ointment, towns nowhere near the desert. So why would he come to Posa?

Micah was still pondering that question when they reached the outskirts of the city. Like Madai, it had a fence around its perimeter and guards at the gates. Micah didn't need to get inside the city, though. He wanted to find Varjiek, and Varjiek would not be in the city; he would be camped somewhere outside the city.

He had nowhere to hide north or south of Posa. The desert was to the south, and the land to the north was nothing but rolling green meadows. The open land did give way to woods east and west of the city along the desert border. All Micah had to do was search the woods for signs of a dragon.

First he needed to take care of his own dragon by letting him eat, since Mertzer's scales were beginning to change colors. He wanted to deny Mertzer dinner due to the frustration he caused earlier, but dealing with a hungry dragon wasn't worth the hassle.

He thus steered Mertzer toward the woods east of the city and released him to hunt for his dinner. While Mertzer hunted for food, Micah hunted for signs of Javan and Varjiek.

Micah wound his way through miles and miles of towering uxe trees until he came across a meadow that housed a quiet little lake teeming with fish. During a quick perimeter search, Micah discovered a dragon-sized patch of trampled grass on the south side of the lake near buried ashes from a small campfire. The ashes were cold, but the bony remains of fish mixed in with the ashes couldn't have been more than a few days old.

"Found you," Micah said, sifting the dirt and ashes through his fingers, "but where did you go?"

He stood and looked around, hoping to find some clue to indicate which direction Javan had gone. "What are you doing, Micah?" He sighed as he chided himself. "Varjiek probably flew out of here, and you can't track an airborne trail."

Frustrated, he turned to head back in the direction he had come knowing he needed the hour of daylight he had left to get back to his rendezvous point with Mertzer. Something, however, was bothering him about the woods further south. Too much light streamed through those trees.

Logic told him to ignore it and get back to Mertzer. His gut told him to investigate. He listened to his gut and sprinted south.

He didn't have to sprint far to find the reason for too much light: dozens of uxe trees had been stripped of their leaves, allowing the fading sunlight to filter all the way through to the ground. Javan would only need to chop down that many leaves if he was preparing for a trip through the desert.

No dragons lived in the desert or in the regions south of Zandador. So why would Javan want to subject himself and his dragon to the dangers of the desert?

"The healing ointment must not be working on that wound. I bet he needs to make his way to Keckrick for medicine."

Micah smiled. A weak Javan would make for an easy target, especially in the desert where the playing field was leveled. If the legend was true, Varjiek wouldn't be able to fly over the land, and Mertzer could run much faster than the Noon Stalker.

Despite their head start, Micah and Mertzer would be able to catch up to them in no time. All Micah had to do was gather a few uxe leaves of his own for the journey, then meet up with his dragon.

If all went well, he would have a Noon Stalker added to his name by morning.

CHAPTER 14
OASIS

More, Varjiek urged, sticking out his tongue that had become as dry and cracked as the land they stood on. The sun had risen a few hours ago, bringing with it the now familiar brutal heat of the desert days. They hadn't been able to find trees or vegetation of any kind in this part of the desert and were forced to simply cook in the sun like they had done all yesterday afternoon.

Javan shook the canteen over Varjiek's tongue, but no water came out. "Sorry, V," Javan said. His own tongue felt like cardboard, and his saliva glands seemed to have stopped working. His shriveled lips made talking painful, and his parched throat made him sound hoarse. "It's gone. Every drop is literally gone."

After losing their uxe leaves yesterday, Javan had rationed their only source of water as best he could. It had gotten them through the hot afternoon and evening, but they were both so drained by the time the sun went down that progress during the night had been minimal. Now they were facing another day of brutal heat with no water to carry them through.

Javan sat down between Varjiek's two front legs and took advantage of the shade Varjiek's head provided. Varjiek, however, had no such relief from the heat. "How close do you think we are to Keckrick?"

I am normally very good with direction, but I do not know anymore. My mind is jumbled, and I feel like everything is moving, even though I am laying still.

"I'm dizzy and confused, too, and this throbbing headache keeps getting worse. We have to keep moving and find water."

Moving will exhaust us too much. We must conserve our energy and wait until nightfall.

"What about food for you? Some of your scales are still golden from yesterday, so I know you didn't get enough to eat. In a few hours, you're going to be super starving."

I am not worried about food. I have a meal waiting to be eaten right here.

"You do?" Javan looked around, saw nothing, then realized Varjiek was referring to him. He jumped up and backed away from the dragon. "Whoa! Wait a minute! You can't eat me!"

Varjiek chuckled. *It is good to see you still have some fight left in you. Now sit back down and relax.*

Javan crossed his arms and stared at Varjiek. What if the dragon did become so hungry and disoriented that he decided Javan would make a good meal?

I promise not to eat you, young Collector. Come sit.

"You better keep your promise." Javan wiped the sweat from his brow and took a step back toward Varjiek. But a bright reflection to the west—like sun bouncing off water—caught his eye. "V, check it out. I see a lake!"

Varjiek turned his head to look in the direction Javan pointed. *I do not think you see what you think you see. All I see is an endless expanse of dirt.*

"No." Javan shook his head and squinted. The reflection remained, and it was surrounded by fuzzy things that appeared to be trees. "I know what I see. That has to be water. It's not that far away. We're gonna survive after all!"

It's a mirage, Javan. You're hallucinating. Come sit and close your eyes.

"That is not a mirage. It's real."

Why can't I see it?

"Maybe you need glasses. Now get up. Let's go."

It is not a good idea. If it is a mirage, we will die of thirst walking in this heat.

"We have two options. We can curl up here and let the sun cook us to death, or we can head toward that water while we still have some life left in us. If it turns out to be a mirage, at least we died trying to do something."

All right. Varjiek rose to his feet. *Let's hope your illusion is real.*

◊　◊　◊

Bored, hot, and unable to sleep, Micah climbed out of the cave at the southern end of Red Rock Canyon just before noon. Wolves howled in the distance, and Mertzer listlessly licked water out of a tiny stream several feet below him.

The sand dunes loomed before Micah, mocking his progress. Micah had wanted to get past the dunes before sunrise, but Mertzer had not cooperated. No matter how hard Micah kicked and whipped the dragon, he refused to run through the desert and maintained a turtle-like pace all night long. Frustrated, Micah had decided to find shelter in the caves of the canyon while it was still dark and cool rather than risk being stuck in the dunes with no relief from the heat during the day.

Even with his hat on, sweat began pouring into Micah's eyes as he scanned the sand around him. He had memorized a map of the desert as a young child and could picture exactly where he was on the map. What the map hadn't prepared him for, however, was the life-draining atmosphere.

A breeze would probably help ease the burden of the hot sun, but the lack of wind made the air feel thick and sticky.

He hated this place.

What if Javan hadn't traveled into the desert? What if those missing uxe leaves were a decoy meant to get Micah off track while Javan actually traveled to Dawn Stalker Territory? What if he was chasing no one in this wretched heat?

As he took a swig of water, he noticed some strange patterns in the sand to his left. Since the black streaks didn't appear to be that far away, and the hill didn't appear to be all that high, he ventured away from the safety of the canyon and up the hill to investigate.

He misjudged both the distance and the incline. The journey took him twice as long as he expected, and the climb required him to constantly hydrate in order to keep going. His canteen was thus empty by the time he reached the first streak.

He didn't mind. What he found would supply him with all the energy he needed to make it back to the canyon where he could replenish his water supply.

He also no longer minded the lack of wind. The dry air had preserved the footprints and fire streaks of what appeared to be a battle between a fire-breathing dragon and a pack of wolves.

Micah smiled and breathed a sigh of relief. Javan and Varjiek were traveling through the desert. That meant Micah was on the right track and couldn't be too far behind them.

He wanted to take off after them right now, especially since he knew no wind indicated a storm was brewing and could blow through at any time. But he knew it would be wiser to stay in the shade the canyon provided and wait until nightfall to travel.

He also needed to make sure Mertzer would have something to eat come dusk. Judging by the amount of wolf footprints in the sand and all the howling he had heard while trying to sleep, food for Mertzer would be plentiful if they stayed put for the rest of the afternoon.

As Micah headed back toward the canyon with his shirt soaked from sweat, he regretted drinking all the water he had brought with him.

◊　◊　◊

The sun made Varjiek's scales too hot to touch, so Javan had walked alongside his dragon all morning long. Varjiek had to adapt his stride to allow Javan to keep up with him, but he preferred the shorter stride to the added weight of a passenger. Now as noon approached, they both walked so slow that it felt like they weren't making any progress at all.

"There." Javan attempted to point and speak, but he was too weak to do either. He could smell the grass and trees and water. He knew he was close. He knew what he saw was real and not a mirage. He just couldn't make his legs go any further. As he tried to take one more step, he dropped to his knees. "Go, V. Go eat. Save yourself."

He hoped the dragon understood him even though he didn't hear his own words pass through what used to be his lips. *This is it*, he thought as he fell the rest of the way to the ground. *I'm going to die. But I got my dragon to water. He is going to live. I am a good Collector.*

With his face laying in the sand, he used what energy he had left to wave Varjiek onward with his left wrist. Then he blacked out, never expecting to wake up again.

Until he did. And he was wet. Drenched. So covered in water he couldn't breathe. He coughed. Breathed in water. Flailed his arms. Kicked his legs. Felt a muddy surface. Stood. Breathed in the air just above the water's surface.

"What just happened?" His throat still hurt from being so dry, but at least he could hear himself form actual words again. He licked his lips, took several more sips of the life-giving water, and looked around.

He found himself standing in a lake surrounded by palm trees and waist high grass, some of which had been trampled by a dragon dragging a body. His body. But he didn't see his dragon anywhere.

"V? Varjiek? Where are you, buddy?"

The only answer he got came from an arrow that flew past his head.

Javan dove back under the water, but that turned out to be a bad plan. He couldn't hold his breath for more than a few seconds and was too drained from the desert walk to swim. So he did the only thing he could think of. He surrendered.

As he resurfaced, he held his hands in the air and shouted as loud as he could, "Don't shoot!"

Men with loaded bows all aimed at him lined the shore. One in the middle spoke. "You are an intruder in our territory. Why shouldn't we shoot?"

"Ummm...valid question." He cleared his scratchy throat and tried to think of something smart to say to avoid being shot to death with arrows. The sun seemed to have fried his brain, however, and he couldn't form any coherent argument.

"Answer or we shoot in five seconds."

"I'm not here to hurt anyone." Javan needed some backup. Where was Varjiek?

"Four."

"I'm just passing through from Zandador." Maybe if he stalled long enough, his dragon would show up and defend him.

"Three."

"All I want to do is get to Keckrick." Javan's heart raced. What if Varjiek had collapsed in the lake and drowned?

"Two."

"How about I say I'm sorry for bothering you and just move on?"

"One."

Javan closed his eyes and braced for the assault, but before he heard any arrows zip through the air, Varjiek's voice cut through the stillness.

I can fly again! He burst up from under the water in the middle of the lake, wings spread, scales golden, breathing fire into the air. He flew several circles above the trees around the lake before coasting back down to hover over the water beside Javan.

"If you shoot me," Javan said, crossing his arms and staring at the leader, "my dragon is going to eat you. Your choice."

The leader lowered his bow, and the others did likewise. "I think we can find something a little less human for your dragon to eat. You look like you could use some food as well. Please. Come join me in my tent for the noon meal."

Javan wasn't sure he should trust a guy who was willing to kill him ten seconds ago, but the thought of eating a real meal inside a cool tent was too tempting to resist.

CHAPTER 15
CLOSING IN

Within hours of sunset, Micah and Mertzer had tracked Varjiek's trail over the dunes, across the flat, cracked earth and straight to a hollow tree. Tiny specs of something littered the ground, so Micah pulled his coat a little tighter and dismounted Mertzer to investigate the area.

He picked up a handful of the specs and studied them in the moonlight. "Shredded uxe leaves. Odd." He brushed the specs off his hands and poked his head inside the tree. A blanket that appeared to be a makeshift bed spread on the ground. "Javan was definitely here, but why did he leave his blanket behind? Nights out here get cold."

As Micah walked around, he noticed a set of dragon tracks and human tracks leading away from the tree. "Hey, Mertzer. Look at these footprints. It looks Varjiek ran away from here, and Javan followed him on foot. Why wasn't he riding his dragon? And why am I talking to mine? It's not like he can answer me." Micah shook his head and hoped this desert trip wasn't making him go crazy on top of feeling paranoid.

At least he knew the source of his paranoia: the windless day and night. He liked the ease of being able to track Javan since no wind allowed all footsteps to remain etched in the sand. But the longer the wind ceased to blow, the stronger and longer the sandstorm would be once it finally hit. What made him jumpy was not knowing when the storm would come. If he and Mertzer got caught in such a storm in this flat area with no tree or rocks to protect them, surviving would be problematic.

They could hide out under the tree and wait for the storm to pass, but they might be waiting for days for a storm that may never come. Besides, Micah had used up his store of patience while waiting for Karl in Madai. "No more waiting." Micah hopped on Mertzer. "We go and hope we're out of the desert before the storm strikes."

His hope was crushed about five minutes later when a gentle breeze ruffled his dreadlocks. One look to his left revealed a wall of sand headed straight for them. "Back to the tree, Mertzer! Back to the tree now!"

Micah had just enough time to dive inside the tree before the storm reached them. And without being told, Mertzer used his body to cover the opening in the tree bark, keeping Micah safe inside the shelter.

"Good dragon," Micah said, patting Mertzer's scales as the rest of his body was battered with wind and sand. "You're a very good dragon."

◊　◊　◊

Javan opened the flap of the tent to the sound of laughter and dancing and music. Night had fallen, and the fifty or so people who made their homes in the oasis were gathered around a crackling bonfire in the center of the small tent village having a grand time.

"We were beginning to wonder if you were ever going to awaken." Lew, the brown-skinned, dark-haired chief who had fed and housed Javan earlier, offered Javan a seat by the fire and handed him a bowl of soup.

"I had a rough day, but I feel like a new man now." Steam emanated from the bowl, and Javan decided the thick broth with chunks of meat needed some time to cool before he took a bite. "That rest did me good. Thank you for your hospitality."

"Sorry for trying to kill you. The few visitors we do get are usually bad men who mean us harm."

"It's forgotten." Javan scooped a spoonful of meat and took a bite. He enjoyed the taste of the spicy meat but didn't dare ask what it was. He could very well be eating something as disturbing as snake or monkey meat, and that would ruin his appetite. "So where's Varjiek?"

Lew pointed to the far side of the bonfire. "Playing with the kids."

Javan looked past the dancing adults to the laughing kids. About fifteen children and teenagers swarmed all over Varjiek. The young ones used his tail and legs as a slide while the older ones threw sticks in the air that he would set on fire with his breath. Why hadn't Javan thought of playing that game with him before? "He looks like he is having fun."

"As are the children. They have never seen a dragon before. Dragons do not travel through the desert." Lew lowered his voice and stared at Javan. "So why are you here?"

"Fair question." Javan had avoided all questions at lunch. His hosts had been too scared of Varjiek to make Javan uncomfortable by interrogating him. Now that they saw Varjiek as a giant toy, they seemed to have lost all fear of him and were back on the offensive. They did deserve answers, though, so Javan resisted the urge to go play with the kids and stayed seated to answer the question like an adult.

"I am a Dragon Collector from Zandador and am competing in the Battle for the Throne. Varjiek is the first dragon in my collection, and we are headed to Keckrick in search of a Dawn Stalker."

"Dragons live in Zandador, not Keckrick."

"I said the exact same thing, but Varjiek insists that a young Dawn Stalker is hiding out in Keckrick."

"Keckrick is a big place filled with mysterious plants and dangerous animals. The humidity can be excruciating, and the people there are at war with one another. How do you plan to find this hidden dragon while battling all those elements?"

Javan's heart sank at the realization that he had no plan. But he was a Collector and could show no fear. He couldn't let Lew know how scared he felt. "I'm just trusting my dragon on this quest." He shrugged, then added, "If you have any ideas, I'm open to suggestions."

"The northwestern shore."

A woman whispered the words in Javan's ear, causing him to jump up and spill the soup all over the ground. "Whoa, lady! You can't sneak up on a guy like that."

The plump old woman with short white hair and a long blue dress laughed at him. "At my age, I can do whatever I want."

"Javan," Lew said, "meet my grandmother Miranda."

"Hello," Javan said, nodding at the laughing woman. "So where did you say I should go?"

"The northwestern shore. One of the few remaining families from the Protector Bloodline lives there. If a dragon is in Keckrick, that family is sure to be protecting it."

"You're sure?"

"I am certain."

"Then I guess--"

Before Javan could finish his sentence, one of the guards rushed up and yelled, "To your tents! A sandstorm is headed this way!"

The music stopped. The kids ran to their parents. And as the people worked together to douse the fire, Lew warned Javan, "Take your dragon and fly away now. This storm could last a few hours or a few days; you won't be able to travel until it passes."

"Yes, sir." Javan shook Lew's hand. "Thank you for everything. You saved our lives. How can we possibly repay you for that?"

"Collect your dragons. Win the throne. And allow us to come live in Zandador."

"Did the Dark King ban you from Zandador?"

"It is a long story that you do not have time to hear right now. Get on your dragon, fly out of here, and beat the storm."

"Okay. But I will be back." Javan nodded at Lew, gathered his things, and took off on the back of his dragon toward Keckrick.

◊   ◊   ◊

Micah huddled under Javan's blanket inside the tree hour after hour listening to the howling wind and the sound of the sand slapping the leaves above him. Both the ground and tree constantly vibrated as a result of Mertzer's body being beaten against the trunk by the wind. He worried that the tree would uproot and expose him to the elements of the sandstorm if it lasted too much longer.

Just when he didn't think his sanity or the tree could endure one more second of the storm, everything stopped. The wind. The sand. The vibrations. All became quiet. In the silent, cold darkness, Micah tapped Mertzer's side. "You can move now. Let me out."

Mertzer groaned and inched away from the opening. Micah crawled out, breathed in the early morning air, and checked on his dragon. He had buried his head under his front legs, but sand still covered his body from snout to tail.

Micah lifted Mertzer's head and softly brushed the sand off the dragon's closed eyes. "You okay?"

Mertzer's eyes fluttered open, and all Micah could see in the black pools staring back at him was pain and sadness. He gulped at the realization that his dragon had feelings. "Sorry you couldn't fit in the tree with me, but thanks for keeping me safe."

The dragon blinked and offered Micah a slight nod. Were they communicating? In a respectful way? Like friends? Could a dragon be his friend and not merely a slave? Omri would say no, but Micah was beginning to believe such a relationship might be possible.

"Think you can run? There should be an oasis not too far west of here. If you can function at even half your normal speed, I bet we can make it there by sunup. Then we can rest in the soft grass under shade of those trees all day long."

Mertzer gave Micah another nod, raised himself to his feet, and shook until most of the sand flew off him. Once Micah climbed aboard, they took off in the direction of the oasis.

Micah allowed Mertzer to set his own pace, a decision Micah soon regretted when Mertzer chose to merely walk. Eventually, however, Micah's annoyance wore off when Mertzer's walk turned into a trot.

His trot never did turn into a run, but they still made it to the edge of the oasis by the time the sun poked through the morning sky. Micah slowed Mertzer to a walk and steered him toward the thick patch of palm trees south of the lake. Before he made it there, though, two young boys blocked his path. One had dark, curly hair, and the other had his hair shaved so short that Micah couldn't tell what color it was.

"Cool! Another dragon!" Curly hair looked up at Micah. "Can we ride him?"

"Ride him? No! Why would you think you can ride my dragon?"

"The other guy let us ride his dragon."

"The other guy?" Micah kept the excitement out of his voice. He had to find out if Javan was still here in a way that wouldn't make these boys think he was a threat.

"His dragon was bigger and could fly," shaved head said, "but your dragon is awesome, too."

"You have to be talking about my friend Javan and his Noon Stalker Varjiek. Are they around?"

"Nah," curly hair said. "They left last night before the storm."

Last night? Micah was so close to catching them! "Do you know where they went?"

"Sure. He went to Keckrick to collect another dragon."

"What?" Micah tried not to show his surprise. "He's going after a dragon in Keckrick?"

"Yeah. I think there's a Dawn Stalker."

"I need to help him find this Dawn Stalker. Do you remember where in Keckrick he was going?"

Curly hair shrugged. "I don't know."

"I do," shaved head said. "My mom said she heard Miranda tell him to go to the coast."

"The coast, huh?"

"Yup." Shaved head looked proud that he knew something curly head didn't know. "So can we ride your dragon now?"

"No. I have to get to Keckrick."

"But Keckrick is like a hundred miles away. Your dragon looks tired, and it's hot out there. You can stay here with us until it cools down again tonight."

"I appreciate the offer, but my dragon is fine. He can run fast. We'll get through the desert before it gets too hot." Micah grabbed Mertzer's reigns and pointed him south. He was too close to Javan to let a little thing like heat stop his progress. "No time for rest, Mertzer. We have to get to Keckrick now."

How about his luck? He would be able to return home with three dragons, not just two. His father was going to be so proud!

CHAPTER 16
KECKRICK

Javan's first glimpse of Keckrick came in the dark when Varjiek landed in the head-high grass of the region an hour or so before midnight. The dragon had used his size and weight to trample out a campground and ensure no snakes or other uninvited critters were hiding where they wanted to sleep.

The wonderful soft feel of the grassy bed enabled Javan to snooze peacefully until after nine that morning. He still felt weak after having the life zapped out of him in the desert the day before, but the good night of rest combined with the breakfast of energizing fruit he brought with him from his new desert friends got his day off to a great start.

Once Javan finished eating and packed up, they had taken to the skies to try to spot the dragon he had come to collect. Although he didn't see any dragons, what he did see from the air amazed him.

"This place is extraordinary." Javan drank in the beauty of the land below him as he soared westward through the sky on Varjiek's back. Every shade of green he could possibly imagine in every sort of shape and size he could think of covered the land in the form of grass, ivy, plants, ferns, and leaves.

Vibrant pink, purple, red, yellow, blue, and orange flowers poked through the greenery on the trees and shrubs in random places. They weren't just any flowers, though. The colors popped as if they were electrified. He wasn't sure if the flowers were actually that gorgeous or if everything appeared brighter after being in the flower-free zone of the desert for the past three days.

In addition to the stunning landscape, Javan spotted a few tigers milling along the streams, heard birds singing from the treetops, and took note of several small villages scattered between the trees.

I do like this land. It reminds me of home. The scale beneath Varjiek's left ear turned from grey to gold. *I know I am going to eat well today.*

"Let's pick up the pace and get to the shore. While you hunt, I can walk the coastline in search of the dragon."

Excellent plan. A patch of scales right under Javan's hands burst into gold. *I am growing hungry and am eager to begin my hunt. Hold on!*

The wind slapped Javan's face and his ears popped as Varjiek went from floating like a lazy eagle to zipping through the air like a supersonic fighter jet on a time-sensitive covert mission. The change of speed also turned the beautiful landscape into a colorful blob that resembled a picture a preschooler might scribble if given a piece of paper and box of crayons.

Javan felt queasy by the time an almost completely golden Varjiek landed on the white sand of the Keckrick coast. Seeing the red ocean wasn't as much of a shock as the first time he saw it more than a month prior further north in Zandador, but he still didn't like it. Oceans should be blue, not red. Some of the things he saw here in the Great Rift just didn't make much sense.

He slid off Varjiek and sat in the sand with his eyes closed hoping the queasiness would soon pass.

Wow! I forgot how much fun flying is. I love that my wings work again! Varjiek flapped his wings, dusting Javan with sand.

"Yeah. That was a real blast." Javan put his head between his legs to keep from losing his breakfast and covered his ears to keep his eardrums from popping out of his head.

Are you okay? I forgot I had a human riding me who might not be able to handle my maximum speed.

"I'll be fine." He waved Varjiek off. "Go. Hunt. Eat. Come back and find me when you're full."

Yes, sir. Goodbye! Varjiek left with a whoosh, and Javan soon found himself being lulled to sleep by the sound of the waves lapping against the sand. Without daring to open his eyes, he laid back, covered his face with his hat, rolled up his sleeves, and enjoyed the sensation of the cool breeze across his skin.

He could search for the dragon tomorrow. Today he was going to simply be a beach bum. As long as he kept his eyes closed, he could pretend the water was blue, and he was just a teenager skipping school to play at the beach.

He liked the idea of letting himself be a normal kid from Earth for one afternoon, not a man on a mission to collect dragons, overthrow a ruthless king and free the people of Zandador. Sometimes that pressure was overwhelming.

◊ ◊ ◊

"He couldn't have made tracking him any easier." Micah stood in the middle of a beaten down circle of grass he and Mertzer stumbled upon a few miles after entering Keckrick. The smashed grass was still green and limp, so the dragon-sized circle had to have been made recently. "But where did he go from here?"

Micah couldn't see anything but grass from where he stood and fought to remember what the map of Keckrick looked like. He hadn't bothered to memorize details, because he never thought he would find himself in this tropical land. He had only put in that kind of effort with the desert map because the desert bordered Zandador, and he wanted to be familiar with any territory bordering his homeland.

Now he was cursing himself for not paying more attention the geography of the other regions in the Great Rift. He closed his eyes and worked to picture the map hanging on the wall of the map room in the castle.

From what he recalled, the middle third of the country was uninhabitable due to the thick rain forest and torrential storms that swept through from the coast to the canyon on a year-round basis. The upper third and lower third also experienced constant rainfall, but the rain forest canopy wasn't as thick, and the storms weren't as brutal as in the middle of the region.

He shouldn't need to head too far south, though. His hunt should take him west toward the shore. And since this grass served as a buffer zone between the desert and jungle-like areas, he may not even need to deal with the humidity, plants, and animals found further south.

"That's what we'll do, Mertzer." Micah got his bearings from the early afternoon sun and turned to face the dragon. "We'll head west straight through the grass."

Mertzer snorted and stared at Micah. His white scales looked dry and crusty from the morning walk through the desert, and his lifeless eyes told Micah he didn't have the heart to take another step without some recovery time.

"We can wait until the morning, though. I want to give Javan time to collect that other dragon, anyway." Micah licked his chapped lips and realized his dragon wasn't the only one who was parched. "In the meantime, I am going to find some water."

He grabbed his canteen from Mertzer's back, then went ahead and unstrapped his bags to free Mertzer from the load he had been carrying for days. Mertzer seemed to appreciate the gesture, because he rolled over and rubbed his back in the grass.

"Stay here until I return. If I'm not back by dusk, go ahead and find something to eat. If I'm not back by dawn, come find me."

Having delivered his orders, Micah drew his sword and began cutting his way south through the grass.

He soon discovered that he enjoyed the challenge of tromping through the grass. His muscles had started to atrophy from lack of use over the past few days, and having to slice his way forward for hours made him feel like he was engaging in some excellent sword training exercises.

He thus found himself a bit disappointed when a swipe of the sword ended the grass covered-land and opened up the world of the rain forest. Here at the outer edge, he could walk through the palm trees and ferns and dandelion bushes without having to forge a path with his sword. He missed both the work and the whirring sound his sword made during the blade-cutting action.

That mesmerizing sound was now replaced with a chorus of chirping, buzzing, and hissing animals. The sounds warned him that he would now have to remain constantly on guard in case one of the animals was stupid enough to bother him.

At least the way the long leaves drooped from the trees and the brightly colored flowers popped along the path made the scenery more pleasant than seeing nothing but grass every which way he turned.

The scenery improved even more when he finally found a stream trickling through moss-covered trees. The cool, clear water acted like medicine for his hot, dry skin as he splashed it on his face, and he couldn't remember ever tasting anything so refreshing when he took his first sip.

After relishing several more sips, he filled his canteen, dodged a leech that nearly attached to his hand, and followed the stream further into the jungle. He figured if he stayed near the water, he would eventually find people. People could provide food for him to eat and a bed for him to sleep on, and he wouldn't have to worry about them reporting back to his father.

All the people here should have a healthy fear of the King due to the trading relations between the regions. Micah wasn't sure of the details, but he knew that if Keckrick didn't meet the quota of medicinal plants Omri demanded, Omri would send a Justice Unit through the portal that connected the two regions. Like in Zandador, the mission of a Justice Unit was to kill and destroy anybody or village who made Omri unhappy.

Micah planned to identify himself as Omri's son and demand food and shelter. If the people didn't comply, he would threaten to have his father wipe them out with a Justice Unit. The plan sounded simple enough.

Then he met the people of the Clartritch Village.

CHAPTER 17
A HOSTILE WELCOME

The stream led Micah right to a village of about thirty or so round huts built side-by-side in a large semi-circle under the rain forest canopy. The identical huts were all made of bamboo and topped with reed-thatched roofs.

Micah couldn't imagine living in such a hut, but he was going to have to endure sleeping in one for the night. He already knew it would be too small and simple to suit him, and he suddenly couldn't wait to return to the castle. He missed the luxury and extravagance of his huge room and soft bed, but at least a night in a hut would be better than another night under the stars.

An arched sign made of vines identified the place as the Clartritch Village. No wall bordered the property, which Micah found odd. Every city and village in Zandador had to be enclosed by walls and guarded by soldiers. Without those walls, people would meander from place to place, talk to each other, and not do the jobs they were assigned by law to perform. That's how Omri maintained productivity and order. Micah thus concluded that the people of Keckrick were not productive and lived in chaos.

His suspicion was confirmed when he spotted a handful of shirtless, barefoot boys with black hair, tan skin, and brown eyes kicking a coconut around a fire pit in the middle of the village. Kids shouldn't be playing. They should be hunting or farming or cooking or learning a trade. He had to put an end to this nonsense right away.

He invaded the circle of kickers, stopped the coconut ball with his foot, and cut it in half with his sword. "Play time is over. I demand to speak with your leader, or this coconut is not the only thing I will destroy with my sword."

After a few seconds of frozen, confused fear, the boys dispersed, each one running to a different hut. Micah smiled, put his sword away, and crossed his arms. He enjoyed scaring kids.

In a matter of moments, men and women began exiting the huts. All of them seemed to share the same tan skin and dark hair, but unlike the boys, the adults were fully clothed. Their clothes, however, didn't match. How was he supposed to tell the leader apart from the commoners if the commoners didn't all wear the same type of outfit like in Zandador?

Maybe they had no leader. He would just have to take charge himself and address the entire tribe. "I am Micah, thirteenth son of Omri, King of Zandador." He pointed to the hut closest to him on the right. "I am going to secure this hut for my own tonight. Whoever lives here will provide my meal this evening.

"The rest of you will entertain me with dancing and music while I eat, and then I am not to be disturbed while I sleep. I expect to eat in one hour. Now get to work preparing my food and entertainment."

With his speech completed, he sat down on one of the benches near the fire pit. But instead of hearing a commotion among the people to comply with his demands, he heard a litany of voices bouncing around the village.

"Spy!"

"We're not fools. We know Omri would never send his son here."

"Which one of the lower tribes sent you?"

"It doesn't matter. He'll never find out how many humminglo plants we have."

"He won't find out because we're going to hang him!"

"Whoa! What?" Micah jumped to his feet but didn't have a chance to grab his sword before being tackled from behind by three men. One of them sat on his back and proceeded to put a noose around his neck. The other two pinned his arms and tied his wrists together.

"For the record," the noose man whispered in Micah's ear, "our humminglo supply is thriving. We will prevail on Transport Day, and your entire region will suffer the consequences."

"What are you talking about? I am not a spy, and I don't care about your humminglo supply! I just want a place to eat and sleep for the night. And I really am the son of Omri. If you hurt me, he will find out and send a Justice Unit to destroy this village!"

"Silence!" The noose man pushed Micah's face into the grass and tightened the rope around Micah's neck. "Men, this one is strong. We need all available hands to carry him to the trees and string him up."

Micah heard a throng of footsteps and felt himself being picked up by dozens of hands. He kicked and screamed and jiggled his shoulders, but he couldn't shake free from his captors.

◊   ◊   ◊

"No." Javan kept walking south along the deserted beach with Varjiek following behind him like a little puppy and nagging him to get back in the air. Ever since Varjiek had regained the ability to fly, Javan couldn't keep the dragon on the ground.

Please, please, please let me fly us around while we still have some daylight left. He leap-frogged over Javan and tried pleading with him face to face. *I'll go slowly so you won't get sick, and you might even find the Dawn Stalker.*

Javan shook his head and once again said, "No. We've had a rough couple of days. Let's just chill the rest of today and start fresh in the morning. Besides, I've never seen the sun set over the ocean. I want to be here on the ground and sitting in the sand to watch it when it does."

You're boring.

"I didn't say you had to sit here and watch the sunset with me."

You mean you want me to explore on my own and find the dragon for you?

"You really want to fly, don't you?"

Varjiek's eyes lit up as he nodded his head. *I feel like a new dragon now that I can fly again, and I'm too excited to stay on the ground. Plus it's all kinds of fun to use my invisibility to scare the animals here.*

"That's mean. And something I've gonna have to watch one day." Javan laughed and decided to give in to Varjiek. "Go. Fly. Have your fun while the sun is still out. Just let me get my backpack first so I can eat while you're frightening the animals."

It won't be all fun; I'll be searching for the Dawn Stalker, too. Varjiek waited for Javan to untie his backpack from the gear stored on his back. *I haven't forgotten that we're on a mission.*

"I was trying to forget, but I suppose I'll keep an eye out for any dragons while I walk. I'll stick to the shore to make it easy for you to find me when you get back."

Yes, sir. I shall return by dark. Varjiek took off with a whoosh, sprinkling Javan with both water and sand.

He brushed himself off and continued his walk. Since Varjiek was out looking for the dragon that may or may not be living somewhere along the northwestern shore near a family of Dragon Protectors, Javan felt free to walk down the beach without thinking of what he needed to do, where he needed to go, or how to collect a Dawn Stalker that could teleport away from him at the slightest hint of danger.

He was also free to explore his surroundings, and his surroundings appeared worthy of exploration up ahead. The palm-tree lined beach gave way to a ragged cliff hundreds of feet high. The rocks of the cliff were as clear as glass and shimmered in the bright sunlight. And the strangest, most beautiful flower he had ever seen covered the base of the cliff, the hill leading to the top of the cliff, and all along the top of the cliff.

Wanting to get a closer look at the flowers, Javan began jogging. He soon found himself past the palm trees and in the midst of head-high flowers with green stems so thick that his fingers barely touched when he wrapped his hands around them.

Thin leaves as long as his arms grew sporadically up the stem leading to the round top that leaned to the side like sunflowers. The petals that lined the perimeter of the circle also reminded him of sunflowers, but these were purple instead of yellow. What truly mesmerized Javan, though, was the web of neon blue strings that burst out from the center of the flower.

Each individual string originated from the base of a petal and stretched downward for about a foot where it intertwined with all of the other strings. Curious about what it felt like, Javan touched one of the strings with his finger. It felt soft and smooth and alive. As soon as Javan touched it, the web immediately retreated to its base where the petals wrapped it in a protective covering.

"Cool," Javan said, touching each flower as he walked by so he could watch them all coil up.

Then something else caught his attention: the sound of a waterfall.

He abandoned his ploy to frighten all the flowers and sprinted ahead. He cut through the last of the flowers right before the land started rising, fought his way through about fifty yards of thick foliage he couldn't identify, and stood in stunned silence at the sight of the most majestic waterfall he had ever seen.

He stood at the right corner of a U-shaped canyon. White water flowed down the curved end of the canyon into a pool of water so clear he could see the bottom and all the fish in between. The straight edges of the U formed the walls of the canyon, were topped with those bizarre flowers, and were made of the same shimmering rocks as the cliffs bordering the ocean.

The clear rocks also formed an island in the middle of the water, and laying on that island basking in the sun was a living, breathing, white-scaled Dawn Stalker. It looked at him, scowled, and said, *You're not Taliya.*

He was about to respond when a female burst through the trees right in front of him and cut him off. "Kisa, leave!" The dragon obeyed and immediately teleported herself away.

Javan sighed and turned his attention to the woman who had delivered the orders. She was about five inches shorter than Javan and wore her black hair in a braided crown atop her head. A machete dangled from her tiny waist, and she held a slingshot in her left hand and a dart in her right.

She had on an unbuttoned long sleeved green shirt over a green tank top and matching green pants. Her outfit allowed her to blend in with the trees, but it didn't camouflage her short, slender figure, gorgeous tan face, and bright blue eyes.

"You must be Taliya." He extended his hand to introduce himself but didn't have the chance. Because right after hearing her name, she lifted the slingshot, loaded it with the dart, and shot him in the neck.

◊   ◊   ◊

They made it halfway across the clearing of the village center toward the trees when shrieks louder than his own pierced the late afternoon air. The shrieks came from the women behind him as three bloodied men burst through the trees in front of him.

One beast of a man carried two smaller, unconscious men. "We need help," the beast said. "It's Cheel and Thia. They're in bad shape."

The men carrying Micah dropped him. He scrambled away and hid under the porch of the nearest hut while his former captors focused their attention on helping the injured.

"We were ambushed by the Negutia tribe," the beast said. "We fought them off, but we're all hurt. Cheel and Thia are the worst. Somebody has to get the healer."

Micah saw a wave of tension wash over the entire village at the mention of the healer. It took a minute, but noose man finally responded. "We have medicine. We can treat them here."

"You can treat me here. Cheel and Thia won't survive without her help."

"People who seek her help return with acid burns, if they return at all. It's not worth it."

Acid burns? Dawn Stalkers breathed acid. The healer must live near the Dawn Stalker Javan was after! Micah stopped trying to untie his hands and listened to the unfolding debate.

"It is if she's their only hope." The beast's voice was stronger now that the villagers had released him from his burden by carrying the injured men into one of the huts.

"No." Noose man stood his ground. "I won't allow it. By trying to save these two, we risk losing more of our own."

"I will go." A woman with a muscular build and long braided hair spoke up. "I can get there by nightfall and have her back here by midnight. She will listen to me."

"I cannot let you go alone."

"Then my sister will accompany me, but we have to leave now. If we delay, Cheel and Thia will be even beyond her help."

"You are sure you can get past her acid-breathing monster?"

"I am certain. She owes me a favor."

"Then get your sister and go. We will do our best to keep Cheel and Thia alive while you are gone."

"Thank you, Swur."

Micah took that as his cue to leave as well. He dashed into the trees and ran back along the stream as fast as he could with his hands tied. When he was certain no one was following him, he stopped, used a sharp rock to cut through the string that held his hands, and removed the noose from his neck.

If he hurried, he could retrieve Mertzer and return to the village in time to follow the healer back to her home. Ironically, he was about to become the spy they accused him of being. This time, though, he wouldn't get caught.

CHAPTER 18
A NEW ENEMY

The first thing Javan noticed when he regained consciousness wasn't that his body lay on a hard wood floor in an uncomfortable ball on his left side, courtesy of his hands being tied to his feet, or that a tight gag around his mouth prevented him from talking.

He didn't register any of that because the burning pain in the right side of his neck made the rest of his predicament irrelevant. He felt like he was being stung with a thousand fire ants all the in the same exact spot at the exact same time, and the stinging kept increasing in intensity.

Since he couldn't scream, he began thrashing his body on the floor instead. All he wanted to do was make the pain stop, but the movement just seemed to make the pain worse.

"I tied you up like that so you wouldn't move." The small warrior woman from the woods talked in a bored tone from across the octagonal room. She was stretched out on her bed reading a book by lantern light. A giant tree dominated the middle of the space, leading Javan to presume they were in some sort of glorified tree house.

"Every time you do move," she continued, "a dose of poison from that dart in your neck enters your system. Once too much poison floods your bloodstream, there is no amount of antidote I can give you to counteract its killing power."

Javan immediately stopped thrashing about and glared at his captor. How could she talk in such a nonchalant way about his possible death? Who was she? Why did she tie him up? What did she want with him?

She appeared to be in her late teens or early twenties. He had a hunch she hid a soft innocence behind her tough exterior, but he didn't care. He didn't care, because he hated her. Although he could get used to looking at her beautiful face, he hated the way she talked, the way she lived, and the way she made him feel like a pitiful, weak, trapped victim.

"All right, trespasser. Now that you have wisely decided to remain still, it's time to talk." She closed her book, plopped it on her bed, and glided on her bare feet over to Javan. "What are you doing on my land? Every inch of ground from here to the coast belongs to me, including the humminglo fields you saw. I will not allow them to be harvested, so trespassing on my land will not help you win the war."

Javan tried to tell her he had no interest in humminglo fields but did want to collect the dragon she called Kisa. The gag, however, turned his response into an unintelligible grunt. She seemed to enjoy the fact that he couldn't speak and waited a moment before reaching for the gag.

She had the knot loosened on the cloth covering Javan's mouth when a pounding sound from below them caused her to pause.

"Taliya, it's Anita." More pounding. "I know you're home. Open up!"

"What is she doing here?" Taliya shook her head in obvious frustration as she retied Javan's gag and patted his cheek. "I guess I'll have to wait to hear your sweet voice. Remember, moving will kill you. Staying still will keep you alive."

With those comforting words, she left the room through a hole in the floor by the tree. Javan assumed a set of stairs wrapped around the trunk, but thanks to the poison dart lodged in his neck, he wasn't about to scoot himself over to the hole to test his theory.

He strained to hear the conversation playing out between the women, but all he could hear were faint whispers and mumblings.

The conversation did not last long or make Taliya happy. She stormed up the steps a few minutes later carrying a cup. "Apparently I have to take a little trip. I'm not sure how long I'll be gone, and I don't need you dying on me before I get back."

She put the cup on the floor, dragged him over to the tree, and cut the vine holding his hands and feet together. His hands remained tied behind him while she propped him against the trunk and used a longer, thicker vine to tie him in a sitting position against the tree. The movement multiplied the pain caused by the dart, and he felt himself start to pass out.

Taliya grabbed the cup she had brought with her, removed the dart and Javan's gag. "Stay with me, stranger. I've got to get you to drink this or I'll never find out who you are."

"Yeah," Javan said, noting that his voice sounded raspy and groggy. "That's why I should drink your mystery beverage. So you can find out who I am."

"Exactly." She smiled, opened his mouth and poured some sort of liquid down his throat that had the consistency of gravy and tasted like sewage. He wanted to throw it up until she encouraged him to keep it down by saying, "I know it tastes terrible, but what it lacks in taste it makes up for in keeping you alive."

Javan forced himself to swallow every drop. It dulled the pain in his neck but made him feel woozy. And sick. And tired. So very tired.

The last thing he remembered before falling asleep was watching Taliya cover him with a blanket and stuff a small pillow behind his head.

◊   ◊   ◊

Micah had had enough of Keckrick. The hot, humid afternoon air caused him to sweat so much that his clothes stuck to his skin, and his hair dripped a steady stream of sweat droplets down his back. Bugs buzzed around him, providing a constant source of annoyance.

When one of the bugs landed on his cheek, he slapped it and flicked its squished body to the ground. He wanted to scream in frustration, but he couldn't without giving away his position. Maintaining a sense of stealth on the back of a dragon in the thick undergrowth of a thriving rain forest while following the three most boring women in the entire Great Rift was tough enough. He didn't need to bring any unwelcome attention to himself.

He had arrived back at the village last night in time to see the healer arrive by canoe with her two escorts, the same women who volunteered to get her and were now taking her home. They had tried to engage the healer in conversation for the first hour or so of their canoe ride, but she would only respond with a word or grunt or nothing at all. The last few hours had been spent in silence, so all Micah had to listen to were the bugs.

Micah did notice that the healer carried herself differently than the village women. She seemed aloof and withdrawn, yet certain of herself and her purpose. Considering her young age and the fact she was shorter than everyone around her, that sense of confidence seemed out of place.

He guessed she was in her twenties, and people in their twenties were supposed to be learning how to follow rules and obey their leaders. They were not supposed to be independent thinkers who were sought after for their healing abilities.

Apparently she was quite good at her job, because the men she came to heal were recovered enough for her to leave the village by noon. It made Micah wonder what kind of medicine was in that bag of hers or if she had some kind of special healing power.

He was also starting to wonder if following her was the right move to make. How could someone so young and so quiet know anything about a Dragon Stalker?

"Stop!" The healer's stern order made Micah freeze, even though she wasn't talking to him. "Anita, pull over to the bank and let me out. Right now."

"Taliya, I can't let you out here." The woman who had volunteered to retrieve the healer yesterday spoke. "Your house is still several miles away."

"I am capable of walking. Now pull over or I will swim to the shore."

"Fine."

Micah watched from a distance as the village women rowed to the shore while Taliya studied the sky. Fortunately they landed on the same side of the stream that Micah was on. He could thus follow Taliya without forcing Mertzer across the water.

When they were a few feet away from landing, Taliya threw her bag onto the ground ahead of her and jumped out of the canoe. "Get back to the village as fast as possible."

"Why?" Anita asked. "What's going on?"

"It's none of your concern. Just get back home to safety."

"We are in your debt for healing Cheel and Thia. Your safety is our concern. We can be back here in a matter of hours with our whole village ready to fight."

"This isn't the kind of fight you're ready for."

"What does that mean?"

"It means the best thing you can do for me is to stay away from me. Promise you will not return."

"But if you're in trouble--"

"I can handle it, but only if you promise to leave me alone."

"That doesn't make any sense. We're at war, and you saw what our enemies did to Cheel and Thia. Even brave warriors like you need help."

"I have all the help I need," Taliya said, fingering a sheer white trinket she wore around her neck.

"You live by yourself. You have no one to help you!"

"Enough arguing. Leave. And if I spot even a hint of you or someone from your village approaching my house, I will not hesitate to shoot. Understood?"

"You would shoot your friends?"

"If you go against my wishes, you are not my friends. Now please go."

"You know where to find us if you change your mind."

"Of course."

"Good bye, Taliya," Anita said, turning the canoe around. "And good luck."

Taliya nodded and watched them row away. After a few minutes of watching the retreating canoe, she left her bag on the ground, blew the trinket around her neck, and began running through the trees while calling for a person named Kisa.

"Finally," Micah mumbled to himself, "something interesting to do." He drew his sword and trotted after Taliya on the back of his dragon.

◊ ◊ ◊

Javan could see his stalker swords and stun ball belt from where he sat tied to the tree. They hung on the wall by a window glistening in the afternoon sun, well out of his reach. He hated knowing that one touch of those blades would easily cut through his bindings, but that he was unable to do anything about it.

That was the least of his problems, though. He needed food to stop his stomach from rumbling, water to soothe his store throat from all the yelling he had done, and healing ointment for his wrists since he had rubbed them raw trying to escape. Most of all, he needed a bathroom. If his captor didn't return soon, he was going to have to deal with the embarrassment of explaining to a beautiful woman why his pants were wet.

"Varjiek!" Javan's hoarse voice was losing its power, but he had to keep trying to get his dragon's attention. "Varjiek, where are you? I need you!"

When he didn't get any response or catch a glimpse of the dragon flying through the trees, Javan dropped his chin to his chest. His situation seemed hopeless and he felt helpless, but he refused to give up. Surrender wasn't an option when he knew God would hear his prayers.

"Please, God," he prayed, "please help Varjiek find me. Please get me out of here."

He waited a few minutes, then once again looked up and yelled, "V! Varjiek! Stop playing around and come blow the roof off this hut."

Hut? You're in a hut? What hut? What are you doing in a hut?

"Haha! Varjiek! You found me!"

Not quite. I hear you, but I don't see you. Or a hut. Step outside into a clearing or climb a tree so I can see you.

"Can't. I'm tied up."

Why did you let yourself get tied up?

"Surprise attack."

How many men did it take? Ten? Twelve?

"Close. One. A woman."

You let a woman capture you? I thought among you humans, men were supposed to be stronger than women. Varjiek's eye appeared in the window. *I'm never going to be able to leave you alone again if you can't defend yourself against one tiny woman.*

"She shot me with a poison dart! Now please get me out of here." Javan beat his legs on the floor. "I really need to go to the bathroom."

I still do not understand why you insist on finding a private spot to relieve yourself. I go when I need to go no matter where I am.

"I know. It's a strange quirk of mine. Just tear the roof off and cut me free with your claws."

Varjiek's eye lit up. *I can burn it off. That would be more fun.*

"No! No fire." Javan looked around at all Taliya's belongings, most of which consisted of books. She wasn't his favorite person, but he didn't see any reason to devastate her by destroying her property. Or turn all of Keckrick against them by starting a raging forest fire. "You should be able to get me free by tearing a hole in the roof."

Fine. Varjiek huffed a puff of smoke. *No fire.*

Varjiek ripped the roof off with his mouth, then daintily reached into the hole and used his sharp nails to free Javan from his bindings.

"Thank you, thank you, thank you!" Javan scrambled to his feet and dashed across the room. He wasn't about to waste time trying to find a proper bathroom. Instead, he climbed on a pile of books, opened a window, and began to empty his bladder into the trees below.

Before he finished, Varjiek interrupted. *Uh, Javan? You might want to hurry up. I found the Dawn Stalker.*

"So did I. Right before I was poisoned." Javan finished his business, retrieved his stalker swords, and looked around for his book bag. He needed his bag. He had food in his bag. "We just need to find this amazing U-shaped canyon, collect the Dawn Stalker, and make our way back to Zandador. Now where did she put...ah. There it is."

He picked up his bag from the bed just as an invisible Varjiek picked him up. "Hey! What are you doing?"

I'm going to drop you on the back of the Dawn Stalker so you can ride her and add her to your collection.

"Let's get to the canyon first. Put me down so I can climb on your back like usual."

That will be unnecessary. What I meant to say a moment ago was that the Dawn Stalker found us. Look down and to your right.

Javan followed Varjiek's instructions. They were about thirty feet high, even with the top of the two-story tree house. The hut was in the middle of a clearing about the size of a baseball field, and Javan spotted a white dragon with black eyes hiding among the green trees on the edge of the clearing to the right of the hut.

"I see her," Javan whispered. "She can't see us, though, right? You're in invisible mode?"

Correct.

"How do we coax her out into the open so I can jump on her back?"

I do not know. You are the Collector.

"But you're a dragon. You should--"

Quiet.

"Excuse me?"

Quiet. I hear something. It is a strange, high-pitched noise that is hurting my ears.

"Where is it coming from?"

I do not know. It stopped. Now I hear yelling. Someone is yelling for...Kisa.

"That's the name of the Dawn Stalker. Taliya must be nearby. Fly a little higher so we can see more of the surrounding area."

Varjiek complied.

When they crested the top of the trees, Javan could see a wide patch of farmland to the left of the hut and in front of a winding river. Although he couldn't hear anything, he could see Taliya running through the middle of the crops and headed straight to the hut. She was not going to be happy when he found him gone and the roof of her hut torn apart.

"We should get out of here."

What about the dragon?

"We'll go back to the canyon and wait for her there."

Where is the canyon?

"Umm…not sure. I was kinda unconscious on the trip from there to here. I do remember that it's near the coast. It should be easy to spot from the air."

Okay. We'll fly to the coast and work our way inland. You should probably get on my back so I don't accidently drop you in the trees.

"Good idea."

As Varjiek eased Javan back into the hut, an animal at the edge of the field behind Taliya caught his attention. He had seen that same animal with a telltale blue streak of scales from the air before when he was riding an okty over Dusk Stalker territory with his mentor Astor. "Mertzer."

Javan watched from the window as Taliya tore through the field toward the hut with Mertzer creeping slowly behind her. Only Mertzer wasn't alone. He had a rider. That rider could only be Micah.

What was Micah doing in Keckrick? Javan's stomach did somersaults and made him feel sick. Had he been followed this whole time? How could he not have sensed that he was being watched?

Javan, we must go. My leg is right by the tree.

"No." He turned around and spoke to the air since he couldn't see his dragon. "We must stay and fight. Micah and Mertzer are here. I can't let them hurt Taliya, and I certainly cannot let Micah capture Kisa."

Didn't this Taliya person hurt you? Maybe she is leading Micah to you and does not deserve your protection.

"Maybe." Javan didn't want to believe Taliya could be on Micah's side, but until he could be sure, he would have to treat her like an enemy.

He did know Kisa was on Taliya's side, so that meant he and Varjiek had to somehow defeat one trained soldier, one amazon warrior, and two dragons. The odds were not in their favor.

"God," he prayed as he watched his approaching enemies, "I thought I needed your help when I was tied up, but I really need it now."

Once he nestled into his spot at the base of Varjiek's neck, he drew his swords and turned his pleading eyes to the sky. "Who should we attack first?"

CHAPTER 19
CLASH OF THE BLOODLINES

"Stay calm, boy," Micah said, pulling back on Mertzer's reigns to keep his speed in check. They needed to stay hidden a safe distance away from Taliya as they tracked her run through the trees, and that wasn't easy considering the agitated dragon didn't seem to like the noise Taliya made whenever she blew into that trinket around her neck.

When she wasn't blowing her trinket or yelling for Kisa, she moved through the trees and leaves and bush with an ease Micah admired. Nothing slowed her down, not even the snake hanging from a branch in her path. She flung the poor thing to the ground and just kept running as though she encountered that kind of danger every day. Then again, perhaps she did.

Before too long, he followed her out of the trees and into a field of waist-high crops. She picked up her pace now that she had no trees, leaves, or snakes blocking her path and ran straight toward a two-story hut built around a huge tree in the middle of a clearing.

He waited at the edge to verify that the hut was indeed her destination. If it was, he could be there in a matter of seconds to question her about the Dawn Stalker. First he wanted to watch and discover why she was in such a hurry to get home.

Only she never reached the hut.

She couldn't have taken more than two steps out of the field when she disappeared. Vanished. Evaporated into thin air.

"Unbelievable," Micah said, urging Mertzer forward. They trampled a diagonal path through the crops and halted at the clearing. Micah shook his head. "Where did she go? It's like she teleported right out of here."

"Or became invisible when she was picked up by a flying dragon." Javan dropped out of the sky above him, kicked Micah in the chest with both his legs, and knocked both of them to the ground. They both rolled twice and stood facing each other, swords drawn and ready to fight.

"Javan. How nice of you to come straight to me. Now I can kill you, claim your dragon as my own, and continue my quest to win the Battle of the Throne."

"That's your plan, huh? You can't handle a little competition and had to come after me and my dragon rather than hunt your own Noon Stalker?"

"Why make things more difficult than they need to be? Getting rid of you is the smart play and easy option."

"Easy? You think I'm going to be easy to kill?"

"Absolutely." Micah lifted his sword and lunged toward Javan, certain this would be a short, quick fight.

◊   ◊   ◊

Javan anticipated Micah's attack, crossed his stalker swords in front of his chest, and blocked Micah's blow. Because Micah was taller, stronger, and fought with a sword wider, longer, and heavier than Javan's two arm-length swords, that one blow shook Javan's entire body and almost sent him to his knees.

But Javan managed to keep his balance and was back up in time to block the next blow. And the next. And the next. His swords were made of a superior steel and allowed him to move with a kind of speed that kept him one step ahead of his opponent. He wasn't getting in any offensive attacks of his own, but he was doing some impeccable defensive work.

He doesn't know I'm here, Varjiek said from somewhere above the fighting men. *I could scorch him for you and end this fight.*

Do not let him hurt Micah, Mertzer said, still standing at the edge of the clearing. *Then I would be obligated to hurt you.*

Do not threaten my Collector, you wingless dragon! Javan, hold your ground. I'll take this Dusk Stalker out, then eliminate the Hunter.

"No, V! No scorching anyone." Javan grunted as Micah backed him into the base of the tree that housed Taliya's hut. Micah went for Javan's throat, but Javan caught Micah's sword between his own and looked straight into Micah's dark eyes. "This fight is between me and him."

"You're right," Micah said. "This fight is between us. You ruined my life, and for that you must pay. I'll take your life, your dragon, and then the dragon you came here to collect."

"That last part I have a problem with." Taliya jumped down from her hut where he had Varjiek leave her moments ago. Although she stood a good foot shorter than Micah, she looked lethal with that poisoned dart aimed at Micah's neck with her slingshot. "I am Kisa's Protector. Nobody is getting near my dragon."

"She's a pretty good shot with that slingshot, Micah," Javan said. "You might want to hop on Mertzer and head on back to Zandador."

Taliya kept her dart aimed at Micah but looked at Javan. "And you might want to leave me alone and let me fight my own battles. If your dragon ever picks me up without my permission again, I will shoot you with another dart and destroy the antidote."

"Looks like this fight isn't just between us anymore, and I don't fight when the odds are against me." Micah pulled his sword away from Javan and stepped back. "Mertzer, it's about time for your evening meal anyway. Kill them both."

Sorry, Javan, Mertzer said. *I should have let you ride me that first time you got on my back. But now I have to obey orders from this man.*

He crouched and sprinted across the field toward his prey.

◊   ◊   ◊

Micah tried not to let the relief show on his face when Taliya interrupted the fight and kept him from killing Javan. Considering how much he hated Javan and how much he wanted him dead so he could take control of Varjiek, and how much he wanted to be ruthless like his father, he thought killing Javan would be easy.

But he had never actually taken another man's life, and the idea of being the one to put an end to Javan's existence made him uneasy. He could delegate the task, though. That he knew how to do. That's what dragons were for.

He watched with a clear conscience as Mertzer charged toward Taliya and Javan. Only the dragon wasn't running at top speed. Why not? If he didn't hurry, Taliya would have time to shoot him with her dart, or Javan would gut him with one of those swords.

"Mertzer, hurry and--" The sudden appearance of a white dragon in the middle of the field stunned Micah and made him forget the rest of his sentence. Mertzer smacked right into the slightly larger dragon and rolled backwards.

"That a girl, Kisa!" Taliya cheered and winked at Micah. "Your dragon is no match for mine."

"My dragon is the superior one." Javan stepped between Micah and Taliya. "Varjiek, uncloak yourself and show these dragons who's boss. Enter the fight and burn whatever you want."

Mertzer barely had time to get back on his feet when Varjiek swooped in and knocked him down again. Mertzer retaliated by snapping up at Varjiek and catching his tail in his mouth.

"Go ahead and eat him for dinner, Mertzer," Micah yelled. "You won't need to eat again for weeks!"

Varjiek apparently didn't like that idea. He shrieked, spun his long neck around, and blew a ball of fire straight at Mertzer's face. Mertzer released Varjiek's tail in time to avoid being burned, but then Kisa turned against him.

She rammed into his side and pinned him to the ground by smothering him with her body. Varjiek landed beside them and used his front feet to keep Mertzer's head and neck immobile.

"No!" Micah began running toward the trio of dragons. "Let him go! We'll leave you alone. All of you. I promise. Just don't hurt him. Let him go. Please let him go!"

The Noon and Dawn Stalker looked at each other. Then at Mertzer. Then at Micah.

A second later, all the dragons disappeared.

CHAPTER 20
BLOWN AWAY

Javan winced when he saw Mertzer bite the scales off Varjiek's tail, cheered when Varjiek broke free, relaxed when Mertzer dodged Varjiek's flames, cringed when Kisa pinned Mertzer and almost yelled when Varjiek teamed up with her. Micah, however, beat him to it.

Micah's desperate pleas for the dragons to spare Mertzer sounded sincere, but Javan wasn't about to trust that promise for Micah to leave them all alone. The heat of the moment had passed, and Micah would be back to his usual, selfish, scheming self. Nevertheless, he did seem genuinely concerned when he stopped in his tracks, turned, and asked, "Where did they go?"

"Probably nowhere," Taliya said. "The Noon Stalker just likes to make himself invisible." She turned her attention to Javan. "Tell your dragon to uncloak himself."

"My dragon isn't the problem." The thoughts of the dragons during the fight were too jumbled to understand, but he did catch Varjiek telling Kisa to teleport them away seconds before they vanished. He said something about saving Mertzer for Javan to collect, so at least Javan knew all the dragons were safe. He just didn't know where they were. "Your dragon is the one that teleported them out of here."

"You don't know that. Kisa wouldn't leave me here alone with the two of you."

"Really? Ten bucks says those dragons are gone, not invisible."

"What is a 'buck'?"

"Nevermind." Javan rolled his eyes at his own stupidity for using an Earthly phrase in the middle of another dimension. "It doesn't matter. Just tell us where Kisa would have teleported to."

"Those dragons are still there," Taliya said, pointing to the seemingly empty field. "Either tell your dragon to make everyone visible again, or walk through the field and prove there are no fighting dragons blocking your path."

"Fine." Javan kept his swords handy and walked straight past the still stunned Micah. He couldn't hear anything Varjiek was thinking and was certain the dragons were gone.

Well, almost certain. Varjiek knew how to block his thoughts from Javan. Maybe that's what he and the other dragons were doing while they tried to kill each other. He better try talking to Varjiek just in case. "V, if you're there, uncloak yourself and let Mertzer go."

Nothing happened, so Javan inched forward with his left-handed sword leading the way. As he approached the singed and trampled grass damaged by the dragons, his sword remained unimpeded by scaly creatures. "See," Javan said, swishing his sword through the air in the middle of the fighting zone, "no dragons. Kisa teleported somewhere and took our dragons with her."

"She wouldn't do that."

Javan turned to find Taliya standing right beside him. How did he not hear her run across the field? He felt taller than usual when he looked down at her and said, "Oh…but she did."

"Are you sure Varjiek didn't fly them out of here?"

"He's strong, but he wouldn't get very far carrying two dragons that I am sure would not have been willing passengers."

"Perhaps Kisa did teleport them. She has that right. She is free to do as she pleases and has no obligation to me. The other dragons are probably thanking her for providing your dragons that same chance at freedom."

"You're wrong." Javan put his swords away and picked up a grey triangular scale that could only have come from Varjiek. The half-inch thick scale filled the palm of his hand and sparkled in the sun. He curled his fingers around the cool scale and scanned the world around him. "Varjiek and I share a bond. He would want me to find him, so you are going to take me to Kisa's home at the canyon where we first met."

"I am going to do no such thing."

The sound of a cracking whip jerked Javan's attention away from the rain forest in time to see Micah wrap his whip around Taliya's waist and pull her to him.

"You will if you want to keep your head." Micah snagged her waist with his left hand, dropped the whip, drew his sword, and held it to her throat. "Take us to the canyon."

◊   ◊   ◊

"Micah," Javan said, putting the scale he had picked up in his pocket, "hurting her isn't going to help anything. Let her go."

"No. I don't take orders from anyone, especially you."

It had taken Micah a few minutes to process everything that happened. Why had he responded with that fear-based outburst when he saw Mertzer go down? Why had he promised to leave the other dragons alone if they spared Mertzer? Why had he stood there like a statue when Javan and Taliya investigated the disappearance? His words and actions made no sense.

He was Micah, the Dragon Hunter. He took charge of every situation and wasn't ruled by such trivial things as emotions. He shouldn't care about Mertzer. Mertzer was a mere dragon.

But Mertzer was his dragon and the closest thing Micah had ever had to a friend. Now his friend might be dead. A strange pain shot through Micah's heart at the thought of losing Mertzer, and it was that pain that finally motivated him to snap back into action by grabbing Taliya.

"Kill me if you must," Taliya said. "If that's what it takes to protect my dragon, so be it."

"That is a bit drastic," Javan said. "Nobody needs to die. We'll leave your dragon alone and take our dragons back to where we came from. Just please help us find them."

"Or we can get Kisa to return here," Micah said, "and battle over who gets to collect her or enslave her. Javan, blow that trinket she's wearing around her neck."

"What? No!" Taliya fought to free herself, but all her fighting did was make Micah hold her tighter. "How do you know about the trinket anyway?"

"I followed you here from the village, so I know that trinket summons Kisa."

"You have a dragon-summoning whistle?" Javan reached over and fingered what looked like a baby dragon tooth hanging from a rope on Taliya's neck. "This is cool. All I have to do is blow it, and Kisa will show up?"

"Yes," Micah said. "Now stop playing and just blow it."

"Okay, okay," Taliya said. "I'll lead you to the canyon."

"Too late," Micah said. "I like my plan better. Javan, blow that thing now, or I will do it for you."

"Ummm…what is that?" Javan's face went pale as he pointed to something behind them.

"Really? You think I'm foolish enough to look?" Micah put his sword back in its sheath so he could take the trinket out of Javan's hands when a cold, unnatural breeze hit the back of his neck. It made him tighten his grip on Taliya and slowly turn his head. "This isn't good."

A ten foot wide wall of white wind spinning end over end hurled toward them, causing the temperature to drop and the wind to gust around them.

He had heard tales of this kind of thing before but had never experienced this weather phenomenon for himself. He did know that if they got caught in its path, it could whisk them hundreds of miles away from where they currently stood. Or rip them to shreds.

"What is it?" Taliya poked her head around Micah, and he felt her gulp. "Oh. White winds. We should probably run."

"Agreed." Micah released his captive, and she sprinted to the left. He and Javan ran after her, staying right on her heels. They had to get past the edge of the wall if they had any hope of escape.

But they didn't get very far before a piece of debris from the windstorm hit Taliya's head and sent her sprawling to the ground.

Javan stopped to pick her up, but Micah kept running.

"Micah, help! She's unconscious."

"So what? Leave her there and run!"

Javan didn't listen to Micah's advice. Instead, the do-gooder draped her right arm over his left shoulder, picked her up, and tried running. He wasn't very successful.

Micah wanted to save himself, but he realized he couldn't leave them, not when she knew where the dragons could be. Irritated, he backtracked and flung her left arm over his right shoulder.

But they were out of time.

"Get down!" Micah tackled both Taliya and Javan, drawing them to the ground with him. Unfortunately, that didn't help them avoid getting walloped by the wall, sucked into it, and becoming part of its spinning destruction as they sailed over the land of Keckrick.

CHAPTER 21
CRASH LANDING

The wall hadn't made any noise as it approached, but now that he was stuck inside the flat tornado between two sheets of freezing wind, all Javan could hear was the blaring of what sounded like a hundred fire engines racing to a fire. The sound made his head hurt, and his eardrums want to explode while the constant flipping and spinning made him dizzy, sick, and delirious.

Nevertheless, he kept his left arm securely locked on the lifeless Taliya. She was the only thing he had to hold onto in the narrow space filled with white, swirling wind. He wasn't about to let her slip away, especially since Micah also retained his grip on her with his right arm.

If given the opportunity, Javan wasn't sure what Micah would do to her in order to get his dragon back. Taliya wasn't exactly Javan's best friend, but he wasn't going to allow Micah the chance to get her alone and torture her.

That seemed liked less and less of a problem the longer they got bashed around inside the wall of wind. Simply surviving took precedence, and Javan began to wonder if getting out of this predicament was even a possibility, so he began praying for deliverance.

God's answer didn't come right away. The wind actually seemed to get stronger and spin faster and lift them higher off the ground the more Javan prayed. But the faster the wall spun, the closer Javan, Taliya, and Micah got to the top end of the wall. If they could reach the top, they might be able to jump out.

Getting to the top was a big if and would require help from Micah. That made it a terrible plan, but at least it was a plan.

Javan reached up with his left hand, tapped Micah on the cheek, and pointed up. Javan couldn't see the expression on Micah's face thanks to the gusts of white wind blowing between them, but he could see that Micah nodded his understanding and started pushing upward with his left arm.

So while pulling Taliya up with them, they worked together to swim through the wind. Javan tried not to let the blue blur of the sky followed by the green blur of the trees distract him from his mission. He instead kept his focus on one white spot at the top edge of the wall and powered through the wind with his right arm to get there.

He made it his goal to reach it before Micah.

As the blue blur appeared again, he found himself inches away from his goal when Micah put his hand on the edge of the wall in the exact spot Javan was aiming for.

Javan didn't have time to be irritated by his loss, so he latched onto the top seconds later and pulled his head into the air above the wall along with Micah. The wind that formed the wall vibrated beneath his fingers. It felt so cold and volatile that he knew he wouldn't be able to hold on long.

"When we see the trees again," Micah yelled through the wailing of the wind, "push down and jump."

"That was my plan," Javan yelled back. As they watched themselves tumble back toward the trees, Javan began counting. "Three...two...ONE!"

They pushed against the wind and jumped. Javan's chest and waist cleared the top of the wall, but as his head hit the trees, he felt his body being sucked back into the wind trap.

Fortunately, he was attached to Taliya, who was attached to Micah, who grabbed a branch and hung on with an amazing display of strength and pulled both Javan and Taliya free from the confines of the wall.

As the wall spun away into the distance, the momentum from the fall forced Javan let go of Taliya and land belly-flop style on top of the rain forest canopy. He grunted on impact, spit out a leaf he accidentally bit into, and tested his limbs to make sure nothing was broken.

Every limb from his fingers to his toes passed the test. He breathed a sigh of relief, thanked God for keeping him alive, and quietly laid there with branches poking his chest until the siren sounds that had penetrated his mind faded away.

"How did we get this far south?"

Javan lifted his head to find Taliya sitting on a branch about five feet to his left. He followed her gaze to see a vast, deep, rugged canyon stretching out ahead of them. Had they exited that wall a second or two later, they would have tumbled to their death on those rocks rather than crashed on the tree tops at the southernmost edge of Keckrick.

"We had a fun trip inside a wall of white wind," Javan said. He didn't bother trying to move yet. He liked the feeling of being still. "It's too bad you slept right through it. You missed all the excitement."

"You two are welcome," Micah said from behind them. "I saved your lives. You can repay me by surrendering your dragons to my custody."

"Not a chance, pal." Taliya stood and turned around. Javan heard her branch start to snap, but she didn't seem to notice. "Kisa is a free dragon, and I'm not about to let you anywhere near her."

"Um...Taliya, is it? You might want to start climbing down. That branch isn't safe."

"You don't get to tell me what to do, either. I am my own—uh-oh."

The branch snapped completely off the tree, and Taliya went down with it. Javan scurried over to where she dropped and saw she managed to catch another thin branch ten feet below him.

"Little help? Please?" She smiled up at him in an attempt to look all adorable and innocent. If that was her ploy, it worked.

"I'm coming. Just hold on."

"Hurry. I think this branch is about to break, too."

Javan made his way down the tree she was hanging on to, perched himself on a sturdy branch, and reached out his hand. "Give me your hand."

"No need." Micah interrupted Javan's rescue by swooping through the air on a vine like Tarzan, grabbing Taliya by the waist and lowering them safely to the ground. Looking up at Javan, he said, "That's how you save a woman in distress."

Javan had never hated anyone more than he hated Micah in that moment.

◊　◊　◊

What a rush! Micah loved the feeling of flying through the air on a vine, catching the tiny little frame of Taliya in the process, and landing them both safely on the soft, fern-covered ground beneath the towering trees. He kind of wanted to climb another tree just so he could swing down on another vine, but he didn't have time to play. He never had time to play.

"Now that I have saved your life twice today," Micah said, "you are forever indebted to me. You can begin to repay your debt by taking me back to the dragons."

"Wow. You sure are cocky." Taliya pushed away from him and crossed her arms. "Who are you, anyway?"

"You don't know who I am?" Micah still wasn't used to people not knowing who he was. His reputation always preceded him in Zandador. Here no one feared him. He didn't like it.

"Obviously not," she said. "I don't ask questions I already know the answer to."

Micah cleared his throat, pulled his shoulders back, stuck his chest out, and spoke with a loud, deep voice. "I am Micah the Dragon Hunter, thirteenth son of the great Omri, King of Zandador."

"That explains your superiority complex, but you might want to keep your voice down." Taliya stood on a rock so she whisper in Micah's ear.

"King Omri is the reason we are at war here in Keckrick. If anyone finds out you are his son, you probably won't be alive very much longer."

"That is nonsense. People revere me."

Taliya laughed and jumped off the rock. "In Zandador, perhaps. In Keckrick, lots of 'accidents' could happen to the great King Omri's son."

His status as Omri's son made him a target? He found that concept difficult to grasp and decided the tiny little woman was simply trying to unnerve him. She probably just wanted to feel important. He would give her that chance. "If I am in danger, I will allow you the privilege of protecting me as you lead me from here to wherever your dragon teleported my dragon to."

"First of all, I am a *Dragon* Protector. My job is to protect Kisa, not you," Taliya said. "Second, you're on your own. I'm not leading you anywhere."

"Good," Javan said, joining them. He sounded angry. "Mertzer is better off without him. My dragon, however, is so loyal to me that I am sure he is already out searching for me."

"And who are you?" Taliya asked.

"I guess we never were properly introduced." Javan offered his hand to the girl. "I'm Javan, a Dragon Collector."

Micah noticed a strange look of shock and recognition flash across Taliya's suddenly pale face as she ignored his hand. When she finally spoke, her voice squeaked. "You said your name is what? And you're a Dragon what?"

"Javan. Dragon Collector." He dropped his hand and looked at Micah. "She probably can't lead us anywhere, because she doesn't know where we are or how to get us back to where we were."

Micah studied the speechless Taliya. "You're probably right. She's just as lost as we are."

"I know exactly where we are." Color rushed back into her cheeks as anger overcame her shock. She brushed some ferns out of the way and began drawing a curved line in the dirt with a dagger she pulled from her boot. "This is the canyon that separates Keckrick from Varzack to the east and the Land of No Return to the south."

The line started in the top right corner of her map area and ended in the bottom left corner. "Judging by the section of the canyon we almost landed in, we are here." She put an X near the curve in the bottom right corner. "We came from here."

She added another X in the top left corner far away from the canyon.

"Great," Javan said. "All we need to do is travel northwest on foot across an entire country to get back to our dragons."

"If only it were that simple," Taliya said. She drew two horizontal lines across the map so Keckrick was divided into three distinct regions.

"To get to my home, you have to go through this middle region of Keckrick known as the Dark Zone. Nobody lives here because it's uninhabitable. Very few people travel through here, because if you go in, you usually don't come out alive."

"Why?" Micah asked. "What makes it dangerous?" He figured if he knew the dangers, he would have no trouble overcoming them.

"The rainstorms. The soggy ground. The abundance of man-eating animals. The lack of plants that are safe for humans to eat. The worst part is the darkness."

"The darkness?"

"Yes. The canopy created by the trees and ivy is so thick that very little light gets through. You lose all sense of direction and time and generally go insane...unless a storm sweeps you away, the ground sucks you in, or an animal tears you limb from limb."

"So I'll fly over it." Micah began surveying the area. "Where can I find an okty?"

"You are a funny man." Taliya poked Micah in the chest with her dagger. "We don't have okties here. Your father doesn't allow us the luxury of air travel in Keckrick. The only way we get places is by walking or by floating on water."

"Okay." Micah pushed Taliya's knife away from him. "Is there a river that will get me through this Dark Zone?"

"Indeed there is," Taliya said. "But you can't just slap a raft on it and float where you want to go. You need a boat. A big boat. One that can withstand the storms. Do you, oh great and mighty Micah, have a boat?"

Javan busted out laughing, and Micah balled his fists to keep from slapping the insolent girl. "You know I don't have a boat."

"Then I suggest you build yourself a hut and learn to live off the land because this," Taliya said, waving her arm around, "is your new home." She put her dagger back in her boot and began walking into the woods.

Micah called after her. "Where are you going?"

"I'm going to find someone who has a boat I can borrow." She spun around and put her hand over her dart gun on her side holster. "If either of you try to follow me, I will shoot you with a poison dart."

"If we travel together," Javan said, "our chances of getting through that Dark Zone alive increase significantly."

"I like my chances just fine on my own."

"So be it," Micah said, "but you might not want to go that way."

"Oh really?" She crossed her arms and cocked her head. "Why is that?"

"Because those spiders behind you don't look very friendly."

◊   ◊   ◊

Javan's eyes widened at the sight of hundreds of peanut-sized black spiders that suddenly dropped by their webs from the trees above and dangled in the air behind Taliya. He had no idea if they were poisonous but wasn't going to stick around to find out. "Run!"

Micah took off on a path to the right of the spiders. Taliya fell into step behind him, and Javan brought up the rear. They zigged and zagged around trees, hurdled rocks and ran over slippery roots. The heat and humidity combined with the sprinting had Javan drenched from his own sweat within minutes.

The sweat didn't bother him as much as the sound of the spiders swarming over the leaves and twigs and dirt behind him. They made such a racket that Javan glanced behind him. All he could see was a wide, pulsating cloud of blackness coming towards them. What kind of spiders chased people?

"They're gonna catch us!" Javan yelled. "Run faster!"

The three picked up the pace and were right on each other's heels when Micah said, "I see a clearing up ahead. We should be able to pick up our pace when we get out of these trees."

"That's not a clearing," Taliya yelled, grabbing Micah with her left arm and reaching out her right arm to stop Javan from running any further. "That's a cliff!"

They were all able to stop before toppling over the edge into the river forty feet below. As they stood there catching their breath, they turned their backs to the edge and watched the approaching spiders.

When they were about a hundred yards away, Javan asked, "Will those things kill us if they reach us?"

"It'll take about ten or twelve bites," Taliya said, "but considering the number of spiders here, that shouldn't take long."

"Then we should jump," Micah said.

"Jump?" Javan looked at Micah. "Are you insane? We have no idea how deep that water is."

"I'd rather take my chances with the water than wait to get eaten by spiders."

"Me, too," Taliya said.

The quick-moving spiders were only twenty yards away. "Fine," Javan said. "Let's jump."

Just as the spiders were ready to crawl up their legs, the trio turned around, screamed, and leapt into the air.

CHAPTER 22
COST OF SURVIVAL

Desperate to get away from the spiders, Micah flailed his arms and kicked his legs as though running in mid-air to force his body as far away from the cliff as possible. Three frantic seconds later, he straightened his legs, anchored his arms by his sides, and braced for impact.

His legs smacked safely into the warm water, but the water burned as it rushed up his nose and into his ears. His dreadlocks wrapped around his face and made it impossible for him to see anything while the current pushed him down and forward.

He held his breath and scrambled against the current. His body flipped and swirled and spun in all kinds of directions. The more he swam, the less confident he became that he would ever reach the surface.

Air. He needed air. He had to breathe in air.

Where was the surface? Had he been swimming down instead of up?

He couldn't die. Not yet. Not like this.

Would anyone care if he died? Would his father? Would he? Was there any kind of life after death?

Before any more disturbing questions had time to flash through his mind, his head popped to the surface. He coughed the water out of his lungs and replaced it with huge gulps of air.

Although his situation had improved, he still found himself surging forward in the middle of the river. Not good. He had seen Taliya's crude map and knew the only place this river could be headed was the deep, rugged canyon they barely avoided earlier.

Taliya and Javan must have realized the same thing. He saw their bobbing heads in front of him, and they were both trying to swim towards the left shoreline. They were closer to the shore than he was, but he wasn't about to let them reach dry land first.

Inch by inch, he made it closer and closer to the bank. He didn't like that he moved forward faster than he moved sideways, but his resolve to free himself from the water strengthened with each stroke.

Up ahead, he watched Javan reach for and miss a low-lying branch that stretched over the water from a sideways growing tree. Taliya made an attempt to grab it. She missed and continued floating downriver.

He intended to succeed where those two failed.

As he approached the branch, he surged his body upward and reached for it with both arms. His left hand slipped off a wet leaf, but his right hand wrapped securely around the sticky bark. "Haha! Got it!"

He swung his left hand back up and found a good grip. After taking a few deep breaths, he let go with his right hand, turned his body halfway around, and re-gripped the branch one foot closer to the shore. Then he made the same move with his left hand.

By continuing the hand over hand movement, he eventually made his way to the shore and plopped himself safely on the dry, grassy land.

Survived. He survived. He survived the spiders. The fall. The water. He was invincible! But what about Javan and Taliya?

He looked downstream and didn't see either one of them past the bend in the river. Could he be so lucky as to have both of them gone? With them out of the way, he had free access to both of their dragons.

Only he had no idea where the dragons were and needed the girl to take him back to her home. Javan, however, was expendable. It would be easier to capture Varjiek by killing Javan than it would be to hunt the dragon on his own, but he would prefer to take his chances with the dragon. Something about killing another human being who wasn't trying to kill him just seemed wrong.

"Please still be alive." Micah picked himself up, shook off what water he could, and ran along the bank of the river in search of the Collector and Protector.

◊　◊　◊

The fallen tree Javan and Taliya had smacked into was starting to crack. "Hurry!" Javan yelled into Taliya's ear. His left shoulder touched her right shoulder, and they were about ten feet from land. "This thing is about to break."

"I am aware. You don't need to tell me what to do. I don't like it when people tell me what to do."

"I'm just trying to encourage you to move a little faster. Otherwise we're gonna be sucked back into the river."

"Stop yelling at me. I'm moving as fast as I can."

Javan took a deep breath, bit his lip, and stared straight ahead while the water slammed into his back. Why was this girl being so difficult? He almost wanted to let go of the log just to get away from her. Then he noticed an insanely long, ridiculously round red snake slithering into the water.

Was it coming for them? Would some other creature get to them first?

"What have we here?" A dripping wet Micah crouched at the river's edge by the roots of the tree Javan was clinging to. An unwelcome creature had gotten to them first after all.

"Great," Javan said. "You're alive."

"Won't be able to say that about you for much longer," Micah said. "As for the little lady, it looks like could use some help. Again."

"I am perfectly capable of getting out of this river on my own," Taliya said, "but if you want to speed up the process by pulling me out, I guess I'll let you."

"The only way you're getting my help now is if you help me get back to my dragon."

The log creaked and jerked forward as the last of the snake's body disappeared into the water. "Okay," Taliya said. "Fine. I'll take you there. Just get me out of this river."

"Gladly." Micah reached out his hand, and Taliya grabbed the lifeline. Within seconds, he had her out of the water and safely by his side. That made three times in one day that Micah had rescued the damsel in distress. Javan found that hero role of Micah's infuriating.

Another piece of the log snapped and sent Javan flying forward. He was now parallel to the land. And closer to the snake. "My turn." Javan's voice squeaked. He couldn't believe he was asking Micah for help.

Instead of reaching out his hand, Micah leaned over the water and looked straight in Javan's eyes. "Unfortunately, I need you dead so I can enslave your dragon. Father's orders. You're on your own."

Javan's heart went cold at the thought of Varjiek becoming Micah's slave, but all he could do was cling to the log as he watched Micah smirk and walk back upstream.

"Hold on," Taliya said. "We can't just leave him there. You have to help him, too!"

"No." Micah calmly walked to Taliya, took her by the arm, and dragged her away with him. She didn't go quietly, though.

"What's wrong with you?" Javan could see her trying to break free from Micah's grip as she protested on his behalf. "Get him out of the water. We're going to need him to get through the Dark Zone. The more people we have, the better our chances of getting through there alive."

If Micah responded, Javan didn't hear what he said. Because Micah and Taliya were gone, leaving Javan alone. In a strange place. Hugging a breaking tree. Being battered by cold water. Unable to move or defend himself.

Something slimy and scaly brushed Javan's leg. "Ahh! Snake!" That was all the incentive he needed to transition from victim to survivor. In one smooth motion, he hoisted his legs out of the water and onto the top of the log so that he was able to straddle the tree.

Without skipping a beat, he pulled himself to his feet and leapt to the land. The log couldn't handle the pressure and broke off. It sailed downstream and seconds later was squeezed to splinters by the massive red snake that had entered the water minutes ago.

Not wanting to wait around for the snake to strangle him, Javan took off in the direction he saw Micah and Taliya go. He wasn't about to leave her alone with Micah, and he certainly wasn't going to let Micah cut off Varjiek's tail.

He knew the hatred he felt toward Micah wasn't healthy, but he let it eat at his heart, anyway. He had to make Micah pay for imprisoning Javan's mother, capturing Mertzer, destroying Gri, and leaving Javan in the river to die.

◊   ◊   ◊

Micah wanted to stuff a sock in the girl's mouth to keep her from saying another word as they searched for a place along the river's edge to set up camp. Her constant chatter about his heartlessness and stupidity and evilness made his head hurt. He almost turned around to get Javan just to shut the girl up, but he knew it was too late. Javan was gone.

Omri would be proud of Micah for leaving Javan in the river. So why wasn't Micah proud of himself? Why didn't he go with his gut, reach out his hand, and help Javan? Why was capturing Varjiek more important than saving a man's life?

Before he had a chance to ponder any more strange questions, something sharp dug into his back. He released Taliya and reached for his sword, but his hand didn't quite touch the handle. Whatever had dug into his back made a low whirring noise and had him completely paralyzed. He could see and hear, but he couldn't move or talk.

"It's about time you let me go," Taliya said. "If we hurry, we might still be able to save Javan."

"No need," Javan said. He walked up from behind and held his sword to Micah's throat. "I managed to get out on my own. But I'm not about to let you take one more step toward Varjiek or Mertzer. Your days of dragon hunting are over."

Micah was strangely relieved to see Javan alive but could tell by the hatred in his eyes that he was a more dangerous enemy than ever. Fortunately, Taliya recognized that as well and inserted herself between Javan and Micah.

"Whoa." Taliya pushed Javan back. "I'm going to berate you, but first I need to make sure I'm not going crazy. Do you hear some sort of whirring sound? I don't know what animal makes that noise, so it's making me kind of nervous."

"You're not crazy. I hit him with a stun ball."

"A stun what?"

Javan picked an odd-shaped ball off his belt and held it up. It was sheer black with two rows of tiny white spikes. "When you throw it with the right spin, it activates the claws that attach to and paralyze the target."

Micah thought stun balls were a myth. He had seen them before, but no one he knew or heard of had ever been able to throw them in a way that made them work. He found himself impressed and furious at the same time; he was impressed with Javan's throwing skills yet furious that he had become a target. All he wanted to do was blink, but that ball in his back was forcing him to keep his eyelids open.

"Interesting." Taliya handled the ball for a minute and returned it to Javan. "Now for the berating. I get that you two don't like each other. I appreciate that because I don't like either one of you. I'm not about to kill you, however, because I need your help *and* his help to get back home."

"If I don't kill him now," Javan said, "he's going to kill me as soon as that stun ball in his back stops stunning him. So move out of my way."

"Do you want to see your dragon again?"

Micah saw Javan's eyes soften at the mention of Varjiek. He cared about his dragon. Micah had never seen that kind of compassion for a beast in the eyes of his father.

"Of course," Javan said. "But I won't if I let Micah live."

"Micah," Taliya said, turning to him, "Javan is going to put his sword away and let you live. In return, you are going to play nice and not harm Javan in any way, shape, or form as we travel from here back to my home. If you do attempt to hurt him, I will refuse to continue the journey, and you will never see your dragon again. Understood?"

Micah glared at Javan through his painful, unblinking eyes. Working with him was a high price to pay for survival, but he didn't have a choice. He thus attempted to nod. His attempt failed.

"I'm going to assume you understand and will be nice." Taliya turned back to Javan. "Do we have a deal? You put your sword away, and we all work as a team to get back to the dragons?"

"Deal." Javan lowered his sword. "But I'm going to let him stay paralyzed until the stun ball shuts off on its own."

"Fair enough," Taliya said. "He deserves some kind of punishment for leaving you in the river like that."

Micah wanted to argue, but all he could do was stand there and plot ways to get back at Javan once they returned to the dragons.

CHAPTER 23
FIGHTING OVER FLOWERS

Micah woke up in his makeshift hammock the next morning and immediately began blinking. He wanted to verify that his eyelids still worked, then he checked his fingers and toes. All good.

The headache that had stayed with him from the time that stun ball dropped out of his back until he went to sleep was now gone. He could think and he could move. Somehow those simple pleasures made his current predicament bearable.

He got to his feet, stretched, and assessed his surroundings. The sun was barely above the horizon, and the temperature was already beginning to rise. Then again, things never really cooled off that much at night. This place was simply hot. All. The. Time.

Javan was sleeping in a sitting position in a tree near the river on the other side of the fire they had used to cook dinner. Taliya had built a shelter for herself between the guys, but a quick look inside the shelter revealed she was no longer in it.

She better not have left him alone with Javan after her big speech about being a team. Feeling a touch angry, Micah tapped Javan on the shoulder. "Wake up. The girl's gone."

"What? Huh?" Javan shook his head and rubbed his eyes. "What's going on?"

"The girl. She's not here. We need to find her."

"Oh. I'm sure she didn't go far. She's the one who wanted us to be a 'team.'"

"Let's check along the river first." Micah picked up his sword and slung it over his shoulder. "I'll go right. You go left. Meet back here if you don't find her. Make sure you take your swords and stay alert. There are all kinds of dangerous animals out here."

"Yeah. Okay." Javan jumped out of the tree and yawned as he strapped his sword belt on. "I'm gonna need a minute or two to wake up before I go anywhere."

"Next time you might want to wake up and look at the ground before you jump. You're standing right next to a scorpion."

Javan screeched and began running in the direction Micah told him to go. That made Micah smile, and he began jogging along the river looking for the girl.

It wasn't an easy run. He had to dodge in and out of trees over snakes and around bushes. He almost lost his footing a few times but managed to keep himself from toppling into the water.

After he turned around and didn't see Javan back at the campsite, he kept running in the direction he sent Javan.

He felt he had gone far enough and was ready to turn around when he spotted Taliya and Javan by the bank of the river more than a mile from the campsite. Taliya was sitting calmly on the grass under a tree. She had her legs dangling over the edge and dancing over the water while Javan paced behind her in a small clearing looking agitated.

"You actually appear happy," Taliya said as Micah approached them. "You must enjoy running."

Micah shrugged and sat beside her. "Never thought about it before. Running is just part of training. And I was trying to find you."

"Here I am."

"I see that. Why did you come all the way down here?"

"Just wandered around a bit trying to figure out exactly where we are."

"Got it figured out?"

"Oh, she has it figured out all right," Javan said. His cheeks were turning red. Micah wasn't sure if that was because he was mad or because he was overheated from his run in the heat.

"What's his problem?" Micah asked.

Taliya rolled her eyes. "He doesn't like my plan."

"Then I probably will. What do we need to do?"

"We need to go that way," Taliya said, pointing up the river to her right. "But first we need to steal that boat." She spun her hand around and pointed down the river to her left.

Micah followed her finger and noticed a large red boat docked on the left bank of the river not too far downstream. It took up about a third of the river's width and appeared to be long enough to fit three full-sized midnight stalkers.

The top deck had a railing around it and doubled as the roof of the twelve-foot high walls that spanned the length of the boat. A walkway encircled the enclosed hub of the boat.

A steady flow of brown-skinned, dark-haired, colorfully dressed people carrying armfuls of plants walked on and off the boat via a wooden plank that led from the main deck to the grass. "It's going to be hard to steal with that many people around," Micah said.

"We shouldn't be stealing anything," Javan said. "Stealing is wrong."

"Getting back to our dragons is the right thing for us to do," Micah said, "so taking that boat is perfectly justified."

"I tried explaining that to him," Taliya said. "He didn't listen to logic."

Javan stopped pacing and folded his arms over his chest. "Your logic is flawed. I think we should ask to borrow the boat."

"They would never agree to that," Taliya said. "Transport Day is less than two weeks away. They need that boat to transport their humminglo supply to Tulkar or they could lose the war."

"Say again?" Javan sounded confused as he sat on the other side of Taliya. "None of that made any sense to me."

"Or me." Micah said. "What are you talking about?"

"I forgot you guys aren't from Keckrick." Taliya took a deep breath and nodded toward the boat. "The people are loading humminglo flowers onto the boat. Those flowers are the reason for the civil war between the Upper and Lower tribes of Keckrick."

"The humminglo is a flower?" Micah shook his head in disbelief. "I almost got hung over those things because one of those Upper tribes thought I was spying on their humminglo supply. What kind of people go to war over a flower?"

"You don't know? You're the king's son, and you don't know?"

"If I knew, I wouldn't ask." Micah made sure to let her hear the edge of infuriation in his words.

Taliya sighed and explained. "Every year on October first, King Omri demands we supply him with humminglo flowers and other medicinal plants that we transport through the portal, which is in the abandoned capital city of Tulkar. As long as we meet our quota each year, he leaves us alone."

"I am aware that my father has a trade agreement set up with all the regions in the Great Rift. I've just never bothered to learn the specifics of each deal."

"Well, the specifics of this year's deal is different. He has increased our quota of humminglo plants tenfold this year and said that he will send his dragons to annihilate our entire population if we don't meet the quota."

"Then why are you fighting?" Javan asked. "Shouldn't all the tribes be united in working to supply as many flowers as possible?"

"You would think so," Taliya said, "but as an added incentive to maximize the supply, the King has promised that even if the quota is met, he will wipe out the entire region of the country that delivers the fewest amount of flowers."

"No," Micah said. He knew his father was ruthless, but he didn't want to believe he was cruel enough to kill people who met his quota demands. "You must be mistaken. My father would never make such an unfair deal."

"Tell that to all the people who have died in this war."

"This war ends now." Javan stood and glared at Micah. "We're going to get you to the portal and back home so you can talk some sense into that maniacal father of yours."

Without another word, he sprinted off in the direction of the boat.

"Umm…what do you think he's going to do?" Micah asked.

"Something very not smart," Taliya replied.

"He's going to get us all killed, isn't he?"

They looked at each other, then scrambled to their feet, and chased after Javan.

◊   ◊   ◊

"What am I doing? What am I doing? What am I doing?" Javan mumbled that same question to himself as he fought through the trees to get to the boat. He had no idea what he was going to say to these people he didn't know regarding a war he just learned about. But he had to do something. He couldn't let Omri annihilate half a country over flowers.

He expected to hear chatter when he got close to the people. Instead, all he heard as he perched behind a tree near the plank was the sound of humming as a mixture of men, women, boys, and girls walked onto the boat with armfuls of plants and off moments later empty-handed.

Javan found the humming soothing. He almost let himself be lured to sleep until he took a closer look at the plants the people carried. He had seen that same purple-petaled, neon-blue stringed flower before; they grew all around the canyon where he first spotted Kisa. Only the flowers at the canyon were mega-sized compared to the two-foot long flowers being carried onto the boat.

What was so special about those plants? Why did Omri want ten times more than he usually demanded? "You're not going to find your answers hiding behind a tree, Javan," he told himself. "Time to be bold and take a risk."

With his head held high and his hands up to show he had no intention of using his swords, he stepped out from behind the safety of the tree and approached the end of the plank. "Excuse me," he said to the woman about to step onto the plank, "where can I find the captain of this boat?"

The plump woman's eyes widened, and she transformed from a sweet little lady to a ferocious warrior. "Intruder! Intruder!" She threw her flowers at his face and body slammed him into the ground. Seconds later, he was surrounded by a dozen or so men who held spears aimed at his head.

"Who sent you?" the woman asked, shoving her forearm under his chin.

"Can't…breathe." He must have gained her sympathy from his faint whisper, because she moved her arm and rolled off his chest.

She picked up one of the flowers she had thrown and pointed it at him. "Now answer my question."

"No one sent me." Javan coughed to search for words to say that wouldn't get him killed. "I came to help. That's why I need to talk to the captain of the boat."

"I think we should get the captain," one of the spear-holders said. "I don't think he's a spy. His skin is too pale for him to be from anywhere in Keckrick."

"Exactly. I'm from Montana." Javan winced at his mistake. He really needed to get used to calling Zandador home and not Montana. "It's kind of a place in the Land of Zandador."

Javan heard someone scurry away. Other than the flowing river water, that's all he heard. The humming parade on and off the boat had ceased, and no one else moved or spoke. He remained still and waited along with everyone else.

"We don't usually get visitors from Zandador before Transport Day." A tall man wearing a wide-brimmed white hat, white shirt, and white pants stepped up and towered over Javan. "I heard you were asking for me. What is your business here in Keckrick?"

"I came to collect a dragon." That news sent a chorus of murmurs through the crowd. He knew he had their attention, so he continued. "It turns out I can also help you win the war."

"Is that so? How do you intend to do that?"

"Two days ago I walked through a vast field of humminglo flowers as tall as me. If you give me and my two friends a ride on your boat, we can take you there."

"You have seen these plants? They are truly as high as your head?"

"I have touched them. They make your flowers look like miniature toys. King Omri would find one more valuable than a hundred of your small flowers."

"Such massive flowers would be valuable and please the king." The captain had the guards back away and helped Javan to his feet. "Where is this field?"

"That's the tricky part. It's on the northwestern shore."

The captain narrowed his eyes, grabbed Javan's shirt, and lifted him up. "Now you are telling stories. You would not have been able to get from there to here in two days."

"Yes. I could." Javan choked the words out. "White winds."

The captain slowly eased Javan back to the ground and let go of his shirt. "You mentioned two friends. I only see you."

Javan called toward the trees. "Micah. Taliya. I know you're there. Come on out, and meet the captain."

Everyone followed Javan's gaze.

No one appeared.

"Tie him up, and throw him in the river," the captain said.

"Hold on! They're there. Give them a second. Please," Javan said, pleading with the captain. The captain held up his hands to signal a hold on his orders, and Javan turned his attention back to the trees.

"Taliya? Micah? I'm sure you followed me and can hear every word I'm saying. If you cooperate, we can hitch a ride to where we want to go while helping these charming people out in the process." It took his stubborn new pals a minute or two, but they finally stepped out from behind the same tree Javan had used for cover.

The people gasped at the sight of Micah. They apparently weren't used to seeing someone with such dark skin. "As you can see," Javan said, "my buddy Micah isn't from Keckrick either. He followed me here from Zandador, and he's going to do something sweet for the people of Keckrick."

"I am?" Sweetness did not exactly ooze from Micah's demeanor. As a matter of fact, he narrowed his eyes and seemed to be trying to incinerate Javan. Good thing he didn't possess the ability to shoot lasers from his eyes.

"You are," Javan said. Since he knew Micah was in no position to hurt him, Javan turned his back on the big man and addressed the people. "You see, Micah has a special relationship with King Omri. If you're able to send him back through the portal with the head-high humminglo flowers I told you about, he is going to convince the King to spare the people of Keckrick."

Smiles spread over the faces of the crowd. Some of them even began clapping. The captain, however, wasn't smiling or clapping. "We have never known King Omri to change his mind about anything. Why would he do so now?"

"Because this man," Javan said, "is King Omri's son." A hush fell over the crowd. Javan enjoyed having the people hang on his every word.

Then the captain barked his orders. "Take their weapons, and put them in the pit!"

"What? You can't do that," Javan said. "We need to be on our way to the head-high humminglo fields."

"I am not yet sure I believe you. Even if I did, I cannot make that decision on my own. We will gather the Council of Tribal Chiefs, let them hear your proposal, and decide your fate. The three of you will remain unarmed in the pit until that time."

The pit? That didn't sound good. And with the way Taliya and Micah were glaring at Javan, he wasn't sure he was going to make it out of that pit alive.

CHAPTER 24
THE COUNCIL'S DECISION

Micah reluctantly surrendered his sword and willingly walked to the pit for one reason: he wanted a chance to strangle the life out of Javan for acting on his own and making their presence known to the locals.

The hike to the pit took about an hour. They passed several humminglo fields along the way, and the last hill they crested provided a sweeping view of the village. The place was at least twice the size of the one he had encountered in the north but lacked any sense of uniformity.

A creek wide enough and deep enough for canoe travel curved through the village. Huts on stilts dotted the shoreline. Huts further away from the creek were built above the ground in the trees. Bigger buildings constructed directly on the ground were scattered in a haphazard fashion among the area.

With no defined perimeter or designated town center, the village appeared to have no structure or organization. How could they expect these people to help when they couldn't even build a decent, sensible town?

"We are here." One of their three spear-carrying guides stopped them halfway down the hill beside a deep, dark, oblong hole in the ground. A thick rope tied around the base of a nearby tree dangled into the pit. "Get in."

"I don't see any stairs," Micah said.

"There aren't any." The man pointed his spear at Micah. "You can use the rope to climb down, or we will throw you in."

Taliya crossed her arms and shook her head. "I'm not about to climb down. I have no idea how deep that hole is or if you'll ever let us out."

"I'll let you know how deep it is," Javan said. He winked at Taliya and used the rope to lower himself into the hole. "I'm at the bottom and can still see you. Plus it's nice and cool down here."

"I don't care," Taliya said. "I prefer the heat up here."

Micah looked up the hill and assessed the guards. Even without his sword, he was sure he could take out the guards and make his escape with the girl. But he wanted to get his hands on Javan's throat. He thus didn't bother with the rope and jumped in after Javan.

The fall took longer than he expected. He nevertheless thumped safely onto the dirt floor and found himself surrounded by dirt walls too high and too smooth to climb up without the aid of the rope the guards were pulling to the top.

A kicking and screaming Taliya landed beside him a minute later. "They threw me in! They actually picked me up and threw me in. Such rudeness!"

Micah stood and ignored her tantrum, but Javan offered her his hand to help her stand. He didn't give her a chance to notice his kindness and pinned Javan against the dirt wall with his forearm. "What were you thinking? Why would you tell them I'm Omri's son? You heard Taliya warn me to keep that a secret."

"I introduced you in a way that would make it advantageous for them to keep you alive," Javan said. He spoke with confidence rather than fear and made no effort to fight back. Micah considered releasing Javan until Taliya stepped up and slapped Javan's cheek.

"Why would you tell them about my humminglo fields? That's where Kisa lives. She loves those flowers. Having them torn up and shipped to another country is going to destroy her home and put her in a seriously bad mood."

"I told the truth," Javan said. "Now these people are considering working with us and taking us where we want to go."

"The truth? What kind of strategy is that? It clearly doesn't work," Taliya said. "These people you think are so helpful put us in a pit and took our weapons."

"Only temporarily," Javan said. "Once we have a chance to present our case before the council, they'll see the wisdom in our plan and have no choice but to team up with us."

"What makes you think I want to go along with this plan of yours?" Micah wanted to tell Javan his plan wouldn't work. Omri never took advice from anyone. However, Micah didn't want to admit that his father wouldn't listen to him. He preferred to let Javan and everyone else think that he had enough sway with his father to change his mind. "I'm sure my father has his reasons for the deal he has in place, and I have no reason to defend the people of Keckrick."

"They're people," Javan said. "Innocent people. You are both in a position to help save them from needless annihilation. Taliya, all you have to do is surrender some flowers; I'll even help you plant more. And Micah, all you have to do is talk to your dad. We'll get our dragons back, Omri will get his flowers, and the people of Keckrick will get to live. Everybody wins."

"He does make a lot of sense," Taliya said.

"Yeah. He does." Micah studied Javan. Choking him wouldn't take long and would eliminate Micah's Collector problem for good.

"Go ahead." Javan's wary brown eyes stared right back at Micah. "Kill me. Show these people you are just as ruthless as your father and can't be trusted. Then see if they ever let you out of this pit alive."

"Nobody is going to kill anybody." Taliya grabbed a handful of Micah's dreadlocks and pulled him away from Javan. "We're in this mess together and have to pretend like we like each other if we're going to convince the council to agree to Javan's plan."

"Fine." Micah rubbed his head to soothe his tender scalp. "I'll let the Collector live and do my part, but I don't have to pretend to like either one of you while we're stuck in here."

"Good," Javan said. "I had no intention of making small talk anyway."

"Small talk?" Taliya cocked her head. "What is that?"

"Umm…idle chit chat. Shallow conversation. Talking about nothing just for the sake of talking."

"Ugh." She scrunched her nose. "That sounds unpleasant. I'd rather sit here in the dark and not say a word."

"Now that is a great plan," Micah said. He sat down, leaned against the cool dirt wall, and closed his eyes. Maybe being stuck in this pit wasn't such a bad thing after all. He hadn't slept well last night and could use some quiet time to recover from the non-stop action of the past few days.

◊   ◊   ◊

Javan dozed on and off throughout the day. He was thankful for the chance to relax, but his rumbling stomach and parched throat began to make the stay in the pit quite uncomfortable.

He also found himself wanting to talk to Taliya. The longer he sat in the dark, the more curious he became about the woman sitting beside him. Who was she? When did she begin protecting Kisa? How did she end up protecting a dragon here in Keckrick? Why did she shoot him the first time she saw him? Did she have a boyfriend?

No matter how much he wanted answers, he kept his questions to himself. If Micah and Taliya could sit in the confined space without talking, so could he. He might go a touch insane, but he was too stubborn to be the one to break the silence.

Before too much of his sanity had a chance to slip away, a voice from above called down to them. "The council has gathered and is ready to hear from you." The rope hit the top of Javan's head, and he used it to climb out of the hole.

His eyes had a chance to adjust to the afternoon sun while Micah and Taliya made their way up the rope. After a much needed bathroom break, six guards led the three guests to a small amphitheater on the other side of the village. Ten rows of grass steps halfway encircled an oval stage.

Seven of the rows remained empty, and the people who filled the first three rows did not match Javan's expectations of what he thought rain forest tribal people should look like. He expected them to be wearing grass skirts, animal jewelry, and bizarre head gear along with an assortment of piercings in their ears, noses, and belly buttons.

Although they did wear layers of necklaces and had their wrists covered with bracelets, they wore regular, colorful clothes as opposed to grass skirts. Javan wasn't sure why, but he found that disappointing.

The captain Javan had met that morning stood on the stage beside a tall, thick, round man whose upper body reminded Javan of a tree trunk. He was dressed in a blue and yellow striped shirt, dark pants, and an odd feathered crown atop his square-shaped head.

"Chief Gale and council members," the captain said, "our guests from the Land of Zandador have arrived." The guards walked Javan, Micah, and Taliya down to the stage and then spread out along the perimeter of the amphitheater to stand watch.

"Welcome." The Chief shook each of the trio's hands and offered them chairs facing the council members. Once they were seated, he continued by addressing the council. "As you all know, the reports from our spies indicate that the north has a greater supply of humminglo plants and is poised for victory if we take no action."

"I agree. That is why my tribe is ready to attack." A female council member in the middle of the second row stood. "We are prepared to send warriors to the north to burn their humminglo fields before they have a chance to harvest them."

"That is foolishness!" A man on the front row stood. "We need their plants to meet King Omri's overall quota."

"Doing nothing is foolishness!"

"Chief Lydia. Chief Paraan. Both of you. Sit. Now." Chief Gale interrupted the argument with such a stern tone that Javan felt the need to lower his head and avert his eyes. He stared at his toes as he listened to the chief address the council.

"We gathered you here today because an opportunity to win the war and save the entire country has presented itself. Our duty as chiefs of the lower eastern tribes is to evaluate the opportunity and choose whether or not to act upon it." Chief Gale touched Javan's shoulder. "Stand and tell us what you told Captain Cyr."

Javan stood, cleared his throat, and prayed he would be able to talk in front of all these strangers without having his voice crack. "Hey. Hello.

So…umm…my name is Javan." His voice wasn't cracking, but he sure was sounding like an idiot. He needed to say something smart that would get the attention of the council. "I'm a Dragon Collector and flew here on the back of my Noon Stalker Varjiek in search of a Dawn Stalker I heard was hiding in your land."

"We have no dragons in Keckrick!" The female chief whom Gale called Lydia was back on her feet. "What kind of nonsense have you brought us here to listen to? The only dragons we need to know about are the ones King Omri will send to destroy us if we lose the war."

"Let's hear him out," another woman from the third row said. "If he's a Dragon Collector, that means he's fighting against King Omri. But I don't see any dragon you claim to have flown here on. Where is he?"

"Good question." Javan took a deep breath and worked to calm his trembling hands. "He's where I left him when I got caught in a wall of white wind and blown here."

"And where did you leave him?"

"On the northwestern shore."

"Tell the council what you saw before the white winds blew you here," Captain Cyr said.

"Right." Javan nodded. "Before I was caught in the white winds, I walked among humminglo flowers as high as my head."

"Head-high humminglo flowers?"

"That's absurd!"

"Those plants never grow higher than one's knees."

"He's telling the truth." Taliya joined Javan and squashed the arguments of the random council members. "These flowers exist and have grown unharvested in a secret location in a place called Fralick for fifteen years. I know because they grow in my fields and are nurtured by me."

"Why have you kept these flowers of yours a secret from your own tribe?" Chief Gale asked Taliya.

"Because I love to watch them grow, and the music they make when you touch them as you walk through the fields is the most soothing noise in the world."

Javan's heart melted at the sentiment in her response, and he wished he had never mentioned anything about her flowers.

"Is anybody believing this?" Chief Lydia pointed at Taliya. "She just admitted she is from Upper Keckrick and thus cannot be trusted. I say we hang them all right now."

"If we hang them," Chief Gale said over the commotion of the crowd, "we'll never know where these humminglo fields are."

"They don't exist!" The rabble-rousing woman stepped between the men in front of her and joined Gale on the stage. "It's a ruse to distract us."

"This is no ruse," Javan said. "These flowers are real, and Taliya is willing to take you to them."

"She is from Upper Keckrick and wants to give her flowers to us?" Chief Lydia sounded dubious. "That makes her either a spy or a traitor!"

"She is neither," Javan said. "All she wants is to get back home, and I want to get back to my dragon, which is near her home. In order to do that, we need a ride on your boat. In order to convince you to give us that ride, we are willing to pay you with huge humminglo flowers."

"That would mean her people in Upper Keckrick would lose the war," Chief Lydia said, "and she would die in the ensuing annihilation."

"What if there is no annihilation?" Javan pointed to Micah. "That's where this guy comes in. Meet Micah. He is King Omri's son."

◊ ◊ ◊

Micah loved the sudden silence that descended upon the crowd at the mention of his name. He slowly stood and took control of the conversation.

"If you are able to get me and these valuable humminglo plants through the portal, I will speak to my father, King Omri." Mertzer would also be a part of that equation, but they didn't need to know about his dragon just yet. He wanted them to understand how powerful he was on his own and how important it was to their well-being to do as he said. "I will tell him how well you served me during my visit here as well as the extra effort you demonstrated to get him the head-high humminglos. I am certain he will then honor my request to spare the people of Keckrick."

"Even if you are Omri's son, the plan is too risky," a bald man on the front row said. "We need our boat here on the river to take our humminglo supply to the portal. We cannot risk sending it through the Dark Zone to get to flowers we aren't sure exist or expect King Omri to change his mind even if they do."

Micah felt his cheeks burn with anger. "Do you dare question my identity and ability to sway my father?"

"Yes, it's risky," Javan said, stepping between Micah and the bald man. "But what's the alternative? Meet your quota, and lose the war anyway?"

"He is right," Chief Gale said. "We must take this risk if we want to survive."

Hearing Chief Gale support the plan calmed Micah. So did the bold words of Captain Cyr.

"I am certain I can get our boat safely through the Dark Zone and back to the portal in time for Transport Day."

"Chief Lydia will join you." Chief Gale put his hands on the woman beside him. "You were prepared to send warriors to Upper Keckrick.

Now you can. Instead of burning fields, though, you can have your people harvest fields our enemy knows nothing about in their own territory."

"Okay." She nodded. "I will lead this trip. But if we get to the northwestern shore and there are no head-high humminglo flowers, I will personally execute these three spies and send my warriors to steal as many humminglo flowers we can find in Upper Keckrick."

"If there is a journey," the bald man said. "Such an undertaking requires a unanimous vote by the council."

"So vote," Micah said through his clenched jaw. His anger was on the rise again after the Lydia woman threatened to execute him.

"Yes. Let us vote," Chief Gale said. "Chiefs of the Lower Eastern Tribes, if you agree to send our main transport boat to the northwestern shore to harvest the head-high humminglos and in turn commit to summoning the use of every smaller boat and canoe and raft from your tribes to get our humminglos to Tulkar by Transport Day, stand."

One by one, the chiefs on the grass steps rose to their feet. Everyone except for the bald man on the front row.

Micah was about to shove Javan out of the way and pull the defiant man into a standing position when Javan spoke to the man. "What would it take to convince you to stand?"

"Nothing." He crossed his arms and shook his head. "We need our boat here carrying the flowers King Omri has demanded we provide. I have been alive too long to believe he would ever change his mind, and getting our humminglo supply to him is our best chance of winning the war."

"Then just make sure I get to my dragon," Javan said. "If our plan fails and Micah cannot change his father's mind, my dragon and I will fight to defend the people of Keckrick."

Why would Javan want to defend these people? He didn't even know them! Plus Javan was no match for his father's dragons. That didn't seem to matter to the bald man, though. After thinking over Javan's vow, the man finally nodded and stood.

"It is decided," Chief Gale said. "Captain Cyr and Chief Lydia will gather a band of warriors and leave at dawn to travel with our guests through the Dark Zone to the northwestern shore of Keckrick."

The Chief then turned to Javan. "Now come, Dragon Collector. You and your friends will be my guests tonight. You have given us cause for celebration, and we must feast!"

CHAPTER 25
JAVAN'S NEW TRICK

As the crowd of chiefs dispersed, Micah tried to make sense of what just happened. Javan convinced the entire council to agree to his plan by telling the truth and giving them hope. How was that possible? Omri had taught Micah the only way to get his way was to use deceit and fear, but Javan's method seemed just as effective. Maybe more so.

Still, Micah wasn't about to surrender his lifelong beliefs. He would stick to the method that had always worked for him and began delivering orders to Captain Cyr. "I want my sword returned to me immediately. I also demand a hot bath. I feel filthy after sitting in that dirt hole all day."

"I am sorry you had to spend the day in the pit," Captain Cyr said, "but it was a necessary precaution. If you follow me, I will take you to the guest house where I am sure you will find the accommodations much more hospitable."

"It better be a cool house with a soft bed and guards outside the door to ensure no one bothers me while I rest."

"He's not your servant, Micah," Javan said. "Stop demanding things, and treat him with a little respect."

"Respect?" Micah grit his teeth and glared at Javan. "He had me thrown in a pit and now wants me to plead with my father to let him live. I can demand whatever I want."

"A bath does sound nice," Taliya said, breaking the tension.

"Of course," Cyr said. "You should have ample time to soak in the hot springs while dinner is prepared. In the meantime, I will have your weapons and a change of clothes delivered to the house."

Micah smirked at Javan and followed Cyr and two of his men through the village at dusk to a large pool surrounded by colorful flowers and bamboo reeds. "The water is hot, so you won't want to soak for long. When you are finished, my men will lead you to the guest house."

"I'm not into the whole communal bath thing," Javan said. "I'll just go back with the Captain and take my turn when you're done."

"Me, too," Taliya said. "I prefer to bathe alone."

"Suit yourselves," Micah said. He waited for them to leave, stripped off his sweaty, dirty clothes, and eased himself down onto the carved out stone bench in the steaming pool.

He slowly leaned his back against the warm rocks that lined the walls of the hot springs. Every inch of his body from his neck to his toes was immersed in the gloriously hot water that cleansed his skin and soothed his muscles. For the first time since the dragon-hunting journey began, Micah felt well-rested and well-pampered.

He just wished he still had his dragon with him. Life felt strange without Mertzer around. Although he wanted to get back to Taliya's house and recover Mertzer, he wasn't in any hurry to leave this place.

Until the feeling of being pampered ended at dinner.

He expected to walk into a magnificent banquet hall in the huge home of the Chief, to sit as the guest of honor at the head of a long rectangular table filled with the most important people in the village, and to be brought plate after plate of food by servants as festive music played in the background.

Instead he walked into a dimly lit hut that was barely big enough to house a dragon. He was forced to sit between Javan and Taliya at a small round table across from the Chief and his wife Esara.

No one else from the village joined them for dinner. No music played while they ate. No servants filled their cups with wine or put platefuls of food at each place. Micah thus had to fill his own cup with water from a pitcher and transfer food from the main dishes in the center of the table to his own plate and bowl.

As if serving himself wasn't bad enough, the scarcity of food was worse. All he had to choose from was some sort of mystery meat, purple-tinted mashed potatoes, and a pot of vegetable soup. At least Esara said it was vegetable soup. It looked more like a bowl of broth with a few carrots floating around in it to justify calling it a vegetable soup. This feast the chief had bragged about wasn't much of a feast at all.

"Umm..." Micah refused to pick up his fork and eat when only half of his plate had food on it. "Where is the rest of the food?"

"Micah, you're being rude," Javan whispered. "Be grateful for what you have and eat."

"No." He pushed his plate away from him. "This is not a fitting meal for the king's son."

"It is here in Keckrick," Taliya said. "We are fortunate they are even feeding us considering how limited food is here because of the king."

"What do you mean? My father can't possibly have anything to do with the food supply in Keckrick."

"Actually, he can," Chief Gale said. "We've had to turn most of our farm lands into humminglo fields in order to meet your father's outrageous demands. Then to make sure the flowers flourish, we have to tend to the fields and guard them against predators. That limits our ability to hunt."

"You can't blame Omri for that. You have plenty of land here and should have used more of it to plant some crops. And if you're hungry, leave the stupid flowers alone and hunt some animals."

"Clearly my friend has no idea what it's like to live in Keckrick." Taliya kicked Micah's shin. "I do apologize for his rudeness, and thank you very much for your hospitality."

"I cooked the last of the food in my kitchen to make this meal for you." Esara stood, reached over the table, and scraped the food from her plate onto Micah's. "We are starting to see many of our people become sick and weak because they do not have enough to eat. If your father's dragons don't kill us, the lack of food might."

She took her empty plate over to the kitchen sink and exited the hut through the back door. Without a word, Gale, Taliya, and Javan copied her, leaving him alone in the hut with a heaping plateful of meat and potatoes.

"Great. More for me." Micah stuffed a forkful in his mouth, but for some strange reason, he had lost his appetite.

◊   ◊   ◊

Two bites. Javan had a chance to eat two teeny bites before Micah's obnoxiousness ruined dinner. As a result, he found himself too hungry to sleep.

His accommodations were cozy enough. He liked the soft bed he sat on in the corner of the lantern-lit room, and he had had fun playing with the lantern. Its round metal base was filled with a cool substance called fire oil and had a thin, inch-wide opening enclosed by a foot tall glass case. Every time he clicked the spark button, metal prongs in the base rubbed together to create a flame that shot through the opening.

Once the thrill of blowing the flame out and reigniting the fire dissipated, he left the lantern lit and listened to his surroundings. The sounds of trickling water and chirping rain forest creatures that wafted into the room from the open window above his head relaxed him.

And thanks to soaking in the hot springs and the fresh set of clothes provided by Esara, he felt clean and comfy. The material of the long-sleeved green shirt and brown pants that looked like khakis was unlike anything Javan had touched before. Although it was tough, it was light-weight and kept him cool in the hot, humid weather.

He didn't like sleeping with a shirt on, though, so he had draped it over the end of the footboard by his stalker sword belt. That still didn't help him sleep. His gurgling stomach and worried mind wouldn't let him rest.

What would Ravier think of Javan's promise to help defend Keckrick? What would Varjiek think? Would the dragon be willing to fight against Omri's dragons?

Javan picked up the scale Varjiek had lost during the clash with Mertzer and Kisa. The half-inch thick triangular scale covered the palm of his hand. Javan wrapped his fingers around it and wondered what his dragon was doing at that very moment.

Had he become friends with Kisa and Mertzer? Had he left them to come find Javan? Did he consider himself free from his obligation to his Collector and return home to Zandador?

Contemplating the answer to that last question disturbed Javan. He sighed, leaned his head against the wall, and was about to close his eyes when the way the light from the lantern beside the bed danced off the handles of his stalker swords caught his attention.

He had never understood why the gap between the end of the handle and beginning of the blade on both swords existed. He thought the thin piece of steel as wide as his palm and half an inch high that connected the blade to the handle was a design flaw. Now that he was holding Varjiek's scale, he had a different idea.

"I wonder…" Javan scrambled to the end of the bed and drew the sword with the grey handle and black and gold blade. He studied the scale and the sword, then carefully slid the scale through the gap. As soon as the point of the triangle touched the steel, it clicked into place. "Huh. That's interesting."

He swished the sword back and forth through the air. The scale remained in place, but Javan wasn't sure what purpose it served. He took it out and swished the sword around again. "I don't notice any kind of difference, but it looks cooler with the scale." He clicked the scale back into place just as he heard a knock on the door.

"Javan? You awake? It's Taliya. Can I come in?"

A girl? Wanted to come into his room? In the middle of the night? He should say no. "Sure," he said. He gripped his sword tighter, hoping that would help his palm to stop sweating.

"I thought you might be hungry, so I brought you food." The door creaked open, and Taliya walked in carrying a tray with a cup and plate on it. She paused two steps inside the room and looked around. "Javan? Where'd you go?"

"I'm over here." He waved with his sword-free right hand.

"Over where?" She scanned the room but didn't seem to see him sitting five feet away from her. "Are you playing games with me? Cause it's not funny."

"You seriously can't see me? I'm sitting on the bed."

"No you're not. I'm standing by the bed. If you were sitting there, I'd be able to see you."

"I think you're the one playing games with me." Javan stood and tossed his sword on the bed.

"Whoa!" Taliya jumped back, bumped into the open door, and dropped the tray. Water from the cup splattered Javan, and the grapes that leapt off the plate began rolling everywhere. "How did you do that?"

"Do what?" Javan wiped the water off his face. "Stand up?"

"No." Her face drained of color and her voice shook. "How did you make yourself appear in the middle of the room?"

"What are you talking about? I've been here all along."

"I know what I saw, and I didn't see you when I walked into this room. I heard you, but I didn't see you until just a second ago."

"That's crazy. I'm not a magician. I can't make myself appear and disappear. Unless..." Javan looked at his sword. Could it be? Did that scale somehow transfer Varjiek's invisibility power to him? "I'm gonna try something. Tell me if you can still see me when I pick up my sword."

"Okay."

Javan rubbed his hands together and slowly reached for the sword. As soon as he wrapped his fingers around the handle, Taliya yelped.

"I guess you can't see me," he said.

"Nope." She backed up and crossed her arms. "I don't like it when people are invisible. Please make yourself visible again."

Javan laughed and dropped the sword back on the bed. "You look terrified."

"I not terrified. Baffled, maybe. But not terrified." She straightened her shoulders and stuck her chin out. "I am not scared of anything."

"Then why did you drop the tray of food and scream?"

"The whole invisibility thing surprised me. That's all." She bent down and began picking up grapes. "I'm guessing it surprised you, too."

"Yeah. Big time." Javan joined her on the floor, eating the grapes as he picked them up. "Thanks for the food. These are good."

"You're welcome. Esara felt bad about dinner and scrounged up what she could from some of the other villagers. She and I ate a lot more than this. When we filled up, she suggested I bring you the leftovers."

"Gee, thanks."

She winked and handed him the plate covered with grapes and a small assortment of other fruits Javan couldn't quite identify. "So are you going to tell our pal Micah about your invisibility sword?"

Javan shook his head while he finished chewing. "No! Definitely not. I'd like to keep this our little secret. Please don't tell anyone, especially Micah."

"All right. I'll keep your secret. But you have to promise to never spy on me in your invisibility mode. I don't want to always have to wonder whether or not you're lurking about."

"Deal." Javan stretched out his hand, and she shook it. Before he let her hand go, he said, "I'm sorry I had to tell them about your humminglo flowers. I didn't realize how important they were to you."

"They are important to me, but it's a smart arrangement. If giving up my flowers means I get to return to Kisa, I guess I can live with that." She pulled her hand away and stood. "Now I'm going to get some rest. You should do the same. We've got a long journey ahead of us. Once we reach the Dark Zone, sleep is going to be scarcer than the food is around here."

"Yes, ma'am." As she closed the door behind her, Javan knew he should heed her warning and sleep in a nice cozy bed while he had a chance. But how was he supposed to sleep when he had just learned he could become invisible?

He picked up his sword and began contemplating all the cool things he could do as an invisible man.

CHAPTER 26
THE IRIA

Micah covered his eyes with his arm to protect them from the sudden burst of light. How could it be morning already? He felt like he had just gotten to sleep.

He groaned, rolled over, and opened his eyes. Much to his surprise, his eyes had to adjust to the artificial light of the lantern on the table by his bed rather than the natural sunlight that wasn't shining through the window on the wall across the room.

Why was the lantern glowing? He had blown the light out. He was sure of it. He demanded total darkness when he slept and would never have left it on. Unless he was more tired than he realized and had zonked out with the light still on. That had to have been the case.

He blew the fire out and settled under the covers in the pleasantly dark room. A minute later, though, the lantern sparked back on.

This time he grabbed the dagger from under his pillow, sat straight up, and looked around. The door near the foot of his bed remained closed. The bench under the window with his clothes and backsword on it remained untouched. Everything seemed normal, but he had the eerie feeling that something was in the room with him. Whatever it was didn't want him to sleep.

Was some sort of spirit in the village angry with him for eating all that food at dinner? It shouldn't be. He had been hungry. He deserved that food. He was Omri's son. He could do whatever he wanted.

"I'm going to blow the light out again," he announced, trying to hide the fear he felt. He had no power over something he couldn't see, and that made him uneasy. To settle his nerves, he did the only thing he knew how to do: he issued a command. "I demand that you leave it off and leave me alone."

Nothing responded. He leaned over, killed the flame with his breath, and waited. Satisfied the spirit was gone and the light was out for good, he laid down. Then he heard the sound of wood scraping the floor and his sword being unsheathed.

"Who's there?" He jumped up and sparked the lantern on. The light allowed him to watch the door open and close on its own. That didn't disturb him nearly as much as seeing the bench tipped over and his clothes hanging on the wall with his sword stuck through them.

Was that a warning? Was he next? Why did he complain about the food? He should have kept his mouth shut and just taken the food offered to him. "Sorry about the food. I won't complain anymore. But you should haunt Omri, not me. He's the reason you have a food shortage here."

The door once again opened by itself. Seconds later, a warm breeze wafted across the back of his neck. Too scared to scream or speak, Micah snatched the top blanket from the bed and ran out of the room.

◊   ◊   ◊

"Javan!" Taliya banged on his door, waking him from a deep sleep. "Get up and get out here. You need to tell Micah his room is not haunted."

Javan chuckled to himself as he recalled Micah running out of the room in his underwear in the middle of the night with nothing but a blanket to wear. This invisibility thing sure had its perks.

"Hello?" More banging. "You awake in there?"

"Yeah," Javan said. "I'm coming." He quickly dressed himself by the light of the rising sun and opened the door. Like the other three rooms in the hut, his door opened directly into the living room. He and Micah had taken the two rooms on the right, and Taliya had taken one of the rooms on the left.

"Finally." Taliya pulled Javan over to Micah, who was sitting in one of the chairs in the living room covered from the waist down by his blanket. "Explain to Micah that ghosts do not exist and that he can go into his own room and get his own clothes and that if he tries to order me to get his stuff for him one more time, I will pull those pretty little dreadlocks out of his head one by painful one." With a huff, she retreated to the kitchen.

"I think you made her mad," Javan said.

"I'm the one who is angry. She wouldn't do what I told her to do."

"She's kinda vicious and could probably follow through with that dreadlock threat. I wouldn't order her around."

"Then you can get my things for me."

"Not a good idea to order me around, either."

Javan turned to follow Taliya into the kitchen, but Micah stood and snagged his arm. "All right. I'm asking nicely. Please bring my clothes and sword. I saw and *felt* things in that room. Creepy things. I can't go back in there."

Guilt ate at Javan's conscience. Micah was spooked because of him. The fear in his eyes made Javan realize Micah was a real person with real feelings, not the cold-hearted, ruthless, evil robot Javan made him out to be.

Javan sighed and started to come clean about his prank when Captain Cyr burst through the front door. "Good. You're awake," the captain said. "Gather your gear. We leave for the Iria in five minutes."

"Yes, sir," Javan said, thankful for the distraction. Now he didn't have time to tell Micah about the prank and could keep his invisibility ability a secret. "We'll be ready."

After Cyr nodded and left, Javan retrieved Micah's clothes for him. They were precisely where he had left them, attached to the wall with the same heavy sword that had sliced through Javan's chest and chopped off Mertzer's tail.

Handling the sword again reminded him how much he hated Micah.

◊　◊　◊

"Welcome to the Iria," Captain Cyr said as he led them across the plank and onto the main deck in the middle of the boat. Micah made sure he was the first person on the boat behind the captain. He didn't like that Cyr was in charge, but he could at least show Javan and Taliya he was ahead of them by positioning himself in the front of the line. And with only three feet between the railing and the red wall twice as tall as Micah, they had to stay in line while the captain walked them around the perimeter.

"This boat is designed to carry cargo," Cyr said, touching the red walls, "so she isn't passenger-friendly. The cargo area inside these walls comprises the bulk of the boat. Right now it is stuffed with humminglo flowers."

The wall gave way to a glass enclosed room at the bow. "This is the wheelhouse and where I will be spending most of my time. When I'm not at the wheel, my second-in-command Andre will be piloting the boat."

Micah studied the room as they walked around it. A podium in the center held a wooden wheel that spanned the distance from Micah's chest to his knees. Wooden spokes that looked long enough to wrap his hand around dotted the perimeter of the wheel, and some sort of device was built into the top of the podium. He wanted to go in to see what that device was, but Cyr moved quickly by the sliding glass door and down the other side of the hundred-foot long boat.

The cargo walls stopped about twenty feet shy of the stern, leaving enough space for an additional ten-foot long room at the end of the boat.

The captain led them into the covered walkway between the two rooms and pointed to the double doors leading into the cargo area. "We don't want to risk any plants blowing away, so please do not open these doors and enter this area for any reason.

"You are free to climb the ladder by the doors, though. It will take you to the deck above where you can find the best seats on the boat in good weather. You'll also notice a hatch under the ladder." He lifted the hatch and let them peek under the floor. "Down here is where you will sleep. You'll also have access to a small kitchen and even smaller bathroom.

"The other place for passengers is in the crank room." He closed the hatch and indicated the room opposite the cargo space. "However, the rumble rocks make hearing anything in that room nearly impossible."

"Rumble rocks?" Javan asked. "What are rumble rocks?"

"I thought you used rumble rocks on your boats in Zandador," Captain Cyr said.

"We do," said Micah. Apparently the Dragon Collector had lived a rather secluded life, and Micah began to wonder what else the Collector was clueless about. "Everyone who is anyone knows what rumble rocks are."

"No need to insult him," Taliya said. She rolled her eyes and turned to Javan. "Rumble rocks are mined from the canyon that divides Keckrick from Varzack. We use them to power our boats."

Javan scratched his head. "I don't understand."

"Let me show you," the captain said, leading Javan into the crank room.

Micah didn't follow them. He didn't care to hear the boring details of how they used rumble rocks to construct paddle wheels that, once cranked, kept turning until the brake was applied. Taliya didn't follow them either, and he joined her by the railing.

"Look at those clouds up ahead," Taliya said, pulling a small bag of berries and leaves out of her pocket. She popped a handful into her mouth and offered some to Micah. "Here. Take some. If that storm starts rocking this boat, these should keep you from getting sick."

Micah refused her offer. "I don't need your berries. I am a mighty Dragon Hunter and have been on boats in storms before. I don't get sick."

"Okay, mighty Micah. Sorry I mistook you for a mere human like the rest of us."

He smiled as she walked away. Even though she was being sarcastic, he liked hearing her acknowledge that he was on a different level than everyone else.

That feeling of superiority faded fast when they smacked into the storm shortly thereafter. The boat didn't handle the rough waters well, and neither did his stomach. The constant queasiness made him feel sub-human, and all he wanted to do was curl up into a little ball and die.

CHAPTER 27
TULKAR

Javan wished he had a window to stare out from his top bunk in the sleeping quarters. It would give him something to do besides study the swaying ceiling, listen to the clock tick, and wonder what the huddled crew members were whispering about at the other end of the long, dimly lit room.

Ten pair of bunk beds lined the walls of the room, and he had been assigned the top bed near the stern and closest to the spiral staircase. Although Cyr had a private room at the bow, his crew filled the first thirteen beds starting at the wall to Cyr's room and leading back toward Javan.

Chief Lydia and her dozen warriors took over the beds on the opposite side of Cyr's crew, and from what Javan had observed, she was not happy about having to sleep in the same room as everyone else. She and her crew were also not happy about being stuck in the sleeping quarters during the storm.

Cyr had ordered everyone below deck except for Micah (who was too sick to walk down the stairs) and the half of his crew he needed to do whatever crew people did to keep a boat like this afloat and moving forward during a storm. Javan knew he knew nothing about navigating on water and willingly followed orders.

Both Lydia and Taliya had protested. Both lost, but apparently their mutual defeat helped them bond. She had given Taliya the bed above hers, and the two seemed to have become fast friends.

Now Javan felt like he was back in high school with the cool kids huddled together and whispering at one end of the room while he got to be the lone social outcast at the other end of the room. On the plus side, the berries and leaves Taliya had given him kept him from feeling queasy, despite the constant rocking of the boat.

"Is that the one who calls himself a Dragon Collector?"

The loud question from one of Cyr's tall, thick-necked, muscle-bound men caught Javan's attention. It had the tone of a taunt, and Javan reached for his swords. He had been bullied enough in school to know when a beating was coming his way, but that was before Ravier had taught him how to use stalker swords.

He hoped he wouldn't have to fight, but he was prepared to defend himself if necessary. He kept his hands on his sword handles and tuned in to the conversation.

"No," another man said. "I think the Collector is the sick one."

"No. The sick one is the king's son. That one down there is the Collector."

A third man interrupted. "You two stop arguing and just go ask him."

"I can't talk to him," the first one said. "He has a dragon!"

"Yeah," the second one said. "He won't want to talk to us."

Javan relaxed his grip. Did he hear that right? Were those big huge men in awe of him? Had they left him out of their circle of coolness because they feared him, not because they thought he was a weirdo or a geek or a nerd? Maybe he was the only cool one in the room, and everyone wanted to be a part of his circle of friends.

Did being a Dragon Collector give him the power to be popular? That was harder to believe than his ability to be invisible! It was also a bigger responsibility. If people paid attention to him and followed him, he better be someone worth following.

"Stay humble, Javan," he murmured to himself. He wanted to be the good kind of popular, not the cocky, obnoxious kind. He rolled off the bed, landed on his feet, and faced Cyr's oversized men. "Yes, I am the Dragon Collector, and I do have an awesome dragon named Varjiek. But I'm also just a regular guy who could use some friends."

He walked down the aisle and held out his hand to the group of six guys. "My name is Javan. Can I join you?"

"We would be honored." One of the men stood and shook Javan's hand. "I'm Kai. This is Mazen, Jaxson, Brigan, Phenix, and Orlan. We are all patrolmen on Captain Cyr's crew. Mind if we ask you some questions about your dragon?"

"Hold on," Taliya said, walking over to Javan. "Chief Lydia and her warriors want to hear about your dragon, too."

Javan looked over to find a dozen more men and women staring at him with rapt attention. Maybe he wasn't ready to be in the spotlight. Maybe he should have stayed in his lonely bunk. But it was too late to retreat now.

"Sure," he said, trying to sound nonchalant. "What do you want to know?"

After a few seconds of silence, the small crowd began peppering him with questions.

"How did you collect your dragon?"

"Do all of his scales really turn the color of gold when he gets hungry?"

"Are you going to enter the Battle of the Throne?"

"Has your dragon ever tried to eat you?"

"What is it like to ride a dragon?"

"Hold on." Javan threw his hands up and quieted the crowd. "Why don't I just tell you my story? Then if you still have questions, I'll answer them one at a time."

Everyone nodded, relaxed, and settled back on their cots to listen to his story. He would share the abbreviated version and leave out minor details like growing up on earth, talking to dragons, and being the answer to the prophecy made thousands of years ago.

Maybe he could do this popularity thing. Maybe if he stood in the spotlight, he could impress Taliya.

◊　◊　◊

Micah's queasiness stuck with him long after the storm subsided late in the afternoon. He thus didn't eat anything all day, and even though he felt better after a decent night of rest on the semi-comfortable cot, he didn't trust himself to keep his breakfast down the next morning.

Once he got out of bed, he bypassed the breakfast table and made his way to the top deck. With the rising sun at his back, he enjoyed the view of the clear blue water ahead and the lush green forests on either side of the river, but he needed to get off the boat. To stand on dry land. To have solid ground under his feet. And to get away from Javan.

That Collector had somehow made himself likeable to everyone on board. At least two or three people were always talking to him, and he seemed to have learned all of their names. Why would he go to that much trouble? Micah hadn't even bothered to learn how many people were on the boat, and he certainly didn't care what their names were.

Micah's sole concern was getting back to Mertzer. He didn't need to make friends with the help along the way. Still, part of him envied Javan and wondered what it would be like to have just one real friend.

Omri would beat him for thinking such things, so he shook the thought out of his mind and reminded himself that he didn't need friends. What he needed were slaves. When he had slaves, he had control and could force them to do whatever he wanted.

As the boat chugged along, the scenery began to change. The rolling hills flattened out, the forest gave way to acres and acres of humminglo fields, and a river flowing down from the north intersected with the east/west river they were floating on.

"You might want to brace yourself, sir." The only other person on the deck with Micah was one of the patrolmen from Cyr's crew. He wore a black leather vest over his beige shirt and carried a bow and arrows. Micah didn't like that the man had bigger biceps than he did. "We'll be making that right turn onto the Derez River, and the change of course can get a bit bumpy."

The stronger man followed his own advice, but he didn't sit on any of the benches attached to the deck. He sat directly on the wooden planks and wrapped his arms around one of the railing posts. Micah couldn't allow a patrolman to tell him what to do, so he continued to lean casually against the railing.

"You're going to tumble over the side as soon as we hit those competing currents," the patrolman warned.

"I will be fine," Micah said. That man really needed to stop talking. He hadn't earned the right to talk to the king's son, much less tell him what to do.

Micah began contemplating ways to teach the people of Keckrick how to behave and submit to his authority when the boat took a sharp left turn, followed by a quick correction to the right.

He lost his balance and almost sailed over the top of the rail. Fortunately, he managed to snag the nearest post with his foot and plop himself down on the deck to prevent a tumble into the water. While the boat rocked back and forth and fought to make the turn north, he hugged the post and tried to ignore the smugness emanating from the patrolman behind him.

◊   ◊   ◊

After being bounced around like a ping pong ball during the turn north, Javan was eager to climb out of the sleeping quarters and onto the top deck of the boat behind Lydia and Taliya. He nodded a hello to Kai and noticed Micah sitting by himself on one of the benches. Everyone else was preparing to dock and unload the cargo.

"We're approaching Tulkar," Lydia said, leading them to the front, "and I want you to see the city from this vantage point."

Stone walls ten stories higher than the boat on both sides of the river loomed before them, blocking the view of anything on the inside.

"Finally," Micah said, stepping between him and Taliya. "This looks like a real city. I didn't think you people here in Keckrick knew how to build walls."

"Excuse me?" Lydia's short spiked hair seemed to jump to attention. "Did you just insult us?"

"Ignore him. He has no manners." Javan put his left hand on Lydia's shoulder to keep her calm. "I would like to apologize for his rudeness. Now please tell me about your city."

"Well," Lydia said, "Tulkar was the first city constructed in Lower Keckrick when our ancestors moved here from the Land of Zandador in the year 500. They came via the portal system that connected this region to every other region in the Great Rift, as well as to Upper Keckrick.

"To keep the portal protected and to commemorate the founding of the city, our people made the city walls to stretch five hundred miles from east to west. The walls only span one hundred fifty miles from north to south due to the natural boundaries like the Dark Zone to the north and the Pheka River to the south."

Javan whistled. "That is one huge city!"

"It was once the largest city in the entire region and a thriving city full of life and ideas and progress. Or so I've been told. I wasn't alive during those days, and this is the only Tulkar I have ever known."

The boat began to slow its speed and floated through two open rusty iron gates with intricate designs that highlighted the trees, plants, and animals of the rain forest. Although Javan expected to see roads, buildings, and people inside the walls, he instead saw an abandoned city that had been reclaimed by the rain forest.

Trees grew through cracks in the stone streets. Ivy covered crumbled and half burned buildings. Some of the buildings were nothing but ashes while others were missing roofs or windows or entire walls.

"What happened here?" Javan asked.

"I thought you said this was your capital city and the largest in the entire region," Micah said. "Why would you let it turn to ruins?"

"It wasn't our choice," Lydia said. "We were commanded to not rebuild after the great fire of 3711."

"Let me guess," Javan said. "Omri gave that command?"

Micah slapped Javan's arm with the back of his hand. "Why would you automatically blame my father? He had barely taken over Zandador at that point. Besides, he maintained the peaceful trading arrangements already established between all the regions of the Great Rift when he won the throne in 3700."

"You're partially right," Lydia said. "For the first decade of his reign, Omri upheld the pre-established trading arrangements. On Trade Day every April first and October first, we provided medicinal plants to Zandador, Varzack, Tirza, and Gibbet. In exchange, Varzack provided stone building materials, Tirza provided wool for clothing, Gibbet provided lumber, and Zandador provided food such as wheat, vegetables, and fruit."

"Ha," Micah gloated, making Javan want to smack the smug look off his face. "Told you."

"I don't think she's finished with her story," Javan said. At least he hoped she wasn't. He needed her to say something that would shatter Micah's idyllic image of Omri.

"There is more to the story." Taliya wiggled her way in the middle of Javan and Micah. "You two just need to be quiet, and let her talk."

"Thank you." Lydia took a breath and continued. "In the spring of 3711, Omri changed Trade Day to Transport Day. He required the regions to transport a designated quota of supplies to Zandador without receiving food in return. We were also to cut off trade with the other regions. If any region didn't meet the quota, he threatened to send his dragons to destroy the major cities and have his army occupy the smaller towns."

As the boat inched along, Javan looked with fresh eyes at the sad city and remembered the destruction he had witnessed at Gri. That vision stuck in his mind as Lydia resumed her story.

"We refused to agree to King Omri's terms, so he sent his dragons to destroy us. His Noon Stalker burned the capital cities of Upper and Lower Keckrick while the other dragons spread through the villages, killing everyone they came across.

"His soldiers followed the dragons, executed our elders, burned our books, and took control of our remaining villages. We were told our heritage as Dragon Protectors was dead and that our future involved supplying Zandador with whatever King Omri demanded. We were forbidden to come to Zandador, use the portal, or protect dragons. If we ever tried to send a representative from the Protector Bloodline to enter the Battle for the Throne, King Omri would burn down the rain forest."

She paused her narrative, leaned her forearms against the railing and folded her hands in front of her as though she needed to contain her anger and frustration. "To remind us of these commands and what happens when we rebel, we were not allowed to rebuild our capital cities. But King Omri promised to remove his troops from our villages if we promised to forsake our heritage, stay out of Zandador, and meet his quotas.

"We agreed and have met his quotas ever since. But if we don't win this humminglo war, my village is going to look like this city in just a few years."

Her somber words hung in the air as the boat halted at a dilapidated dock in the middle of the crumbling city.

CHAPTER 28
UNSETTLING QUESTIONS

Micah quietly bypassed the line leading to the cargo room after descending from the top deck with Javan, Lydia, and Taliya. Cyr had ordered everyone to assist with unloading the humminglo plants, but that sounded like tedious work. Besides, he was a guest on the ship and the one who would save Keckrick from annihilation. He deserved the kind of special treatment that allowed him to watch rather than work.

He walked to the bow of the boat to hide from the crowd, leaned against the rail, and observed his surroundings. A dozen docks on both sides of the wide river stretched about ten feet into the water from a bed of stones on the shore. The Iria had pulled up to the first dock on the western shore, and although its old decking showed signs of neglect, it was the only dock that didn't look like it was about to crumble under the weight of a feather.

As for the city itself, everything on the eastern side looked bleak and lifeless. On the western side, however, tents set up on grass between broken buildings indicated that Tulkar wasn't a completely abandoned city.

Other signs of life included large wagons sitting empty on the uneven streets and the thirty or so people who inhabited the tents. Most of them had joined the effort to unload the humminglo plants, while a handful of boys and girls fished from one of the docks further upstream.

None of that mattered to Micah. He didn't want to set foot in Tulkar.

The listless atmosphere of the city depressed him. As much as he had wanted to get off the boat at the outset of the day, he now felt the overwhelming desire to stay on board and keep churning forward.

Why? He had seen ruined cities before, cities he had led the charge to destroy under orders from his father. Tiny towns, anyway. Towns like Gri.

With that destruction still fresh on his mind, he recalled the screams of the people as they ran from their homes. He felt their terror as they watched Mertzer stomp through the streets, crush buildings with his feet, and spew poison in every direction.

Part of him craved the chaos. He loved having the power to control a dragon, destroy homes, and instill fear in people all around him. That was the part of him he felt obligated to nurture because that was the part of him that made his father proud.

His father wouldn't be proud of the part of him who let the people of Gri escape. He hadn't let Mertzer crush a building until he knew it was empty, and he had ensured no people were within range of Mertzer's poisonous breath before ordering him to spray the surrounding area.

He hadn't been taught to value anyone's life save his own, so why had he allowed the people in Gri to live? And why did the death of those soldiers in Fury's Pass still haunt his dreams?

Now as he scanned the remnants of Tulkar, he wondered how many people died when Vasilis had charged through here. Would they have had a chance to escape, or did the walls they had built to protect them end up trapping them instead?

Why did he care? Why had Lydia's story upset him? Why did he want to keep going and pretend like he had never seen this city or heard the tale of its destruction?

"You should be helping unload the cargo." Captain Cyr approached Micah from behind.

"No, I shouldn't." Micah kept his forearms on the rail and locked his hands in front of him. He had to remain cool and composed and not show any evidence of the questions tormenting his soul. "I don't do work that is meant for common people."

"Do you eat?"

Micah creased his brow and looked back at Cyr. "Of course."

"Then you will work."

"Excuse me?"

"If you want to eat any morsel of food on this boat at any time between here and our ultimate destination, you will help me and the rest of the crew unload the cargo. We all do our part, and 'all' includes you."

"I am King Omri's son." Hearing himself claim his identity helped eradicate those unsettling questions in his mind and restore his heartless nature. "I take orders from no one."

"I am Captain Cyr. This is my boat, and my rules apply. No work means no food, no matter who you are. It's that simple."

"You have to feed me. Otherwise I will not talk to my father and ask him to spare your people."

"You have to work. Otherwise you will not eat."

Micah turned around and crossed his arms over his chest. Was this really happening? Was the captain threatening him when he should be cowering before him the way everyone in Zandador did? "You do understand who I am, right? You know that my father would not be pleased to hear that you attempted to make me work or refused me food."

Cyr stepped forward and whispered in Micah's ear. "You do understand that it's going to take six or seven days to get through the Dark Zone to the northwestern shore. That's a long time to go without food." Before Micah could reply, Cyr patted Micah's shoulder and walked away.

As Cyr's footsteps faded, Micah's stomach rumbled, reminding him that he hadn't had anything to eat in over twenty-four hours. "Fine," Micah grumbled. "I'll work. But I will tell Omri about this torture."

He tramped down the walkway toward the cargo room, but the sight of the ruins around him made him rethink his definition of torture. Perhaps unloading a few plants from a boat wouldn't be a horrible way to spend his day. After all, it sure beat having his home destroyed or losing his life to a dragon.

◊ ◊ ◊

Although Javan soon worked up a sweat in the sweltering heat, he enjoyed the work of unloading the cargo. The crew from the boat, along with those temporarily living in Tulkar until Transport Day to assist with the harvest, worked to a cadence, and Javan quickly fell into step with their humming rhythm, making him feel like part of the group.

Into the cargo room. Out down the plank. Across the dock. Lean over the wagon. Drop the load of humminglos. And back to the cargo room to get another load.

Wheelbarrows or forklifts would have made unloading the plants more efficient, but Javan didn't mind the monotonous nature of the work. He even decided to make it fun by adding in some shuffle steps and snaps between loads, and the rest of the crew began to copy him. Until Micah broke the pattern.

"Are you the one who told Cyr to force me to help?" Micah stepped in front of Javan as he was about to enter the cargo room.

"No," Javan said. Warning bells sounded in Javan's mind. Micah seemed angry and ready to fight. "He asked where you were. I told him I saw you walk toward the front of the boat. I had no control over what he chose to do with that information."

"He threatened to deny me food if I didn't work."

"Then you better work." Javan kept his voice steady to keep from antagonizing Micah and pointed into the room. "We still have half the space left to unload."

Micah growled his displeasure and stepped inside. "What are we supposed to do?"

"It's easy," Javan said, following Micah into the warehouse. Dried leaves and flower petals covered the floor until about the halfway point; stacks of flowers that reached from the floor to the ceiling filled the rest of the space. "Walk down to Mirela, and hold out your arms. She'll give you a bushel of flowers, and you take them out to the wagons at the end of the dock. Then you come back for more."

"Ugh." Micah shuddered. "I shouldn't have to do this."

"Why? Are you not strong enough to carry a few flowers? Should I tell the captain that this work is too strenuous for your weak muscles to handle?"

"Me? Weak? Ha!" Micah huffed and stomped down to Mirela, the long-haired, wiry woman in charge of the cargo.

"Another worker," she said. "Nice. Thank you for helping."

"You're not welcome. Just give me some flowers," Micah said. She frowned and put a bushel in his arms, but he didn't move. "More."

"If you insist." She added a second bushel so that his arms were full from his waist to his chin.

"One more."

"But you won't be able to see."

"I can handle it." He glared back at Javan as she put a third bushel in his arms. He reached up and smashed the flowers down so they were just below his eye level. He turned around and paused as he walked by Javan. "Let's see how many you can carry, Collector boy."

"Oh, it's on," Javan said. He stepped up to Mirela and held out his arms. "Load me up." The fun, easy workday had just become a serious competition between him and his worst enemy.

◊ ◊ ◊

Micah walked across the shaky but secure boardwalk and dumped the final load of humminglo plants into the wagon. "Done!" He pumped his arms in the air and waited for Javan to toss his final load into the wagon as well.

Javan had only been able to carry half of what Micah could handle, and Micah needed to make sure Javan knew he had won the unofficial battle. "Don't try to beat me in any competition. Ever. You won't win."

"You're taller," Javan said. "You should be able to carry more humminglo plants than me. But I'm smarter. I'll be sure to use that to my advantage in the competition that really counts."

"I'd rather be taller and stronger. Your intelligence didn't do you much good when we fought over Mertzer." Micah ran his finger down Javan's chest, mimicking the action he took when he cut him with his sword. "You're the one who has a scar, not me."

"Keep underestimating me." Javan narrowed his eyes and slapped Micah's hand away. "I dare you."

"I'll take that dare." Micah smiled and nodded toward the cooking fire on the ground next to the dock. The smell of fried fish wafted through the air, making Micah's mouth water. "Now go fetch me some lunch. I earned it by beating you."

"Get your own food," Javan said, jumping from the dock to the ground. "I'm not fetching you anything."

Micah laughed and jumped to the ground as well. Lunch wasn't quite ready, so he returned to the dock, took his shirt off, and dipped it in the cold river water to wash away his sweat and the debris from the countless number of humminglo plants he had carried off the boat.

Even though it wasn't a glorious victory, he was proud of himself for making the Collector look puny in comparison to him. Perhaps now the crew would shun Javan and give Micah the reverence he deserved.

He put his wet shirt on his overheated skin, splashed his face with water, and took a stroll down the street by the wagons now overflowing with humminglo plants. Apparently the temporary dwellers in the city planned to drive the wagons to the portal and keep the plants stored safely in buildings there until Transport Day.

Micah reached up and touched one of the purple petals of the plants. Why did his father need these flowers? What purpose did they serve? And why hadn't he told Micah about Transport Day and this entire arrangement with Keckrick?

Micah almost wanted to ride to the portal with the crew so he could return home and get answers to his questions, but he knew he needed to retrieve Mertzer and win both Varjiek and Kisa first.

Increased levels of laughter and chatter drew Micah back to the dock. No one noticed him as he picked up one of the plates on the makeshift table by the fire. They were too busy sitting on the dock swapping stories with Javan as they ate their fried fish.

How could that be? How could they still accept and respect Javan when Micah had made him look so weak and worthless? What was it about the Collector that drew people to him?

Micah knew Javan's ability to get people to like him made him a genuine threat to both himself and Omri, and anyone who threatened Omri's power had to be eliminated.

CHAPTER 29
THE BOOK

"Easy, girl." Javan rubbed the trunk of the skittish miniature elephant. It was slightly taller than a horse but easily twice as wide. Its straight white tusks popped against its dark grey skin, and it had tried more than once to use those tucks to stab Shria, her handler. "We're not going to hurt you. We just need your help pulling a wagon."

"That won't work, Javan," Shria said from the other side of the fence. The young woman had her sword drawn and stood ready to fight. "She's always been trouble. I'm not even sure why we keep her around."

"Ah, she's a sweetie." Javan never took his eyes off the elephant. Being in this moment made him glad he chose to work with the crew on the ground to get the wagons ready to take to the portal rather than nap along with Captain Cyr and his crew. These elephants were awesome. "She's just a little scared. All we have to do is keep her calm and explain what we need her to do."

"She's an animal. Why would we need to explain anything to her?"

"Because she can understand." Javan tried to read her mind the way he did with Varjiek, but he heard nothing. He would just have to read her eyes the way he did with his horse Storm. "In a minute, I'm going to open that gate. You're going to follow me calmly down the street. When we get to the wagon, you're going to stand by your brother and let me put a harness on you. You probably won't like it, but it won't hurt you. I promise. It's just a way for us to connect the wagon to you so you can show off that strength of yours. Got it?"

The elephant gave Javan a slight nod, so Javan nodded back and walked over to the gate. As he reached for the latch, Shria tried to stop him.

"What are you doing? She'll run away if you let her out of that gate without the chain attached to her collar."

"No. She won't. Trust me."

Shria backed off, and Javan opened the gate. Without looking behind him, he began walking the few blocks toward the waiting wagons. He could tell by speechless Shria and the heavy steps of the elephant that his new friend was following him.

Once he reached the last of the seven wagons, he turned around, coaxed the elephant into place, and patted her side. "Good girl," he said. "Now you behave for these nice people, and I promise they'll take good care of you."

The elephant snorted her acceptance and let Shria's men hook her up to the harness without any protest.

"Unbelievable," Shria said, approaching Javan. "We've never been able to get her to cooperate without a fight before. Are you sure you don't want to stay here with us and take charge of the animals?"

"I appreciate the offer, but I'll need to be on that boat when it ships out at sunset. I miss my dragon."

"That's too bad." She reached for his hand and held it between her own. "We will miss you."

The touch of her hand turned Javan from a confident animal tamer to awkward teen. His cheeks flushed. His stomach turned a few somersaults. He tongue lost all power to form words. He wasn't used to getting this kind of attention from women. Then Taliya spoiled it.

"Javan, there you are." She charged across the street, grabbed his wrist, and jerked his hand away from Shria. Smudges of black ash dotted her face, arms, and clothes. "Come with me. I need your help with something important."

"Whoa. Stop." He tried to pull away from her grip, but she wouldn't let go. "I'm in the middle of something important here."

"No, you're not." Before he could protest further, he found himself being dragged over the stone streets and into a dark, crumbling building two blocks away.

◊　◊　◊

Micah couldn't believe what he saw from the top deck of the Iria. Was an elephant really following Javan down the street? Of its own accord? Without being led by a chain?

Certainly not. Javan had to have been holding a rope and guiding the elephant. The rope was probably just too thin for Micah to be able to see from his vantage point.

As he squinted to try to see the rope, a sudden movement several blocks to the left of the wagons caught Micah's attention. Was that Taliya? Why was she wandering through the city ruins on her own?

She wasn't exactly wandering. She walked as though she was on a mission, marched straight up to Javan, snatched him away from his admirers, and took him back to where she had just come from. He kept an eye on them as they crawled under a pile of rubble a few minutes later. What were they up to?

He wasn't sure, but he was definitely going to go find out.

◊　◊　◊

Javan crouched under another broken beam in his quest to keep up with Taliya. He coughed the dust out of his lungs and brushed a spider web out of his hair. "I'm pretty sure this place qualifies as a condemned building that we shouldn't be poking around in. We should get out of here before the part of the ceiling that is still intact collapses on us."

"We're not leaving until I get what I came for."

"What could you possibly need in this place?"

"You'll see." She stopped in what appeared to be the corner of the building, moved an empty shelf out of the way, dropped to her knees, and felt the floor with her hands. "This is it."

"It's what? You are acting very strange. Are you always this strange?"

She looked up and held out her hand. "I need to borrow your dragon scale."

"Excuse me?"

"The dragon scale. The one you keep in your pocket. I need to borrow it."

"What makes you think I have it in my pocket?"

"Because it's not with your stuff on your bunk. I checked."

"You went through my stuff?"

She shrugged. "I needed the scale."

"That doesn't give you the right to rummage through my things."

"It's not like I stole anything. Now can I please borrow the scale? I promise to give it right back."

"Why do you need it?"

"Enough with the questions." She reached into Javan's left pocket and retrieved the scale. "It will be easier to show you."

Taliya fit the scale into a triangle-sized hole in the floor and turned it. After hearing a click, she lifted a square door in the floor, creating an opening just big enough for a person to climb through. "It worked!" She put the scale back in Javan's pocket. "Now all we have to do is find the book."

"What book?"

"No more questions!" She reached her legs into the hole, landed on a ladder, and scrambled down. "You coming?"

Javan wasn't sure he wanted to follow. The last time he entered a dark hole in the ground, he wound up in an entirely new dimension. "I think I'll wait for you up here."

"Fine. Collectors aren't supposed to know this room exists anyway."

A secret room no other Collector knew about? Now he had to descend into the darkness to satisfy his curiosity. He leaned into the hole, found the ladder with his feet, and made his way down rung by rung.

"Nice of you to join me." Taliya sparked an old lantern to life, flooding the room with light.

Javan squinted, covered his eyes, and blinked until he could see clearly. "What is this place?" Rows of shelves filled with books and glass containers showcasing dragon scales stretched out before them.

"This is the Protector's Den. Every Protector who has taken a dragon egg through the portal and returned with a dragon documented every step of the process from finding the egg to releasing the dragon into the wild." Taliya ran her fingers across the spine of the books. "That's what these books and jars are: the journals of the Protectors and the shed scales of the dragons kept here as mementos."

"Why keep this place a secret?"

"Because we're Protectors. We protect our knowledge."

"How did you know it was here?"

"The building above us was once the grandest library in the Great Rift, and I knew the Den was hidden below this building. I've never been to Tulkar before, but when I realized we would be stopping here, I had to find out for myself if this place really existed."

"Why? Did you want to find Kisa's story? Is that the book you are looking for?"

"No. Her story isn't here."

"I thought you just said--"

"I just said her story isn't here." She stiffened, turned, and began walking forward. "The book I want should be in the center of this room."

Javan wondered what sore spot he hit with his innocent question, but he didn't press the issue further. She held the only source of light, and he had to keep up with her as she charged through the rows of books labeled with names of dragons. He scanned the titles as he followed her, hoping to find a book titled <u>Varjiek</u> or <u>Mertzer</u> or <u>Silverspike</u> or <u>Skylark</u>. None of the names, however, seemed familiar.

"Oh, wow." Taliya worked her way to the middle of the room and slowly approached a round, waist-high column decorated with dragon scales and topped with a dome glass lid covered with dust. "This has to be it."

"It has to be what?"

Without looking at Javan, she handed him the lantern and brushed the dust on the glass away. A thick black book with gold lettering entitled *Portal Codes* sat on display under the glass. A slight gasp revealed her excitement, and she attempted to lift the lid. It didn't move. "It's stuck. I can't believe it's stuck. I need that book!"

"Whoa. Chill. Let me try." Javan returned the lantern to Taliya, stretched his arms, and rounded his shoulders. "This is a man's job."

"Please. I may be short, but I'm not a weakling. You won't be able to get the lid off, either."

It was glass. How heavy could it be? "Watch me." He put his hands on the bottom edge of the dome lid and lifted. With the exception of dust, nothing moved. "I think it's cemented on. Nobody is getting this book out of here."

"Watch me." Taliya slammed the lantern onto the glass. The glass cracked, so she hit it again. More cracks appeared, and the light began blinking on and off.

"What are you doing?" Javan grabbed her arm before she could strike the glass a third time.

"I'm getting my book."

"You're stealing the book. I don't think it was meant to leave this place."

"Times have changed since it was sealed in here. I am one of the last people in the Protector Bloodline, and this book contains knowledge I need to learn so I can carry on my heritage. Now let me go."

A muffled horn blasted through the dry air.

"That would be the Iria," Taliya said. "The captain is signaling us that they are about to leave. We better hurry if we want to be on that boat when it cruises out of here."

Javan didn't want to be an accomplice in the theft of a book, but since no one had been here for hundreds of years, and since Taliya's heritage gave her rights to the book, he supposed taking the book wouldn't actually be stealing. "Fine." He let her go, took the lantern, and smashed the glass himself. It shattered into thousands of pieces and killed the light in the process.

"Thank you!" She gave Javan a quick hug and picked up the book.

"Don't thank me yet. We still have to navigate our way out of here in the dark, crawl back through the rubble, and make it to the boat before it leaves."

"Then stop talking and start walking." She latched onto Javan's hand and held onto it as she began pulling them back in the direction they had just come from.

He wished they had another lantern and more time. He wanted to find Varjiek's story on these shelves. He also wanted to learn more about how Protectors went about finding dragon eggs, taking them through the portal, and caring for newly hatched dragons. On the plus side, he kind of liked holding Taliya's hand.

As he closed the door to the Protector's Den and helped Taliya move the empty shelf back on top of it, he realized he wouldn't ever have a chance to return to this place. But all hope was not lost. He had access to the knowledge he desired, and she was crawling through the rat-infested rubble with him at this very moment.

CHAPTER 30
NO MORE DAYLIGHT

Micah studied the opening of the building he had watched Javan and Taliya enter. With one well-placed shove, he could send the precariously balanced bricks collapsing on one another and trap the two of them inside.

The boat horn had already sounded once, indicating the captain was ready to leave. Could Micah convince him to leave without Taliya and the Collector on board?

Probably not. The girl could lead them to the humminglo fields, and everyone wanted to see Javan ride his dragon. He should let them live. Besides, he wanted to find out why they went into the building in the first place.

The horn blasted again. If they didn't get to that boat, the captain might leave them all behind. Where were those two? Were they stuck? Was he going to have to rescue them? He really didn't want to go in there, so he was relieved to hear their voices.

"We're almost there," Taliya said. "That light up ahead has to be the doorway."

"We would be able to move faster if you would let me carry that book for you," Javan replied.

"For the last time, I am not giving up my book."

A book? Micah scratched his head and hid around the corner. They jeopardized their lives for a book? What book could possibly be that important? And how did Taliya know that book survived the book-burning fires of 3711?

Javan and Taliya emerged from the rubble a few minutes later. He peeked around the corner and noticed the big black book in Taliya's hands. That's all he had time to notice, because they began sprinting back to the boat without bothering to brush off the dust and debris they had collected from their exploration.

Micah ran a different route and beat the pair to the boat. He made it to the top deck in time to watch them run down the dock, but he didn't see either one of them carrying a book.

How could that be? Why would they go to all the trouble to locate the book only to leave it behind? It made no sense. They had to have snuck it on board.

A final horn sounded before the boat rumbled to life. As it took off in the light of the setting sun, he made his way down to the main deck. There were only so many places on this boat to hide something, and Micah was determined to find that book.

◊   ◊   ◊

Despite Micah's determination, he had no luck finding the book. He had waited for everyone except the patrol on the night watch to go to sleep before beginning his search, but it yielded no results. Perhaps Taliya had left the book in Tulkar after all.

Micah managed to get a few hours of restless sleep, but not knowing what the book contained or where it was hidden bothered him too much to allow him to sleep peacefully. He thus decided to burn off his frustration by running laps around the outer walkway of the main deck.

He had been running for a solid hour when the captain stopped him at the bow of the boat. "Hold up, Micah." Cyr handed him a cup of water and pointed to the river ahead of them. "You're going to want to see this."

Micah took a few deep breaths and swallowed half the water in the cup. "What am I looking for?"

"The sunrise."

Micah rolled his eyes and gave the cup back to Cyr. "I've seen plenty of sunrises. I'd rather keep running."

"Wait." Cyr put the cup back in Micah's hands. "Watch."

A ray of light to their right poked through the sky. The dense trees along the riverbank that stood twice as high as the boat kept the light from dancing on the water.

As the sun slowly rose higher and turned the sky beautiful shades of red, orange, purple, and pink, the landscape around them escaped from the shadows and stunned Micah with its bright green beauty.

Branches of trees draped over the edges of the river and made Micah feel like the trees were bowing to him as they floated along. "You were right. The sunrise was worth watching."

"That not the only reason I wanted you to see it."

"Oh?"

"Take a closer look at the landscape to the north. Notice how the trees grow taller and thicker?"

Micah finished his water and inspected the land ahead. Sure enough, the towering trees created an impenetrable-looking wall on either side of the river. And instead of the branches dangling over the sides of the river, they reached over the river, intertwined with branches from the opposite side, and effectively created a ceiling above the water. "Yeah. So?"

"So that's the entrance to the Dark Zone." Cyr coughed and wiped his brow with his forearm. His skin seemed one shade paler than usual, and he was sweating more than Micah. "Once we go under that canopy, we won't see the sun again for days."

"Ah." Micah returned the empty cup to Cyr and took a step sideways. He didn't want to catch whatever sickness the captain was suffering from. "I think I'll walk a few laps to cool down while I can still enjoy the sunlight."

"Good idea." The captain returned to his wheel, and Micah walked away as fast as he could. He hated being sick and hoped he hadn't lingered around the captain too long.

A lap later, new worries flooded his mind when the boat floated under the canopy of the Dark Zone that Saturday morning. It immediately felt darker than midnight, and the swarm of bats that swooped down and quickly dispersed into the darkness around them made Micah think that they were warning the other animals about the human intruders.

He needed his sword. He would feel safer if he had his sword in his hands.

◊　◊　◊

According to the pocket time piece Javan had won from Kai in a stun ball throwing contest, noon on Sunday was sixteen minutes away. At least he thought he was reading the square clock correctly by the lantern light above his bunk.

It didn't have an hour, minute, or second hand. What tracked the time was a mini rumble rock that ticked from corner to corner. The distance from corner to corner represented one hour, and every time it made a full revolution, it chimed. It chimed once at 4:00 a.m., twice at 8:00 a.m., three times at noon, and so forth until chiming six times at midnight.

If he was reading the clock correctly, it meant that Varjiek was eating, the sun was shining somewhere above them, and they had been immersed in darkness for nearly twenty-nine hours. During that time, he had lost all sorts of physical fitness contests to one member of the crew or another. Whether it was push-ups, pull-ups or sit-ups, he just wasn't quite strong enough to outperform his insanely fit competition.

Micah hadn't participated in any of the games, which was a good thing. He probably would have won, and that would have just given him bragging rights and made him even more obnoxious than usual.

Losing contest after contest was damaging Javan's pride, though, so he suggested the stun ball contest late the previous night. He offered to give one to the person who could throw it with better accuracy than him, but no one even came close. Kai thus gave Javan his time piece as a prize for his superior throwing skills.

Today hadn't been as fun. Energy levels had dropped, and everyone wanted to simply laze around. All Javan had done since waking up was watch time tick away.

Needing to do something, he went in search of Taliya. Which wasn't challenging. He figured she would be in the empty cargo room reading her book she had him sneak on board under his shirt, and that is precisely where he found her.

"It's hot and musty in here," Javan said. "How can you sit here and read?"

"It's the only private place on the boat." She looked up at him and frowned. "At least it was."

He ignored her veiled attempt to tell him to leave and sat against the metal wall beside her. "Is your book any good?"

"It's complicated. Lots of patterns to memorize."

Javan remembered watching his mother activate the earth portal and how she almost killed them by entering the code wrong. Good times. "Tell me something. Why bother memorizing those patterns when you may never have a chance to use them?"

"I saw my father activate the portal once, and I've been fascinated by it ever since."

"Wait. That portal is in Zandador, and I thought no one from Keckrick has been allowed in Zandador for almost five hundred years. Surely you're not older than that."

"No, not even close." She chuckled and shook her head. "But I never said I was born in Keckrick."

Javan waited for more details. When none came, he asked another question. "So are you from Zandador?"

"I lived there for the first seven years of my life."

"Why did you move to Keckrick?"

"To keep Kisa safe."

"And where did you get a dragon?"

"My father."

Javan closed his eyes and took a deep breath to keep from banging his head against the wall. Her short answers were driving him crazy. "You know," he said, turning to face her, "I have nothing else to do today. I am just going to keep asking questions until I get answers. The sooner you tell me your full story, the sooner I'll leave you alone to memorize your patterns."

"Fine." She closed her book and put it on the floor. "What do you want to know?"

"What happened when you were seven that brought you and Kisa to Keckrick?"

"A good friend of my father's needed help getting her newborn baby through the portal to keep him out of the king's clutches."

"Interesting." Javan's heart began to race. This story had a familiar ring to it. "What was the friend's name?"

"Does it matter?"

"It might." His heart pounded as he waited to hear his mother's name.

"Sorry. I don't remember. I do remember holding the baby while my father activated the portal and the other two men with us stood guard."

"Do you remember anything special about the baby or the names of those men?" Surely she was talking about Kenton and Ravier.

"No. No names come to mind. And it was night, so I didn't get a good look at the baby, either."

"Ah. Okay." He had hoped she had noticed the baby's unusually green eyes. "What happened next?"

"My father took the baby and went through the portal with one of the men and his Noon Stalker, but the baby wasn't the only thing he took with him."

"What else did he take?"

"Two dragon eggs: one Dusk and one Dawn. The dusk egg never hatched, but he returned with an adorable little Dawn Stalker five days later."

"Kisa."

"Yup."

"That's why Kisa's story wasn't in the Protector's Den."

"Exactly. Tulkar had already been destroyed. Plus my father wanted to keep Kisa's existence a secret. So he sent me and her to live in Keckrick with my great-grandparents, and they taught me how to protect her."

"How long ago was that?" Javan wanted her to say fifteen years. Then he wouldn't need names of the people involved to verify that he was the baby in that story.

"Ummm…I guess it's been a little over fifteen years now."

"You won't believe this, but I was there that night you watched your father go through the portal."

"Yeah. I know. You were the baby I held."

Javan's eyes widened. "How did you know that?"

"The baby's name is the one name I remembered." She smiled, but the smile only lasted for an instant. It vanished by the sudden rocking of the boat and a mad scramble of people outside the door.

Javan opened the door to discover half the crew trying to squeeze into the crank room. "What's going on?"

Kai pointed to the water. "Whirlpool. If we don't speed the boat up, we're going to be sucked into it, and it will break this boat apart in a matter of seconds."

CHAPTER 31
WHIRLPOOL

Micah took another bite of his sandwich. Now that everyone had darted upstairs, he could finally eat lunch in peace. He wasn't sure what the big emergency was that drew them away, but he sure was glad to see them go. Let them deal with the darkness. He didn't want to emerge from this room until he could see the sun again.

"You're eating?" Taliya sprinted the short distance from the ladder to the table, took the sandwich out of his hands, and threw it across the room. "How could you be eating when everyone's help is needed in the crank room?"

So much for peacefulness. "I don't see you helping."

"That's because I'm a tiny little thing who would just get in the way trying to turn the crank. You, on the other hand, are strong enough to do some good."

"There are plenty of strong guys on this boat." He left his sandwich on the floor, lay on his bottom bunk, and covered his eyes with his arm. "What's the big emergency, anyway?"

Taliya moved his arm. "We're approaching the center of the Dark Zone where the Clesi, Yarmu, and Derez Rivers meet. The different currents form a wide whirlpool at their collision point. If we don't pick up enough speed to skirt around the whirlpool and catch the current of the Clesi River, we're going to get sucked into the vortex and be torn to shreds."

Micah gulped. "Maybe I should get upstairs to the crank room and see if they need my help."

"Maybe." Taliya pulled him off the bed. "Go!"

The day was as dark as night on the deck above the sleeping quarters, but light poured out of the open door to the crank room. Micah pushed his way inside and tried to make sense of the confusion.

Two waist-high columns jutted out of the floor in the center of the room. A steel wheel with a pole long enough for five men to hold was attached to the outer side of each column.

A bulky man with a long beard on a bench on the left side of the room barked orders to the ten men cranking the wheels. Fortunately he had a deep voice, or no one would have been able to hear him over the deafening noise of the rumble rocks below them. "Right side, maintain. Left side, switch!"

The exhausted men on the left let go of the crank, and four fresh men stepped up and took over the wheel. "You!" The leader pointed at Micah. "Join them."

Micah nodded and slid to the end of the row. He caught the pole on the second rotation and began turning the wheel with his new teammates.

"Good work, men. Keep it up. We're going fast enough, but something's wrong. We should be turning, but we're not."

Cyr. He had been sick yesterday. Perhaps he had become too weak to turn the captain's wheel with enough force.

"Fill my spot," Micah said. "I think I know what the problem is."

Despite a chorus of protests, Micah abandoned the crank, ran along the dark walkway, and burst into the wheelhouse. Sure enough, the captain was crumpled on the floor behind the boat's wooden steering wheel in a state of delirium. "Micah," he whispered. "Thank goodness. Turn the wheel to the left. Now."

"Yes, sir." He eased the captain out of the way, grasped two of the wooden spokes, and turned the speeding boat to the left with as much force as he could muster. Only the boat didn't seem to be moving to the left. It kept getting sucked further and further to the right. "It's not working, captain!"

"It will. Keep turning, and hold it steady. Just don't turn too much. We need to end up on the northern Clesi River, not the southern Yarmu."

"How am I supposed to tell which river is which? It's too dark to see anything!"

"Use the compass on the navigation stand above the wheel. It should be pointed northwest, not southwest."

"Got it." The needle on the compass pointed more north than west, so Micah kept turning the wheel. His muscles ached from the strain, and he could hear the swirling of the whirlpool get louder and louder. "I can't do this!"

"Sure you can. I can feel the boat changing course. Stay strong."

The captain didn't know what he was talking about. According to the compass, they were still headed north. This was it. This was the end. He was going to die in a watery grave because he couldn't turn a wooden wheel far enough to the left.

"One more turn, Micah," the captain said. "Give me one more turn."

"Okay." With a final show of strength, Micah forced the wheel one complete turn to the left. At that exact moment, the boat's speed picked up, the needle on the compass began pointing towards the northwest, and the sound of the whirlpool began to fade.

"Ha! I think that did it! I think we're in the clear and on the right river." Micah looked back at the captain only to find that he lay unconscious on the floor.

CHAPTER 32
YELLOW SEA

Three days of darkness. Two torrential storms. One narrowly avoided whirlpool. So far this trip through the Dark Zone had been mostly depressing, intermingled with a touch of adventure.

Javan didn't know how much more darkness he could handle. He felt irritated all the time, and that crankiness seemed to be an epidemic that affected all thirty people on board. Except the captain. Cyr remained in critical condition thanks to a spider bite, and Taliya had volunteered to help the resident doctor Dreix tend to him. He thus hadn't seen or spoken to her since their private conversation two days ago.

Andre had taken over the captain's duties, and in a strange twist, Micah steered the boat when Andre needed breaks. Micah had been behaving like a team player and decent human being since the whirlpool incident. He was even starting to learn people's names, but that was probably because everyone now considered him a hero.

Javan still didn't trust Micah and did his best to stay out of Micah's way. He hated seeing the crew treat Micah with a sense of respect and awe knowing Micah didn't deserve such treatment. He was the kind of man who beat innocent people with a whip and used his dragon to destroy entire towns. Steering a boat away from a whirlpool to save his own life didn't make up for any of that.

In an effort to combat his bad attitude, Javan locked himself in the empty cargo room and practiced slicing through the air with his stalker swords for several hours following breakfast on Tuesday morning.

Pushing himself to the point of exhaustion helped restore his sense of self, but his internal alarm bells went off when he felt the boat slow down. That couldn't be good.

He sheathed his swords, wiped his sweaty hair away from his face, and stepped outside. And into the faint light of day. Were they through the Dark Zone already? How had they turned a week-long trip into only three days?

He didn't care. He just wanted to bask in the sunshine. He climbed the ladder to the top deck and ran to the front railing. Sure enough, a break in the canopy up ahead allowed the sun to shine through the trees.

"Sun!"

"Beautiful sight, isn't it?" Phenix, the guard on patrol, came and stood beside Javan. He was almost a foot taller than Javan but as thin as a paper clip.

"Yes, indeed. So why are we slowing down? Shouldn't we be speeding up to get to the end of this miserable Dark Zone?"

"Oh, that's not the end of the Dark Zone. That's just the Yellow Sea. It marks the halfway point."

"Halfway?" Javan's shoulders drooped. "You mean to tell me that after we cross this sea, we're gonna be back in the darkness?"

"You got it. The good news is that we'll anchor here for a couple of hours to replenish our water and food supply. Then it will take the rest of the day to get across the sea, so we get a whole day of sunshine. And rumor has it that the Yellow Sea is one of the most beautiful places in the Great Rift."

As if on cue, the boat drifted out from under the canopy and onto a vast body of golden water that sparkled in the gloriously hot sunshine.

"Wow." Javan could see nothing but water in front of him while trees with giant drooping leaves and brightly colored flowers towered around the edges of the sea behind him.

The boat anchored to a stop within swimming distance of the shore, and schools of tropical fish glided through the water below. Then Kai, Mazen, and Orlan jumped in the water and scared the fish away.

"We're allowed to swim here?" Javan watched as Phida, Grux, Bree, and Kloe from Lydia's crew dove overboard as well. "Let's go join them!"

"You go ahead," Phenix said. "I'm on duty and have to keep an eye out for dangerous animals."

"Yell if you see any snakes, and I'll try to create a big enough splash to get you wet from here."

"I don't think any water will reach me up here, but you can try."

Javan quickly made his way down to the main deck and dropped his sword belt on the floor outside of the cargo room. He stripped his shirt, shoes, and socks off, left them by his swords, and jumped over the railing into the cool, refreshing water.

◊　◊　◊

Micah floated on his back with his eyes closed and let the sun beat down on his bare chest. He hadn't been thankful for much in his life, but he sure was thankful for this simple thing called sunshine.

He could hear Javan, Kai, and Orlan splashing around him. Until they suddenly entered silent mode. Which made him nervous. So he opened his eyes. Just in time to see them throw a fat, red, oversized fish right on his stomach.

The weight of the fish sent his whole body underwater. The terrified creature flipped and flapped and finally swam away, and it took Micah a minute or two to regain his composure after the brief battle with the fish.

"I wish I had a video of that!" Javan was treading water three feet away from Micah and couldn't stop laughing. His buddies on either side of him looked confused, though.

"What's a video?" Orlan asked.

"Um…well." Javan coughed and calmed himself down. "It's a recording that you can watch over and over again. I just think it would be neat to have, you know, so you could show it to people who weren't around to see it for themselves."

"That's stupid," Micah said. "Even if you could 'record' things, no one would want to watch three guys throwing a fish on top of another guy floating in the water."

Javan scrunched his nose. "I could probably get a video like that to go viral."

"Go what?"

"Nothing." Javan scooped water up in his left hand and poured it back into the sea. "Hey, did you notice that this water is actually clear? It's the yellow coral on the bottom of the sea that makes the water appear yellow."

"Of course I knew that." Now that Javan had pointed it out. Which made him mad. He didn't like that the Collector was more observant than him. He needed to come up with something to make himself once again feel superior. "I bet I could beat you to the bottom, tear off a piece of it, and return to the surface faster than you."

"That's not a great idea," Kai said. "In this clear water, the bottom is further down than it appears."

"I wasn't challenging you," Micah said. "But if Javan wants to use that as an excuse to not lose to me in yet another competition, so be it."

"There is no way you can beat me," Javan said. "I am an excellent swimmer."

"As am I."

"Then test your skills by swimming to the shore and back," Orlan said. "Going down is a good way to drown."

"I won't drown." Micah resumed floating on his back. "Javan might, but I won't."

"Only one way to find out." Javan pushed Micah's ankles into the water, forcing him to an upright position. "Let's do this."

Micah smiled and took a series of deep breaths to fill his lungs with air. "Kai, you tell us when to go."

"Do I have to participate in this?"

"Yes!" Micah and Javan said in unison.

"All right. But I refuse to come rescue either one of you."

"I won't need you to," Micah said.

"Enough talk." Javan took a few deep breaths of his own. "Just say go."

"Go."

Micah drank in as much air as he could and dove into the water. Down he went, gliding through the water with the sleek speed of an arrow. He picked a prickly piece of coral as his target and was halfway to it when Javan pulled ahead of him.

Micah increased his kicking power, but Javan remained in the lead. He was running out of breath, his ears were starting to pop, and the coral was still way out of reach. Javan's leg wasn't, though. One tug at this depth, and the Collector would be done.

Without a second thought, he wrapped his hands around Javan's right ankle and yanked. Bubbles exploded around Javan's head, indicating that he opened his mouth and tried to breathe. His eyes widened in fear as he looked back at Micah, and he shot up toward the surface.

Micah continued his descent, now certain of victory. He willed himself to the bottom and reached for the piece of coral he had originally targeted. But the second he snatched it, the long tentacles of a snake-like creature snatched him.

CHAPTER 33
ATTACK OF THE SEA MONSTER

Air. Boat. Hide. If Javan could reach the surface, breathe in air, and make it to the boat, then he could hide from that hideous monster tracking him and Micah.

What was that thing? How fast could it swim? Would he and Micah be able to get away from it?

Javan assumed Micah was right behind him, but he didn't dare look down to verify his assumption. He held on to the little breath he had left and kept his burning eyes on the surface.

Kick. Stroke. Kick. Stroke. Kick. Stroke. Faster and faster he went, praying he could get to the surface before that yellow creature could attack. He kept expecting those long tentacles to wrap around his legs and drag him down, but he broke through the top of the water before that happened.

He gulped in as much air as his lungs could handle and focused on the boat ahead rather than the monster below. His friends were yelling at him to swim, so he swam, the adrenaline to propelling him forward. As soon as he made it to the rope that dangled over the side, Kai and Orlan pulled him up. He collapsed on the deck by his swords, laid on his back, and took a moment to enjoy being alive.

He enjoyed it even more when Taliya smothered him with a hug. "I'm glad you made it."

Between breaths and with his eyes closed, he asked, "Where's Micah? Did he get away?"

When she didn't answer him, he sat up. Everyone else was lined along the railing staring out at the water. Not saying anything. "It's not good, is it?"

"No. And they won't help him. No one will help him."

"Maybe I can." Taliya helped him stand and walked with him to the railing.

He saw what he feared he would see. Thirty feet away, the dark yellow animal that had the head of a crocodile, the body of an anaconda, and the tentacles of an octopus engulfed Micah. Micah appeared to be fighting, but considering the strangling power of the snake-like body, he wouldn't be alive much longer.

◊　◊　◊

At first, Micah thought cutting the tentacle of the creature with the coral was a grand idea. After all, it had let go of him and allowed him to swim away. Almost to the surface. Almost.

It knew Micah needed air. It let him think he could get it. Then it attacked.

This time Micah had no way of defending himself. Dozens of its tentacles covered Micah's body, sending electric shocks through his system. Following the brief, paralyzing shock, it released its tentacles and coiled its body around Micah from his shoulders to his toes.

Then it slowly began squeezing him.

He tried to break free. He pushed and kicked and shoved. But he had no air to breathe and no way of defending himself. Even if he did have a weapon at hand, he had been deprived of oxygen too long to keep fighting.

This was how he was going to die, crushed underwater by a monster he couldn't even name.

He closed his eyes, bowed his head, and accepted his fate.

◊　◊　◊

"Raise the anchor," Andre said, backing away from the railing beside Taliya and under the covered area beside Javan's swords. "Cristiano, start the rumble rocks."

"We can't leave!" Taliya dashed across the deck and moved to block the crank room. "He might not be dead yet. We have to save him!"

"We don't even know what that thing is out there," Andre said. "It's getting closer and closer to this boat, and we can't risk it attacking anyone else on this crew. Now step aside, and let Cristiano's men get to the crank room."

Javan glanced at his swords at Andre's feet and back at the water. If Micah hadn't warned him about the monster by tugging on his leg, that could be Javan out there. Now God was tugging on his heart to save Micah. If he didn't take action immediately, he would think too much and be too scared to take any action at all.

"You're the one who needs to step aside." Javan nudged Andre to the side, picked up his swords, and dove into the water.

He utilized the breaststroke to cover the short distance to creature, careful to not cut himself with his swords as he swam. By the time he got close enough to do something, the monster had Micah in some sort of death spin parallel to the surface of the water. Javan wasn't quite sure how to stop the yellow blur, so he did the only thing he could think of. He stabbed it with both swords.

The monster stopped spinning as the water turned red. An instant later, it poked its head above the water and roared like a lion. Uncoiling itself from Micah, it searched for the new threat. And set its eyes on Javan. "Uh oh."

Its snakelike tail wrapped around Javan's waist, and its crocodile head lurched up and over Javan. He stared into the back of its throat as it opened its jaws and covered Javan's head. So it didn't see Javan lift his arms or hear him scream as he crossed his swords across one another straight through the creature's neck.

Blood spurted everywhere, and he felt the monster's teeth scrape his back before he could throw the severed, smelly head off of him and into the water. Without pausing to freak out, he pried the tail away from his waist and dove into the blood-stained water to retrieve Micah's lifeless body.

CHAPTER 34
RECOVERY

Flashes. Micah could only stay alert long enough to experience flashes of life. Javan pushing on his chest. Kai and Orlan carrying him. Taliya applying cold cream to his tender ribs. Cyr force feeding him soup. Lydia demanding he recover so he could return to Zandador.

None of the flashes made sense. He should be dead. Why didn't he die?

Thinking hurt. Breathing hurt. Existing hurt.

Sleeping. He liked sleeping. The pain went away when he slept. He wanted to keep sleeping. To sleep and never wake up.

Until the nightmares began. Nightmares of black dragons. Yellow monsters. Burning fire. Red water.

But it was the screams that truly tormented him. The screeches of children running from their homes to escape the dragon. The shrieks of women being beaten for breaking Omri's law. The cries of the men caught in Fury's Pass.

"Stop!" He covered his ears and sat straight up. "Stop the yelling!"

"Micah." Taliya's soft voice broke through the madness. She sat on the end of the bed and eased his hands away from his head. "It's okay. Nobody's yelling here. All is quiet. You're safe."

As he struggled to turn his shallow breaths into deeper, more controlled breathing despite the fear and pain, Micah took in his surroundings. He sat on a soft bed twice as wide as his bunk in the sleeping quarters. It stretched from wall to wall in the small room that had two exits: a ladder on the left end of the bed leading up and a door on the right end of the bed leading out.

A lantern dangled from the ceiling, and no light poured in from the round window in the wall above the chair across from the bed. He wasn't sure if that meant it was the middle of the night or if it meant they had progressed further into the Dark Zone.

"Where am I?"

"Captain's quarters. He said he beat his spider bite in here, so this was the best place for you to recover from your battle with that monster."

He rubbed his eyes and tried to scoot back. But he couldn't move without pain.

"Careful," Taliya said. "You bruised or broke just about every rib in your body."

"That explains the pain." He grimaced and leaned against the wall. "How long have I been in here?"

"A day and a half."

"So that's day darkness outside."

"Yup. After your little adventure, we cranked the boat up and continued on our way."

"I don't remember much about my 'adventure.' You'll have to fill me in on the details. How did I fight that monster off and then get back on the boat?"

"You think you fought the monster off on your own?"

"Of course. That's what I do. I battle big monsters and win."

"Hmm."

"'Hmm?' What does that mean? 'Hmm.'"

"That means your arrogance is not going to let you believe the truth."

"I have to be arrogant. I am Omri's son."

"Even Omri's son needs help from time to time."

"What happened? Did some of the men and women risk their lives to save me? I guess they would feel indebted to me. I did save us all from the disaster of the whirlpool."

"And one man saved you from the clutches of that monster."

"Courageous of him."

"Extremely. Not only did he slice the head clean off the monster, he plummeted to the bottom of the lake to get your unconscious body, dragged you back to the boat, and had everyone take turns doing this thing he called chest compressions until you came back to life and spit water in his face."

"I'll have to apologize for that. So who was it? Kai? Mazen? Datnara?"

"None of the above." She cocked her head to the side and said the one name he never expected to hear. "Javan."

◊   ◊   ◊

As he had for the past day and a half, Javan lay in his bunk on his left side. Bandages covered the long scratches on his back and another bandage covered his eyes like a blindfold.

He wouldn't have needed the blindfold bandage if he hadn't worn his contacts in the water. He had lost his left contact altogether, and something microscopic had lodged itself under his right contact, scratching his cornea.

Taliya was the only one who had seen his eyes since the incident. She had flushed his puffy eye with a solution she concocted in the kitchen and patched him up without making one comment about his brown eyes suddenly looking like glowing emeralds.

The eye pain had finally subsided that morning, but he wasn't ready to take the bandage off. Once he did, he wouldn't be able to hide his shiny green eyes from anyone ever again.

When he was in Gri, he had adapted to living without his contacts. But that was in a controlled environment with people he trusted. Out here in the real world, he would be known as the freaky green-eyed guy.

That disturbed him more than the fact that he was almost eaten by a sea monster and left him too shaken up to celebrate his victory with the crew.

"Hey, monster killer." Taliya tapped him on the shoulder, and he rolled to his right side. "Micah's awake. He wants to talk to you."

"I don't feel like talking to anyone right now." As long as he wore the blindfold and couldn't see the people he was talking to, he preferred to keep to himself. "Didn't you tell him I'm blind?"

"You are not blind." Taliya ripped the bandage off his head. "Just as I suspected. The swelling is gone, and your eye looks perfectly healthy."

"No." He sat up and tried to wrap the cloth around his eyes again. "I have to keep my eyes covered."

"That's why I brought you these." Taliya took the cloth and replaced it with a pair of sunglasses. "I don't know why you want to camouflage those gorgeous eyes of yours, but these glasses should protect your eyes until you're ready to show people who you really are."

"You think my eyes are gorgeous?"

"Just put the glasses on, and follow me."

"Yes, ma'am." Javan donned the shades, bounded off the bed, and followed Taliya to the captain's quarters at the opposite end of the room.

◊　◊　◊

Micah had to fight through the pain to take deep breaths. Dreix had offered him medicine to minimize the pain during his exam, but Micah declined. The medicine would make him sleepy, and Micah did not want to sleep.

The doctor ordered him to stay in bed until they arrived in Fralick and to keep applying the cold cream to his chest to speed the healing process. Considering how much it hurt to move, he decided to obey those orders.

Shortly after Dreix left, Javan arrived. "Hey," Javan said, closing the door behind him. "You wanted to see me?"

"Yeah." Micah was taken aback by the Collector's sunglasses. "What's with the dark glasses? There's no light outside, and it's not all that bright in here."

"Scratched my cornea. Makes my eyes sensitive to light."

"Oh. I broke my ribs. Makes my lungs sensitive to breathing."

"You always have to one up me, huh?"

Micah shrugged. Then grimaced when the casual movement sent a wave of pain through his body. "I did get hurt worse."

"True. But that does remind me." Javan tossed a ball of yellow coral on the bed. "I won."

Micah fingered the coral, impressed with the Collector for following through with the bet. He wasn't about to tell him that, though. "I reached the coral first, but I dropped my piece when that monster strangled me."

"That's what you have to say to me?" Javan shook his head and opened the door to leave.

"Wait. Close the door. Have a seat. Please. I need to ask you something."

Javan sighed, shut the door, and sat in the chair. "What?"

"Why?"

"Why...what?"

"I was a dead man. We are enemies. I imprisoned your family, destroyed your town, and left you to die. Twice. Once when I sliced you open, and once when I wouldn't pull you out of the river. You should hate me. Plus with me out of the way, Mertzer would be yours. So why did you save me?"

"I do hate you, but it was the right thing to do."

"The right thing? How do you determine the difference between right and wrong? Had the situation been reversed, the right thing for me would have been to let the monster kill you."

"I know. We operate by a different set of values. For instance, I value human life, even the lives of people I hate. You value your life and no one else's. That may feed your pride, but I'm guessing it leaves you feeling empty, lonely, and unfulfilled."

Micah squirmed under the distressing truth of Javan's words. How did the Collector know how empty and lonely he felt? And where did Javan's values come from? Did they offer him a sense of fulfillment?

In a softer voice, Javan continued. "As much as I despise you, I saw a hint of goodness in you when you tugged on my leg and warned me about that monster."

"That's why you saved me? Because I tugged your leg?" Had Micah not tried to cheat, would Javan have done what he did? Should he tell Javan the truth?

Javan rose to his feet so that he was standing at the end of the bed. "That creature could have just as easily attacked me, and I knew God would help me save you. I was right."

"God? Who is your God?"

"You really want to know? You don't just want to bash my beliefs?"

"I am curious about your beliefs. I've never known any god but Omri, and he has never helped me save anyone."

"In that case--" Javan's answer was interrupted when the boat jerked to a sudden stop. "Great. I wonder what's wrong now."

"Let's go find out." Micah started inching his way off the bed.

"No." Javan pointed at Micah. "You stay. I'll be back later so we can finish our conversation."

"Good. I'd like that."

Javan nodded and opened the door. Micah couldn't let him leave without telling him one more thing.

"Hey, Javan."

He poked his head back through the door. "Yeah?"

"I'm pretty sure my own father wouldn't have risked his life for mine, so thank you."

"You're welcome."

He left, but Micah called him back. "And Javan?"

"Yeah?" This time he answered from outside the room.

"The people of Gri? They all survived. I didn't let Mertzer crush any buildings until I saw the people retreat into the woods."

He wasn't sure Javan heard him until the Collector returned to the room a minute later. "Thank you. I still hate you, but thanks for telling me that."

"Then we are good because I still hate you, too. Now go do your hero thing and fix whatever's wrong with the boat. I would if I wasn't so sore and tired."

"A true hero's work is never done." Javan smiled, nodded, and left the room.

Micah leaned his head back and closed his eyes. But the shrieks wouldn't let him rest. Because these shrieks didn't come from his memories. They came from the crew on the deck above him.

CHAPTER 35
AMBUSH

Empty? That's was odd. At any given time, ten to fifteen people hung out in the sleeping quarters to rest, chat, or eat in the dining area. But when Javan walked out of the captain's room, he found himself alone in the big space. Where was everyone?

He speed walked through the room and was about to climb the ladder to the upper deck when Taliya and Jili the cook came down and elbowed him out of the way.

"What's going on?" Javan asked. "Why did we stop?"

"Frogs," Taliya said. "Lots of frogs. They're clogging the paddlewheels."

"Here." Jili handed him a jug of water. Strands of her white hair had escaped from its bun and hung over her wrinkled face. "Fill every pot, pan, and bowl you can find."

"Okay. But why?"

"Frogs hate salt," Taliya said, scrounging through the cabinets and putting bowls on the table, "so we're going to pour salt water on them."

As Javan filled the bowls with water, Jili added scoops of salt. He had one bowl left when the screams from above sent chills down Javan's spine. "What kind of frogs are we dealing with here?"

"Poisonous ones." Lydia appeared at the bottom of the ladder. "But they're not our only problem. Get your swords. You're needed on the top deck."

"For what? I was helping here."

"Go." Taliya took the water from him. "We have this under control."

Javan strapped on his sword belt and followed Lydia to the first deck. Only he couldn't see a thing through the sunglasses. He felt like a blind man in a dark cave surrounded by shrieks and cackles and hisses. It disturbed him, so he perched his shades on top of his head. Although it was still dark, he could at least make out Lydia's shadow. "What's with all these noises?"

"We're under attack." A big bird flew under the roof, cawing loudly as it grazed both their necks with its wing. "See what I mean!"

"That was a bird." Javan talked slowly to help Lydia grasp her overreaction to the situation. "Birds aren't scary. Why is everyone terrified?"

"One bird isn't scary. Dozens of them pecking at your face, pulling your hair, and biting your hands can be a good reason to scream."

"That's what's happening?" Javan gulped and listened to the banging and screeching around and above him.

"Yes. The animals seem to have created an ambush for us. Frogs are attacking from the water, birds from the air, and we're still not sure what's trying to get to us from the land. Plus the wind is picking up. The weather is about to turn on us, too."

"Wonderful." He leaned to the side and noticed countless pairs of shimmering eyes moving about through the rustling trees on the shore. His heart rate started to spike as a gust of wind tipped the boat from side to side. "What can I do?"

"I've got my archers on the top deck shooting whatever moves on land, but the birds are making that mission difficult. You and I are going to fend them off to free the archers."

"We are?"

"Yes. You might want to put those sunglasses back on to protect your eyes."

Javan took her advice, drew his swords, and followed her up into the chaos. Even through the dark glasses, he could make out shapes of birds as small as sparrows and as big as eagles swooping down and around and on the six archers.

One landed on his head and pulled a chunk of his hair out with his claws while another rammed straight into the fresh wound on his back. "That's enough of that!" Javan waved his swords in the air like a madman, blazing across the deck and chopping at any bird he could reach.

"Need some help, please!" Bree, a five foot nine lean, muscular woman not too far to Javan's right was trying to load her bow. Several birds pecking at her hands made that task difficult.

"I've got you covered." Javan charged over, stabbed one bird, and shooed the others off. "Quick! Take your shot."

She loaded her bow, lined up her shot, and let the arrow fly. "Got it!"

The arrow lodged right between the eyes of a tiger in mid-leap. It splashed in the water before it could reach the boat.

"Nice shot."

"I'm not sure how much good it did. I'm almost out of arrows, but I can spot more than thirty animals bigger than that tiger from here. If we don't get this boat moving soon, we don't stand a chance."

Javan kept his swords raised and moving as he surveyed the land. He couldn't see what Bree saw, but when he turned his attention back to the deck, he could see the birds winning the fight against the humans.

They seemed to be growing in number while more and more of Lydia's brave warriors emptied their quivers and resorted to hiding under the benches, crying like babies and praying for help.

Javan turned his gaze upward. He could only see the dark canopy of the rain forest, and he could only manage a simple prayer of his own. "God, this sure would be a good time for a miracle."

◊　◊　◊

Another yelp. Another thump. Another warrior fallen. According to Micah's count, that made five men down, and that was just in the area above his room. How many more had fallen throughout the boat? What was the cause of their demise? How long would it be before the danger reached him?

He eyed the spear hanging above the door. Surely that wasn't as heavy as his sword and would be a weapon he could handle even in his weakened state. If he could grab it and get himself up that ladder, he could join the fight rather than wait to die.

Rain began beating against the window of the rocking boat by the time he scooted himself off the bed. The sharp pains radiating from his chest and the queasiness emanating from his stomach made him want to lay back down. Then he spotted the influx of colorful, thumbnail-sized frogs squeezing under the door.

He forgot about the pain, jumped on the bed, snatched the spear, and darted up the ladder before any of those poisonous things could touch him. The ladder led him straight into the wheelhouse right behind the wheel. What he saw from there made him want to take his chances with the frogs.

Five whimpering men and women with torn clothes, bloodied bodies, and distressed faces huddled together on the deck, trying to protect themselves from the rain and birds and threat of the electric eels circling in the water below.

Additional animal threats lurked on either shore, so getting off the boat wasn't an option. He could, however, get the injured people inside the safety of the glass room. The only problem was that he would have to risk his own life in the process.

That was a big problem. Why would he want to endanger his life to save people he barely knew? Because he could. Unlike with those men he lost in Fury's Pass. He had been helpless to do anything there. Here he had a chance of saving everyone, including himself. Before he talked himself out of taking action, Micah slipped out the side door.

The rain smacked him in the face, and the wind tried to knock him to his knees. Nevertheless, he stood his ground, yelled to distract himself from the pain, and used the spear to beat the birds away. "Go, go, go!"

Andre took charge of the downed crew that included Mirela, Phenix, Helena, and Orlan. Under the protection of Micah's spear, they helped each other crawl to the door. Once they were all inside, Andre hollered for Micah. "Get inside! Quick!"

"Coming!" He took a few steps toward the door but slipped on the wet decking of the rocking boat. His broken ribs slammed into the railing. The overwhelming pain caused him to drop the spear, and he crashed into a defenseless heap on the wood.

The birds began pecking and clawing at his back. Until a terrifying roar caused them to squawk. Flutter in startled circles. Then fly away just as the canopy ripped open and a stream of fire shot down from the sky.

◊ ◊ ◊

"Varjiek!" As the birds flew away, Javan threw his hands in the air and waved his swords at the invisible dragon. What perfect timing for a perfect miracle. "You found me!"

All the animals found you. A ring of fire around the boat was the only thing that gave away the dragon's location. *Getting rid of them is going to take some time. This rain keeps killing my flames.*

"We've been battling the animals and rain long enough. It's all you now, Varjiek." He sheathed his swords and began pulling people out from under the benches. "Let's get inside, everyone. My dragon has it from here."

Animals screeched and howled from the land as Javan, Lydia, and her team of archers scurried to the ladder and down to the main deck. Once on the main deck, Taliya directed the beat up crew into the cargo space rather than the sleeping quarters.

Javan was the last one down, and when Taliya urged him to follow everyone else inside, he refused. "I'm staying right here. I have to make sure Varjiek is okay."

"I understand. Just knock if you want in."

"I will." He couldn't let her go in yet, though. "Hey, Taliya?"

She paused with her hand on the doorknob. "Yeah?"

"What happened with the frogs? Did you and Jili get rid of them?"

"Mostly."

"Mostly?"

"We unclogged the paddlewheels, but some of the frogs made their way into the crank room and the sleeping quarters. We can't crank up the boat or go below deck until we figure out how to get rid of those things."

"Wonderful."

"Stay alert out here. The doors are sealed, but those little frogs may find a way to get through anyway. Don't touch any of them. We've already lost Cristiano and Brigan. We don't need them killing anyone else."

"Thanks for the warning." Javan choked back the tears until Taliya left him alone on the deck. He sank to the rocking floor, locked his arm around the bottom rung of the ladder, and let the tears roll over his rain-soaked cheeks as he mourned the loss of his two friends.

CHAPTER 36
THE AFTERSHOCK

The storm raged on for more than an hour after Micah crawled inside the crowded wheelhouse, along with the five folks he had helped crawl in before him. They used their shredded clothes as bandages to patch each other up and sat in agonized silence against the glass wall waiting for the storm to end.

None of them were in good shape, yet none of them complained. They shared the same scrapes, cuts, and bruises inflicted by those enraged birds, and that seemed to give them a sense of camaraderie. Which was a new experience for Micah. He didn't much care for the pain he felt with every breath, but he did like feeling as though he belonged somewhere.

Eventually the howling wind eased to a gentle breeze, the rain gave way to the sun, and the boat settled into a stable position on the calming water.

Andre spoke first. "That sun is going to set soon, and we'll be in the dark again." He pulled himself up using the navigation pedestal in the middle of the room. "Let's go assess the damage while we still have daylight."

One by one, Mirela, Orlan, Phenix and Helena stood, but Micah let out an involuntary whimper when he tried to stand.

"You've done enough," Mirela said, putting her hand on his shoulder. "Why don't you stay put until we can get the doc in here to see you?"

"No." Micah shook his head. "I'm part of this crew. I'm coming with you."

"Then you're going to need some help." Mirela offered her bandaged hand. His first instinct was to ignore it and get up on his own, but the concept of receiving help intrigued him. Why would she want to assist him without being ordered to? Is this what friends did for one another?

He held his breath, took her hand, and let her pull him up. She was surprisingly strong and didn't waver one bit, despite being nearly a foot shorter than him.

"Thanks," Micah said, testing his balance. He felt a bit wobbly until Mirela put his arm around her shoulder and helped him out to the walkway in front of the others. From there, he was able to use the railing as a crutch while hobbling toward the stern of the boat.

"Check out the sunset," she said, nudging Micah from behind.

Micah had never paid much attention to sunsets before. He didn't see the point in starting now, but he glanced up through the dragon-sized tear in the canopy anyway. "Oh. Wow. That's beautiful." The purple and pink smudged sky brightened his spirit, and he decided he would have to start noticing sunsets more often.

"Oh my! Talk about wow." Mirela nudged him again, this time directing his gaze to the shore. "That's a dragon!"

The grey-scaled Noon Stalker swooped down and cleared a space among the trees for himself with his long tail, sharp teeth, and strong legs. Once he curled into the spot, he nestled his wings alongside his body and stretched his neck across the water.

"Varjiek!" Javan appeared from under the covered walkway ten feet ahead of Micah. He stretched his hands over the railing, but Varjiek's head was too far away for Javan to touch. "I can't believe you fought off all those animals. You were awesome!"

Why was he praising his dragon? Dragons didn't respond to praise. All they understood were orders from their masters.

"That's tempting." Javan continued talking like he was having an actual conversation with his dragon. "I want to ride you out of here, but I can't. I have to finish what I've started with these guys."

Varjiek snorted and turned his head away from Javan.

"Don't be like that. I want to hear what's happened with you since we were separated, but things have gotten complicated." The dragon swiveled his head back toward Javan. After a slight pause, Javan carried on his one-sided conversation. "Really? That's...no. I can't. But we'll get there a lot faster if you stick with us and help us out."

"Javan?" Micah closed the distance between him and the Collector. As he approached, he noticed that Taliya, Cyr, Kai, and Lydia were standing behind Javan. They looked concerned about the Collector's sanity as well. "Did that bird attack make you crazy? Why are you talking to your dragon as if he can talk back?"

"I didn't realize I had company." Javan bit his lip and adjusted his sunglasses. "I thought everyone was still inside."

"No," Taliya said. "You have an audience. Can you really hear what Varjiek is saying?"

Javan scrunched his nose and ran his fingers through his hair. "Maybe."

"That's preposterous," Micah said. "The dragon hasn't said anything. Dragons are animals. Dragons don't talk."

"Of course he doesn't talk," Javan said. "But he does think, and I can kinda read his mind."

"Impossible." Micah had heard that some Collectors had the ability to read the minds of their dragons, but Micah didn't believe those rumors. "No one can read minds, especially the minds of dragons."

"The Collector who is the answer to the prophecy can," Taliya said.

"The prophecy?" Micah knew about the prophecy. The prophecy is the one thing that scared his father. Omri had banned Dartez to the Land of No Return because of the prophecy. Dartez with his shiny green eyes was the threat, not Javan. Javan had brown eyes. "He can't be the answer to the prophecy. His eyes are brown."

"Are they?" Taliya asked.

"Yeah." Micah hadn't memorized the man's eyes, but he knew they weren't green. "Well, they might be blue or black. But they definitely aren't a bright emerald green color."

"Javan," Taliya said, "show him. Take off your glasses."

"No!" Javan crossed his arms and shook his head.

Taliya stepped up and put her hand on Javan's elbow. "It's time to stop hiding. People are going to see the true you eventually. Might as well be now."

"I'm not ready," Javan said.

"I am." Micah had to put an end to this nonsense. He reached out and jerked Javan's glasses off his face.

He nearly fainted when he saw a pair of gleaming green eyes staring back at him.

◊   ◊   ◊

Exposed. Javan felt exposed. Vulnerable. Freakish. He had to escape. Now. He turned away from the stunned Micah and turned to Varjiek. "Let me on. I want to leave."

You said you wanted to stay.

"I changed my mind." Javan could feel the stares of the crew. He had to get out of there before they had a chance to taunt him about his eyes. "Let's go."

As you wish. Varjiek spread his wing over the water so that its round edge reached the railing. Javan jumped on, slid down the slick wing, and stopped himself at the base of the dragon's neck.

"Where are you going?" Taliya yelled her question from the boat, but Javan didn't have the courage to respond. He needed to get away from her. From all of them.

He leaned forward and spoke to Varjiek. "Make me invisible, and fly us out of here."

Done. Varjiek launched off the ground and shot straight up through the opening in the canopy he had created earlier. Javan clung to Varjiek's neck, closed his hated eyes, and relished the feeling of the warm wind blowing through his tangled hair. Until Varjiek's thoughts cut into his pity party.

What is this prophecy that made you change your mind about coming with me?

"The prophecy? Oh, I don't care about that. I care that my eyes make me look like a mutant." Javan sighed, sat up, and drank in the beauty of the colorful sunset as Varjiek coasted over the top of the dark green canopy that looked thick enough to walk on. "No one will want to be around me when my eyes look like this."

I see nothing wrong with your eyes.

"People will. They'll make fun of me, call me names, and make me feel like an outcast."

How do you know?

"I've been to high school. I know how cruel people can be."

I do not understand. You don't want to feel like an outcast, but didn't you make yourself an outcast by flying away from the people on that boat?

"No. I..." Javan couldn't think of a way to defend himself against Varjiek's logic. It did seem silly to run away because he didn't want to feel like an outsider when in fact running away made him an outsider. Wouldn't it be better to be known as the freak who did what he said he would do than to be known as the guy who deserted his friends?

I did not hear your response. How am I wrong?

"You're not wrong. I am."

Does that mean we have to go back? I could take you to Kisa first. After you collect her, we could return to help your friends.

"How long do you think that will take?" If Javan could get to Kisa before Micah and Taliya, he could ensure he made that dragon his.

A day. Maybe more. Kisa has to decide she likes you before she'll let you ride her.

"She told you that?"

Yes.

The thrill of adding another dragon to his collection excited him. He had to get to Kisa. Fast. "Take me to her."

Yes, my Collector.

The last of the light was fading as they soared over the northern border of the Dark Zone, but it was enough light for Javan to notice movement on the ground below. "Slow down, Varjiek. Circle back to where the river exits the Dark Zone."

Varjiek turned around and followed the river back to the border. *What are we looking for?*

"That." Javan pointed to the tents along both banks and the armed people patrolling the area. "The crew on the Iria is out of ammunition. They'll have no way of defending themselves when they get here."

Shall I destroy these people then?

"No! They're as innocent as the people on the boat. Nobody needs to get hurt, so I have an idea."

We're not going to collect Kisa, are we?

"Not yet."

Then what's your plan?

Javan smiled. "We're going to make the Iria disappear."

◊　◊　◊

"How did he make his eyes look like that?" Micah finally found the ability to speak after Taliya led him into the cargo space and sat him down along with the rest of the battered crew. The dozen or so people who were still well enough to walk were in the sleeping quarters hunting frogs.

"His eyes have always looked like that." Taliya dabbed a cut on Micah's shoulder with a wet cloth. "Apparently he lost the covers he wore on them to make them look brown when he went for that swim in the Yellow Sea."

"That can't be," Micah said. He needed a different explanation, one that didn't point to Javan as the fulfillment of the prophecy. "Those can't be his real eyes. He can't really hear what his dragon is thinking. He can't be the answer to the prophecy."

"Why not?"

"Because my father has devoted his life to ensuring that no one can or will fulfill that prophecy."

"Javan seems to be a pretty good candidate. He is 'a young Collector whose eyes shine like emeralds and whose ears can hear the thoughts of any dragon.'"

"He never said he could hear the thoughts of any dragon, just his Noon Stalker. It is true that some Collectors have the ability to hear the thoughts of their own dragons, but no one has ever been able to hear the thoughts of a dragon who isn't a part of his collection. And if you're going to quote the prophecy, don't forget the last part."

"The part about him entering the competition in final months of a Battle for the Throne year? I think he did that."

"True, but he hasn't collected all four dragons yet. Even if he does, the prophecy states that the Collector must unite the four opposing Bloodlines to defeat the reigning King. That means that you, me, and some Destroyer out there will willingly fight with Javan against my father."

"You're not the only one of the Hunter Bloodline left, and I'd rather stand with him than with Omri."

"You sure you're going to have that chance?" Micah had to help Taliya see what a mistake opposing Omri would be. He almost considered her a friend, and he found the thought of her being tortured or killed because she stood against his father unpleasant. "How can Javan unite us when he flew away and left us here to die? That's not someone I want to follow. If I ever get back to Zandador, I think I'll stay loyal to my father."

"Javan will be back."

"Why would he come back? He has free access to our dragons. Once he collects them, he'll go after a Midnight Stalker. We'll never see him again."

A startling thud from something crashing onto the deck above them rocked the boat and prevented Taliya from responding. No one moved as the boat resettled. They all simply shared anxious glances and braced for the next animal attack.

Then the tension broke when the door burst open, and Javan stepped through it. "Miss me?"

His green eyes glowed in the dim lantern light, and Taliya seemed to be the only one who wasn't too entranced by Javan's eyes to speak. She suddenly turned from Javan's defender to his interrogator.

"Why did you leave?" She threw the cloth in Micah's lap, stood, and crossed her arms. The more she talked, the angrier she sounded. "We have all kinds of problems here, and you just flew away the first chance you got."

"It's a good thing I did," Javan said. "Once we get out of the Dark Zone, we'll have new problems to deal with."

"What do you mean?"

"Warriors from Upper Keckrick are guarding the river at the edge of the Dark Zone. There's enough of them to take us out as soon as we reach their territory."

"Wonderful." She dropped her arms and softened her voice. "We can't divert our path, and with all of our ammunition depleted, we can't defend ourselves."

"That's why I'm back. I have a plan."

"Let me guess," Micah said. He could see where this was going. Javan returned so could brag about having his dragon wipeout the imminent threat. He wanted the crew to think of him as a hero. "You're going to have your dragon take out the warriors before they can take us out."

"That's one option," Javan said, "but I have a better idea. With Varjiek's help, we're going to make the Iria invisible and float right past them."

"Really?" Taliya took a few steps toward Javan. "Varjiek can cloak the entire boat?"

"It will take a lot of his energy, but he says he can do it."

"He says he can, huh?" Micah still wasn't convinced Javan could communicate with his dragon. "What else does he say he can do?"

Javan walked to Micah, leaned down, and whispered in Micah's ear. "He says he can whip you with the spiked end of his tail for whipping Mertzer, but I told him to leave you alone because the people of Keckrick need you to talk to Omri."

Micah's blood ran cold. No one knew about that whipping except Mertzer. The only way Javan could know was if Mertzer told Varjiek, who then told Javan.

The Collector could hear his dragon's thoughts. Javan just might be the answer to the prophecy. If that was true, Micah could never return to Zandador without first killing Javan. But how could he kill Javan after he had saved Micah's life, then returned to save the entire crew?

The dilemma caused a pounding headache, and he could no longer think. "Sleep," Micah said. "I need sleep." He leaned his head against the wall, closed his eyes, and shut himself away from the world that had brought him face to face with his father's greatest fear.

CHAPTER 37
THE FINAL STRETCH

Taliya put her hands on the passed out Micah's neck and checked his pulse. "What did you say to him?"

"I just told him something Varjiek told me." Javan nodded toward Micah. "Is he all right?"

"For now. He has a fever, and I'm sure he's in an incredible amount of pain with those broken ribs. The rest will help him." She stood and pointed to the door. "Can I talk to you outside?"

"Sure." When they were alone under the covered walkway, he asked, "What's up?"

"Is Varjiek the only dragon you can talk to?"

"Huh?" That wasn't the question he was expecting. He thought she would grill him about leaving or want to discuss his eyes.

"Varjiek. Is he the only dragon you can talk to?"

Javan didn't want to answer, not when he couldn't read her expression. Although they were only standing a few feet apart, all he could see was a dark shadow in front of him. The determination in her voice, however, told him she wasn't going to drop the subject until she got her answer. "No."

"So you could hear Kisa's thoughts?"

"Yes. And Mertzer's. And every other dragon I've come across. So what? It's not that big of a deal."

"Not that big of a deal? I have devoted my life to protecting Kisa so that she would be safe from Hunters and Destroyers. But I knew I would never be able to protect her from the Collector who could read her thoughts." Her tear-stained voice began to shake. "I thought I'd be ready to give her up for the good of Zandador when he came along. Now that you're standing right in front of me, it's all too real. I don't know what I'm supposed to do with my life without Kisa around to care for."

"Please don't cry." He reached out to hug her, but she backed away. "I haven't collected her yet. I can find another Dawn Stalker."

"You came to Keckrick for Kisa, and you better not leave without her. I don't want to see her become Micah's slave."

181

"Maybe you could--"

"My life is here. Not in Zandador. Just promise me you'll treat her well."

"Of course." He'd promise anything to get her to stop crying.

"Good." She wiped her cheeks and cleared her throat. "I need to get back to the wounded. At least my work as a healer will always give me something to do." She gave a half-hearted laugh and walked back into the cargo room.

Javan let her go, but he decided he wasn't going to leave Keckrick without both her and Kisa.

◊   ◊   ◊

Micah slept fitfully that Wednesday night. Breathing hurt. The bird-inflicted cuts burned. But the headache was the worst. He felt like his brain was swelling at the same time his skull was shrinking, and he couldn't do anything to prevent the imminent explosion.

Taliya checked on him every now and then. She propped a pillow between his head and the wall, covered his legs with a blanket, and cut off the shreds of his tattered shirt in an attempt to make him more comfortable. It didn't work, especially once the boat began moving again shortly after midnight. He felt every vibration of the moving boat and just wanted someone to knock him out until the ride was done.

"Good news," Taliya said, rousing him with a wet cloth to his forehead early Thursday morning. "We made it out of the Dark Zone and past the guards at the border undetected."

"Wonderful." He took a sip of the water she offered. "How long until we get to the dragons?"

"It's about a day's journey between here and home."

"Another day?"

"Yes. It should be an easy trip. We have daylight, and Varjiek will continue to cloak us so that no villagers spot us. The toughest part will be going without food."

The mention of food made Micah's stomach rumble. "Why do we have to go without food?"

"The frogs got into our food supply and tainted everything. We don't have any food left that's safe to eat."

Great. Now all Micah wanted to do was eat. "This is going to be a very long day."

"If you feel like moving, you should head down to your bunk along with the rest of the injured crew. We're pretty sure we killed all the frogs."

"Pretty sure?" Micah noticed that he and Taliya were the only ones left in the cargo space, but he didn't want to take any chances of coming into contact with one of those poisonous frogs. He adjusted the pillow behind his head and rearranged the blanket on his lap. "I think I'll stay here."

"Then at least let me give you something that will help you sleep."

"What have you got?"

"A mixture I made from the doc's supply of plants and berries." She picked up a small bowl and showed him the greenish goo inside. "It's got a thick consistency and not much of a taste, but it will keep you sedated and still so you can heal."

"It looks gross."

"Just try it." She globbed some on a spoon and raised it to his mouth. "Open. You need to sleep."

"Fine." He did like the idea of disregarding the world for a while. That thought prompted him to open his mouth and eat the goo. Within seconds, his entire body went limp, and he drifted into a deep sleep.

He stayed asleep until he felt the boat rumble to a stop. He immediately reached for his sword, then remembered he had left it in the sleeping quarters below. Great. How was he supposed to defend himself if another animal outside that door wanted him dead?

Micah listened for the frantic activity associated with any kind of attack. Hearing nothing out of the ordinary, he slowly made his way to the exit. Maybe they weren't under attack. Maybe they had reached their destination.

As he stepped outside, he discovered he could breathe with minimal pain. He needed to find out what Taliya put in that paste she had shoved down his throat. Whatever it was seemed to have done wonders for healing his internal wounds.

And the scenery did wonders for healing his spirit. The sunshine alone was enough to make him smile, but the way it sparkled off the water trickling down the bronze mountainside to the left of the boat made his heart smile. He could see the world again, and he never wanted to return to that dark, dark place in the middle of Keckrick.

"Micah, what are you doing up?" Taliya approached him from behind. "I was just coming to check on you."

"How long have I been asleep?"

"A little over a day. You feeling better?"

"Much. So we're here? Back at your home?"

"Close. The river ends here. It splits off into streams that aren't wide enough or deep enough for the Iria. We'll be hiking to Fralick, which is about five miles north."

"You don't sound very excited."

"I'm not. The white winds already destroyed my house. Once the humminglos are harvested, this place won't feel like home anymore, for me or for Kisa."

"So keep them."

"What?"

"Keep the flowers. Take the crew to the wrong place, and say some other village got to the fields before we did."

"That would work out well for me, but it's not the deal I made. The only way to keep Omri from annihilating half of Keckrick is to deliver these plants to him." Taliya looked up at Micah. "You are still going to keep your end of the deal, right? You're going to talk to your father and convince him to spare the people?"

"Yes." Micah nodded. "Yes, of course." He just didn't tell her that he planned to capture her dragon first. Otherwise he wouldn't be able to convince his father to spare him.

CHAPTER 38
CHANGE OF PLANS

Javan rolled over in his bunk when the boat slowed to a stop at 8:30 Friday morning. He had been up late the night before keeping a lookout with Varjiek and wanted to sleep for ten more minutes. Or an hour. Another hour would be good.

"Javan!" Lydia's commanding voice crushed Javan's hope for more sleep. He rolled back over and saw her charging down the aisle from the direction of the captain's quarters. Bree and Grux, the tall, flat-faced warrior on her crew, marched quickly behind her. "Javan, get up. You have some explaining to do."

He groggily sat up and dangled his legs over the side of the bed. "Is it about Varjiek? What do you need me to explain?"

"This has nothing to do with your dragon." Lydia moved to the end of the bunk and addressed her two warriors. "Get him down from there."

Bree and Grux each grabbed an arm and pulled Javan down. "Whoa," he said, "why the harsh treatment? What's the problem?"

"The problem is that you set us up to lose the war."

"What? What are you talking about?"

"Don't play stupid. We're at the end of the river, and there are no head-high humminglos anywhere to be seen. You brought us here for nothing!"

"The plants exist," Javan said, trying not to panic. He had no idea where the humminglo fields were if the river didn't take them straight to the fields. "Taliya said they were in a secret location; she never said they were at the end of the river. Let's just find her and have her tell us where to go from here."

"She's probably checking on Micah in the cargo space," Bree said.

"Grux," Lydia said, "get the captain and Andre. Tell them to meet us in the cargo area. Bree, bring Javan. You two are coming with me."

"I can walk on my own," Javan said, pulling his arm away from Bree. "You don't have to treat me like a prisoner."

"You are a prisoner until we get some answers." Lydia motioned to Bree. Bree once again took hold of Javan's arm, dragged him to the ladder, and had him climb up after Lydia but before her.

Javan thought about yelling for Varjiek as he transitioned from the ladder to the deck, but he wanted to wait to play the dragon card until Taliya had a chance to explain. He was sure she would be able to get them back in the crew's good graces.

Fortunately they didn't have to work hard to find her. She and Micah were standing at the railing staring at the stunning waterfall to the left of the boat. Bree shoved Javan toward them, and that got their attention.

"What's going on?" Taliya asked.

"You tell us." Captain Cyr approached from the walkway along the side of the boat. Andre, Dreix, and Mirela were right behind him.

"Tell you what?"

"Taliya," Javan said, "it seems our friends have some concerns about the humminglo fields they thought would be here but aren't."

"If the fields were here," Taliya said, "anyone could find them. But if we hike about five miles north, you'll see more humminglo plants than you know what to do with."

"Hike?" Lydia stepped in front of Taliya. "We're going to have to hike? For five miles? Through that wild territory? How are we supposed to get to the fields, harvest the plants, and get them back to the boat in time to get to the portal in Tulkar by Tuesday?"

"We're not," Cyr said. "We may be able to travel faster since we'll be going with the current, but it will take us until Tuesday to get all the plants we need to the boat."

"So we use Varjiek to transport us and the plants," Javan said. "It won't take any time at all for him to fly five miles, and he'll easily be able to carry large loads of plants on his back."

"Still," Andre said, "the harvest itself will take several days. We'll never be able to make it back through the Dark Zone by Tuesday. This whole trip was a mistake."

"Not necessarily." Micah spoke for the first time. "Isn't there another portal in Upper Keckrick?"

"Yes," Taliya said. "In Nahat. It only takes a little over two days to get there by boat from here."

"You want us to take our crop to the portal in Upper Keckrick?" Lydia did not sound pleased. "That's suicide."

"No," Javan said. "It's a great plan. We just have to get these plants to Omri. Whether they come from the portal in Upper or Lower Keckrick doesn't matter because Micah is going to have a chat with his father."

"The people of Upper Keckrick don't know that," Cyr said. "They will kill us before we have a chance to get to the portal."

"Not if Varjiek and I come with you to make sure the boat gets to Nahat safely." Taking that trip would delay his plan to collect Kisa, but he needed to see this mission through to the end.

"That could work," Andre said.

"It will have to work," Cyr said. "It's our only option."

"Then I'm going to get Varjiek." Rather than move, Javan held his hands up. "Unless I'm still a prisoner."

"Get your dragon," Lydia said, "but you are still my prisoner until I see those humminglo fields."

"I guess you'll be making the first trip with me," Javan said.

"And me." Taliya hooked her arm around Javan's. "You need to know where to go, and there's someone I need to see before all these people show up."

Javan was happy to oblige. If he knew where Kisa was living, he may be able to collect her before he had to leave again for Nahat.

◊   ◊   ◊

Micah's headache returned as he watched Varjiek fly away with Javan, Taliya, and Lydia. If they found the fields, harvested the flowers, and got them to Zandador by Transport Day, everyone would expect him to be able to change his father's mind about destroying half of Keckrick. Micah knew that would never happen. These people were doomed. He would be, too, if he didn't find Mertzer and capture both Kisa and Varjiek.

"All right," Cyr said, cutting into Micah's thoughts. "I want everyone up on the top deck and ready to go by the time Javan returns."

"What about Micah and others still recovering from their injuries?" Dreix asked.

"It would be tough to help with the harvest since I can't even breathe without pain," Micah said.

Cyr nodded and modified his orders. "Micah, you stay on the boat and oversee the transfer of the plants from the dragon to the cargo space. Those in the worst shape will stay here with you. We need everyone else in the fields cutting or bundling humminglo flowers until that cargo space is full."

"Yes, sir," Bree said. "I'll take the doctor and rouse those who are in their bunks."

"Andre, Grux, and I will gather the scythes from the supply compartment," Mirela said. She took her left arm out of the sling it was in and tossed the sling on the deck. "We'll make sure the blades are sharp and ready for use."

"Good." Cyr clapped his hands twice. "Let's move. I'll meet you all up top."

An instant later, Micah found himself alone with nothing to do. Which suited him just fine. He had no intention of staying on board to help with the harvest. His job was to take care of himself. That meant finding Mertzer.

First, though, he needed to hunt down clothes and food.

He would wait until the sleeping quarters were clear, then recover his boots and sword while snagging a spare shirt from one of the crew's belongings. Once most everyone was gone, he would lower the ramp and exit into the forest where he was sure he would be able to locate something to feed his growling stomach as he searched for Mertzer.

He took a deep breath and hid in the shadows of the walkway as he studied the path he would take through the trees. On his own. Away from the common people. Just like he was used to.

Contemplating his solitary escape amidst the bustle of activity below and above him helped him feel like his old self. He only had one problem with that.

He wasn't sure if he liked the selfish, lonely, empty man he used to be.

◊   ◊   ◊

"Amazing," Taliya said. Her arms were wrapped around Javan's waist as they flew high above the humminglo fields. The large purple flowers covered the land below, broken up only by a handful of streams that wound their way through the fields and emptied into the U-shaped canyon where Javan had first laid eyes on Kisa. "I've never seen these fields from the air before."

"This is unbelievable!" Lydia sat behind Taliya and couldn't contain her excitement. "I shouldn't have doubted you. You are definitely NOT my prisoners anymore!"

"Good to know," Javan said. "Where would you like to land?"

"At the far end of the field," Taliya said, "as far away from the waterfall as possible. That area is soggy and full of snakes."

I do not think that is accurate, Varjiek said. *I think she is just trying to keep us from getting too close to Kisa's cave.*

Javan agreed with Varjiek's assessment but didn't see the harm in keeping Kisa safe. "Take us down to the far end of the field, Varjiek," Javan said. "You may need to trample some flowers to create a space to land."

Okay, but hang on. We're going to have some fun before we land.

"What do you mean?"

Varjiek didn't respond. He just picked up speed as he flew in a huge circle around the wide fields. Javan latched onto the dragon's neck a little tighter, and Taliya squeezed Javan's waist a little tighter as well.

They went around the fields again, but this time Varjiek flew lower and faster. Soon they were hovering just above the flowers, and the wind from

Varjiek's wings seemed to bring the flowers to life. The neon blue strings in the middle of the purple petals went from their downward droop to an electrified, raised position facing the sky. The petals danced around the strings, creating a rich symphony of melodic sounds.

When Varjiek landed in a small clearing at the edge of the field, Javan, Taliya, and Lydia sat awestruck on the dragon's back as they watched and listened to the musical plants. Without the wind to keep them playing, though, the plants soon drooped to their normal position.

"That was cool!" Javan wanted Varjiek to take another spin but figured he would sound too much like a kid if he asked that of the dragon. Instead, he cleared his throat and forced himself to become serious. "It's too bad we have to cut these flowers down."

"True," Lydia said, sliding off Varjiek, "but they are sure to please King Omri."

"Just what I live for." Taliya let go of Javan and joined Lydia on the ground. "Let's get to chopping down my plants so the great King Omri will be happy."

Lydia ignored Taliya's bitterness and looked up at Javan. "It shouldn't take long to get everyone else here as long as Varjiek doesn't do that spirally flight around the fields each time."

"Direct flights there and back. Gotcha."

Varjiek snorted. *That's boring.*

"I know," Javan said, "but she is right. We don't have much time to get these flowers harvested."

"What?" Lydia asked.

"Nothing. I was talking to Varjiek."

"Oh. Okay. Well, you get on back to the boat, and we'll work on a plan on how best to get started."

"Yes, ma'am." As Varjiek lifted him into the air, Javan noticed Taliya looking longingly in the direction of the canyon. She was worried about her dragon.

How was he supposed to collect Kisa knowing how much that dragon meant to Taliya? He couldn't. Even though that would deem this entire trip to Keckrick a bust, he was willing to find another Dawn Stalker to collect if that would make Taliya happy.

Was a happy Taliya more important that winning the Battle of the Throne, though? To him, yes. To the people of Zandador? Probably not.

He shouldn't have to make such tough decisions at his age. Too bad Varjiek couldn't fly him back to Montana where all he had to do was go to school and play football. He missed being a carefree teenager!

CHAPTER 39
HARVESTING THE HUMMINGLOS

So quiet. So alone. So hot.

Micah sat on a rock by the stream he had been following for the past few hours and took his backsword and shirt off. Both had been rubbing against his bird-induced scrapes, causing an annoying amount of discomfort. He wanted a few moments of relief before continuing his search for food and Mertzer.

Being alone in the woods seemed strange after spending nearly a week on a boat surrounded by people day in and day out. He missed being part of the group and almost wanted to go back to help with the harvest. That wasn't an option, though. He was Omri's son. He had a dragon-hunting mission to fulfill on behalf of his father. He couldn't waste any more time with people now that he was near dragons again.

Unlike in the Dark Zone, the sun filtered down through the thin rain forest canopy, enabling Micah to see the ferns and shrubs and palm trees surrounding him. Upon closer inspection, Micah realized some of the palm trees bore huge clusters of fruit.

"Food!" He unsheathed his sword, walked a few steps to the nearest tree, and chopped off a cluster of round green balls. He picked one off and took a tiny bite. Sour! But tasty. He popped the entire ball into his mouth, winced as he chewed the sour treat, then found himself surprised by a juicy burst of sweet flavor that satisfied his thirst as well as his hunger. "That's surprisingly delicious."

After eating the twenty or so balls on the cluster, he chopped down several more clusters. He was halfway through devouring his third batch when he heard branches breaking and trees snapping and animals squealing.

He dropped the fruit and picked up his sword, ready to fight whatever dangerous animal was headed his way and causing all the commotion. The ground began to shake at the same time he noticed a big white blur weaving through the trees not too far in front of him.

Flashbacks to the sea monster squeezing his body and birds clawing at his skin triggered fresh sweat that trickled down his forehead and stung his eyes. Those attacks made him realize he wasn't immune to death. What if this time he couldn't escape death's clutches?

He wanted help. He needed help. Only he had no one to call on. His father was too far away to hear him, and he had yet to find Mertzer. What about Javan's God? Would Javan's God hear him and help him? What should he say? How should he pray?

"Umm...God?" Micah looked up, hoping that Javan's God was somewhere in the heavens. "Please don't let me die."

Micah wasn't sure God heard him because the blur staggered to a stop. "Not good." Micah held his breath and braced for an attack. Until he realized he was looking at his massive, muscular, white-scaled dragon. "Mertzer!"

Relief flooded Micah's system. He didn't need help from a God he couldn't see. He also wasn't going to have to return to Zandador as a dragonless Dragon Hunter. Better yet, he could focus on how to capture Kisa and Varjiek since he had Mertzer back in his possession. He was going to make his father proud after all.

Micah put his sword away. As the dragon approached, he noticed stacks of giant humminglo flowers strapped to Mertzer's back with vines. "Why are you carrying humminglos? You're my dragon. You shouldn't be doing anything without my permission or a direct order from me."

Mertzer bent his long neck and stared at the ground.

"Did Javan put you up to this? How did he get you to cooperate?" Micah's next thought caused him to shudder. "Can you talk to Javan?"

The dragon slowly lifted his head and met Micah's eyes.

"You can talk to Javan. He convinced you to help with the harvest, just like he did with his own Noon Stalker."

That meant Javan could talk to any dragon, just like the Collector spoken of in the prophecy. So what should Micah do about it? Should he eliminate the Collector and ensure his father's place on the throne? Or should he give Javan the chance to collect Kisa and overthrow Omri?

Where did that last thought come from? Why would he even think about giving Javan such a chance? Yes, he was a decent guy who cared about people and treated his dragon with respect. That didn't matter. Javan remained his worst enemy. Micah must remain loyal to his father. That's what he had been taught. That's what he had been trained to do.

But had he been taught and trained to do the right things? Was staying loyal to Omri the right choice?

"I need to sort this out," Micah told Mertzer. He didn't know how to deal with these foreign feelings of uncertainty and doubt. He needed to find a way to restore his confidence. "Go ahead and take these plants to the boat, then come right back here for me." Mertzer nodded and continued his speedy zig zag through the rain forest.

By the time he returned, Micah would have a decision. And a plan.

◊　◊　◊

Javan dragged another bundle of humminglos to the growing pile near the edge of the woods. Mertzer should have been back for another load by now. Where was he? Had Micah reclaimed him when he got to the boat and refused to let the dragon return?

Varjiek wasn't around, either. After transporting most of the crew to the fields, he took off to hunt his noon meal. He was taking longer than usual. Then again, he had been expending a lot of extra energy and probably needed extra food.

The thought of food made Javan groan. He couldn't remember the last time he ate and was starting to feel lightheaded after working out in the heat with only a minimal amount of water to keep him going. Taliya had volunteered to hunt food for everyone since she knew the area, but like the dragons, she had yet to return. He had a hunch her delay was related to her own dragon, and he wanted to sneak away to find her and Kisa. That sounded like a lot more fun than bundling humminglos.

At least he wasn't cutting the flowers anymore using that annoying scythe. With its curved blade that projected to the side at the end of the long wooden shaft, the scythe looked just like the weapon carried by the Grim Reaper. In light of the fact that they used the tool to kill the humminglo flowers, it was a fitting metaphor.

What irritated Javan, however, was that the tool was made for right-handed people. Thanks to the angle of the blade, he had to hold the top handle in his dominant left hand and the middle handle protruding from the central part of the shaft in his weaker right hand. Twisting his body to the left while guiding his blade with his right hand through the lower stems of the flowers felt awkward and ineffective.

So Javan had been glad when Mertzer showed up just as Varjiek left to hunt his noon meal. The Dusk Stalker had approached Javan asking to help, and that gave Javan a reason to work on gathering and bundling the cut flowers with Kloe and Bree rather than operate the scythe.

"Mertzer's back!"

Javan turned at Bree's high-pitched exclamation to find Micah emerge from the trees on the back of Mertzer. Great. He had reclaimed his dragon. What would he do now? Use Mertzer to hunt Kisa or continue to help with the harvest?

Javan walked away from his piles of flowers to greet Micah. "We weren't expecting to see you out here. You must be feeling better."

"Not really." Micah glared down at him from atop the dragon's back. "I needed to come remind you that Mertzer is my dragon. I decide what he does and does not do."

He is right, Mertzer said. *I should have awaited orders from my master.*

"I apologize." Javan's heart broke for Mertzer. If there was any way he could free Mertzer from Micah, he was going to find it. "I didn't think you would have a problem with your dragon helping with something that would benefit your father. Besides, I didn't order him to do anything. He volunteered to help."

"That is nonsense. Dragons don't think for themselves. They have to be told what to do."

"Not in my experience."

"Really? You're telling me that Mertzer just came up to you and offered to carry humminglos to the boat?"

"Basically. Varjiek knew where he was and told him we needed help. He thus showed up and asked what he could do."

"He asked?" Micah sat up a little straighter. "Are you telling me you can read my dragon's thoughts, too?"

He's testing you. He's already figured out you can communicate with me, and it scares him.

Rather than answering Micah's question directly, Javan shrugged. "Maybe."

Micah just stared at him, making Javan wish he had the ability to read Micah's thoughts as well.

◊ ◊ ◊

Micah didn't want it to be true. It was bad enough accepting that this Collector could read the thoughts of any dragon, but Micah certainly didn't want to believe dragons had the ability to think for themselves. That's why they had to be hunted. They required human masters to think for them.

And Micah controlled Mertzer. Javan needed to understand that reality. "Whether or not you can read Mertzer's thoughts doesn't matter," Micah said. "He belongs to me and my father, and there is nothing you can do to change that."

"True," Javan said. "But that doesn't mean you can't change the way you treat him. He's not a mindless weapon. He's a living being with thoughts and feelings."

"He's an animal, and I can treat him however I choose."

"Like when you almost got him and your father's other dragons killed fighting a Midnight Stalker?"

"How do you know about that?"

"Mertzer told me."

"Oh?" Micah felt betrayed and wanted to punish the dragon for conversing with the Collector. "What else has he told you?"

"I don't care who told who what," Lydia said, marching up and interrupting the conversation. "All I care about is getting these flowers loaded on Mertzer's back. We have to keep this process moving, or we'll never finish the harvest."

"I'm done talking," Javan said, "but we may need to wait for Varjiek. I'm not sure Micah wants Mertzer helping with the harvest."

"Why not?" Lydia asked, looking up at Micah. She showed no fear of Mertzer, and Mertzer was probably telling Javan all sorts of secrets. When had Micah entered a world where people didn't fear dragons, and dragons could talk to people?

Micah sighed. He was going to have to allow Mertzer to transport humminglos in order to keep the peace with Lydia. It wasn't part of his plan, but he could adapt. "We can't add a load of flowers until I unload the food."

"Food?" Lydia inched closer to Mertzer. "What food?"

"Fruit I found on the way here." He tossed a cluster of the fruit down to Lydia.

"Bitterberries!" Lydia shoved a handful in her mouth and shivered until she swallowed. "Here, Javan. Try one."

"Are they good?" Javan picked a berry and popped it in his mouth. After his bright green eyes teared up from the sour taste, the sweetness must have kicked in because he relaxed and smiled. "Weird but awesome. Thanks, Micah."

Lydia turned and whistled to the crew working in the field. "Micah brought bitterberries. Come eat!"

As the dozens of people dropped their tools in the partially harvested humminglo fields and swarmed toward Micah, he wondered what had compelled him to bring them food. That wasn't the kind of thing he had ever done before. People were supposed to provide food for him, not the other way around.

What was happening to him? When had he lost his edge and started thinking about helping other people? His father would be so ashamed.

Micah needed to reconnect with his ruthless self. The way to do that was to hunt Kisa. So while he left Mertzer with the crew to transport flowers, he would utilize the distraction of the harvest, slip away, locate Kisa, and chop off her tail.

CHAPTER 40
CELEBRATION

Javan threw the last branch on the oversized pile of sticks and leaves in the middle of the flattened humminglo fields and backed away. "Now, Varjiek!"

The dragon whooshed down from the night sky, fire streaming from his mouth. The flames engulfed the debris gathered from the floor of the rain forest and created an instant bonfire designed to celebrate the end of the harvest. The weary warriors from Lower Keckrick cheered at the sight, and Cyr addressed the crowd around the fire once the cheers died down.

"Getting here was not easy. We lost two good men along the way, and many more of you suffered serious injuries. Then we had to work tirelessly for the past two days to harvest these humminglo plants. Yet we have accomplished the impossible by filling our cargo space with more than enough plants to meet King Omri's quota!"

Whistles, claps, and joyous shouts rang through the air. Several people showered Javan with friendly pats on his back, and Javan added a few claps and whistles of his own to the fun. Micah stood further away. In the shadows. Arms crossed. Looking cranky.

He'd been acting strange since arriving on Mertzer the day before. He would disappear for hours at a time, then reappear, and pretend to help bundle the flowers so he could eat whatever Jili had cooked, then he would disappear again. Javan knew Micah had been searching for Kisa and had been tempted to follow Micah rather than stay and help with the harvest.

He only stayed because he knew from experience that Taliya was a good Protector, and he trusted her to keep Kisa safe. Taliya had been disappearing for long spells as well, and Javan hadn't seen her since late that afternoon. Just as Cyr resumed his speech, Javan noticed her walk up on the opposite side of the fire from Micah.

"Our mission is not done," Cyr continued. "We still have to travel through enemy territory to deliver our cargo to the King. Even with the protection of Varjiek, we must remain alert and ready to fight should the need arise. If we don't reach Nahat by Tuesday, we will have no families or homes to return to."

A heavy silence fell over the now somber crowd. Javan could feel the tension, hear the shifting of feet, and see the worry on the faces of his friends. He wanted to promise them all would turn out well and that they had nothing to worry about, but he knew better than to make a promise he wasn't sure he could keep.

"Before we leave in the morning," Cyr said, clearing his throat and speaking in a more upbeat tone, "we get to enjoy tonight. Relax around the fire, fill your bellies with Jili's stew, and dance to Orlan's music!"

Orlan began playing a deep, thumping bass on his small wooden hand drum he brought over to the fields from the boat. Kai, Bree, Andre, and Kloe lined up and danced in a uniform rhythm to the beat while the rest of the crew created a half-circle around them and clapped in tune with the drum.

The dancing didn't seem to interest Taliya, so Javan excused himself from the commotion, picked up two bowls of stew, and took one to Taliya. "Thought you might be hungry."

"Thanks." She gave him a half-smile, took the bowl from him and sat on the ground. She swirled the spoon around the bowl but didn't eat anything.

He ate a bite of his own soup and sat beside her. "You okay?"

"I will be. Just thinking about how much I'm going to miss this. Being around people. I might even miss you."

The firelight made her eyes sparkle, and that made Javan's stomach flip flop.

He suddenly felt too nervous to talk. He forced a spoonful of stew in his mouth, chewed the tiny chunks of meat more than he needed to, and swallowed. That helped him regain his composure enough to speak. "You don't have to stay here. Why don't you come with us?"

"My home is here."

"Your home is in pieces on the ground."

"I can rebuild. And replant. I want to see these humminglo fields come to life again. Just promise me something."

"What?"

"Promise me you'll take good care of Kisa."

Javan shook his head. "No."

"Excuse me?" Taliya clanged her spoon against the bowl. "Why not?"

"I can't take care of a dragon who doesn't belong to me. She's your dragon. You are the one meant to protect her."

"You're wrong. I have never taken any of her scales. She is a free dragon and belongs to no one. My mission has been to protect her only until the Collector with emerald eyes comes for her." Taliya put her bowl down and stared straight into Javan's eyes. "I've been protecting her for you."

Javan gulped. "You have? You're okay with me collecting her?"

"No. I'd rather keep her safe here. But that's just me being selfish. The people of Zandador and all those in the Great Rift need you to collect Kisa." She put her hand on his and squeezed. "You've proven your worth on this trip. I trust you now, and I know she'll be in good hands. I just need to hear you promise to take good care of her."

He squeezed her hand back. "I promise."

"Thank you. Now finish your soup, and call Varjiek. We need to get to Kisa before Micah does."

Javan forgot about the soup and ran around the fire to the spot where he last saw Micah standing. Only Micah was nowhere to be seen.

Panic began to overtake Javan. Was he about to lose another dragon to the Hunter?

◊　◊　◊

Micah abandoned the celebration before he could get any of Jili's soup in his stomach. Now he was going to have to find something to eat on his own. In the dark. And eat it cold. That didn't sound nearly as appealing as a hot bowl of soup filled with tender meat and wild parsnips.

If he had stayed, he would have wanted to dance. If he had danced, he would have felt relaxed, joyful, and content to be part of the group. If he felt those things, he would never be able to carry through with his risky plan.

He traipsed away from the fire and utilized the moonlight to navigate his way around the humminglo stumps to the nest Mertzer had made for himself at the edge of the trees. The white dragon rested peacefully in his temporary home on a soft bed of flowers. He had devoured his dinner a few hours ago and liked to take long naps after his evening feasts.

Tonight the dragon's nap would have to be cut short. Micah only had until dawn to prepare the trap for Kisa, and he needed Mertzer's speedy legs to transport him to the trap's location.

He also needed Javan to follow him. His plan wouldn't work without Javan following him.

CHAPTER 41
HUNTING KISA

"Varjiek?" Javan's voice wavered as he stared at the formidable waterfall the dragon was on track to fly them into. A thick, unforgiving rock wall waited behind the waterfall. "You might want to pull up so you don't kill us."

"Relax." Taliya squeezed Javan's waist a little tighter from her seat behind him. "I think your dragon knows what he is doing."

The lady is right. Varjiek tucked his round wings halfway into his body and skimmed across the water that filled the bottom of the horseshoe canyon where Javan had first spotted Kisa. *Now duck your heads. We are about to get wet.*

"What? No! This isn't a good idea!" The roar of the waterfall smothered Javan's response. Varjiek kept his course, and Javan had no choice but to lean forward, bow his head, and pray for deliverance.

Water pounded the back of his head for three breathless seconds. Then a breeze rushed over his wet skin as Varjiek glided to a stop, and the sounds of the waterfall continued behind him. He opened his eyes and inhaled the surprisingly clean air of the vast, bright cave that splintered off into a handful of wide tunnels.

The ground consisted of hard-packed dirt while the jagged walls around and above them were made of the same reflective rock as the outside of the canyon. As Javan looked around, he could see a hundred images of himself, Taliya, and Varjiek glimmering off the walls and ceiling.

Welcome to Kisa's home. She may spray you with acid if you startle her awake, so let me go find and wake her.

"Okay," Javan said.

"Okay to what?" Taliya's words echoed behind his own.

"Varjiek is going to find Kisa." Javan spoke softly to minimize the echo effect. "He wants us to stay here and wait."

"I want to explore the tunnels with him. I've never actually been in here before."

"We can explore after Kisa's awake." Javan slid down Varjiek's leg and reached his hand up to assist Taliya. "We may end up covered in acid if we startle her."

"I guess you're right." Taliya zoomed down the other side of the dragon, completely ignoring Javan's effort to help her. "I can see why Kisa likes it in here. She can stare at herself from every angle."

Stay put, Varjiek said. *I'll bring Kisa to you. She may want to ask you a few questions before she'll let you ride her.*

Javan swallowed and patted Varjiek's leg with his sweaty palm to let the dragon know he heard him. He was too excited and nervous to speak. The excitement came from the prospect of collecting another dragon. The nervousness arose from being left alone in a cave at midnight with a beautiful woman.

◊　◊　◊

Micah didn't even try to bring Mertzer to the water's edge. The last thing he needed right now was a paralyzed dragon, so he left Mertzer in the woods far enough away from the sights and sounds of the waterfall to keep the dragon from freaking out.

Why Mertzer feared water made no sense to Micah. It also made Micah a little sad because he had no one to share the beauty of this spot with. The walls of the U-shaped canyon drank in the moonlight and seemed to glow in the darkness. The glowing walls allowed him to see a myriad of colorful fish swimming in the clear deep water that filled the floor of the canyon.

The waterfall at the curved end of the canyon, however, proved to be the most striking aspect of the area. The cascading water mesmerized him as he sat under the cover of the trees on the land across from the waterfall, and he caught himself nodding off more than once.

Where was Javan? Why hadn't he even tried to find Kisa? Surely between Varjiek and Taliya, he could figure out that the dragon lived in the cave behind the waterfall. He had figured it out yesterday afternoon without any help. Then again, he was a remarkable Dragon Hunter. He didn't need help finding dragons.

A rough wind rustled the trees, and Micah looked up to see a dragon whoosh down and skim across the water. He heard Javan yell some incomprehensible words just before Varjiek flew them into the waterfall.

"Finally." Micah rose to his feet and brushed the dirt off his pants. "It's about time you started acting like a Collector."

He began his short hike back to Mertzer, confident he wouldn't lose Kisa to the Collector tonight. He wasn't sure where the Dawn Stalker was, but he knew she would not be in her cave. A few well-placed crickets in her home earlier successfully exploited her natural fear of insects, and he doubted she would want to return to that cave anytime soon. Maybe not ever.

She would want to eat in the morning, and Micah knew where to find her feeding grounds. If Javan had any sense at all, he would also be waiting for Kisa there come dawn.

Micah's trap would be ready for them both. If he worked efficiently enough, he might even have enough time to get a little sleep between now and then.

The lure of sleep caused him to pick up his pace. How things turned out in the morning would determine his future, and being well-rested would help ensure victory.

◊ ◊ ◊

Taliya wandered around the main room of the cave, tracing her fingers along the wall as she walked with her head down and shoulders drooped. She wiped her eyes a couple of times, and Javan wasn't sure what he was going to do if she started crying in front of him.

"So...ummm...uhhh..." He tried to coax himself to speak, but no intelligent words came out of his mouth. Why had he lost the ability to talk?

"Maybe when Kisa's gone, I can make this my home." Taliya sniffled through the words, and Javan just let her talk. If she was talking, she wouldn't be crying. "It's cool and dry. It'll keep me safe from storms and wild animals. Plus it won't rip apart if another wall of white winds blows through here."

"Yeah." *Clever response, Javan.* He rolled his eyes as he chided himself. *She's gonna think you're super smart and compassionate now.*

"Unless you're a dragon who can teleport or fly," Taliya continued, paying no attention to Javan, "this cave isn't the easiest place to get in and out of. That could be a problem."

Javan wanted to tell her to stop moping and just agree to return to Zandador with him, but she had already turned down that offer. He didn't want to be rejected again. So he strode over to the entrance of the middle tunnel that Varjiek had taken and changed the subject. "How big is this cave? Surely Varjiek should have been able to find Kisa by now."

"That's what you're thinking about?" She marched across the room and turned her misty blue eyes on him. "Haven't you heard anything I've said?"

Trouble. He sensed trouble. He didn't know how to talk his way out of girl trouble! "Umm. Well. I just thought--"

"What? What did you think?"

"Varjiek is lost. I need to go find him."

I am not lost. Heavy dragon steps reverberated through the cave as Varjiek poked his head through the tunnel left of where Javan and Taliya stood. *Why is the girl crying?*

Javan shrugged his shoulders. "I don't know."

"What don't you know? What is Varjiek saying?" She lost the tear-stained edge to her voice and sprinted to the front of Varjiek's tunnel. While trying to look down the tunnel past Varjiek, she continued. "Did he find Kisa? I don't see her. Is she okay?"

"Calm down. If you give me a minute to talk to my dragon, I'll let you know what I find out."

She huffed. Crossed her arms. Bit her bottom lip. And finally walked away.

I was only gone for a few minutes, Varjiek said. *What did you do to upset her?*

"Nothing." At least he didn't think he did anything wrong. He would do a mental replay later to uncover any potential mistakes. At the moment, he wanted to focus on Kisa rather than Taliya. "Where's Kisa? She change her mind about talking to me?"

I am uncertain how to answer those questions.

"Why are you uncertain?"

I was unable to locate Kisa. All I found were crickets.

"Crickets?"

"Oh, no." Taliya returned to Javan's side. "If crickets found their way in here, Kisa won't be back anytime soon. She's terrified of insects."

"Great. How are we supposed to find her?"

"We wait until morning. She loves dragon fruit and always makes that part of her meal. I can take you to her feeding grounds before dawn."

It's a good plan, Varjiek said. *Trying to find her in the dark would be a waste of energy.*

"What about Micah? If he gets to her first..."

"He doesn't know where she is, either," Taliya said. "He's also still weak from his injuries and is going to need to sleep tonight. He'll probably try to capture her at dawn. He knows where her feeding grounds are located."

Javan clenched his jaw and looked back and forth between Taliya and Varjiek. "Then we better make sure we beat him there."

CHAPTER 42
DAWN

Micah wanted to stretch. Loosen up. Walk around. Yet he didn't dare move from his perch under a tree halfway up a hill overlooking Kisa's feeding grounds. The dragon was already overdue, and he needed to remain perfectly still until she showed up to keep from spooking her in any way. That was also why he had ordered Mertzer to stay away.

The faint light of the predawn sun exposed the cluster of dragon fruit trees at the bottom of the hill a few miles west of the canyon. None of the trees with their thick trunks, curvy branches, and long, skinny leaves grew higher than ten feet tall, and that had made it easy to dust them all with the debilitating powder while riding atop Mertzer through the trees earlier that morning.

The fruit itself dangled from every branch in the form of blue buds, tiny green dots, or fully ripe yellow balls the size of his head. The ripe fruit hung from the branches by jagged red leaves that looked like flames shooting toward the sky. The leathery exterior was too tough for a human to peel or bite into, but dragons had no problem ripping the fruit open and devouring the juicy contents.

Micah hoped he had used enough of the powder to keep the Dawn Stalker from teleporting but not so much as to damage her organs. He would find out soon enough. A sudden flurry of birds flying away from the middle of the trees signaled the dragon's appearance. Not all of them got away.

Micah silently made his way toward her as she chewed a mouthful of birds. The row of spiked scales down her back had turned a dark red, her stomach burned a pinkish color, and more than half of the white scales along her legs and sides had changed to streaks of purple and orange.

This dragon was hungry. He drew his sword and paused about twenty feet away from her, not willing to get any closer until she took a big whiff of the powder he had left for her. He also wanted to lure Javan out of hiding. Although Micah hadn't seen Javan, he was certain the Collector was around and about to make a daring attempt to collect Kisa.

At least he better be around and try to collect Kisa. Micah's plan depended on it.

◊   ◊   ◊

"There she is." Taliya's whisper barely registered in Javan's sleepy state, but her tap on his shoulder caused him to look in the direction she pointed. "Isn't she beautiful?"

Javan shook his sleepiness away and focused on the orange and purple-streaked dragon standing among the trees. They were close enough to her to hear the bones of the birds she crunched in her mouth. The sound made Javan cringe and reminded him to proceed with caution, especially since Varjiek wasn't around. Javan had tasked his dragon with making sure Mertzer didn't interfere with the Kisa collection process.

Nevertheless, not knowing where Micah and Mertzer were made Javan nervous. Keeping his voice low, he asked, "Do you see Micah anywhere?"

"No. That doesn't mean he's not here, though."

"Right." Javan checked his black and gold sword. Varjiek's scale was in place, so as long as he kept a hold of the handle and Taliya stayed in contact with him, they would remain invisible. Once he made his move toward Kisa, however, Taliya would be exposed.

Still hungry. The dragon swallowed her snack, sat up on her back legs, and plucked a yellow ball off a tree with her front claws. *Now for my real meal.*

Kisa brought the ball up to her mouth and opened her jaws. She lingered before biting into it. Cocked her head. Turned the fruit over and over in her claws. Then sniffed it. *What is that smell?*

She tossed the fruit away, plucked another one, smelled it, and tossed it away.

"What is she doing?" Taliya asked.

"She's confused about the smell of the fruit."

"Dragon fruit doesn't have an aroma."

"Apparently it does today." Javan picked a yellow ball hanging in front of him and took a whiff. It reminded him of breakfast on Christmas morning when the whole house smelled like cinnamon rolls. "Smells sweet. And spicy. Like cinnamon."

"Cinnamon?" Taliya snatched the fruit and put it up to her nose. "Micah must have found my cinnamon trees. This is bad."

"What is bad about cinnamon?"

"It will mess with her mental synapses. She won't be able to teleport for several minutes, longer if she eats the fruit. You have to go ride her. Now!"

Taliya pushed Javan toward the dragon whose thoughts had become too jumbled to make sense of. Reasoning with her wasn't going to be an option. How was he supposed to collect her if he wasn't an invited rider?

When he stumbled to a stop under her upraised front legs a second later, he realized he wouldn't have time to talk to her anyway. Because Micah was standing at the other end of her body. In front of her back leg. Beside her tail. With his sword raised.

Javan had one shot to save Kisa. If he missed, he would lose the dragon forever. So he better not miss.

He pulled a stun ball off his belt and fired it at Micah.

CHAPTER 43
STUNNED

Could it really be this easy?

Micah lifted his sword over Kisa's tail and smiled. All those hours of peeling the cinnamon bark, drying it out, crushing it, and sprinkling it on the dragon fruit trees proved to be a brilliant plan and well worth the effort. Rather than recognize the smell as harmful, Kisa just kept inhaling more and more of the powder. She didn't even notice when he walked right up to her tail.

Nor did Micah have to contend with Javan. A battle with the Collector would have been the ideal scenario, but he could make this alternative work. One slice of this disoriented dragon's tail, and he would be halfway to fulfilling his dragon-hunting mission.

So why was he hesitating when he should be slicing through those red and orange and purple scales? He had a job to do and had to stop allowing his conscience to get in the way of taking action. "Now, Micah. Just do it."

He began to bring his sword down, but a familiar whirring noise followed by a prick in his side instantly paralyzed him.

Stun ball. Javan. Defeat.

Excellent. Now he could follow through with his original plan.

Javan didn't sheath his sword until the stun ball lodged securely in Micah's side. Then he wasted no time by running past Micah onto Kisa's tail and past her hind legs. She must not have liked the feel of his human footsteps on her scaly body, because she roared, stood straight up on her back legs, and flopped her tail.

He latched onto her red spikes with both hands, kept his feet firmly planted on either side of the spikes, and began climbing straight up. "Settle down, girl," he yelled as he climbed. "If you don't let me ride you, he's gonna cut off your tail!"

Cave. Home. Waterfall. Beach. Mushrooms. Flowers. Lake. Ahhh! Still here. Strange smells. So hungry. Can't move. What's on me? Must get it off!

205

She twisted her body back and forth, and Javan lost his grip with his right hand halfway to the base of her neck.

"I'm a Collector. Your friend. I can help you." Javan fought to get his right hand back in place.

"Let him help you, Kisa." Taliya's voice stilled the dragon. "Just put your legs down and walk away from these trees as fast as you can."

Taliya? Sweet Taliya. What is happening?

"I'll explain everything to you," Javan said. He took advantage of the stillness and scurried upwards. As he nestled into a smooth spot at the dragon's neck, he continued. "Right now you have to get away from these trees and Micah. Go!"

"Listen to him. Get out of here."

Yes, Taliya. Kisa dropped her front legs and staggered on all fours out of the cluster of cinnamon-covered dragon fruit trees. She trampled several bushes and zigzagged her way toward a lake.

"Why don't you stop here, take some deep breaths, and see if that helps clear your head?"

Water. Thirsty. Hungry. Hot. Swim.

"Swim? No. No swim!" But she wasn't paying attention to him. She dashed across the field and charged into the lake.

Javan managed a deep breath before being submerged in the water. He wanted to bail but couldn't. He had to stay on the dragon until they forged a bond. He just wasn't sure he had enough air in his lungs to make that happen.

◊ ◊ ◊

Kisa's tail whacked Micah's tender ribs and sent his immovable body to the ground. Unfortunately, the fall did not loosen the stun ball from his side, so he had to listen helplessly from the grass floor as Taliya and Javan convinced Kisa to let Javan ride her.

Micah felt relieved when the dragon finally sauntered away. Her back leg had come close to crushing his head several times. Being stomped to death by a dragon would have been a humiliating death for a Dragon Hunter.

"I'm not sure I should let you get up." Taliya pried his sword from his hands and pointed the tip at his throat. He stared at her through unblinking eyes, wondering if she had it in her to finish him off. He hoped not. Death by his own sword wielded by a woman Protector was a far more humiliating end than being stomped to death by a dragon.

"You had time to cut off Kisa's tail," she said, "but you didn't. It's almost as if you were waiting for Javan to come collect her. I don't know if that makes you a good guy or if that means you have a far more devious plot in place."

The whirring stopped. The stun ball released, restoring Micah's ability to move. He didn't. He simply blinked and kept his eyes on Taliya.

"Remember what you've seen here in Keckrick. The famine. The fighting. The destruction. Your father is an oppressive king who needs to be stopped. I think you know that. I think that's why you hesitated when you had a chance to cut off Kisa's tail."

Is that why he hesitated? Did he think Javan would make a better leader than Omri? What kind of son did that make him? How could he live with himself if he turned against his own father? He wouldn't have to live long because Omri didn't allow traitors to live.

"I see the good in you, but I'm not sure you see it in yourself. So you and I are going to travel to Nahat together. I'm going to make sure you go through that portal and plead with your father on behalf of the people of Keckrick." She leaned a little closer, making sure the point of his sword touched his skin. "And if you so much as look at Javan or his dragons the wrong way, I will make you wish Javan had left you to die in the clutches of that sea monster."

Taliya dropped the sword by his head and walked away. He closed his eyes and let his tense body rest.

He did have a wish at the moment. He wished he was the good guy she thought him to be. But he was Omri's son. His fate was sealed. He had to stay true to his father.

CHAPTER 44
A BUMPY RIDE

Kisa swam effortlessly through the water. Twirling. Gliding. Spinning. Eating whatever fish crossed her watery path.

Javan's ride was not as effortless. He clung to the dragon's neck with his legs and arms. He kept his eyes wide open and his mouth firmly shut. His nose burned. His ears popped. His chest hurt. But he wasn't going to let go of the dragon.

Surely she would need air soon. He would tough it out until she resurfaced. At least that's what he thought until he saw the school of silver piranhas wider than the length of Kisa's body baring their teeth and headed their way.

Javan kicked the dragon.

The fish swam closer.

Javan kicked some more.

Kisa turned her head.

Sharp fish teeth dug into Javan's left calf.

He grimaced. Air escaped from his lungs. Water filled them.

Another fish dug into his shoulder.

He screamed. This time air filled his lungs. From inside Kisa's cave. She could teleport again!

Javan gulped in the air as he ripped the tenacious fish off his shoulder and leg. Pain from his torn flesh made it difficult to maintain his position on the dragon. He needed to find a way to patch his wounds, but he didn't have time. Because she teleported again.

To a flowery meadow. Javan could hear water trickling over rocks in the distance. "Where are we? This looks like...Zandador?"

Kisa didn't linger long enough to answer him. She just popped to the waterfall at the end of the river where the Iria was docked. Javan had enough time to wave at his friends aboard the boat before Kisa transported them to the beach, a field of giant mushrooms, the mowed humminglo fields, and onto the rock in the middle of her canyon.

Javan felt woozy from the series of jumps. Teleportation wasn't as cool as he expected. He wanted off this ride.

I have never had a human sit on me before.

Javan noticed Kisa staring at their reflection in the clear water. He leaned to the side and let her see his face. He had to keep her in one place long enough to calm his queasy stomach. "I've never been to that many places that fast before."

Me, either. I felt out of control. Now I feel... She cocked her head to the side and met the reflection of Javan's eyes. *Safe.*

"Good." He held her stare, smiled, and nodded. His queasiness gave way to a sense of ownership and belonging.

I also find myself wanting to serve and protect you, but I am not sure why. I am not old and wise like Varjiek. I am a young dragon who knows not much about Zandador or fighting or people.

"I am a young Collector who knows even less. How about we figure things out together?"

I can agree to that, but you must do one thing for me. Kisa spun her head around so that she was looking directly in Javan's eyes. *You must bring Taliya with us.*

"I already asked her to come with me. She refused."

Ask her again.

"What if she still says no?"

Ask until she says yes. Kisa turned her head away from Javan and stiffened her neck. *Despite this bond I now feel with you, I will not leave this place without her.*

Great. How was he supposed to get Taliya to change her mind? That seemed like a more difficult task than fending off that entire school of piranhas with his bare hands!

CHAPTER 45
CLEAR THE WAY

Micah had the power to resist. One swift move would eliminate Taliya and have him riding back to the Land of Zandador on the fast feet of Mertzer. He chose to keep his power in check, however, and utilize Mertzer's speed to get him and Taliya back to the Iria. He wanted to play the part of the good guy long enough to get the humminglo flowers to his father.

What of Javan? Had he managed to stay on Kisa and form that collector's bond with her? And why did Taliya help Javan ride her? Wasn't she supposed to protect the dragon from both Collectors and Hunters?

As Mertzer sped through the trees and bushes of the rain forest, Micah decided to keep his questions about Taliya to himself. The more he understood her, the tougher it would be to turn against her.

The sun had yet to peek above the horizon by the time they reached the docked Iria. "Whew!" Taliya exclaimed, letting go of Micah's waist. "I'm not sure which is more fun: flying on a dragon or riding on a speeding one."

Micah's chest puffed with pride. "Mertzer may not have wings, but he does feel like he flies over the ground."

"That gives me an idea." She slid off Mertzer and waved him down. "Come on. We need to talk to Cyr."

"About what?"

"Just come." She put her hand on her sling. "Don't make me shoot you."

"Fine." Micah lifted his hands as if in surrender, ordered Mertzer to stay where he stood, and dismounted the dragon. A few minutes later, he and Taliya were in the wheelhouse with Cyr, Andre, and Lydia. Hands tied. At knifepoint.

"What have you two and Javan been up to?" Lydia glared up her sword at him, and he hated feeling so vulnerable. "None of you came back to the boat last night, and a few minutes ago, Javan popped in and out of here on a Dawn Stalker!"

"She regained her ability to teleport, and Javan was still riding her." Taliya sounded relieved. "Good."

"Good?" Cyr stepped in front of Taliya. "You knew we had a wild dragon lurking near us this whole time?"

"Yes. Her name is Kisa, and I made sure she posed no threat to your people. But she's not wild anymore." A hint of resignation laced Taliya's words. "She's now part of Javan's collection."

"Javan has gained another dragon?" Now Andre spoke up. "That makes him twice as powerful as he was before. Do you think he will still return and assist us on our journey to Nahat?"

"Yes," Taliya said. "He is a man of his word. I am sure he will use both of his dragons to see you safely to Nahat. In the meantime, Micah and I will ride ahead on Mertzer to clear the way by telling the villages of our plans to save Keckrick."

"Hold on," Micah said, turning to Taliya. He didn't like being blindsided by her scheme. "We're going to do what?"

"The people of Upper Keckrick need to know what's happening," Taliya said. "Your dragon is fast enough to get us from village to village to explain what's going on and still make it to Nahat ahead of the Iria. They'll listen to me and believe what I'm saying when they see you with me."

"It would be beneficial to make peace with the locals," Cyr said. "I would prefer to not fight our way into Nahat."

Lydia lowered her sword. "It is a good plan."

"So untie me." Micah found himself wanting to help and be the hero who prevented bloodshed. Plus it would give him more time to heal physically before having to take Javan out of the game for good. "The sooner we leave, the better chance we have of success."

◊　◊　◊

"Where are they?" Javan picked up the stun ball that had briefly paralyzed Micah and looked around the grove of dragon fruit trees Kisa had brought them back to. But he saw no signs of Taliya or Micah.

Was Taliya safe? He knew he shouldn't have left her here alone with Micah. If something happened to her, he would never forgive himself.

Javan sprinted back through the trees to the spot where Kisa was pacing, being sure to keep a safe distance away from the smell of cinnamon. Most of her scales had turned colors by now, and he could see the hunger in her eyes.

You are still alone. Where is Taliya?

"She's not here," he said, trying to gauge whether or not Kisa considered him food. "Maybe she went back to the boat. Take me to the Iria, then go eat."

Kisa nodded and bent her front legs so Javan could easily climb aboard. He used her front leg as a step and stretched to reach the spike at the base of her neck. Before he could pull himself up and swing his leg over her side, he found himself on the shore downstream of the Iria. "That was quick."

I will eat you even quicker if you do not get off and allow me to hunt.

"Right." Javan let go of the spike and slid to the ground. "Return here when you are full. We'll then begin our trip to Nahat."

Just make sure Taliya comes as well. With that, Kisa disappeared.

"No pressure there," Javan said. "I don't even know where she is."

I do. Varjiek uncloaked himself from his position in the air above Javan and landed in Javan's path.

"Varjiek!" Javan smiled and hugged the dragon's muscular front right leg. "I just had the most amazing morning!" He stepped back so he could see the dragon's face. "I hung on to Kisa as she teleported from place to place, and we bonded. She's part of my collection now. I guess that kind of makes her your little sister."

Hmmm. Perhaps. Does that mean I can order her around?

"That is a big brother's job."

Good.

"She won't come with us unless Taliya does, though. You said you know where Taliya is?"

She is on her way to Nahat.

"She can't be gone." Javan pointed at the boat. The movement made the fresh wound in his shoulder open up again. Irritated by the trickle of blood, he cut a piece of cloth off the bottom of his shirt and held it over the cut. "The Iria is still here."

She is not traveling by boat.

"Then how is she getting there?"

On Mertzer.

"You mean she's with Micah?" Javan felt betrayed, only this was worse than when Gesha turned against him to reveal the location of Gri to Omri. This betrayal cut too deep to describe.

They're using Mertzer's speed to reach the villages between here and Nahat. Taliya believes she can get her people to unite with those from Lower Keckrick and clear a safe path for the Iria.

Hope crept back into Javan's heart. "You sure that's why she went?"

I am sure.

"But you can get from village to village faster by flying. Why didn't she ask me and you to take her?"

She knew we need to remain with the Iria to ensure its safety.

"Then you stay with the boat." He had to find a way to get to her. Fast. He had to know if she was on his side or Micah's. "I'll take Kisa and catch up with them."

Kisa will never be able to match Mertzer's speed.

"So we'll leave Kisa with the boat, and you'll take me." Javan threw the bloody piece of cloth on the ground. "Taliya could be in danger. I can't let her be alone with Micah."

Taliya is a strong woman and a loyal friend. Varjiek nudged Javan with his nose. *She surrendered the dragon she protected into your care. She would not betray you. Trust her. Let her trust us to get these humminglo flowers to Nahat.*

Javan grasped the wisdom of the dragon's words. He knew he needed to put his personal feelings aside and do what was best for the greatest amount of people. He knew it was the right choice, but it certainly wasn't the easy one.

"Fine," Javan said. "Let's get the Iria to Nahat." He just hoped Taliya would be waiting for him there and that she would be impressed by his decision to stick with the Iria rather than come after her.

CHAPTER 46
JOINING FORCES

"No." The word sounded rougher than Micah intended, but at this point he didn't care. Covering more than a thousand miles in two days over rough terrain in brutal humidity on the back of a dragon had his shirt glued to his cuts with sweat and his broken ribs radiating pain throughout his body.

While the intermittent stop at the villages along the way had served to ease the physical distress, having to play nice with the hostile people such as the tall, striking chief with broad shoulders and a neatly trimmed beard standing before him at the end of the second day of travel ate at his conscience and had zapped him of all ability to cooperate.

Micah folded his arms over his sore chest and squinted into the setting sun while facing Taliya and Anley, the chief. "Mertzer goes with me." He hadn't been racing toward Nahat in such a painful manner only to leave his dragon behind at the last minute.

Anley mirrored Micah's folded arms and responded in a deep, deliberate tone. "We must leave now if we are to join with the Iria and prevent bloodshed at the gates of Nahat."

"Micah," Taliya said, "we have to get you to the portal by tomorrow, and the river stands between us and Nahat. Mertzer is too terrified of water to swim across, and there is no other way to get him to the other side. You can come back for him after you talk to your father. Right now we have to get on Anley's boat, intercept the Iria, and take the river the rest of the way to Nahat."

"I want to get to the portal more than anyone here," Micah said, "but I cannot return to Zandador without Mertzer. My father would assume the people of Keckrick captured the dragon and will have the entire region destroyed as punishment."

"So tell him the truth," Taliya said.

"My father is not always interested in the truth of a situation." Micah looked beyond Taliya and studied the blue-streaked dragon lurking in the trees just west of the village. Soon streaks of green, purple, and pink would emerge. Micah needed to let the dragon hunt, but first he had to find a way to get Mertzer to Nahat. "Does the river become more narrow between here and Nahat?"

"No." Anley shook his head. "It becomes wider after the split."

"What split?"

"About ten miles from here, the Ishom River which flows east forks off into the Aron River, which flows southeast and takes us through Nahat."

"Yeah," Taliya said, "but the Ishom takes a slight turn north and becomes much more narrow as it flows through the hills north of Nahat."

"Narrow enough for a dragon to jump over?"

"Yes." Taliya smiled. "Yes. I believe Mertzer could make such a jump. Then it is not far from there to the northwestern gates of the city."

"The northwestern gates?" Anley's brown face crinkled into disdain. "No one uses the northwestern gates anymore."

"Why not?" Curiosity made Micah forget about the sweat dripping down his face.

"They were permanently sealed after the destruction of the city. No one has used them or even been to that section of Nahat in centuries. You will not be able to enter the city from there."

"Maybe people can't," Micah said, relishing the challenge, "but have you ever seen the damage the poison from a Dusk Stalker can do to iron?"

◊   ◊   ◊

"It's dark," Javan said, urging Kisa forward along the riverbank. Clouds covered the moon and stars, making the early hours of the night seem more like the darkest hours of the morning. "You can't even see it."

Yes, but I can feel it. She slowed her steady pace and drew to a stop. *I need to wash off before continuing.*

"Kisa, you've taken like twenty baths in the last two days. Letting a speck or two of dirt stick to your scales is not going to hurt you." Javan tried to keep the irritation out of his voice. He liked the adventurous, upbeat attitude of the dragon, but he didn't much care for her obsession to keep herself clean. "Forget the bath and keep going. We need to catch up with the Iria."

Kisa huffed, stuck her nose in the air, and plodded onward. She made a show of swishing her tail and shaking her body in an effort to rid herself of whatever dirt she believed was currently defiling her pristine white scales. It made for an uncomfortable ride, and Javan was about to give in and let her go for a swim when she calmed herself and crouched as low to the ground as she could get. *I hear Taliya.*

Javan tuned his ears to the sounds around him. He could make out the flowing water of the river two steps to his right, the rustling of leaves from the woods to his left, and random howls, chirps, and slithers of unseen animals all around him. But no Taliya. "Are you sure? I don't hear anything except the sounds of the rain forest."

I am certain. It is the whistle she wears around her neck meant for my ears only.

"Ah." Why hadn't she blown that whistle a few nights ago when they couldn't find Kisa in her cave? "Follow the sound. Take us to her."

Kisa spent the next few minutes weaving through trees and over roots and around rocks. She kept her ears attuned to the noise Javan couldn't hear until he ordered her to stop as they rounded a bend in the river. "Whoa. Hold up here."

Up ahead, boats of varying sizes spanned the width of the river. Torches burned brightly from the bow of each boat, and people milled about on the decks as if waiting for something.

"It's about time you got here." Taliya stepped out of the darkness and positioned herself in front of the dragon. "I thought I was going to have to blow this whistle all night."

"Hello to you, too." Javan could only make out her shadow, so he slid off Kisa in order to meet her face to face on the ground. "And you could have blown that whistle the other night in the cave to bring Kisa to us. Why didn't you?"

"She was still mine to protect at that point. You needed to go to her; I couldn't bring her to you."

"I guess that makes sense," Javan said, accepting Taliya's explanation.

Tell her she has to come with us to Zandador, Kisa said.

Javan ignored Kisa and nodded toward the water. "What's going on? This looks like a blockade. Are the people not going to allow the Iria through?"

"Now that would mean I failed in my mission to unite Upper and Lower Keckrick." She let go of the whistle, patted his chest, and winked at him. "I'm too lovable to fail in such a mission."

Javan relaxed a little, but he still had some unanswered questions. "Where's your best bud Micah? And what's with all the torches?"

"Micah is *not* my best bud, but he did get us from village to village and do a good job of convincing the people he is on their side. Right now he's on his way to Nahat. He had to take a different route because Mertzer doesn't deal well with water."

"That's an understatement." Javan recalled the way Mertzer froze on the beach the night Javan attempted to collect him. Had the dragon not been so scared of the water, Javan would have been able to ride away on him before Micah arrived and cut off his tail. "But what about the blockade?"

"It was the only way we could think of to stop the Iria, and we lit the torches to make sure the Iria could see us since we can't see her."

"Why not just clear the boats out of the water and allow the Iria to sail smoothly all the way to Nahat?"

"The gatekeepers are more likely to let her through if she has a local escort. That's why we're here. To escort the Iria to Nahat." She wrapped her arm around his elbow and led him to the edge of the water. "It's hard to escort a boat we can't see, and I have a hunch the Iria is already here. The boat may be invisible, but that doesn't mean she's quiet. Can you have Varjiek uncloak the Iria?"

What if this was a trap? What if she only wanted the boat uncloaked so her people could attack the crew and steal the humminglos for themselves? "I don't think that's such a good idea."

"I'm on your side, Javan. I promise."

Javan's gut told him to take a chance and believe her, but his experience with Gesha told him women couldn't be trusted and that he needed to run far, far away.

You can trust her, Kisa said. *I always have.*

Javan had to make a decision. He wasn't sure he should trust Taliya, but he was sure he didn't want to live in fear of trusting his gut.

He uncurled her arm from his, took a few steps downstream of the blockade, and addressed a dragon he couldn't see. "Varjiek! Varjiek, if you can hear me, uncloak yourself and the boat!"

CHAPTER 47
SLITHERING GUARDS

Reaching the hilly terrain hadn't been a problem. Finding a place for Mertzer to leap over the river on a moonless night proved to be the challenge. So Micah decided to hunker down for the night on a soft patch of knee-high grass between two hills. The valley was just the right size for Mertzer to nestle into, which pleased Micah. The dragon deserved a cozy place to sleep after all the running he had done over the past few days.

Micah, on the other hand, found himself too troubled to sleep. He would have to face his father in the morning to ask him a favor, despite having gained no additional dragons on Omri's behalf. That alone would put him on his father's bad side and could prevent Omri from even talking to him.

If Micah could get Omri to listen to his plan, though, he would be able to save Keckrick. He would also eliminate Javan in the process. That should make him feel powerful and happy, but for some reason, the idea of killing Javan made Micah feel nothing but guilt and dread.

Morning came way too soon for Micah's liking. He rubbed his bloodshot eyes and hiked up the nearest hill. Reaching the crest brought with it a view of desolate rolling hills as far as the eye could see.

Grass filled the valleys that river didn't wind through, but the hills themselves were covered with the rotting stalks of harvested humminglo plants. The sad sight hurt his eyes and overwhelmed him with the sense that he was standing in a mass graveyard. It wasn't so much the death of the flowers that concerned him; it was the death of all those who had lost their lives because of the flowers that made him shudder.

When had he become so sensitive? This attitude was unbecoming and would never do in the presence of Omri. Micah shook it out of his system, marched himself down the hill, and mounted the sleeping Mertzer. "Mertzer, wake up." He kicked the dragon as hard as he could. "Time to move."

Mertzer roared to life, sprung to his feet, and littered the ground with a stream of poison.

"Okay. Maybe that wasn't the best way to wake you up." He patted Mertzer's neck as his way of apologizing and climbed on the dragon. "But we do need to get going. I think I spotted a good place to cross the river not too far from here."

Mertzer snorted, stretched, and began trotting through the valley that paralleled the river. After they passed the fifth hill, Micah nudged Mertzer up the next one. "Yup," Micah said, looking down at the river from the top of the hill. The water took a sharp turn through the hills and appeared to be barely wide enough to fit two canoes through. "You can make that jump. You'll be able to build up plenty of momentum running down this hill. Just keep going when you get to the bottom and leap over the gap. From there, it's a straight shot to Nahat and back home to Zandador."

The dragon bristled at Micah's final words, and Micah could feel a chill run through Mertzer. Micah could tell the dragon didn't want to cooperate, so he reached for his whip that hung from his belt.

Before he unhooked the whip, he remembered what Javan said about dragons having thoughts and feelings. Maybe beating them into submission wasn't the best way to get them to take action.

"Don't worry, boy," Micah said, abandoning the whip and stroking his neck instead. "I'll make sure you're treated well." He leaned forward, wrapped his arms around Mertzer's neck, and slammed his heels against the dragon's scales. "Now get me to Nahat!"

Mertzer jumped into motion and flew down the hill toward his biggest fear. Micah fully expected Mertzer to stop short of the water. He had shown the dragon a touch of kindness, and that kindness was certain to be repaid with rebellion.

But instead of slowing down near the bottom of the hill, Mertzer sped up, transferred all his energy into his hind legs, and leapt over the river. He cleared the water by a body length and kept right on running as if solid ground had been under his legs the whole time.

Pride in his dragon for dealing with his fear surged through Micah and propelled him all the way to the gates of Nahat.

◊ ◊ ◊

It feels so good to be off that boat and back in the air! Varjiek coasted through the early morning sky with his wings wide, head high, and tail wagging behind him. *I'm glad your girl showed up last night and freed me from having to keep the boat cloaked.*

"Correction," Javan said, making sure to hang on tight in case the dragon decided to start flying in loops. "Taliya is not my girl. If she was, she wouldn't have chosen to ride on the lead boat with that guy named Anley."

Is that why you're so grumpy? You're mad she didn't come back to the Iria?

"I'm not grumpy or mad." The moment the words came out of his mouth, Javan knew they weren't true. "Okay. Maybe I am. Just a little. But that's because I promised Kisa I would convince Taliya to return to Zandador with us. I can't convince her of anything if she won't let me talk to her."

She will if you save her people.

"That's out of my control. If Micah doesn't come through--"

Then we will fight.

"I don't know anything about fighting a war."

All you have to do is sit on my back and yell. Varjiek let loose a long streak of fire that burned the clouds above them. *I will take care of the fighting.*

"Hopefully no one will have to face your fire-breathing wrath." Javan smiled and tapped Varjiek's shoulder. "Now that you've had a chance to spread your wings and breathe a little smoke, let's get back to the boat. We have to make sure those humminglo plants get safely to the portal today, or Micah will have nothing to negotiate with."

As they banked back toward the Iria, Javan's thoughts turned to Micah. Would he follow through with the plan, or was he too bitter over the loss of Kisa to do anything to save the people of Keckrick?

◊　　◊　　◊

Once the humminglo fields gave way to the grass as high as Mertzer's legs, Micah had been able to spot the walls of Nahat in the distance. Fortunately the grass didn't slow Mertzer down, and Micah had found himself in front of the gates to the city within an hour of having woken that morning.

Taliya had explained that the city was shaped like a large, wide J, and that Micah would be entering in the top left corner of the J. The portal, however, was located in the middle of the hook along the river in the lower part of the city. So once inside, he would still have a bit of a journey ahead of him.

Vines covered the iron gates and surrounding stone walls that stood three times higher than Mertzer's head. Countless numbers of snakes slithered in and out of the vines, making him feel helpless and terrified. Micah could feel their eyes on him and could hear their hissing grow louder and louder.

He knew he should tell Mertzer to blast them with his poison, but he wasn't sure he wanted to enter the city they seemed to be guarding. What if they had taken over the abandoned buildings and tried to squeeze the life out of him the way that sea monster had done?

Reliving that scene rendered him breathless and unable to speak. Mertzer shifted back and forth, awaiting orders. Micah wanted to tell him to run away, but he couldn't form the words.

More snakes gathered below them on the ground.

The hissing became so loud it hurt Micah's ears.

Then a long red snake with golden specks bared his fangs and flung itself off the top of the gate straight at Micah's head. Micah reached for his sword, but he didn't need it. Mertzer snatched the snake in mid-air with his jaws and tossed it to the side. Without pausing to get permission, the dragon stomped the legless creatures on the ground while smothering the gates with his poison from top to bottom.

The snakes that could scurried away. Those touched by the poison wouldn't be scurrying anywhere ever again.

After a moment or two of silence, Mertzer kicked the gates and backed up as the iron crumbled to the ground. He tilted his head to look at Micah, and Micah nodded to urge him forward.

From now on, Micah would let the dragon take control during life-threatening situations. He had earned that right. More importantly, he had earned Micah's respect.

CHAPTER 48
NAHAT

Two steps inside the city walls made Micah realize he had been foolish to fear snakes living in this place. Nothing lived here other than the occasional weed or daring shrub that was brave enough to poke through the hollow houses and blackened buildings.

How long had it been since someone strolled down these pebbled streets? Had it always smelled of loneliness and death? Or had it once been as vibrant as the villages he and Taliya had visited on the way here?

Micah recalled the faces of the people he had met along the way. They looked up to him with admiration and respect rather than fear and disdain like the people of Zandador who knew him well. But the people here in Keckrick didn't know him. They thought he was a good guy. They believed he could and would help them.

He knew that if he didn't interfere, his father would turn all the villages Micah had visited into death towns like this one. For what? Flowers? He couldn't let that happen.

Standing up to his father wouldn't be easy, but it was necessary. People's lives depended on it. "Okay, Mertzer. I've seen enough. Speed it up, and head south. We have to get to that portal as soon as possible."

That's all the nudging the dragon needed. In the next instant, the abandoned buildings became nothing more than a blur as Mertzer raced down the empty streets.

◊   ◊   ◊

"Are we there yet?" Sounding like an impatient kid on a long road trip, Javan slumped against the railing of the top deck of the Iria. They had clearly not arrived at their destination, but with the morning half gone and no Nahat in sight, he felt compelled to ask the question anyway.

"Shouldn't be too much longer," Lydia said, pacing behind him.

"Better not be." Orlan stood on Javan's right and casually sharpened the tip of his spear. "I'm ready to get off this boat and back home to my family."

"I'm ready to be free of these folks from Upper Keckrick," Lydia said. "They claim to be 'escorting' us, but I believe they will attack the first chance they get."

"I'm not so sure." Javan couldn't argue that the dozens of boats in front of and behind them did provide a sense of captivity, but he also wanted to give Taliya an opportunity to prove herself trustworthy. "They had a chance to attack about an hour ago when Varjiek flew away to find food."

"Perhaps." Lydia strolled to Javan's left and surveyed the boats in the water ahead of them. "We'll find out their true intentions soon enough. Look. The city is coming into view."

Javan looked beyond the boats and observed two towering gates with wavy bars of iron blocking the passage through the water into the city. A stone arch with the city name of Nahat engraved into it stretched over the gates and rested on top of the intimidating rock walls that surrounded the city.

Warriors armed with bows and arrows also stood guard atop the walls, prompting Javan to check the sky for Varjiek and the land for Kisa. He couldn't spot either dragon, although he didn't really expect to see them. Kisa liked to sleep after eating her morning meal. He had thus instructed her to get her rest, then follow the river, find a good hiding spot outside the city gates, and wait for him to come get her after they delivered the plants to the portal.

As for Varjiek, he was too focused on feeding himself to worry about the humans. He knew he wouldn't be seeing Varjiek until after noon. Still, what good did having dragons do Javan if they weren't around to help in threatening situations like this?

The boats ahead of them slowed to a stop as they approached the gates, and the Iria did the same about a hundred yards away from the lead boat. Taliya and her new buddy Anley stood on the bow of the rectangular boat and addressed the lead warrior on the wall while holding a few of the humminglo plants they had borrowed from the Iria last night. Javan strained to hear what they were saying, but he was too far away to make sense out of the mumbled shouting.

"I don't like this," Lydia said. "Those archers on the wall have a huge advantage. We have to take that advantage away by striking first, especially since we only have a limited amount of arrows left after that animal attack in the Dark Zone."

"Just wait," Javan said. "This the first the guards have heard of our plan. Let Taliya do her thing and talk us into the city."

"It's taking too long."

"It's been two minutes. That's not long enough to even explain the short version of the plan."

"Fine. She has two more minutes. Then we attack."

Before Javan could say anything else, Lydia stormed away. Seconds later, he heard her warriors scrambling into place behind him and along the lower deck.

"Hope your girl comes through," Orlan said. "Lydia loves to fight."

"You have to tell her to wait."

"Stand in the way of Lydia and a fight? I'm not crazy." Orlan touched the tip of his spear and seemed satisfied with its sharpness. "If those gates don't open in less than two minutes, you better find cover, because arrows will be flying." He patted Javan on the back and walked away.

A tense minute passed.

"Please open the gates," Javan prayed. "Please have them open the gates."

The gates remained closed and the dragons nowhere to be seen as thirty more seconds ticked away.

With twenty seconds to go, the soft rustling of arrows being pulled out of quivers hit Javan's ears. Not good. He had to stop this before it started. He turned to yell at Lydia's warriors to put their bows down, but the creaking of the opening gates cut him off.

He turned back around and melted against the railing as the boats began drifting through the gates. They had avoided this fight, but would they be able to prevent an onslaught from Omri and his dragons?

CHAPTER 49
SPECIAL DELIVERY

A boom followed by a flash of pink that shot into the sky caused Micah to pull up on Mertzer's scales. The dragon slid to a stop on the cobblestone road between two empty tents. "The portal," Micah whispered, feeling lightheaded after the sudden stop. He gave himself a moment to get oxygen to his brain and assess his surroundings.

Rubble from the city's destroyed buildings rotted behind him. The road he and Mertzer stood on wound through a field of deserted tents and ended at the edge of a river. A bridge with gaps in the railing and more than a few missing pieces of stone arched over the water at a height just high enough for a boat as big as the Iria to pass under.

Docks that led directly into long, flat-roofed mud buildings lined the opposite side of the river with one exception: a wide space between buildings to the left of the bridge. That is where the flash had come from, so that is where the portal had to be located.

Micah could make out specks of people scurrying in and out of buildings as well as piles of plants in the open area around the portal. He could also make out the all-too-familiar sounds of whips cracking and soldiers shouting.

He didn't see any of Javan's dragons or the Iria, however. "Looks like we beat them here. Guess we'll have to sit and wait. But waiting is boring." Micah rubbed the stubble on his cheeks as he thought through his options.

They could storm over the bridge, take over the portal, and go home. Only Micah wasn't quite ready to return Mertzer to his father. He also needed a bit of bargaining power if Omri didn't approve of Micah's plan.

That left him with the waiting option, but he could wait a little closer to the action. "All right, Mertzer. Here's the plan." Micah dismounted, adjusted his sword strap, and checked his whip. "I'm going to head back to Zandador with the huge humminglos once the Iria arrives. You stay here to rest and take cover in the rubble. If I'm not back by dusk, you're free to leave the city to hunt. Just be sure to return to this area so I know where to find you."

Mertzer didn't move, so Micah slapped the dragon's leg and pointed to the rubble. "Go!"

The dragon dropped his eyes, sighed, and wandered toward the ruins. "Take care, my friend," Micah whispered. He then mirrored the dragon's sigh and sprinted toward the bridge.

◊ ◊ ◊

The contrast between the green world teeming with life outside the gates and the drab world devoid of any kind of plant life inside the gates astounded Javan. Block after block of blackened buildings assaulted his eyes from every angle, and the depressing atmosphere of the city made the tension on board the Iria right before the gates opened seem like the party of the century.

Dark clouds overtook the sky, and Javan wanted it to rain. His tears alone weren't sufficient; the sky needed to cry over this place. Nevertheless, the clouds choked back the rain.

They floated through the graveyard called Nahat in silence for nearly an hour. Sections of Javan's mind began shutting down, and he felt his sanity slowly slipping away. Mercifully, it all came rushing back when he spotted a jumbled campsite full of tents on the left hand side of the river and dozens of intact mud buildings connected to docks that looked like warehouses on the right hand side of the river. Life did exist here!

They passed thirty-three buildings before their escort led them to a dock just shy of a sad-looking bridge. If a butterfly landed on it, the thing might just collapse into the water.

"Why didn't we build our portal right on the water?" Kai's voice carried up to Javan from the lower deck. "It sure would make Transport Day much easier."

Javan transferred his eyes from the bridge to the ground. A loud mix of people and animals scurried between wagons and around humminglo plants between the building where they docked and the next building along the river. No one walked on the huge white circle in the middle of the building, though.

Although much of it was covered with stacks of humminglo flowers, he recognized the white circle made of Dawn Stalker scales from the portal in Zandador he and Astor had used to travel to Dusk Stalker territory. Like that portal, this one had a radius of at least twenty feet and could easily accommodate a dragon. Unlike that portal, though, this one only had two triangle holes, not ten.

One triangle hole marked the center of the circle, and Javan concluded that linked to the central portal in the basement of the castle. The other triangle hole was located south of the castle link and had to represent their current location.

If Javan recalled correctly, putting scales shed by a seven-year-old Dawn Stalker into those triangle holes activated the portal. He didn't understand why the scales shed by the Dawn Stalker at age seven had more power than the ones shed at age six or eight or eighty, but there were a lot of things about dragons and this dimension he didn't understand.

For instance, why did this portal only have a link to the castle? That seemed strange and unfair for the people here in Keckrick.

"What is the meaning of this?" A gruff, white-haired man with specks of red in his long beard dressed like one of Omri's soldiers cracked his whip on the dock and stood in the way of Cyr de-boarding the Iria. "All of your cargo ships should have arrived by yesterday to undergo quality inspections before transport to the castle."

"We encountered a few delays," Cyr said. "It's not even noon yet. You have plenty of time to inspect our crop now. I think you'll be pleased and eager to make an exception."

"King Omri doesn't allow exceptions."

"He will today." Micah approached from out of nowhere and bounded up the steps to the dock.

The soldier's face turned whiter than his hair. He dropped his whip, trembled, and bowed.

"Stand up, and step aside," Micah said. "I need a sample of this special delivery to personally present to my father."

Shock glued Javan to the deck. Micah had made it to Nahat ahead of them yet waited for them to arrive? He could have abandoned their deal and made the soldiers send him back to Zandador right away. But he hadn't. Why?

Maybe he had developed a conscience while in Keckrick. Or maybe he wanted to take credit for finding the super huge flowers. Javan knew how to find out. He would simply put Varjiek's scale in his stalker sword and become Micah's invisible shadow when Micah traveled back to Zandador.

But first he had to see a girl about protecting his dragons during his absence.

CHAPTER 50
BACK TO ZANDADOR

"Welcome aboard, Micah." Cyr held the gate open for Micah but let it slam back into the waist of the cowering soldier attempting to follow him. "It's good to see you."

"Thanks." He nodded and headed straight across the deck to the door of the cargo area. "Let's get a batch of these flowers loaded onto the portal, so I can begin negotiations with my father."

"Micah, sir, I can't allow this." The soldier opened the gate for himself and marched over to Micah. His voice cracked and his words shook, making him sound weak and unconvincing. "Only crops that have been inspected can be sent through the portal."

"These crops have passed my inspection."

"How is that possible? How is it possible you are even here?" He lowered his trembling voice to a whisper. "We all thought that you were…"

"You thought I was what?" Micah used to relish the fear he invoked in people. So why did this man's obvious distress make Micah uncomfortable?

"Dead, sir." The man bowed his head. "We thought you were dead."

"Oh?" Micah chuckled. "Whoever started that rumor is obviously mistaken. Since I am very much alive, I outrank you and am ordering you to have these plants unloaded and transported to Zandador as fast as possible."

"You are certain they meet King Omri's standards?"

Micah wanted to ask what those standards were and what Omri was doing with these plants, but he didn't want to reveal his ignorance to the cowardly soldier. "Open the door and see for yourself."

"Yes, sir." The man slowly opened the door. And gasped. "I have never seen such large humminglos! Where did you find these? King Omri is going to be so pleased!"

"Of course he is." Micah hoped the soldier was right, but he kept the doubt out of his words in order to retain his authoritative tone. "You have ten minutes to get the first batch unloaded and onto the portal."

"Thank you, Micah," Cyr said, shaking Micah's hand. "We owe you our lives. If there is ever anything we can do for you, let us know."

"I will." Micah returned Cyr's strong handshake and exited the boat without saying goodbye to anyone. Although he had grown to care about the crew, he had a reputation to uphold and couldn't let the soldiers see that he had made friends among the natives.

As Micah walked toward the portal, he felt like he was walking away from the only friends he would ever have for the rest of his privileged life.

◊   ◊   ◊

Javan activated the invisibility mode of his stalker sword and slipped off the boat just behind Micah. Ten minutes didn't give him much time to find and chat with Taliya. Too bad the electronically challenged people in this dimension didn't have cell phones. Being able to call or text Taliya at a time like this would come in handy, especially considering the chaos that gripped the ground around the portal.

Soldiers scattered among the people emptying wagons full of plants and yelled at and pushed the workers. The mules pulling the wagons snorted and stomped and kicked up dust. Large dogs carried flowers on their backs, and other random animals such as pigs and chickens roamed about with no discernable purpose. Flies and bees buzzed around the smelly animals and dried out flowers piled all around the white circle.

The clouds kept the sun from beating down on the messy scene, but Javan preferred the blazing sun to the stifling humidity. If he wasn't in such a hurry to find Taliya, he'd take a dip in the river to cool off.

Four minutes ticked away before he finally located Taliya among the crowd. She was standing at the bottom of the bridge and loading her slingshot. He followed her eyes to a young soldier shouting at an old man shriveled on the ground from obvious fatigue.

The soldier deserved to be shot with one of her sleeping darts, but Javan couldn't let Taliya get arrested. He was too far away from her to keep her from shooting, so he opted for Plan B.

Making sure to remain invisible while keeping his sword close to his body, Javan sprinted toward the soldier. He rammed the soldier from behind and sent him tumbling face first into a pile of humminglo plants as Taliya's dart whisked through the air. The dart lodged into the dirt not far from where the soldier had been standing, just missing a squealing pig.

Before the surprised soldier could figure out what happened, Javan retrieved the dart and ran toward Taliya. "Shooting at soldiers?" Javan asked as he approached the bridge. "How is that going to help keep the peace?"

Taliya startled to attention and hid her sling. Then her brain must have registered what was going on because she relaxed and said, "That soldier is so mean that even his buddies wouldn't have been upset if he took a little nap."

"You might have a point."

"And you might be easier to talk to if you let me see you."

"Fine." Javan put his sword back in its sheath and handed her the dart. "Better?"

"Much." She put the dart back in her pouch. "You pushed that soldier, didn't you?"

"Yes." A loud bang and flash of pinkish purple momentarily rendered him deaf and blind. Once the swirling colors fizzled and his hearing returned, he noticed the soldier from the boat ordering a parade of people to place the Iria's cargo on the portal.

"I hate the way these soldiers treat us," Taliya said, twirling her slingshot in her hands.

"I agree." Javan put his hands on hers to keep her from fiddling with the slingshot. "So help me stop them."

She shook her head. "I already told you that I'm not coming with you."

"You don't have a choice."

"Excuse me?" She jerked her hands away from his. "Are you trying to order me around?"

"No. No, that's not what I meant." Javan brushed his hands through his hair and tried to salvage his plea to recruit Taliya. He had to hurry. Micah was taking the scales he needed to activate the portal from the white-haired soldier.

"Here's the deal," Javan said, talking fast. "Kisa doesn't want to come back to Zandador without you, and neither do I. You're smart. You're strong. You know all kinds of things about dragons that I am clueless about. I need you on my team. I can't win the throne without you. So please. Please join me."

"Uh." Taliya rolled her eyes. "I can't handle this begging nonsense. If you promise to stop sounding so desperate, I'll come with you."

"Awesome!" Javan gave her a quick hug. "Can you please look out for the dragons? Varjiek should show up anytime, and Kisa is hiding in the forest outside the gates. I'll be back as soon as possible."

He drew his invisibility sword and began sprinting away.

"Wait. What?" Taliya tried to grab him, but he was already out of her reach. "Where are you going?"

Javan paused and turned toward her. "To Zandador. I have to make sure Micah upholds his end of the deal."

"Then you better hurry." Taliya pointed to the portal. "Micah just put the first scale in the Nahat slot."

"Oh, no. Gotta go." Javan spun around and ran through the crowd as Micah walked across the portal and bent down among the surrounding piles of humminglo plants to put the scale in the center slot.

◊　◊　◊

Micah knelt in the center of the portal, closed his eyes, and took a deep breath. The sweet aroma from the flowers around him calmed his nerves, and the cool triangular scale he held in his hand revived his sense of control. The scale gave him the ability to travel without relying on a boat or dragon to get him where he wanted to go.

He should want to go back to Zandador, so why was he hesitating? In a matter of moments, he could be standing in the presence of his father to deliver a flower that supposedly would make Omri very happy. Omri would be even happier when he heard Micah's plan to give the king power over two more dragons.

Pleasing Omri had been Micah's sole objective in life, and now he finally had a chance to meet and surpass his father's expectations. Micah should be elated, not hesitant.

He had to forget about the people here and what it felt like to have friends. "Move on, Micah," he mumbled to himself. "Better things are waiting for you in Zandador."

A gust of wind toppled a pile of flowers in front of him. He ignored the mess and placed the scale in the center slot. A pop turned his world orange, and he felt himself being pulled through the wormhole that led to the Land of Zandador.

CHAPTER 51
FAMILIAR FACES

Javan jumped onto the portal and into a pile of humminglo plants seconds before Micah inserted the destination scale in the middle slot. He heard a gentle pop rather than the loud bang he expected and became lost in a swirling bath of orange streaks.

The streaks spun faster and faster and seemed to suck him through a hole like a pin being devoured by the hose of a vacuum cleaner. The spinning made him dizzy, and the dizziness made him queasy. He had to close his eyes and cover his mouth to keep from re-tasting his breakfast. He didn't want to find out what would happen when an invisible man puked in a portal.

He kept his eyes closed even after he felt the spinning subside to give his body time to adjust to being still. Gawking sounds of oohs and aahs floated through the air, accompanied by actual words of awed strangers.

"Unbelievable."

"Impossible."

"Miraculous."

Javan thought the people's words referred to the plants, but when he opened his eyes and adjusted them to the brightness of the place, he noticed that the eight soldiers in the cavernous oval room all had their gazes fixed on Micah.

It took Javan a moment to realize that the light came from the portal beneath him. It glowed a dazzling yellow, then shifted to varying shades of pink, purple, red, and orange before returning to yellow.

A three-foot high wall in front of him that curved with the shape of the portal was also covered with Dawn scales and radiated the same colors as the portal. An array of equally colorful buttons topped the six foot long and two foot wide wall. The only man not in a soldier's uniform stood on the other side of the three foot high wall and spoke the first real sentence.

"Leave it to Micah to deliver a batch of humminglos unlike anything we've ever seen before." His commanding voice had a familiar ring, and the green shirt he wore over his wide shoulders made his hazel eyes shine against his tan skin. His well-trimmed beard added an air of sophistication that his bushy dark hair detracted from.

"Hello, Vince." Micah puffed out his chest and picked up a plant near Javan's head. "I came across them while hunting dragons in Keckrick and knew they would please my father."

Vince. Why did Javan know that name?

"Strange that your hunt took you to Keckrick, but these may please your father more than ten thousand dragons ever could." Vince stepped over the wall and reached for a plant Javan was sitting on. Javan rolled out of the way and kept himself from grunting when his back hit the wall. And when he remembered why he knew Vince.

This man was his great-grandfather. The family traitor. The reason his father was banished to the Land of No Return and his mother was imprisoned by the Dark King when she was pregnant with him. But he was also the one who orchestrated his mother's escape several months ago and sent her to find him.

"This is incredible." Vince inspected the plant from top to bottom, then gave a handful to a nearby solider. "Take these to Barath's lab for immediate testing."

The soldier nodded and exited the room. At the same time, the rest of the soldiers began unloading the plants remaining on the portal and sending them through a hole in the floor in the back of the room to what Javan guessed was a sub-basement storage area.

"I'll have Barath conduct some tests to be sure," Vince said, ignoring the commotion, "but I believe one of these plants is valuable enough to save an entire region. Did they come from Upper or Lower Keckrick?"

"I prefer to save that information for my father," Micah said. "Where is he?"

"In the throne room discussing battle plans with the captains of the Justice Units."

"Great." Micah stepped through the piles of plants and made his way toward the door. Javan stood and followed him but had to pause mid-step when Vince's words stopped Micah.

"I should warn you that your replacement is in that meeting," Vince said.

"My replacement?"

"King Omri appointed your half-brother Theo as Captain of the Dusk Stalker Unit a few days ago."

"What? Why would he do that?"

"No one has heard anything from you for three weeks. You and the Dusk Stalker Mertzer were presumed dead. The land mourned your loss at your funeral last week."

"My funeral? Everyone thinks I'm dead?" The horror on Micah's face caused bubbles of laughter to burst inside Javan's chest. He had to hold his breath to keep from expelling his squeals of delight and therefore revealing his presence.

Too bad invisibility didn't come with a sound proof feature. Refraining from laughing made his lungs hurt, but he was able to regain his self-control once Micah began moving.

"It is good to see that you are very much alive," Vince said. "What of the dragon?"

"Mertzer is well and waiting for me in Keckrick. I will bring him home once I speak to my father."

"Then go. You will need to take the stairs. The lift to the top floor is currently being repaired."

"Great." Micah left the room in a hurry, and Javan had to scramble to keep up with him.

◊   ◊   ◊

Micah charged down the dark basement hallway and up the spiral staircase that wound through the center of the castle. How could he be replaced? By Theo? That older half-brother of his was a skinny, conniving weasel who hated everyone. He would make a terrible leader and would enjoy torturing Eli. The Dusk Stalker had always been trouble, but he didn't deserve Theo's brand of cruelty.

Then again, Micah had never been the epitome of kindness and mercy. Memories of the harsh words he had spoken and painful punishments he had carried out in Omri's name humbled him and slowed his pace to a crawl by the time he reached the seventh floor.

Had people mourned for him at his funeral? Or did they cry tears of joy because they knew they would never have to see him again? Had anyone even tried to find him, or had they just presumed he was dead when he didn't return to the castle?

He passed floors eight and nine and stopped on the staircase leading to the top floor of the castle. He looked at the flower in his hand and thought of the people depending on him back in Keckrick. He wanted to do right by them, and the only way he knew how to do that was to maintain a touch of his old, heartless self.

He dragged his heavy legs up the final flight of stairs, walked across the marble floor under the dome glass ceiling, and approached the soldier standing guard at the entrance to the throne room. Clearing his throat, he said, "I'm here to see my father."

The same scrawny man Micah had shoved aside upon his return from Gri spoke in a quivering voice. "He's...ummm...he's." The man dropped his spear and nervously picked it up. "The king is in a private meeting. He doesn't want to be disturbed."

"Please inform him that his son has returned from the dead." Micah patted the man's shoulder. "I think that is a legitimate reason to disturb him."

"Yes, sir. Yes, yes, of course." The man nodded in agreement and opened the doors. He took a step inside the room and announced, "King Omri, you have a guest."

"How dare you open those doors and speak to me!" Omri's words made Micah cringe. He had forgotten how angry his father could get at the slightest intrusion. "No guest is important enough to interrupt my meeting."

"What about this one?" Micah stepped in front of the soldier and held up the humminglo flower. "And I come bearing gifts from Keckrick."

"Is that a…" Omri's words trailed off as he got up from his throne, walked past his four captains, crossed the room, and took the flower from Micah. "It's beautiful. How did you find this, and are there more like it?"

"It's a long story, but there are plenty more like it." Micah's heart sank. He hoped his father would hug him, rejoice in his return, and welcome him home, but Omri focused his attention on the flower. That made Micah's next words easier. "They can all be yours. Under the right conditions, that is."

◊   ◊   ◊

"The right conditions?" Omri slapped Micah across the face and ordered the four other people in the room to leave. After they walked out and closed the doors behind them, Omri said, "You know I don't deal well with negotiations or threats."

Javan watched in shock from his hiding spot ten feet away from Micah as Omri punched Micah in the gut, then pulled back on his dreadlocks, forcing Micah to bend backwards and look up at Omri. "I want all the flowers like this one in my possession by the end of the day."

What was wrong with this man? He hadn't even bothered to say hello to the son he thought was dead. No wonder Micah had grown into such a jerk. His father valued flowers more than the life of his own child.

"Hear me out, sir." Micah strained to speak. Javan found himself wanting to pull Omri's hair to get him to let go of Micah. "You know I would never dare threaten you."

Omri yanked Micah's head back further. "I'm listening."

Micah continued without attempting to fight back. "The conditions I alluded to involve eliminating the Collector and gaining both a Noon Stalker and a Dawn Stalker."

Javan almost let the sword that gave him invisibility slip out of his hand. He regained his grip before dropping it. Javan had never felt so gullible. The man he felt sorry for a few seconds ago wanted to kill him and take his dragons.

Micah was just as ruthless as his father, and Javan wasn't about to let him get anywhere near Varjiek or Kisa. He thus needed to get back to Keckrick ahead of Micah, but with the doors already closed, he couldn't sneak out of the room.

He found himself stuck, and his blood ran cold when he heard the details of Micah's plan.

CHAPTER 52
MICAH'S PLAN

Micah's scalp felt like it was being ripped off his head, and his body screamed from being contorted into an unnatural position. Yet he said nothing and let his father yank his hair. If he begged for relief or attempted to retaliate, Omri would simply inflict more pain.

Micah focused on his breathing while he let his words penetrate his father's ego. Finally, Omri released Micah's hair and sauntered to the other end of the room. He glided up the red carpeted steps to his throne and sat on the black cushion of the oversized, gold-plated chair that sparkled from the sunshine streaming through the windows behind it.

"Tell me your story," Omri said. He gently placed the humminglo flower across his lap. "The short version that ends with me gaining two more dragons and an abundance of these giant flowers."

"After I sent the Justice Units back to the castle from Midnight Territory, I began tracking Javan." Micah clicked his way across the hollow room. Omri hadn't invited him up on the platform sit in any of the captain's chairs on either side of the throne, so he stopped at the bottom of the stairs. "I found him in Keckrick."

"Keckrick?" Omri slapped his hands on the arms of his throne. "How did he know about the humminglos? Was he attempting to harvest them for his own use? How many of these giant flowers does he have in his possession?"

"None. He doesn't care about the flowers." Omri's mini-tirade made Micah more curious than ever about the humminglo plants, but he suppressed that curiosity in order to deliver his well-rehearsed speech. "He collected a Dawn Stalker and is attempting to use his growing power to take over control of Keckrick."

"What?" Omri's roar rattled the statues of Omri's tailless dragons that stood in the four corners of the room. "How did he collect a Dawn Stalker? My army has been guarding the entire perimeter of the Dawn Territory to prevent him from collecting any more dragons."

"How is irrelevant." Micah didn't think Omri needed to know about Taliya hiding Kisa, and he certainly wasn't going to admit that he watched

237

Javan ride away on Kisa. "The fact remains that Javan has two dragons and is using them to unite Keckrick in a fight against you."

"That is a war he will not win!" Omri leapt to his feet. "I will wipeout that entire rebellious region. Gather the Justice Units and--"

"No." Micah had never interrupted Omri before. He held his breath and waited for his father's reaction.

Omri cocked his head and hissed his response. "What did you just say to me?"

"No." Repeating the word instilled courage in Micah. "The way to win is to do nothing."

"Oh?" Omri crossed his arms and shot daggers at Micah with his eyes.

Micah could tell Omri's patience was gone. He needed to talk fast. "You want the humminglo flowers, Javan, and his dragons. All the people of Keckrick want is to live. Javan is giving them that hope. You can, too. Let them live. Instead of wiping out Upper or Lower Keckrick based on who provides more flowers, take their super flowers, and let them all live."

"Interesting proposition, but that doesn't eliminate Javan or get me his dragons."

"It does if you give them a choice."

"What choice is that?"

"Tell them they can surrender Javan for execution by my hand or suffer total annihilation by yours."

CHAPTER 53
JAVAN'S PLAN

An involuntary gasp escaped Javan's lips. He quickly covered his mouth to keep more unwelcome noises from getting through. Sound carried well in this mammoth room as evidenced by the fact he could hear every word the two men spoke at the opposite end of the room. If he could hear them, they would be able to hear him.

"I am not convinced." Omri picked up the flower he had dropped and returned to his seat on the throne. "Repealing my original command to destroy the half of Keckrick that provides the fewest flowers will make me look weak."

"On the contrary," Micah said. "You become stronger than ever. You gain the entire humminglo supply—including the super flowers—without having to send one dragon through the portal. The people will view your repeal as mercy and work harder in the coming years to keep you supplied with humminglos. They will willingly surrender Javan to save themselves, and once I slay the Collector, his dragons become yours."

Javan wondered if the people would turn him over that easily. They knew he was willing and able to fight for them. Wouldn't they want to fight for a chance at freedom? Or was survival more important? Would they rather live even though it meant living as Omri's slaves?

"That last part is brilliant," Omri said. "Although I agreed to abide by the law and not harm the Collector, you are not bound by those restrictions. Executing him would end the Battle for the Throne, and the additional dragons would make me more powerful."

Javan could end the battle as well. In his current invisible state, he could execute both Omri and Micah before anyone else became aware of anything these men were currently plotting. Maybe. The concept of killing men in cold-blood didn't sit well with him.

"You agree with my plan, then?" Micah put one foot on the bottom step, then immediately moved it back to the floor. "You will spare Keckrick in exchange for their super flowers and Javan?"

A movement near the statue of the Midnight Stalker in the left corner of the room near the throne caught Javan's eye. He could see the leg and tip of a sword of someone hiding under the statue.

So much for his execution plan. Despite being invisible, Javan doubted his ability to take out two men at once. He certainly wasn't skilled enough to take out three people.

"Yes." Omri leaned back on his throne. "Get me the super flowers and Javan's dragons, and I will spare the people of Keckrick."

"Yes, sir." Micah nodded and began walking back toward the exit.

Javan gripped his sword tighter. As long as he held the sword, no one could see him. He could sneak out of the room behind Micah, exit the castle, and head to Midnight Stalker Territory to collect a Midnight Stalker. If he never returned to Keckrick, the people would never have the option of turning him over to Micah.

But if they didn't have that option, Omri would order a complete genocide of the people of Keckrick. Was Javan's life more valuable than millions of people?

What about the people of Zandador? Javan's death would ensure Omri remained on the throne. His sole mission in life was to overthrow Omri. If he failed, the people of Zandador were doomed to live under Omri's oppressive rule for 500 more years.

At least they would be alive. The people of Keckrick wouldn't have that privilege if Javan ran away. He needed to return with Micah and surrender himself on behalf of Keckrick.

Micah yanked the doors open. Javan tiptoed in that direction as Micah disappeared into the hallway, but the guard pulled the doors shut before Javan could get through them.

Not good. Not good at all.

CHAPTER 54
THE POWER OF THE HUMMINGLO

Micah leaned his wobbly body against the railing and began his staircase descent to the basement. He did it. He actually did it. He had stood up to his father, presented his case, and convinced Omri to change his mind. The people of Keckrick would survive. Javan wouldn't, but wasn't killing one person better than slaughtering an entire population?

Yes. The logical answer had to be yes. Micah just wished he didn't have to be the one to carry out the execution. The idea made his stomach turn. He thus felt sick by the time he reached the basement.

The moldy smell from the dank walls sparked a piercing headache. He couldn't return to Keckrick. Not yet. Not until he felt strong and healthy again. Resting in the lounge on the ground floor should help him recover. Maybe he would even have the servants fix him some soup to settle his stomach.

Micah changed directions and climbed up two steps when he noticed a light seeping into the basement hallway from the end opposite the portal room and near the entrance to the Dragon Quarters. The light came from Barath's lab.

That old man liked to talk. He would gladly babble about the humminglos to Micah, and Micah could finally discover why these flowers were so important to Omri. Curiosity cured Micah's nausea and headache. He traipsed down the hall and barged into the lab without knocking.

The vastness of the lab surprised him. It spanned the entire length of the castle and half its width. Dozens of workstations scattered around the open space were divided only by strategically placed columns that kept the castle from collapsing. Men and women dressed in the standard brown garb of Zandadorian citizens worked in pairs around the workstations dissecting humminglo flowers.

Most of them were too entrenched in their work to notice him standing at the door. Disbelief washed over the faces of the few who did look his way. While he let them try to figure out if they were seeing a ghost or the real live version of himself, Micah scanned the room for Barath.

He spotted the half-bald black man with a well-trimmed white beard hunched over a long table in the back left corner of the room. One pair of glasses rested on top of his head, one pair perched on the end of his nose, and one pair dangled from a chain around his neck. He wore a white coat over his red shirt and was carefully cutting the web-like strings off one of the super flowers.

"Tell me, Barath," Micah said, leaning over Barath's shoulder, "what makes this flower so special?"

"Micah?" Barath dropped his knife, stumbled off his stool, and poked Micah's chest. "Is that really you? You are alive?"

"Yes."

"Welcome back from the dead." Barath flung his arms around Micah's waist and gave him a brief squeeze. "Your father will be pleased. You must go see him right away."

"I just saw him." A pang of guilt hit Micah's heart. This man whom Micah had mistreated and mocked was the only one who had given him a warm greeting. Micah made a mental note to start respecting this old man.

"Good, good," Barath said. "Did he send you to inquire about my test results? I don't have them yet. I'm working as fast as I can, but--"

"It's okay," Micah said. He eased Barath back onto his stool. "King Omri didn't send me here. I came on my own."

"Oh? Why? You don't usually like to visit me."

"I do today. I want to learn about these flowers. I know they are important to my father, and I want to understand why. Can you explain what makes these flowers special?"

"Oh, many, many things. The aloe from the leaves is used to make healing ointment. The petals are crushed and used in lotions to relieve headaches. But it's the substance found within the strings of the flower that is most interesting."

Barath cut a section of string off the flower and squeezed the clear liquid inside the string into a small glass. "Smell." He handed the glass to Micah.

Micah swirled the liquid around and inhaled. "I don't smell anything."

"Exactly. It is undetectable. You can put it in any beverage or on any food, and it blends in. No one is ever aware that they are consuming it."

"Is this poison?" Micah put the glass on the table and took a step back. "Does my father want all these flowers so he can harvest undetectable poison?"

"No." Barath chuckled. "It is harmless to one's health."

"Then what's the point? What does it do?"

"Hmmm. How to explain this?" Barath leaned his elbows on the table, locked his fingers together, and tapped his thumbs against each other. "You know how you cut off the tails of dragons to gain control of its will?"

"Yes."

Barath picked up the glass. "This does the same thing to humans."

"What? I don't follow."

"Mind control, Micah." Barath tapped the glass. "If you were to drink the contents of the cup, it would cut off your free will, and allow me to control your mind. You would do whatever I told you to do and would be powerless to resist my commands."

"That's why Omri wants all of these flowers? He wants the power to control people's minds?"

"Oh, yes. Think how much easier it will be to rule the land. He won't have to use his dragons to instill fear in people. He can simply issue orders and expect them to be followed without backlash or rebellion."

"Wonderful." Complete and total power over people. That used to be Micah's big dream. Now it seemed arrogant and wrong.

Barath leaned back over his table and fingered the super flower. "These super flowers seem to be more potent than anything I've seen before. Extracting the substance will take some time, but we should be ready to begin widespread distribution by the first of the year."

"That soon?" Micah pasted a smile on his face. "My father will be happy to hear that." He patted Barath's back and left the lab.

His headache returned with a vengeance. What had he done? And could he stop it?

CHAPTER 55
SECRETS AND DILEMMAS

Javan bit his bottom lip and stared at the wooden doors blocking his exit. What would happen if he opened the doors? It might startle Omri, his mystery guest, and the soldier guarding the entrance, but they couldn't exactly see him to stop him. Plus, he doubted they would automatically assume an invisible man was wandering through the castle opening doors. He just had to be quick about it and get away before they realized he had even been there.

He placed his hand on the cold steel knob. But he didn't turn it. Because a female voice started a conversation with Omri that Javan wasn't supposed to hear.

"It sounds like your son is going to take care of the Collector problem for you," the woman said. "Does that mean you no longer require my services?"

Javan turned to find a tall woman approaching Omri from the direction of the Midnight Stalker statue. Her red tank top showed off her toned caramel colored skin. It almost matched her auburn hair that couldn't decide if it should be curly or wavy and hung just past her shoulders. Both those reds paled in comparison to the ruby handle of the large axe she carried in her right hand.

"No," Omri said, sitting on his throne. "It simply means we will need to amend the terms of our arrangement."

"How so?"

"I want the two dragons Javan has that will soon be mine. Once Micah returns with them, kill him."

Did Javan hear that right? Did Omri just take out a contract on his own son's life?

"I am a Destroyer, King Omri. I kill dragons. Not people."

"You kill whomever I order you to kill!" Omri slammed his hands on the arms of his throne. "I cannot allow Micah to live. I've already had his funeral. His return from the grave would make me look foolish. Buying the silence of those who have seen him today is going to be humiliating enough."

Javan had to warn Micah. Wait. When? Right before Micah killed him? Why should he warn Micah when Micah wanted him dead?

He couldn't let Micah kill him. Not now. If Omri was willing to have his own son murdered, what would stop him from annihilating Keckrick once he got the supply of super flowers he wanted? The best way to stop Omri was to win the Battle for the Throne.

"Understood." The woman nodded. "What about the rest of the dragons?"

"Stick to the original agreement." Omri got up, wandered over to the wall of windows, and stared outside. "Destroy them all. The only dragons you are not to touch are the seven who belong to me."

"Yes, sir." The woman turned, and Javan couldn't take his eyes off her face as she walked toward him. He expected her to be old—like thirty or forty—but she didn't look a day over sixteen. Her big brown eyes, dainty round nose, sleek cheekbones, and full red lips combined to make her into a striking beauty.

Only she had no life in her eyes, no hint of playfulness or whimsy. She had that all-business-all-the-time kind of attitude about her. Boring. Disturbing. And sad.

An impish desire to cut through her icy demeanor suddenly washed over him. So as he followed her out of the room, he tugged on her hair, whispered "Gotcha!" in her ear, and sprinted down the spiral staircase before she had a chance to retaliate.

◊ ◊ ◊

Standing on the portal while Vince punched in the code to send him back to Upper Keckrick, Micah appeared calm and confident. But that was an illusion. He felt jumpy. Uncertain. Torn between two worlds.

If he saved Keckrick, the people of Zandador would lose their minds.

If he saved Zandador, the people of Keckrick would lose their lives.

Neither one seemed right or fair or wrong, so how was he supposed to choose? The people of Keckrick taught him what it meant to care, but he called Zandador home. He couldn't turn his back on his home.

The dilemma raged on as the light flashed and the portal transported him to Keckrick.

CHAPTER 56
FAMILY REUNION

Javan paced back and forth in front of the door to the portal room. Every few minutes, he would hear a slight pop and see bright flashes of light shoot out from under the door. That was always followed by a flurry of commands and a scurry of shuffling feet as the soldiers inside the room worked to unload the fresh arrival of humminglos and prepare for the next shipment.

He would be able to get inside the room easily enough, but he would never be able to use the portal to transport him back to Keckrick. Not on his own. For that he needed help.

Vince could help him. But would he? And how was Javan supposed to ask? The man never left the room, and he was the guy in charge. Everyone would notice if Javan attempted to approach him.

No one wandered the halls, though. They could have a private conversation right here if Vince stepped out of the room. Getting him out of the room was the trick, but after a little more pacing and a few desperate prayers, Javan figured out how to do just that.

Making sure to remain cloaked, he cleared his throat, beat on the door, and opened it. With the deepest voice he could muster, he yelled, "Vince, King Omri wants to see you right away."

"Now?"

"Yes." Javan nodded even though no one could see him. "Right away."

"He probably wants an update on the humminglo supply," a man near Vince said.

"Probably." Vince tapped the man on the shoulder. "You're in charge until I return. I shouldn't be long."

"At least you have good news to deliver," the man said.

"If I didn't," Vince said, smiling, "I'd send you."

The man smiled back as Vince left the room. Javan closed the door behind him and let him take about ten steps down the poorly lit hallway before talking to him. "King Omri didn't really summon you."

Vince stopped and spun around. "Who said that?"

"I did." Javan walked to within three feet of Vince and sheathed his sword, allowing himself to become visible.

"Whoa." Vince stumbled backwards. The wall caught him and prevented him from falling. "Who are you? How did you do that?"

"Do what?"

"Appear out of nowhere."

"It's my little secret. You have a secret, too."

"I do." Vince stood tall and seemed to regain his composure. "I have many secrets. Which specific one are you alluding to?"

"I know you helped my mom escape from here."

"Quiet!" Vince covered Javan's mouth with his hand, looked up and down the empty hallway, then back at Javan. "You're Javan?"

Javan nodded, and Vince slowly removed his hand. After what seemed like a ridiculously long minute of staring at each other, Javan spoke. "Hello, great-grandfather. It's good to meet you."

◊   ◊   ◊

Micah shuddered as the transporting lights of the portal faded and the heat from Nahat hit his skin. Portal travel always made him woozy, and it took him a minute to regain his balance.

"Micah. Sir." The soldier Micah had scolded on the dock greeted him with a bow. "We weren't expecting you to return."

"We were." Taliya spoke up from the other side of the portal. Javan wasn't with her, but Cyr and Lydia were. None of them bothered to bow. "What did your father say? Is he going to spare us?"

"King Omri is willing to negotiate." Micah sounded as cold and authoritative as possible. Although his emotions were churning beneath the surface, he had to portray the heartless, domineering leader the soldiers knew him to be. "Gather the people while I retrieve Mertzer. I will announce the terms of the agreement once I return."

"Please don't make us wait," Taliya said, stepping forward. "What are the terms?"

"You can wait. I won't be gone long." Micah took her arm and pulled her close enough to speak only to her. "Make sure Javan is here when I return. I won't make any announcement without him present."

"Why? Do Omri's terms involve Javan?"

"Just make sure he is here." Micah let go of her arm and pushed his way through the crowd. He still felt woozy, but that feeling had nothing to do with portal travel and everything to do with his upcoming encounter with the Dragon Collector.

◊   ◊   ◊

"It's not good to meet you," Vince said, making Javan feel unwelcome. "You shouldn't be here. It's not safe. Why are you here?"

Javan didn't want to answer the question since his own relative didn't want to meet him. However, he needed this man's help. He couldn't let his hurt feelings interfere with the situation. "I followed Micah back from Keckrick. Now I need to return. Can you help me get back?"

"Keckrick? Why were you there? Why do you want to go back?"

"My dragons are there."

"Dragons? Plural? You've collected another one?"

"Yes. A Dawn Stalker." Javan kept his answer short and asked a question of his own. "Can you help me get back or not?"

Vince shook his head. "I need a lot more information first."

"I would love to chat, but I'm running out of time. If I don't get back and face Micah, the people of Keckrick are in trouble. Just give me the scales I need to activate the portal. I can do my invisibility thing to sneak into the room and transport myself to Keckrick."

"This portal doesn't use scales."

"What?"

"This is the main portal in the system. It's operated by a control panel. You have to know the right codes in order to use it."

"So give me the codes."

"The codes are complicated." Vince sighed and crossed his arms. "I can help you, but I will have to go to Keckrick with you."

Javan liked that idea. He could use the support of an older, wiser family member. "Fine."

"But you will be on your own."

"What do you mean?"

"I won't be able to help you in any kind of public setting. Until you win the throne, I have to maintain the ruse that I am loyal to the king and act accordingly. Understood?"

So much for that support he wanted. "I understand."

"Good. And I didn't mean what I said before. I am glad we met." Vince roped Javan into a bear hug, then pushed him away. "Now make yourself invisible, and follow me."

Javan wiped a tear away and obeyed his great-grandfather.

CHAPTER 57
ONE LAST RIDE

Micah trudged through the tents on the other side of the river, thankful for the chance to be alone and think. The exercise and fresh air improved his mood and spurred an idea he hadn't considered before.

What if he didn't choose Keckrick or Zandador? What if he hopped on Mertzer, ran away, and let everything sort itself out?

Omri would still get his super flowers. The thrill of dominating people's minds would distract Omri from the thrill of killing, and the people of Keckrick would be spared annihilation. Omri would gain total control over the people of Zandador, but at least they would be able to live.

Javan would also be able to live. He would have no chance of winning the throne as long as Micah and Mertzer stayed hidden through the end of the year, and that would effectively eliminate him as a threat to Omri's power. The Great Rift was a big place, and Micah could find somewhere to hide for two months.

But would he have a home to return to? Would Omri ever let him back in the castle knowing Micah failed to execute Javan?

Micah kicked a rock on his path. Running away wasn't the answer. He had to face his problems.

He had to face Javan.

◊　◊　◊

Javan waited for the whirling, swirling sensations of portal travel to fade before uncurling himself from the little ball he had folded himself into. Vince didn't seem to need any time to recover, though. He took immediate charge of the area the same way he had taken charge of the portal in Zandador.

"King Omri is pleased with the super flowers you've been sending, but he wants more. I am here to oversee these valuable shipments and make sure none get left behind."

While Vince distracted the soldiers, Javan wobbled to his feet, stumbled into the crowd, and sheathed his sword. He no longer needed to be invisible, and he enjoyed having both hands free again.

"Javan!" Taliya grabbed Javan's hand and pulled him out of the crowd to a quiet spot under the dock. "What happened in Zandador?"

"Micah hasn't told you yet?"

"No. He said he would make an announcement after he brought Mertzer back. He was looking for you, too. He won't tell us anything without you present. I was worried when I didn't see you return with Micah."

"I got hung up but found someone willing to help me return."

"So what happened? Micah said Omri was willing to negotiate. Is that true?"

"Yes, but things are more complicated than Micah realizes. I need to talk to him before he makes that announcement. Where's Varjiek?"

"I don't know. I haven't seen him."

That's because I haven't wanted to be seen.

"Varjiek?" Javan ran out from under the dock and looked around. "Where are you?"

Up here. Varjiek uncloaked himself just long enough to let Javan see him sitting on top of the building attached to the dock he stood beside. *And I am not happy with you.*

◊　◊　◊

"Mertzer." The dragon had dug out a bed for himself among the rubble and lay snoozing on his side in a dirt hole. "Mertzer, wake up."

Mertzer lifted his head, peered at Micah through alert eyes, and moved himself into a sitting position. He studied Micah as if awaiting orders. Micah sure was going to miss this dragon.

"We're going to take one last ride across that bridge to the portal. No matter what happens, you are to back me up. Do not try to stop me, and do not engage in any fights with Javan's dragons."

Confusion mixed with curiosity filled the dragon's eyes. He wanted more information, but Micah knew better. This dragon could talk to Javan, and he didn't want Mertzer spoiling his surprise.

"You understand your orders?"

Mertzer bowed his head, closed his eyes, and slowly opened them again.

"I'll take that as a yes." Micah climbed on Mertzer's back and directed him toward the bridge.

CHAPTER 58
OMRI'S TERMS

Although it required serious upper body strength, Javan pulled himself onto the roof from the handrail of the dock. He lay in a heap on the hot mud roof and addressed his invisible dragon through strained breaths. "Thanks for the help, buddy."

You didn't need my help traveling to Zandador. You shouldn't need my help to climb on a roof.

"That's why you're upset? Because I went to Zandador without you?"

You are my responsibility. I cannot keep you safe if I do not know where you are.

"I thought you were my responsibility."

Nonsense. I became responsible for you the moment you landed on my back. That's what makes our relationship work. It does not work when you disappear without telling me where you are going.

"Ah. Okay." Javan stood and brushed the dirt off his clothes. Varjiek felt left out. Javan could fix that. "Sorry I took off without you. I would have told you, but you weren't back from eating. I saw an opportunity to follow Micah, and I had to take it at that moment."

Varjiek snorted.

"It's a good thing I went." Javan didn't like arguing with an invisible dragon. He couldn't tell if Varjiek was still upset. Since he wasn't responding, Javan kept talking. "I learned some things I need to tell Micah about. We need to go find him before he finds us."

Too late.

"Too late? What do you mean?"

I mean he is here.

"Javan!"

Javan turned to find Micah yelling for him atop the bridge. He was sitting on Mertzer and demanded the hushed attention of everyone in the vicinity. "Javan, stay right there. I have news for you and the people of Keckrick from the King of Zandador!"

Before Javan had a chance to respond, Mertzer sped down the bridge.

◊   ◊   ◊

The people on the ground dashed out of Micah and Mertzer's way, clearing an easy path to the building where Javan stood. Why Javan stood on top of a building made no sense to Micah, but it did make him easy to find and would make a good stage.

The building wasn't much taller than Mertzer, so with very little effort, Micah jumped from the dragon's back to the flat rooftop beside Javan. As he looked down at the crowd awash with fear and uncertainty, he felt as powerful as his father must feel when addressing the people of Zandador from the platform in Stalker Square.

His father fed off the fear he inspired in the people, but it made Micah uncomfortable. He could put names to the faces he saw. Cyr. Lydia. Andre. Dreix. Bree. Orlan. Kai.

They weren't soulless objects he had power over. They were his friends. He found himself wanting to say something to alleviate their fear and put them at ease. "I have spoken with King Omri on your behalf," Micah said. He paused to let the anticipation grow. Then, with a booming voice, he made his grand announcement. "He is pleased with the super flowers!"

The fear of the people turned to smiles, and the tension gave way to cheers.

"Micah," Javan said, "before you say anything else, we need to talk."

"No." Micah kept his eyes on the crowd but his voice low enough so that only Javan could hear him. "I found a way to spare Keckrick. If that is what you truly want, you need go along with whatever I say."

"You don't know the whole story. Your father--"

"My father," Micah said, ignoring Javan and speaking to the people, "has agreed to spare the lives of all of Keckrick!"

He let the people yell and holler and slap each other on the back for a moment before quieting them. "He only asks for one life in return."

With sweaty palms, Micah reached behind his neck and drew his sword as he turned toward Javan.

CHAPTER 59
A WILLING SACRIFICE

"No!" Taliya screamed from the dock, and Javan heard her trying to scramble her way onto the roof.

Javan, Varjiek said, *this man means you harm. Step aside, and let me take care of him.*

"Micah…" Javan stayed planted and raised both his hands to signal surrender to Micah. If given the chance, he believed he could persuade Micah to let him live. "You don't have to do this."

"Yes." Micah's voice shook. Droplets of sweat poured down his face. "Yes, I do."

"If you kill me--"

"If I kill you, my father wins." Micah placed his sword in Javan's hands. The heavy sword knocked Javan off balance as Micah dropped to his knees and put his hands behind his back. "That is why you must kill me."

I didn't see that coming, Varjiek said. *What are you going to do, young Collector?*

◊   ◊   ◊

Micah lowered his head, closed his eyes, and waited for the steel to strike the back of his neck. But the blow never came. Perplexed, he locked up and found Javan standing in a frozen state of disbelief. "Go ahead," Micah said. "Kill me. Take Mertzer. Win the throne."

"I…I don't understand."

"It's not hard. You need a Dusk Stalker. Mertzer is the last Dusk Stalker alive. The only way you can collect him is if you kill me."

"I get that. What I don't get is why. The deal you made with Omri involved my execution in exchange for letting the people of Keckrick live."

"No one else was in that room." Chills ran down Micah's spine. "How did you know about that?"

"That's irrelevant. What matters is that I know the real deal. So why are you changing the terms?"

"Because I found out what my father is doing with the humminglo plants."

CHAPTER 60
ANOTHER WAY

"What Omri is doing with the plants changed your mind?" That's not the answer Javan expected. He assumed Micah had learned about the Destroyer. "So it had nothing to do with the Destroyer?"

"What Destroyer?"

"Nevermind." Javan shook his head, tossed Micah's sword aside, and pulled Micah to his feet. "What's Omri using the humminglo flowers for?"

"When the liquid from inside the web of the flower is consumed, it somehow cuts off a person's ability to think for themselves. My father plans to use this substance to control the Land of Zandador. He won't need an army to enforce his laws, and he won't need dragons to inflict punishment. He'll gain complete and total power over everyone."

"Mind control?" Taliya had succeeded in reaching the roof and walked over to stand beside Javan. "Are you sure?"

"I wouldn't be willing to die if I wasn't sure," Micah said. "And I am sure my father won't bother destroying the people of Keckrick once he gets his hands on their entire supply of super humminglos. The flowers are more important to him than anything else."

"This doesn't make sense," Javan said. "You like having control over people. You should be trying to harness the power of the humminglos for yourself, not be asking me to usurp your father."

"My father is wrong. People matter. You taught me that." Micah drew the stalker sword from the scabbard hanging on Javan's right hip, pointed the tip at his chest, and forced Javan to hold the handle by smothering Javan's hands with his own. "But my father thought I was dead and didn't care. My death should bother him. It will if you kill me and take Mertzer."

Javan's chest heaved up and down. All he had to do was push the sword in a few inches. Mertzer would be his, and he would be one dragon away from becoming the King of Zandador.

"Don't do it, Javan." Taliya put her hand on Javan's shoulder. "You're not a murderer."

"What other choice do I have?" Javan kept his eyes glued on Micah's. The man wanted to die. He wanted to die because he felt alone in this world. That was a terrible reason to die, especially if a worse fate waited for him in the next world.

Consider all your options, Mertzer said. *I may be the last Dusk Stalker alive, but Protectors know how to find the eggs our females have hidden.*

Javan shifted his gaze to Taliya. He thought of the book she had taken from Tulkar and the story she had told about Kisa's birth.

"Javan, stop stalling." Tears dripped down Micah's cheeks. "Put an end to my agony. Please."

"I will. But not by killing you." Javan yanked his hands free from Micah's grip, put his sword away, and reached out his hand for Micah to shake. "Join me. Be part of my team. Fight with me and Taliya to overthrow your father."

"No. Mertzer can never be a part of your collection as long as I am alive. You need him."

"No. I need you on my side." Javan smiled. "I know of another way to collect a Dusk Stalker."

"There is no other way. You have to--"

"You have to shut up and trust me."

◊　◊　◊

Micah cocked his head and narrowed his eyes. The Collector seemed sure of himself. What if he did know of another way to collect a Dusk Stalker?

Micah had to risk trusting him. Only it would make him an outcast, just like Karl. He thus wouldn't be able to follow through with his promise to speak to Omri on his brother's behalf. Because Micah couldn't return home. Ever. Omri wouldn't allow it if he didn't bring him more dragons, and Micah had lost the will to hunt the creatures.

So if Javan wouldn't kill him, Micah had no choice but to join him. He would just have to find another way to repay his brother for helping him in Madai.

"All right," Micah said, sealing his fate. "I'll trust you."

He stuck out his hand, grasped Javan's, and shook, marking the first time in the history of the Great Rift that the Hunter Bloodline and the Collector Bloodline joined forces.

Keeping them united over the coming months would prove to be a far more difficult challenge.

END OF BOOK TWO

NOVELS BY D.K. DRAKE

The Dragon Stalker Bloodlines Saga

BOOK 1: <u>**The Dragon Collector**</u>
BOOK 2: <u>**The Dragon Hunter**</u>
BOOK 3: <u>**The Dragon Protector**</u>
BOOK 4: <u>**The Dragon Destroyer**</u> *(coming soon)*

ABOUT THE AUTHOR

D.K. Drake brings you entertaining, engaging, wholesome adventures too packed with action to leave room for eye-rolling sappiness or mind-numbing fluff.

She is a Christian, a foster parent, and an avid runner. One of her goals is to run some sort of race in every state and (almost) every continent (no thanks, ice-covered Antarctica!).

She lives with two of her sisters in the great state of North Carolina and encourages you to trust God, believe in yourself, and fight for your dreams.

Get Exclusive Access to More {FREE} Stories Today!

Want to know a secret? Then come a little closer. That's it. Now lean in. Listen closely with your eyes because I'm typing these words with a whisper...

D.K. Drake doesn't exist.

I made her up. Just like I make up the characters in my books. In other words, D.K. Drake is my pen name. Why did I choose to write under this pen name? What do the "D" and "K" stand for? What is my true identity?

I answer all those questions and more for those who want to be email buddies. When you become one of my email buddies, you get FREE access to the D.K. Drake starter library that includes the short story "Cops, Robbers...and Dragons?" (This is the story that sparked the idea for the entire Saga!)

You'll also get notified about new books and deals, have a chance to join the Advanced Reader Team, and keep up with my real-life adventures as an author, a runner, and a foster parent. All you have to do is visit **www.AuthorDKDrake.com** and sign up to the Insiders mailing list for FREE today.

A PERSONAL STORY FROM THE AUTHOR

I love making up stories and living in the world of my imagination. But the story I most enjoy sharing is the true story of the day I accepted Jesus Christ as my Savior. So I want to share that story with you now...

As I listened to my mother read the Bible to me and my three older sisters before bed that night, I realized something important: I was a sinner.

I may have only been four years old, but I knew right from wrong I knew it was a lot easier to choose to do the wrong thing than to do the right thing. I knew when I did something wrong, I got in trouble.

I knew my natural tendency was to tell lies to cover my mistakes. I knew my natural tendency was to be impolite to those in authority over me. I knew my natural tendency was to be selfish rather than look out for others.

So when I heard that "all have sinned and fall short of the glory of God (Romans 3:23)," I knew that verse was talking about me. I had sinned. That meant I had fallen short of God's glory.

When I heard that "the wages of sin is death, but the gift of God is eternal life in Christ Jesus our Lord (Romans 6:23)," I knew I was deserving of death but wanted God's gift of eternal life.

When I heard that Jesus said, "I am the way, the truth and the life. No one comes to the Father except through Me (John 14:6)," I understood that believing in Jesus was the only way to experience that eternal life and see the kingdom of God.

So when my mother finished reading the Bible that night, I asked her what I needed to do to be saved.

She sent my sisters to bed and sat down with me with her Bible open. She made sure I understood I was a sinner in need of God's forgiving grace. She made sure I understood that salvation comes by grace through faith, not by anything I do.

I told her I understood and wanted to ask God to save me. We thus knelt side by side along the couch, and she prayed with me as I asked God to forgive me and save me.

Then something wonderful happened: God saved me! The instant I asked for salvation, I felt His presence wash over me. I felt different. Renewed. Alive. I didn't quite understand it at the time, but now I realize that presence I felt was the Holy Spirit. He came to reside in my soul at that moment, and He has never and will never leave.

I was still a sinner, but now I was a sinner saved by grace. My sin nature still lived in me, but now so did God in the person of the Holy

Spirit. Now I was equipped to fight my sin nature, and the battle between my fleshly desires and my Godly desires is a battle that will rage within me until the day I die.

As I fight that battle, I have learned to structure my life in such a way that allows me to stand strong in Christ. I do that by making seeking Him, serving Him, and sharing Him my number one priority in life.

I find great comfort, joy, and delight in living for God and obeying His commandments. I am far from perfect and still get derailed from time to time. I have made more mistakes in my life than I care to admit and have disappointed my God in ways that break my heart to recall.

But I serve a gracious, forgiving, loving God. He made me. He saved me. And he gave me gifts to use, dreams to pursue, and people to love along the way.

That's what makes life fun. Seeking God. Serving God. Sharing God. And loving others.

If you haven't experienced the kind of fun, peace, and joy that comes from knowing God, I encourage you to open your Bible and seek Him today.

Don't have a Bible or aren't sure how to seek God? Then contact me by sending an email to **dk@authordkdrake.com**. I would love to hear from you!

AUTHORDKDRAKE.COM